"What he trusts in is fragile;
what he relies on is a spider's web.
He leans on his web, but it gives way;
he clings to it, but it does not hold."

JOB 8:14-15

A STORY OF LOVE, FAITH & LIFE-CHANGING CHOICES

LEANING
ON A SPIDER'S WEB

Jennifer
Rees Larcombe

InterVarsity Press
DOWNERS GROVE, ILLINOIS 60515

©1991 by Jennifer Rees Larcombe

Published in the United States of America by InterVarsity Press, Downers Grove, Illinois, with permission from Hodder & Stoughton, England.

InterVarsity Press® is the book-publishing division of InterVarsity Christian Fellowship®, a student movement active on campus at hundreds of universities, colleges and schools of nursing in the United States of America, and a member movement of the International Fellowship of Evangelical Students. For information about local and regional activities, write Public Relations Dept., InterVarsity Christian Fellowship, 6400 Schroeder Rd., P.O. Box 7895, Madison, WI 53707-7895.

Cover illustration: John Walker
ISBN 0-8308-1374-8

Printed in the United States of America ∞

Library of Congress Cataloging-in-Publication Data

Rees, Jennifer, 1942-
    Leaning on a spider's web/Jennifer Rees Larcombe.
       p.   cm.
    ISBN 0-8308-1374-8
    I. Title.
PR6068.E375L4   1993
823'.914—dc20   92-38137
                                         CIP

16	15	14	13	12	11	10	9	8	7	6	5	4	3	2	1
05	04	03	02	01	00	99	98	97	96	95	94	93	92		

ACKNOWLEDGMENTS

This book is very much a family venture; it is about a town and a road like the one where we live and the characters and incidents have been created over many a meal. Without the help and advice of my husband Tony, son and daughter, Justyn and Sarah, Tanya Aydon my cousin and my aunt Geraldine Webster it could never have been written. The patience of the rest of the family has also been amazing over the last year! Because of my dyslexia problem the final stages of correcting and checking took countless hours of work, and I am greatly indebted to our friends Liz and Nick Manning who cheerfully undertook this enormous task. Although many of the places mentioned are real and some of the incidents are based on fact, all the characters are fictional.

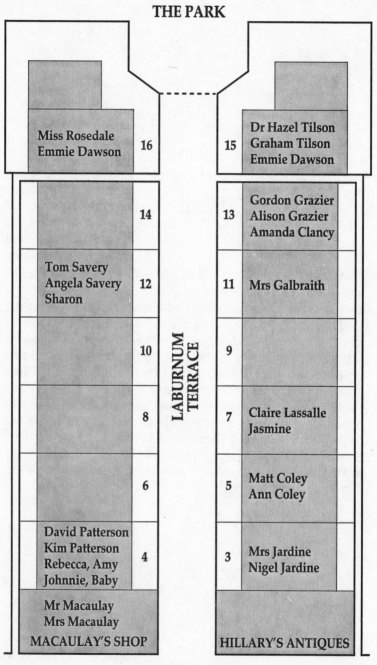

THE PARK

Miss Rosedale
Emmie Dawson
16

15
Dr Hazel Tilson
Graham Tilson
Emmie Dawson

14

13
Gordon Grazier
Alison Grazier
Amanda Clancy

Tom Savery
Angela Savery
Sharon
12

11
Mrs Galbraith

10

9

8

7
Claire Lassalle
Jasmine

6

5
Matt Coley
Ann Coley

David Patterson
Kim Patterson
Rebecca, Amy
Johnnie, Baby
4

3
Mrs Jardine
Nigel Jardine

LABURNUM TERRACE

Mr Macaulay
Mrs Macaulay
MACAULAY'S SHOP

HILLARY'S ANTIQUES

BAKER'S HILL

GOOD FRIDAY

Five thirty was perhaps a strange time to take a walk in the park on Good Friday morning. Later in the day the media christened it 'Bad Friday', but as she picked her way down the hill, the day still felt good to her.

In the valley lay the lake, and by the fading light of the tired moon it looked like liquid silver. In spite of its beauty she turned her back upon it and began to climb the steep path through the tangled rhododendrons.

When she emerged at last she had reached her favourite spot at the top of the hill, where the beech trees towered above their blanket of springy turf. At that time in the morning, they had no substance and were nothing yet but grey shadows.

From here she could look back at the hill on the far side of the lake and see the road where she lived lying beyond the park railings. It looked so peaceful, still lit by its amber streetlights with her neighbours asleep behind their curtains. Such an ordinary little terrace, yet so much had happened there since Good Friday a year ago.

The sky above the town was beginning to flush with the approaching dawn, but as she looked up she saw something strange. For a moment she thought the morning star itself had exploded.

For the rest of her life, the next few seconds were repeated in her dreams over and over again. The unearthly streak of light sweeping towards her. The noise which shook the ground and rattled the beech trees as if they had been frail stalks of grass. Then the uncanny silence which was the worst part of all.

1

When she finally opened her eyes, the pretty cul-de-sac which had been her home was lost in swirling dust and smoke. Flames leapt and danced, spreading their ghastly reflection on the innocent surface of the water. 'The lake of fire,' she thought absently, but surely this was not the end of the world? The beech trees were still standing.

She began to run, not away to safety but down across the valley and up the far side of the hill towards home, like a startled rabbit diving instinctively for the warren.

'This isn't real,' she told herself. 'It's a dream − a mistake, this kind of thing would never happen in a place like Welbridge.'

Something outrageous was protruding from the end of the terrace. Her mind told her it was the corpse of a great fish, but reason recognised the blazing forward fuselage of a wingless aircraft.

'It's ruined the park railings,' she thought indignantly. She could not, at that moment, allow her mind to recognise the total devastation which lay in the monster's wake.

THE PREVIOUS GOOD FRIDAY

5.30am

A year before, on Good Friday morning, the milkman had been the first person to enter Laburnum Terrace. Actually she was not a milk*man* at all, but no one could have guessed her gender because her body was buried under so many layers of warm clothes. Backwards and forwards she lumbered between her milk truck and the Victorian doorsteps. If anyone had woken and peered out at the murky gloom, they might well have thought she was a shapeless Egyptian mummy.

'All right for some,' she thought with an indulgent smile, 'lying in. Most of 'em won't budge for hours yet.' But these were *her* people and in an affectionate, motherly way she did not begrudge them their Bank Holiday treat. Welbridge Dairies sent out a milk*man* on Saturdays to do its financial business so Babs never actually met anyone from Laburnum Terrace, but she knew them well – in her imagination.

'Funny how much you can learn about people by their milk order,' she mused as she dumped a heavy crate down on the step of Number Four. 'Nice ordinary family this – untidy though,' she added as she retrieved yesterday's empty crate from beneath a heap of tricycles, scooters and red wellington boots.

Laburnum Terrace was the favourite part of her round because the road had fascinated her from childhood. Every weekend she had walked along this sleepy cul-de-sac on her way to the park which lay at the far end. As

3

she had peered up at the pretty little Victorian villas with their decorative twirls and twists she had grown to love each one of them.

"Health freaks this lot," she said as she crossed the road and placed the usual order on the doorstep of Number Five. The only way the garrulous Babs coped with such a solitary job was by talking to herself incessantly throughout her entire round. "Two pints of skimmed milk, carton of fresh orange and two plain yoghurts. Probably a nice young couple with no kids – yet." She gave them a nod of approval, then swept past the next house with a contrasting snort of disgust. There was no point in looking for notes on the step of Number Seven; they never deigned to use the services of Welbridge Dairies. Mrs Macaulay from the newsagent had told Babs they were vegans, a definite insult to her bottles of good healthy cows' milk.

"Got a little girl, too," Mrs Macaulay had added, "fancy bringing her up on nuts, seeds and fizzy water!"

'Pretty house, though,' thought Babs, 'all those frilly old-fashioned curtains and little window boxes . . . hullo, whatever's that?' The beam of her torch had picked out something scrawled on the wall between the front door and a hanging basket of winter pansies. Large red letters stood out angrily against the immaculate white wall, A WICH LIVS HEAR said the message with a happy disregard for spelling.

"Kids," clucked Babs, "but all the same, there's no smoke without fire . . . vegans, indeed!"

As soon as she pushed open the gate of Number Thirteen she saw a piece of paper neatly curled inside a spotless milk bottle. 'Now what's wrong?' Yes, she might have known it – yet another complaint.

Please would you kindly remember to put these covers over the bottles to prevent the birds getting the cream. I have already requested this many times before.

4

As Babs rammed the plastic tops on to the bottles in a series of vicious little snaps she visualised Number Thirteen. She'd be a great gorilla of a woman with a top-heavy bust.

'I wonder why I bother with this job really,' she thought as she rearranged the crates in the back of her truck as noisily as she dared. 'It's not worth the money, no one cares about their milkman.'

Something was propped up against the empty bottles at Number Fifteen, the last house on the right of the terrace. Babs steeled herself for another complaint, but what a difference! A tiny home-made card was tucked inside a minute envelope and a hand-painted primrose gleamed up at her through the beam of her pencil torch. It said in spring green ink:

Happy Easter. Thanks for being my alarm-clock. When I hear you I know it's time to start moving.

'Well, that's nice I must say,' thought Babs as she burrowed under layers of woollies to put the card away safely in her pocket. Perhaps the job was all right after all. 'Alarm-clock now, am I?' As she smiled up at the house a dim, rosy light went on behind the curtains high above her head.

Her float had its nose pressed against the park railings now and the two terraces receded behind it. 'Very cosy,' thought Babs appreciatively, 'but it's these two end houses I've always liked best. I'll buy one of 'em when my boat comes in.'

One hundred and twenty years ago the builder had allowed himself a treat when he decided to round off his terrace with two minute Victorian mansions – perfect in every fussy detail. Disdainfully they turned their backs on the smaller houses behind them and looked proudly out over the park through their corpulent bay windows and elegant façades. They were the only houses in the road to have large gardens, enclosed by the same iron

5

railings which surrounded the park. The one on the right (where the rosy light now showed) had been restored to its former glory, while its twin on the opposite side of the road looked as if it had been untouched by human hands for at least a century.

"This is the house I'd choose," remarked Babs, as she gave the rusty iron gate an affectionate pat of welcome. The fact that the gate was open should have warned her that something was wrong, but she was too busy with her memories to be observant. It was here, at this very gate, that it had happened. Of course she had only been a tiny girl then. Colour, that's what she saw as she pressed her fat cheeks against the iron bars, glorious colour, far better than anything the park had to offer.

"So you like flowers too, do you?" An elderly lady with a watering-can in her hand had bent down and looked at her, and no one had ever smiled at Babs like that before. The next minute a huge bunch of sweetpeas were placed in her sticky fists. To a gardenless, town child a bouquet of her very own felt like a gift straight from heaven and at that moment, the child Babs had discovered joy.

"That's my old lady," she would say a few years later as she and her teenage friends lounged round the entrance to the park, smoking their first cigarettes and whispering about boys. They would always giggle at the poor old girl as she waged an energetic war on her weeds, but Babs never forgot that smile.

When she came back here as a milkie, five years ago, 'her old lady' must have conceded the final victory to those bullying weeds and closed her front door on them in defeat. Gleefully the brambles and nettles had occupied their coveted territory, and now, thought Babs, as she walked across the overgrown garden, 'it's just an ugly jungle.'

Somewhere inside this decaying memory of Victorian gentility the old lady still existed, but the only evidence Babs had of that was the note that was always waiting for her on the doorstep.

6

On went the torch yet again, illuminating the exquisite spidery writing that had been learned in this very house when both the pupil and the century had been as young as each other. "No milk today, thank you."

"There!" snorted Babs. "It's taking her four days to get through one pint now, she's not feeding herself properly. Ought to be safe in a home, not shut up alone in a big house like this. Falling down round her ears and full of nasty creepy-crawlies." She put her mittened hand on the peeling door to steady herself and, to her surprise, it swung open against her weight. "Silly old so-and-so, she must have forgotten to put the catch down last night," scolded Babs affectionately. "I'll have to see if I can do it for her before someone just walks in." She squeezed her woolly bulk inside and began to grope behind the door for the Yale lock.

A dim light shone from the room at the far end of the shabby hall, casting weird shadows round the mouldering head of a great stuffed stag. Cobwebs decorated its ancient antlers and Babs had the oddest feeling that it was appealing to her with its dusty glass eyes.

"Oh, Gawd," breathed Babs. "Wish I was home with a warm cuppa tea." Just then her fur-lined boot crunched against something hard, and at long last alarm bells began ringing inside her head. On the door mat lay a poker with a heavy brass knob. She directed the beam of light down on to it and she stiffened. Jam, that was her first thought, strawberry jam. Yet she knew instinctively that the sticky substance which covered the poker was something far more sinister.

It was then that she saw the feet. They were sticking out of the doorway under the stag's head. Panic enveloped Babs. If she ran now she could be in Albert Gardens delivering milk in one minute flat. After all it was the police who found bodies, not milkmen. But suppose she wasn't dead. The memory of sweet peas and an even sweeter smile checked her on the door-step.

"Oh, all right then," she said to the ancient stag, and slowly she began to edge her way across the hall.

Something happened to Babs between the front door and the long dead 'Monarch of the Glen'. All the countless hours that she had spent watching murder thrillers on TV had not been wasted after all. Suddenly she became the efficient detective who was usually at the centre of all her favourite programmes.

"Mustn't touch anything in case of fingerprints," she warned the stag sternly. "Or move anything either, not till the police get here."

The body wore a dressing-gown that had been new in the nineteen-twenties, and it lay on its back in the doorway. The face that had once smiled at a child in the summertime was now unrecognisable. "It's not really her," remarked Babs briskly, "just an old overcoat she's left behind." The vicar had said that at her Gran's funeral.

'Phone. That's what I need now,' thought the cool detective inside the milkperson's disguise. As she looked round the room she noticed the devastation. Antique drawers had been yanked from desks and chests, their contents strewn heartlessly over the faded Turkish carpets. Pictures and mirrors had been wrenched from the William Morris wallpaper and the glass of the exquisite china cabinet had been brutally smashed.

"It's not fair," snorted Babs, "I bet she loved her old bits and pieces. I hope they killed her *before* she had to watch them doing all this."

A faint noise behind her momentarily transformed the detective back into a petrified milkman. Had the stag groaned or was someone still lurking in the house? Babs would never have believed she could be so relieved to see a corpse move. She pulled a rug and a cushion from an upturned armchair.

"Thought you was dead, luvvy," she muttered apologetically. "You are cold!" The eyes were open now and the swollen lips were making feeble attempts at communication.

"It's all right, it's only the milkman. Just let me get this cushion under your poor old head. Where is the phone?" she added in the loud slow voice with which most people irritate the old and disabled. "I suppose they disconnected it, they always do that. I'll have to leave you a moment, luvvy. I'll be straight back – promise."

Laburnum Terrace had never looked so dark or so unfriendly as Babs ran back towards her deserted float. The nearest phone box was right across the park and probably out of order. All was darkness again at Number Fifteen, the person who had left that card must have gone back to sleep again with the blissful realisation that it was Bank Holiday. All the same it was worth a try. The gate and the path were a mirror image of the ones behind her but no weed dared to show its face in this immaculate garden. The front door positively gleamed with shiny new paint.

"Come on, come on," puffed Babs urgently, "wake up for gawd's sake." A light came on in the hall and streamed through the stained glass that surrounded the door, but there was no noise from inside.

"It's only the milkman," called Babs reassuringly through the letter-box. "Sorry to wake you, but I need help."

A chain slid back cautiously, slowly the door swung open and there on the threshold stood Emmie. Babs drew back in surprise, the perfect Victorian house had a ghost to match. Certainly Emmie looked the part in her frilly cotton night gown. Her long silky blonde hair, with its middle parting, made her look as if she had stepped straight out of a Jane Austen novel.

'A puff of wind would blow her away,' thought Babs, suddenly conscious of her extra pounds of fat, but she heard the new detective's voice say,

"The old lady from Number Sixteen's been attacked, I need an ambulance and the police." Emmie's big 'china doll' eyes widened in sudden sympathy.

"I'll ring," she said decisively. "You go back to her and

I'll bring you over some tea." A wave of enormous relief swept over Babs and her chin wobbled ominously. "And a good nip of brandy, too," added the 'ghost' as she patted Babs' well-padded shoulder.

"Well," sniffed Babs as she scuttled back to her post, "this'll teach me to go envying people their cosy little lives." What with witches, robberies and ghosts in Victorian nighties, her imaginary people were not quite as she'd pictured them.

6.50 at Number Twelve Laburnum Terrace

"Dad! Mum! There's an ambulance in the road and policemen *everywhere*! Do you think there's been a murder?"

"Go away," groaned Sharon's father from the depths of his duvet. "I don't care if there's been a blasted massacre, it's Bank Holiday."

"Can I get dressed and go and see?" persisted his daughter.

"Go where you like, so long as you shut up. That child's a nosy little toad," added Tom when Sharon had banged the bedroom door. "She'll go too far one day, you'll see." His wife was asleep, she seldom listened to a word he said.

7.30 at Number Fifteen

Emmie was very cold and shaken when she finally waved good-bye to the milk-float. She ignored Sharon who watched her ghoulishly from her ringside seat on the garden wall. 'Surely that policeman didn't need to ask me all those silly questions,' Emmie thought as she unlocked her front door. PC Blackett had given her the uncomfortable feeling that he was more interested in her flimsy night attire than her answers.

Sharon had enjoyed seeing the battered body of Miss Rosedale wheeled past her on the stretcher, but the sight had affected Emmie deeply. 'How could any human being possibly treat a defenceless old lady with such brutality?' she wondered. 'Specially in a sleepy old town like Welbridge.'

Slowly she climbed up the two flights of stairs to her flat. This was not her house, she only provided the Tilsons with pin-money. They had converted their attic into a tiny apartment which had become Emmie's world. From the little dormer window that thrust its way cheekily through the eaves she could just see PC Blackett and two other policemen scrambling round among the tangle of brambles that mounted siege against Miss Rosedale's French windows. They looked cold too.

'I'd better have a hot shower before I freeze,' but Emmie had always hated showers. After a shock like that she needed a long hot bath . . . but dare she? They were away until tonight, they would never know.

Guiltily she crept down to the floor below. Her landlords were not the kind of people who ever said, "Do use the bathroom – the deep freeze – the washing machine." Emmie always felt that their expensive possessions were sacred objects – the household gods.

She often had tantalising glimpses of their bathroom looking like something out of a glossy magazine. Deep pile carpet, oval bath, mirrors everywhere and soft fluffy towels. With an envious sigh, Emmie turned on the taps.

It was odd lying there, surrounded by someone else's things, immersed in their exotic bath bubbles and wearing their shower hat. On the shelves by the basin stood Hazel's luxurious cosmetics all lined up like glamorous model girls awaiting the cat-walk. They certainly earned their keep; Hazel, at thirty-six, was still extremely attractive.

'Her possessions and her looks, those are the things that matter most to Hazel,' she thought as the water-level crept over her shoulders. 'I wish I knew what matters

11

most to me.' The tragic fate of the old lady in the house opposite had jarred her into thinking more profoundly than usual.

She pressed the button which operated the six underwater whirlpool jets and tried to regain her equilibrium. 'When I marry Edward, I'll have a bathroom exactly like this . . . but perhaps softer colours might be more restful . . . Whatever was that?' As the roar of the jacuzzi died away, she could hear loud voices in the hall and her heart sank as she recognised their clipped accents only too well. Someone was coming upstairs now with firm confident steps and she clutched the bubble mountain for protection and cursed herself for not closing the bathroom door.

"Well, I can see there's no need to urge you to make yourself at home." The voice was as irate as Emmie knew it would be.

"Look, I'm sorry, but you see I was most terribly cold."

"We left the heating on for you," replied Hazel.

"Yes, oh yes thank you, but you see . . ." Mentally she was cursing herself for being so shy with doctors. "The old lady over the road was attacked, and they needed me to help." Hazel's expression conveyed her disbelief that anyone could ever want Emmie's help over anything but she flung back her long red hair with a characteristic gesture of dismissal.

"If you wouldn't mind too much, I'd rather like to use my bathroom. I've got to go in to work, apparently there's a staffing crisis at the hospital."

'I'd hate to be a patient when you're on duty,' thought Emmie, 'but as you're a pathologist, I suppose I wouldn't know much about it if I were.'

It was then that she remembered she had come down without her own towel. The heated rails which contained Hazel's were on the far side of the room and she was showing no sign of a tactful withdrawal. She followed Emmie's embarrassed glance and said icily, "You'd better use one of our towels. I'm sure you intended to anyway."

Swathed awkwardly in fluffy luxury, Emmie padded up the stairs leaving a trail of footprints on the thick carpet. Below she could hear Hazel's voice complaining about her behaviour to Graham. 'I've tried so hard to get on with them,' she thought as she pulled on her warmest sweater and jeans. 'Trust me to mess it all up. The trouble is they love things and use people. That has to be the wrong way round, surely. But perhaps I'm the same, it's just that I don't have so many things to love.'

As she filled the kettle in her little galley she was still thinking of the old lady across the road. 'There has to be another dimension to life,' she told herself as she waited for it to boil. 'Something that goes beyond work, food and sex, but somehow I never seem to discover what it is.' Sometimes, when she indulged in her favourite hobby, painting flowers, she almost discovered it, but when she tried to put a mental hand round the floating idea it bobbed away and eluded her grasp. She had once tried to explain it to Edward who had roared with laughter and christened it her 'Spiritual Quest'.

'Edward never will understand anything like that,' she realised with a sense of sadness. The steaming kettle reminded her she was hungry and sent her rummaging into the cupboard like a mouse in search of food. Breakfast was not a meal she usually had time to remember. There was only that box of cornflakes Edward had insisted on buying, and Emmie frowned. It was rather annoying to open a cupboard and be confronted by your own face grinning at you from the side of a cereal packet. Of course that Brightways brief had been the biggest contract her design studio had landed for ages. Her boss had asked her to portray a nice little family, father-mother-boy-girl sitting round the breakfast table all smiles and comfortable respectability. She had actually dared to point out that the vast majority of the buying public would not be happy middle-class family units.

"Come up with something better then," he had growled. 'I stayed up all night to produce a visual for this,' she thought, as she held the packet at arm's length. Through a sea of rippling corn, splashed with vivid scarlet poppies and blue cornflowers wandered a golden-haired girl. She carried a basket full of corncobs on her arm and she looked away to the distant hills with an expression of deep contentment on her delicate oval face. Yes, of course, it had been a self-portrait, but Emmie was not vain, she had simply wanted to convey the way she felt when she walked alone in the countryside.

Somehow it had worked and the high echelons of Brightways had loved it. Not only had it won the contract, but it secured for the studio the brief for Brightways' new range of low fat dairy produce.

"I never thought my life would be reduced to this," sighed Emmie. "Cornflakes and cottage cheese, and I wanted my flowers to hang in the Royal Academy."

Somewhere downstairs the door banged again and the sleek BMW purred into life. 'I'm sick of them all!' she realised suddenly as she scooped her half-eaten bowl of revolting cardboard flakes into the sink. 'Sick of them downstairs, sick of the boss and his endless deadlines, and yes . . . I'm sick of Edward too.' She had not allowed herself to realise it until now, and the thought made her sit down suddenly.

'Don't be an idiot,' said her sensible side. 'You're going to marry Edward, and live happily ever after. All you need is a bit of space today. Ring and tell him you're going to do some painting, then you could pop to Whippendell Woods and find some violets for a still life.'

"That's right," Emmie agreed with herself. "All I need is a chance to be alone, then I'll cope with the lot of them."

8.05 at Number Thirteen

The milk bottles (in their plastic hats) were collected from the doorstep with a snort of astonishment.

"Well, so he's read my note at long last." Alison

Grazier walked back into the kitchen with the same air of efficiency with which she managed everything in her life. Her husband Gordon was eating grapefruit at the kitchen table. He looked defeated. It was not that he disliked the fruit – he perpetually resembled a man who had given up on life a long time ago.

Only breakfast was allowed to be eaten in the kitchen of Number Thirteen, but even for this simple meal there was always a clean white cloth on the table.

"But, dear," Gordon sounded desperate, "it's going to be fine today, and there's so much to do up at the allotment this time of year."

Alison poured half a pint of milk into a dainty china jug, while two red spots appeared on her cheeks – red flags which signalled danger for Gordon.

"We went over all this last night," she spoke slowly, as if addressing an imbecile. "You can go up there tomorrow while I'm flower arranging at church. Remember we decided we must go out into the country this afternoon because flowers are always cheaper in those roadside nurseries. We also agreed that if we were going in that direction we might just as well drive on to Eastbourne and put in a visit to Auntie Madge. Our good deed done for the day."

Gordon felt he had done too many good deeds on too many days already and he loathed Eastbourne and Auntie Madge equally.

Alison spotted his mulish expression and decided to change tactics.

"I don't think you realise," she said carefully, allowing a note of martyrdom to colour her voice, "just what an honour it is for me to be asked to decorate the church for Easter Day."

Gordon was defeated, he knew Alison's status in the church's pecking order was all important to her. So he pushed away the thought of a peaceful afternoon pottering among his vegetables and bit miserably into his perfectly cooked slice of bacon.

8.10 at Number Five

By ten past eight the display of health foods which Babs
had left on the doorstep had been removed and deposited
in the fridge – all except one pint of skimmed milk which
Matt drank straight from the bottle. He felt he had earned
it after fifty press-ups. Now he was showered and draped
Roman style in a large white towel. 'Life's good,' he told
himself as he swallowed his vitamin pills. Only two more
weeks now to the London Marathon, and their training
programme was bringing them both up to peak at just
the right moment. A challenging sixty-mile cycle ride was
on their schedule for the day, and Matt loved a challenge.

Softly Ann came into the kitchen behind him. Her long
dark hair was also wet from the shower and her body
positively glistened with health.

"You shouldn't wander about the house in the
altogether," complained Matt. "Laburnum Terrace is far
too nosy."

"Kiss me good morning, then I'll go and dress," she
said, sliding into his arms. Had an artist been searching
for models to portray Adam and Eve he would hardly
have sought them in the back kitchen of a Victorian villa,
but he would have been amply rewarded had he done
so. Standing together in the spring sunshine, Ann and
Matt were perfect specimens of humanity.

"Come on," Matt sounded impatient. "We've got a
lot of miles to cover today."

"Training's all you ever think about," sighed Ann.
"But I still like being married to you."

"What about the years we were together before,
weren't they any good?"asked Matt.

"They were good, but this is better."

"Now you've finally trapped me, eh?"

"Matt, I'd die if you ever left me," Ann looked up
anxiously into his lean face.

"What kind of a man would be fool enough to leave
a girl with a body like yours?"

"But suppose . . . suppose my body wasn't beautiful any more, would you still love me then?"

"Don't be ridiculous, just keep exercising and eating right and you'll stay beautiful and healthy. It's as easy as that, if only people would see it." Ann was not listening.

"Don't look round darling," she said as she stared out of the window over his shoulder. "But the alley's simply crawling with policemen."

Three helmets were bobbing about in the no-man's-land that ran between the backs of Albert Gardens and Laburnum Terrace where no one but the dustmen ever went. Under the helmets were three very interested faces which now appeared in a row above the back fence. All three showed every appearance of enjoyment.

Matt swore as he groped for his towel.

"The big one's coming in through the gate," Ann snatched the seersucker cloth from the kitchen table and sent the empty milk bottle flying.

"Sorry to intrude, sir," began a slightly pink PC Blackett when Matt grudgingly opened the back door. "I wonder if you would mind answering a few questions?"

Matt and Ann, shivering in the draught, *did* mind, but it was rather too late to say so.

No, they had never even heard of Miss Rosedale, no they had heard nothing unusual in the road or the alley last night, and yes they would get in touch if they remembered anything.

As PC Blackett returned to his colleagues and their dustbin search he was beginning to feel this was his lucky day, first Emmie in her frilly night clothes and now the garden of Eden, and people told him police work was dull!

9.10 at Number Four

Across the road two small girls were removing the heavy crate from their doorstep. One was rather smaller than the other, but they both had the same bright red faces and bobbed black hair.

"You go that end and lift it carefully," ordered the older girl. "We don't want broken bottles this morning, do we?" Being the oldest of a family of four was a weighty responsibility for a six-year-old and it had aged Rebecca considerably.

"Daddy's taking us to the zoo tomorrow, zoo tomorrow, zoo . . ." sang the younger girl shrilly and promptly fell over the doorstep.

"Now just look where you're going, and anyway," added Rebecca with crushing finality, "that's a silly song, 'cos he's taking us today, not tomorrow and it's the seaside not the zoo."

The kitchen at the end of the passage would have been a beautiful room if anyone ever had the time to tidy it. The stripped pine dresser, copper pans and antique chairs had been much enjoyed when they had first arrived, but that was four babies ago, and no one had noticed them since.

Johnnie, strapped firmly into his high-chair, looked at his mother speculatively. Her back was towards him as she bent over the changing pad, coping with his baby brother's diaper. This was his chance to attempt something he had long wanted to do, so he began at once to shampoo his hair with his porridge.

"Thank you, girls," said their mother without turning round. "What would I do without you?" she added, grimly maintaining her studied performance of calm efficiency.

"Mummy!" Rebecca's voice rang with smug enjoyment. "Just look what Johnnie's done *now*." Kim swung round still clutching the dirty diaper, the third she had changed that morning. Her enforced calm was visibly rocking, any minute now she'd . . .

David, her husband, had been searching the cluttered backyard for buckets and spades, but he appeared in the doorway just in time to read the danger signals.

"Come on, old chap," he said, scooping his son from the high-chair, "let's hose you down."

"One day I'll murder that child," muttered Kim. She had always expected to be such a good mother, after all she had her teacher training and a good knowledge of child psychology, but somehow the reality of motherhood was not quite like the books implied it should be.

"You two girls, go and see how beautifully you can tidy your bedroom," she said as she ordered her body to relax. "The quicker we get the jobs done the sooner we can go."

"Can we take our Easter eggs for the picnic?" Amy asked hopefully.

Kim allowed her face to register exaggerated horror, "They're for Easter Sunday, it's hot-cross-buns today."

"But I don't like currants," replied Amy tragically.

"But you do like egg sandwiches," said Kim, "and I'm going to make some, if I ever get the chance. Really I wonder why we bother to go out at all," she added as she wiped up the milk Johnnie had spilt on the floor. "Getting ready makes me too tired to want to go."

"Don't worry, Mummy, 'cos Daddy's used to coping with lots of children at school," said Rebecca brightly, "we're only a little handful to him."

"There are two meanings to the word handful," replied her mother with feeling.

10.25 at Number Thirteen

"Excuse me, sir," said PC Blackett, "would you mind if we asked you a few questions?" Gordon Grazier jumped. Why should he feel like a criminal he asked himself furiously. He was doing nothing wrong, polishing the windscreen of his own car, outside his own house in his own Sunday-going-to-church suit. He was the branch manager of a respectable building society who had never broken the law in his life. So why should he always feel guilty whenever a policeman spoke to him? The effect of twenty years with Alison perhaps?

There were actually two policemen standing behind him, and one held a large clipboard in his hand. Gordon locked his beloved car carefully and straightened up to the full extent of his diminutive height.

"Last night," began PC Blackett, sounding like a tape recording, "Number Sixteen, Laburnum Terrace, was forcibly entered, and a Miss Rosedale was seriously injured. Quite a number of items seem to have been removed, therefore we would like to know if you heard anything unusual between . . ." and he consulted his clipboard, "between three and five this morning?"

"No, oh no," replied Gordon, trying not to squeak in his nervousness. "We sleep very soundly, never heard a thing until the alarm-clock went off. Poor old lady," he added more gently, "I didn't know her, but I knew *of* her of course. Is she badly hurt? People always said she was sitting on a gold mine in there."

"Did they indeed, sir," said PC Blackett underlining the polite statement with a heavy ring of suspicion. Gordon watched him make a note on his clipboard and bit his tongue.

"Perhaps you'd like to ask my wife," he parried hopefully and conducted the two officers into the hall which instantly seemed far too narrow to contain them. He could see Alison standing in front of the mirror in the front room adjusting her church hat and contorting her face into the expression of refined piety he knew she felt should accompany it.

"Dear dear," she said when the 'tape recording' had been played to her, "I must hurry and inform the vicar before he robes. He'll want to say some prayers for her, I'm sure."

'She always enjoys being first with the news,' thought Gordon. 'Her neck's going red with anticipation.'

"No, I never heard anything at all last night. Miss

20

Rosedale is on our list of 'shut-ins' of course. I help the vicar with his visiting, you know, so I pop in often."
Gordon shot her a quick glance. The statement was far from true and her neck flushed a slightly darker shade. He knew for a fact that she had only 'popped' once in Miss Rosedale's direction and had met her match.

"So obviously you were aware of the valuable content of the house then," said the young policeman suspiciously.

"Content?" said Alison blankly.

"The things Miss Rosedale had — antiques, silver, china — that kind of thing."

"I can't say I noticed anything but the mess," replied Alison with a fastidious sniff. "Needed fumigation, that place did."

"You can't remember telling anyone about the contents can you?" PC Blackett was known in the force for his persistence.

"Young man, are you suggesting I planned this robbery?" The red spots were back on Alison's cheeks and Gordon winced.

"Certainly not, madam, but it's easy to make a casual remark to someone, perhaps the man who comes in to mend your sink . . ."

"I am not in the habit of talking to plumbers," replied Alison frostily.

"No, perhaps not." PC Blackett looked her up and down coolly. His brother was a plumber.

When the door shut behind them, Alison went back to the mirror to smooth her hair and her feelings.

"Hurry now, Gordon, I do want to catch the vicar." Gordon did up the top button of his white shirt and slowly tied his sombre tie. The misery of the long Good Friday vigil ahead was already chilling his spirits. He was so thin the pews made his bottom hurt and the lofty Gothic building diminished him still further.

"Amanda's late," he said sourly.

"No she's not," snapped Alison. "She works so hard

all week I gave her breakfast in bed. Here she is now. Come on, my sweet.''

As his daughter walked down the stairs Gordon found himself wondering why his wife never used that caressing tone when she addressed him. Amanda was pink and plump and vaguely reminded him of a prettily dressed pig, but she was the one joy in Alison's life.

"You'll look lovely singing in the choir with your hair done up like that," she said.

Alison had her hand on the door-catch when the phone rang. With a very unchristian expression of annoyance, she lifted the receiver.

"Hello." It was more a bark than a greeting, but instantly her voice changed to honey. Gordon, brushing dandruff from his lapels, looked sideways at her sharply. Even her accent had climbed a few rungs up the social ladder.

"Yes, yes, of course we could, we *are* just off to church now . . . but this afternoon perhaps? Yes, you'll give us more details then, of course . . . What? You want us to take her *today*?" The voice lost some of its smooth sweetness, but Alison checked herself firmly. "Poor child . . . yes naturally we will do all that we can." Her pious face was firmly pinned back into place now and Gordon sensed she was enjoying herself as she slowly replaced the receiver.

"That was Mrs Gray, the social worker. After all those months of interviews, they've got a child for us at last."

As they walked up the terrace on their way to St Mark's church Emmie passed them in her yellow Fiesta bound for the woods. They did not acknowledge each other.

10.30 at Number Seven

"Mummy, *are* you a witch?" Jasmine Lassalle had been standing in her mother's bedroom doorway for at least five minutes, mustering all her eight-year-old courage to ask that vital question. Claire, sitting at her dressing-table, had almost succeeded in moulding her thick black hair into the elegant style of the Edwardian era. The impact of the question, however, sent her hair rippling back down over her shoulders, showering the carpet with hairpins.

"Now look what you made me do," she said with a cluck of annoyance. "And who put that silly idea into your head anyway?"

"Sharon." For a week now the conversation in the playground had haunted Jasmine and the memory of Sharon's sharp foxy face as she hissed, "your mum's a witch," had disturbed her sleep. Sharon was 'clever', she always knew everything that went on in Laburnum Terrace, so she had to be right about this too.

"I wish you didn't have to spend so much time with that abominable child." Claire frowned at her reflection as she patiently began to rebuild her hair.

"But I have to go *somewhere* after school," pointed out Jasmine hastily.

"You could come round to the salon," mumbled Claire through the three hairpins she was holding in her mouth.

Jasmine's heart sank to her blue sandals – she hated her mother's hairdressing shop, steamy hot and smelling of peroxide. Sharon was bearable because of her nice ordinary mummy and the nice ordinary teas which she provided. *White* bread and *shop* cakes – a girl could get very tired of home-made brown bread with 'bits' in it, and organically grown carrots – not to mention soya milk. There was the telly, too.

She looked tensely at her mother's face in the glass. She certainly didn't look like a witch – witches had white hair and pointed chins. Mummy was forty-five, so of course she must be terribly old, but her hair was black and shiny and she was very beautiful because she put on so much make-up. Jasmine sighed uneasily. In spite of her looks, she had to admit that Mummy wasn't like other people's mummies – they didn't wear floating black clothes and billowing silk scarves. They didn't spend their weekends wandering round the countryside with twigs in their hands looking for energy lines. When someone was ill, *other people's* mummies called the doctor, not that man with the sweaty hands who 'had a gift of healing'.

"*Are* you a witch, Mummy?" she persisted urgently. The doobell rang and Claire jabbed in a final hairpin with a sigh of relief.

"Quick, they're here already. Take your anorak," she called as she followed Jasmine down the stairs. "And here's some money for emergencies, but don't you dare buy any ice-cream."

The sight of a whole carload of children from Number Four made Claire shudder. 'Four under six!' she thought as she watched Jasmine squeezed in among the beachballs and cricket bats. 'But how odd to offer Jasmine a day out at the sea.' She hardly knew the Pattersons except that they lived over the road and the 'mum' came to the salon to have her hair cut. Why should they put themselves out for her?

As she stood in the middle of the road waving goodbye, the chilly breeze whipped her flowing skirt round her long slender legs.

'They're just a nice ordinary family, so why do they always make me feel so uneasy?' she asked herself. Perhaps it was their aura, a subtle danger in their vibrations? 'But what does it matter?' she thought. 'They're giving me a whole precious day of child-free peace.'

She had been planning it all week. She would spring-clean the house from attic to cellar, shift all the accumulated winter rubbish and then perhaps . . . As she turned towards the house she froze like a graceful Edwardian statue in the middle of the road. She was looking at the red letters on her wall which had startled Babs four hours earlier. "A wich livs hear."

Embarrassment was her first emotion. How many of the neighbours would have seen that? It could have an adverse effect on her business. Then fury pushed

24

embarrassment aside. Spinning round to face Number Twelve across the road she was just in time to see a foxy head duck down behind the low garden wall.

"Of course," she muttered grimly, "the Abominable Sharon!" Two strides from her long legs and Claire was towering over the cornered culprit.

"Where are your parents?" she demanded curtly.

"Still in bed," retorted Sharon, truthful for once.

"Then you'll just have to come over and clean my wall for me yourself." Claire's voice was dangerously quiet.

"I will if you promise not to . . . look at me."

"I'm not in the habit of putting the 'evil eye' on people, but if I ever felt tempted, I would certainly start on you! Now come and I'll find you a scrubbing-brush and some hot water."

Ten minutes later the job was done, leaving only a faint pink smudge on the white plaster, but somehow all the joy had gone out of the day for Claire. She stood frowning in the middle of her kitchen as her energy and good intentions oozed out of the soles of her shoes.

Jasmine's accusing eyes and Sharon's vandalism had forced to the surface of her mind a conflict which had been pricking her like a buried thorn for nearly two weeks.

"I must get out of this polluted town," she muttered. Spring-cleaning would only serve to push the thorn back down again to jab at her later on. "Come on, Boris, we'll go to the woods, I'll be able to think there." The German shepherd dog who had been looking up hopefully at her sprang to life, as if he had been released from a binding spell.

Soon Claire's little Renault was nosing its way down Laburnum Terrace and out into Baker's Hill. She glanced automatically at her salon – empty, dark and thoroughly cleaned – waiting for a busy Saturday tomorrow. The opposite side of the road was dominated by the grotesque Victorian bulk of St Mark's. Its bell was ringing dolefully, calling the faithful to their Good Friday service. There was that impossible couple from Number Thirteen. He was tiptoeing along in a black funeral suit and she was . . . horrors! Which of the girls had done that woman's hair yesterday? The new one? She really must speak to her about it, that shade of chestnut was outrageous and those frizzy curls! Yet she distinctly remembered Mrs Grazier smiling as she paid the bill. Just for once she had not complained, perhaps she actually wanted to look like that! And what a way to spend a Bank Holiday, cooped up in a Victorian mausoleum, worshipping a dying god. Claire shivered and put her foot down harder on the accelerator.

She would have been horrified a year ago to see herself drive her spotless car down a muddy track, or worse still to watch as she pulled on green boots and scrambled over a stile. Even now she had to remind the 'townie' she had always been that living close to the earth was the only way to complete wholeness. All the same she was far too absorbed in her thoughts to notice the green spikes which promised bluebells next month. Neither did she see the white faces of the wood anemones which had so delighted Emmie when she had walked down this same path a little while before.

Claire had been walking for some minutes when she reached the fork. Two little paths led away in different directions, one down to the stream (which Emmie had taken) and the other up to the badger's set. Which way should she go? She leaned her back against the lichen-softened trunk of an ancient oak while she savoured the decision at length. Over her head the birds sang and the scent of the old Goddess Earth rose invitingly from under her feet. Into her mind floated an image of Mrs Alison Grazier's frizzy head bowed in worship. 'Sanctimonious hypocrite!' Making everyone's life a misery. What sort of a god was it that she spent so long worshipping?

'What sort of a god do I worship?' The question came to her as softly as the spring breeze and for some reason Claire shivered.

The two paths at her feet split sharply away from each other and reminded her of the decision she had come here to make.

Boris galloped away on his own business and slowly she slipped down on to the mossy softness at the foot of the tree and gave her mind permission to travel backwards. She had just been an ordinary hairdresser a year ago, coming home to the soaps on television and the ironing.

"Mummy, *are* you a witch?" The childish question came back to her like a repetitive birdsong. "*Are* you a witch?" Well, of course she wasn't. It was still just a new absorbing hobby, but if she let it go on any longer it would become her whole life, pushing Jasmine and the business out into an antechamber. Was she willing to allow anything to change her so radically? But did she have an alternative? Being beautiful and helping others to be so had been Claire's entire life. When Michael had left her two years ago she realised that her looks were leaving her too. Grey hairs could be eradicated by someone with her skills, but her face? The mirror told her relentlessly that she was fading like a rose picked a week ago.

There had always been men in Claire's life, she had divorced two of them, and had not married Michael. At twenty-eight he had been fascinated by his craze for the 'older woman', but not so pleased when their relationship had led accidentally to a squalling, nappy-dependent baby. He had stuck domesticity for six years, but a fluffy young blonde had pulled him back into the world of childless freedom and left her alone with the baby-sitters' bills, the Brownies and the school lunch-box.

'I was going out of my head with boredom,' she reminded herself. 'I had to have something new and absorbing to give my life shape, and I certainly found it – through Roger.' He had opened a door for her into a world she had never dreamed could exist. A smile began to ease the tension from her face and she relaxed against the tree-trunk.

She had been twisted up in agony for weeks, after falling downstairs one morning. The doctor said there was nothing wrong with her back – his X-rays proved it.

"So why, in heaven's name, does it go on hurting?" she had demanded across his surgery desk.

"Tension," he had replied blandly. "You're probably a bit depressed too – single parent – your age perhaps. The pain is all in the mind."

"You look awful," a client had said a few days later as Claire had been struggling to perm her hair.

She had looked at her reflection over the woman's head, and the face that looked back at her was haggard, careworn and defeated.

"You haven't been well for weeks, dear," continued the client. "You're in pain all the time, aren't you?"

"The doctor says it's depression that's causing the pain," Claire had growled. "But you'd think anyone would have the common sense to see it's the other way round."

"You ought to go to Roger," the woman had replied enthusiastically. "My dear, he's marvellous. He has the most incredible psychic powers."

Three days later Claire had driven down the little lane with the high flower-tangled banks. Roger's cottage had once been a watermill, and nestled by the stream at the bottom of a forgotten valley. It reminded Claire of an elderly cat sleeping in the evening shadows after years of hard work. As she got out of the car the pungent scents of an evening garden had woven round her like a spell – she was stepping backwards in time. Welbridge was only twenty minutes away, but it felt like a thousand years.

It was dusk, on a warm summer evening and Roger had just lit the oil-lamps – he never felt the need for electricity. Bunches of fragrant herbs hung from the beamed ceiling, roses filled a bowl on the gnarled oak table, and all around the sleepy cottage the evening song of the birds provided a superior alternative to a modern stereo.

"My dear, you are in pain, I can see it in your eyes."
Those were the very first words Roger had ever spoken
to her, and they pierced her shell and made her want to
cry like a hurting child. "Come on in and let me do
something for you." It had not mattered that Roger was
bald and ageing, he had an 'other world' quality about
him which made everything she had always held as
important seem shallow and meaningless.

He had placed her on a three-legged milking-stool by
the ingle-nook, lit a fire of apple logs and dried lavender
and then poured her a glass of his own cowslip wine.

The warmth of the fire and its gentle flickering light had
soothed her miraculously and she felt herself relax at last.

Slowly he had reached over from the armchair where
he sat and placed his hands on her back. A strange
warmth had coursed through her entire body. Gently he
began to caress her neck, behind her ears and along her
slender shoulders. It was not like the touch of other men,
a prelude to something they wanted from her. Roger was
abstracted; it was almost as if he was silently communing
with himself, trying to feel his way to the heart of her
misery. The whole experience had been beautiful, and
she knew instinctively that he had entered and possessed
her spirit. It had belonged to him ever since.

The sky was full of stars when she finally drove home
to face an angry baby-sitter, but a week later when he
phoned to see how she was, her back was no better.

"I'm sorry," he had said gently. "You're obviously
going to need a course of at least twelve sittings to undo
this damage." Claire had not been sorry at all. The weeks
which followed felt like a honeymoon.

A chilly little breeze brought her back into the present
again, and she forced herself to stop and think when the
conflict had begun, this war between an ordinary little
provincial hairdresser and the new creature that was
emerging like a dragonfly from a grub.

Perhaps it was the evening when she had felt she was
floating right out of her own body and away from Roger's

caressing hands suspended weightlessly among the wood smoke. The sensation had been profoundly exhilarating, but when she found herself sitting once again on the milking-stool she had felt awkward and ruffled.

"What happened?" she had demanded.

"It was your Awakening," Roger had said. "Your spirit being set free from the confines of your body."

As she had driven back to Welbridge that night she had vowed never to go back to Roger's cottage again. She was getting out of her depth; better to stick to a world she could organise and understand. Two days later she had lifted a heavy box in the store room and pain had seared once again through her back. She had hobbled round in stony-faced endurance for a fortnight. Then back to Roger she had gone with a feeling of relief which mingled oddly with a new delicious sense of fear. 'Suppose there really is another world out there beyond Laburnum Terrace.'

She had sold her grandmother's diamond brooch to pay his fees, but what did that matter?

"Right across the globe," Roger had told her with a strange glow in his pale eyes, "enlightenment is coming. People are discovering new ideas, rediscovering them actually, most are older than time itself. Humans are uniting to pool their discoveries, sharing the long-forgotten cosmic energies that have lain waiting deep in the heart of old Mother Earth."

"I've read about the New Age in the papers," said Claire. "Is that what you mean?"

"That's just a media word, an umbrella term," he replied with a contemptuous shrug, "to cover all the exciting things which are uniting a diversity of forces." Claire's starved mind was struggling. "The sign of Pisces is on the wane, the fish badge of Christianity has had its day. Now Aquarius is ascending, giving the world a new beginning. We must each fulfil our own human potential; for me this is through the power of healing."

"I'd like to know more about all this," said Claire breathlessly.

30

She had read nothing but glossy magazines for years, but she positively devoured the books he lent her each week. She grew so excited about ley lines and the healing power of crystals she hardly slept for weeks.

Roger suggested she took up yoga for both her physical and spiritual pain and drastically changed her diet. Best of all he introduced her to the Group.

'I never would have believed that there were so many interesting people tucked away in a dull place like Welbridge,' Claire had thought the first time Roger had taken her to 'a gathering'. She had been to many since, but she had never lost the exhilaration of the first time they all clustered round someone's log fire and knocked ideas about, like billiard balls, deep into the night.

Gradually her whole life style had changed. Oven chips and beefburgers disappeared from her freezer and were replaced by sprouting mung beans on her window ledge and stoneground bread rising by the stove. Her smart business-woman's clothes were sold and natural fibres filled her wardrobe with wholesome vitality and subtle colour. She burnt her sealskin handbag.

No, the buried thorn had not started to trouble her until recently, when Roger had startled her by saying, "You have to face the fact, my dear, you are psychic – a born healer."

"Me? I could never do what you do."

"My dear, you could, you have the gift. Didn't you realise, you are surrounded by the green aura?"

"But I'm such an ordinary kind of person, not like the others in the Group."

"No, you are not like them," he had quietly replied, "but *they* are the ordinary ones. *You* are the one with potential." He had taken her hands in his and gently lifted their palms to his lips. "Let me teach you all I know," he had said, and the reverent look in his eyes had made her feel young and beautiful again.

"Do you want to receive this power, my dear? Are you willing for the cost?"

"Cost? What cost?" The business woman in Claire was instantly suspicious.

"There is always a cost, my dear, but who can say what it will be?"

Back in the wood again, Claire stood up stiffly, and turned her cheek towards the oak tree for comfort. Life had suddenly become so complicated. Did she really want to launch out into a new career at her age? It might take months, even years, to learn all she would need to know. How could she afford that much time *and* keep the business going? And there was always Jasmine . . .

She had told him she would think about it, but that was two weeks ago. The decision had to be made. If she turned back she would lose his friendship and respect. Like Cinderella at the stroke of midnight she would have to return to the monotonous drudgery of Laburnum Terrace. But what had he meant when he said, "there is always a cost"? What if she burnt her bridges behind her and then discovered something sinister waiting for her in this New Age which Roger offered?

Claire shook her slim shoulders angrily. These silly doubts were nothing more than the dying squeaks of a mousy little hairdresser. The two woodland paths lay waiting at her feet, she must take one or the other just as she must decide today which path to take in life — safety or danger? Boredom or adventure?

"What the hell?" she said out loud, "Grasp your chance, my girl, or you'll end up a lonely old woman like Miss Rosedale up the road. Adventure and power are what you've always wanted and you'll never find that under a hair-dryer." So with new resolve in her step she whistled Boris and took the path up towards the badger's set.

11.45

Emmie walked slowly down Laburnum Terrace wearing the expression which helped sell Brightways cornflakes by the ton. Her boots were covered with clay but her hands were full of violets. On the wall of Number Three sat a young man, and the artist in her was instantly intrigued by his face. 'He ought to make TV commercials with a smile like that,' she thought. As she walked by, he leaned forward and touched the flowers in her hand, almost reverently. For some reason Emmie found herself smiling back at him, in spite of her usual reserve.

"It's no use trying to talk to Nigel." Behind her Sharon's bicycle brakes grated harshly. "He's handi-capped." A surge of annoyance flooded Emmie. Why was this obnoxious child allowed to get under everyone's feet?

"You have to put the words into his head first, you see," explained Sharon. "Like this." She turned to the young man on the wall and bellowed, "Minibus, Nigel?"

"Minibus," he nodded happily.

"Going on the day-centre outing, aren't you."

"Day-centre outing." He looked ecstatic.

"You see?" Sharon sounded like a conceited professor explaining a complicated procedure.

At the end of the road a small red bus jerked to a halt. As Nigel scrambled in he was greeted by a chorus of delighted welcomes from the other beaming occupants. They clapped their hands and cheered as he slid the door shut behind him.

"Isn't it sad?" said Sharon, mimicking her mother. "They spend all day making stools and things." Emmie looked at the excited faces smiling out of the windows of the van, and Nigel's hand waving cheerfully as he disappeared up Bakers Hill. She wondered if it really was sad that a human being should be so happy.

12 noon

By midday Matt and Ann Coley were miles from Laburnum Terrace, pedalling up a steep lane which wound its way up to the top of the Downs near Eastbourne. Most people would have been forced to walk that gradient, but they merely stood high on the pedals of their light racing bikes. Neither of them noticed the primroses which decorated the high banks on either side of the lane.

The summit felt like the crown of Everest itself when they finally reached it, but only a skylark applauded their achievement. A solitary Ford Escort was parked there, facing the magnificent view, but both its occupants were fast asleep. Matt took out his stop-watch, "We've cut five minutes off last week's record. I think we deserve a bit of lunch." He took a waterproof cape from his saddle-bag and spread it out on the ground squashing a carpet of violets. As they lay side by side, munching their muesli bars, the plaintive sound of a bell tolling down in the valley was wafted towards them on the breeze. An ancient church, nestling in the rippling skirt of the Downs, was summoning the scattered population, just as it had done for centuries.

"People seem to worship all kinds of things," said Ann, who for some unaccountable reason was thinking of the neighbours back in Laburnum Terrace.

"I don't worship anything," said Matt, peeling a banana.

"Yes you do, you worship that great body of yours."

"Well why not? Health's the only thing that counts. If people would only realise their bodies can be made to do as they're told, we'd hardly need the NHS."

Ann smiled, she loved him, complete with the 'bees in his bonnet'. She lay down and wriggled closer to him. He had always been so forceful, he made life happen to him while she had always been the type who waited for life to happen to her. Never mind, while she could creep along through life in his shadow, perhaps people wouldn't realise how timid she felt.

Babs woke up with a snort and peered out of the window of the Ford Escort. The good thing about a milk round was that it left you with the rest of the day free, but the trouble was you were too tired to enjoy it.

"Come on Ron," she said, poking her husband with her elbow. "Time we made for Eastbourne, I fancy some fish and chips."

"Nice looking girl that," said Ron sleepily, "what a figure!" Babs watched Ann climb back onto her bicycle and ride away behind Matt down the hill.

"Bodies aren't everything," she said, pulling her sweater firmly down over her spare tyres. "It's happiness that counts."

1.15pm

The Patterson family from Number Four were discovering that Camber Sands was not the best choice for an April outing with small children. Kim sat huddled behind the canvas wind-break, breast-feeding the baby and trying to prevent Johnnie swallowing any more fistfuls of sand. The unrestrained wind hurled itself off the sea and turned the baby's button nose to Christmas scarlet.

"Do you remember when we were first married?" she said. "We used to grab our swim stuff and a couple of Mars bars and just come down here for the day."

David, who had spent an hour lugging carrycot, picnic box and heavy bag of paraphernalia over the sand-dunes, smiled appreciatively. To say David Patterson was a man of few words would have been wrong. He was a man of almost no words at all, yet he communicated with the world most successfully by means of an expressive face and an infectious laugh. He lay peacefully on one elbow and smiled as he watched the three little girls digging feverishly in the sand. They were creating an intricate sand village, and Jasmine, although the eldest, was certainly not in charge – Rebecca always took that role automatically.

"I think Jasmine's frightened of something," whispered Kim, "she always looks . . . haunted somehow. What's she like at school?" David sipped tea from the plastic lid of the thermos and frowned. He taught the fourth year so Jasmine would not be in his class for three more years, yet now Kim mentioned it he had noticed the way she skirted round the edges of the playground like an ethereal shadow.

"She enjoyed her picnic lunch though." Kim was used to doing all the talking in their conversations. "She positively wolfed down those egg sandwiches, not to mention the hot-cross-buns. There's nothing wrong with her appetite, yet she's as thin as a matchstick."

"Daddy, can we go to find the sea now," said Rebecca. The job of site manager had begun to pall.

"Good idea," said Kim brightly. "The baby needs his nap and he'll settle better if you all go away. Johnnie can ride on Daddy's shoulders," she added hopefully. The book she had brought in the hope of some peace was positively burning a hole in her beach-bag. Fortunately the tide was so far out it had almost disappeared over the horizon. It would take them ages to reach it. "Books and motherhood don't mix well," she sighed.

Over the sparkling wet sand ran Rebecca, her flat feet sending splatters of mud up her solid legs.

"Come on, Amy," she called over her shoulder. Jasmine walked stiffly along beside David. She liked being with grown-ups more than other children and Rebecca's bossiness was beginning to grate.

David looked down at the waif who walked beside him and wondered again why she was so frightened, and he cursed himself for being so bad at conversation. Jasmine looked up at him and felt cross with herself for being too shy to ask the question that burned so painfully in her head. Over the damp, ridged sand they walked in silence, their spirits trying in vain to make contact while Rebecca urged them on impatiently.

'She ought to have ballet lessons,' thought Jasmine. 'Mummy says they make you graceful,' but somehow she simply could not picture a cart-horse like Rebecca up on her points. She's lucky to have a nice lumpy mummy who makes egg sandwiches and a dad who laughs all the time. It isn't fair. Mummy never had time now for the things Jasmine enjoyed and the evenings weren't cosy any-more since the television had gone.

They were crossing a little stream which meandered its way out to meet the tide, when it happened. It was not as shallow as it appeared, and Jasmine would have stumbled into deep water if David had not grabbed her hand.

"That scared you," he said, smiling down at her. Her face was expressionless but her ice-cold fingers clutched his warm ones as if she never again meant to let them go. Touch did far more for their relationship than words could ever have done, and Jasmine was still holding David's hand by the time the first feeble little waves came creeping over the mud to curl themselves about their boots. Life in Laburnum Terrace might feel threatening, but Jasmine realised there was safety to be found with this man. She wished she dared ask him if witches were true.

3.30 at Number Thirteen

"Well, what a strange Good Friday!" Alison Grazier's voice was muffled, because she had crawled under the spare-room bed in order to damp-dust the already spotless skirting-board. Gordon could see nothing 'good' about it whatsoever, as he teetered on the top of the step-ladder trying to hang a pair of curtains. Sweat poured off his face and he was very thirsty indeed. The thought of the tins of beer he always kept in his shed at the allotment did nothing for his temper as yet another plastic curtain-hook snapped in its bed of rufflette tape.

On the way to church this morning, when Alison had said, "We can't possibly go out to get the flowers this afternoon," his spirits had lifted, only to be dashed when she decreed that instead they must spring-clean the spare room.

"The child is arriving for good at four o'clock," she had added with relish. Gordon could imagine how much she was going to enjoy telling her circle of admiring church friends that her latest campaign to reform teenage delinquents was about to begin. "They've had to remove her instantly from her home because of . . . her step-father," she added darkly. However, she would divulge no more details, leaving Gordon to sit through the service feeling like a child excluded from the facts, on account of his tender age.

As he wiggled a new curtain-hook into place he looked down at his wife's ample backside as she reversed out from under the bed, and a look of pure loathing flitted across his mild face. Fostering this defenceless kid was just another of Alison's great schemes for reform. She would take her apart, piece by piece, clean her out, and then thrust her out upon the world remodelled, a dull little robot just like Amanda. Why could Alison never accept anyone or anything just as it was? She always wanted to improve on it and stamp it with her own impress. If she ever got into the office she would reorganise every system and procedure in the organisation, and the worst of it was – she would probably be right. The thought made Gordon shudder.

"I can't think why you make such a mess of hanging curtains, you always seem to end up with horrid uneven gaps, don't you?"

'You ought to try doing the job yourself sometime,' thought Gordon.

"That's it then," she said, looking round the room with satisfaction. "There's only the switch on the bedside lamp to mend when you're finished up there. Oh dear, you did leave a lot of smears when you cleaned the window."

"Why couldn't Amanda have given us a hand?"

"Don't be silly, dear, you know how much homework she gets – she's entitled to a holiday."

Gordon knew that if he pointed out how hard he worked in order to pay for the expensive private school which set the homework, Alison would only say, "Our Amanda's education is worth a little sacrifice."

She moved a china dog on the window-ledge a centimetre to the left, and then glanced at her watch. "We've only got half an hour to get ourselves ready, and I haven't even started on the tea. It's funny," she added almost shyly, "but I really feel I'm beginning my life's work, today."

Gordon was still fiddling ineffectually with the lamp switch thirty minutes later when the front doorbell rang loudly.

"She'll have to do without!" he growled, thrusting the lamp back on the table and ignoring the shrill cry of "Gordon!" from the bottom of the stairs.

He went into the bathroom and locked the door on the female voices below. He didn't want a stranger living in his house, looking at him at breakfast in the morning and using his toothpaste. He felt like staying in the bathroom for the rest of the night and reading his library book on the art of rotation in the vegetable garden.

"Gordon! Gordon!" This time the voice was accompanied by a sharp rapping on the bathroom door. Hiding the book in the dirty-clothes basket, Gordon squared his shoulders and pulled back the bolt.

By the time he had changed his sweaty shirt, Mrs Gray, the social worker, was already in the kitchen whispering confidences to Alison.

"Go on into the front room and keep the child talking while I get the details," ordered his wife. 'Keep her talking . . .' What did one say to girls of fourteen? He'd never practised on Amanda.

The next few minutes were preserved in Gordon's mind and played back frequently like a precious video. Looking back he often felt he was never the same man

39

again. She was sitting stiffly poised on the edge of the settee with her back towards him. The television was on, but Alison had neglected to turn up the sound. As the door opened she sprang nervously to her feet and spun round to face him. As she did so, her long black hair swirled out and billowed round her face like an advert for a hair conditioner. Two huge terrified eyes surveyed him through the narrow gap her hair left when it finally settled to rest.

"Er . . . how do you do . . ." began Gordon, not quite sure if he should shake hands. 'She's so small,' he thought, and his stiff shoulders relaxed. All his life was spent looking up at people who were bigger than he was. Here was someone who was actually looking up at *him*.

She held out her hand and he took it gently. It felt fragile as it lay in his, quivering. The other day he had noticed a fledgling which had fallen from its nest in the hedge which flanked his allotment. The vicious ginger cat which had always reminded him of Alison was standing over it beginning its sadistic game, while the baby bird squeaked wildly for its mother.

He had enjoyed putting his boot into that cat's frizzy ginger fur and when he stood cupping the terrified bird in both hands its body had felt just like this little hand. She must feel as if she's been yanked out of her nest, too. Would Alison tyrannise over this child like the ginger cat? He wouldn't be able to protect her. Or would he?

"I . . . er . . . hope you'll be happy here . . . Clancy," he said awkwardly. Two rows of incredibly long lashes fell over her dark eyes and as she dropped her head demurely the curtain of hair swung across her face like the end of Act One.

"I'll . . . go and give them a hand . . . with tea . . ." he stammered and ran out to the kitchen like a soldier diving for cover.

"She's so young," he remarked rather breathlessly to Mrs Gray, "so young to be . . . you know." The social worker eyed him with the pitying stare of the professional who has lost all sense of surprise.

"The police aren't going to charge the stepfather. We can't prove anything conclusively, but in this kind of case it's better to be safe than sorry."

"We'll soon put her to rights," said Alison with the confident assurance of total ignorance.

7.15

It was getting dark rapidly outside now and yet Claire did not want to pull down the kitchen blind while her hands were covered in flour. Jasmine was upstairs in her bedroom sulking as usual. When the Pattersons had brought her home she had asked to go over and play with Rebecca. 'TV and a junk-food tea, that's the real attraction,' thought Claire grimly, as she pounded the lump of wholemeal dough.

Someone was out in the back alley. It was not that she heard anything, she simply felt she was being watched. Slowly she wiped her hands, and flicked off the kitchen light. Was this how the old lady at the end of the road had felt, before her attackers had burst into her house? Claire was afraid of physical violence – a woman living alone is always vulnerable. As she crossed to the window she was sure something moved out there in the dusk.

"Boris," she called urgently. Downstairs he ran from his nest on her bed, his bristly hackles raised. He had heard something out there, too. "Go on boy, get them." Boris's grandmother had been a police dog and she would have been proud of the way he scaled the backyard gate. A piercing scream shattered the peace of Laburnum Terrace, and the dustbins the police had so carefully searched that morning sounded as if they were going down like bowling pins.

Claire frowned; the scream had sounded distinctly feminine. Fumbling with the gate-catch she hurried out

41

into the alley where Boris was standing proudly over the fallen enemy and a mound of scattered rubbish.

"Sharon! How dare you spy on me!"

Sharon did not want to say she had been trying to see Claire making spells, "I was looking for our cat," she offered instead.

"Cat!" snapped Claire. "You haven't got a cat! I'm taking you right back home to your parents."

Tom and Angela Savery were enjoying a pleasant evening by the television – their favourite occupation. It was ended abruptly by the shrill summons of the doorbell.

"Tell them to go away," said Tom crossly.

"It's Claire," called Angela from the front door. "She wants a word with you."

"Tell her to come back later."

"I shall do no such thing," Claire's voice was shrill. "You are disgusting parents! Leaving your child to scribble graffiti and act like a peeping Tom!"

He heaved his large stomach out of the chair and followed it to the front door. The money Claire paid for babysitting Jasmine came in handy, but no one was going to call him names.

"If you're talking about what she wrote on your wall, I don't blame her," he shouted. "Lots of people round here would agree."

"How dare you!" Claire had not meant to raise her voice too, but the tension she had been under recently caused her self-control to snap. Boris, absorbing her mood, leapt about the pavement behind her, barking wildly. The curtains of Laburnum Terrace began to twitch like the sniffs of disapproving noses. Several people decided that it was time to put out their milk bottles.

"You certainly aren't fit to be babysitters," finished Claire when she had shouted a great many other things. "Jasmine will be coming to the salon with me from now on."

"Well really!" said Alison Grazier, dusting the already spotless front window sill of Number Thirteen. "I've never trusted that hairdresser woman. Fancy behaving like that in the street. She's beginning to let the whole Terrace down with her funny ideas.''

Jasmine, who was watching the proceedings from her solitary bedroom, knew that she hated her mother.

11.15

The Terrace was deserted now. Once again the curtains were closed tightly and the streetlights softened the corners of the quaint little houses that Babs the milkperson thought were so cosy.

At Number Four Kim pulled the covers over her head in a vain attempt not to hear the baby bellowing in the next room. 'If only I could stop being a mother, just for twenty-four hours,' she thought wearily.

''Kim,'' came David's voice through the darkness. ''We've got to do something for that kid Jasmine.''

''Do what for her?'' replied Kim with muffled irritation. ''I already feel like the old woman who lived in a shoe.''

Clancy, lying in the spotlessly clean back bedroom of Number Thirteen, allowed the smile of innocent sweetness which she had worn all day, to take a well-earned rest. This place would do her nicely. That woman was a bit of a pain, but she would soon have the little Gordon man eating out of her hand. Toffee-nosed Amanda would have to be taught a lesson, but that wouldn't be too difficult. The food was great and as for this bedroom – well if only her mates on the Charbury Estate could see her now! She had risked everything to get herself here, now all she had to do was play her cards right and she'd be laughing.

11.45

Matt and Ann Coley had been asleep for two hours

already. Early nights were part of their training programme. Just as Claire finally climbed into bed in the next-door house, Ann sprang up, grappling with the duvet.

"Matt, Matt, don't leave me!" she screamed.

"Shut up," he mumbled sleepily, "you'll wake the whole Terrace."

"I must have been dreaming," she said as she lay down again. Yes, of course that was all it was, just a silly dream. A gigantic stage-curtain had descended, wrapping her in its velvety folds. Her legs and arms were hopelessly tangled and Matt was walking away off the stage, leaving her alone – pinned down and immobile. She put out a hand and felt for him in the darkness, but he was sound asleep.

Midnight

Emmie lay stiff and straight under her frilly bedcover. 'This has got to stop,' she thought with finality. The moonlight slanted through the dormer window, silvery and beautiful, but it served only to illuminate Edward's head, lying on the pillow beside her, tousled and sweating.

How had she ever got herself into a mess like this. She had been eating a cheese sandwich when it all began. She could see herself now, leaning over her drawing-board, cursing Bea's constant whistling – too busy to stop for a proper lunch. Then the office door had exploded with sudden force and in hurtled the boss waving his arms like a football fan after a hat-trick.

"They're biting," he yelped as he hugged Bea and deftly dodged her indignant slap. He had been wooing Health Care International for some time – they wanted a glossy house magazine. A monthly contract of that size could be the studio's bread and butter for years to come.

"They liked your visuals, Emmie," he beamed. "I'm

taking their Mr Soames out to lunch at the Welbridge Hotel in thirty minutes and you're coming too. Go home and put on something . . .''

"Sexy?'' Bea had finished acidly. "Sure you wouldn't like me to come along too? All 238 pounds of me?''

Emmie had fallen in love with Edward before they had finished the prawn cocktails. Or had she simply fallen in love with the culture, beauty and music his glittering world seemed to contain? Listening to him talk had made her own life seem so grey and narrow. In spite of her startling good looks she had always been too shy to make relationships with men, so when he had asked her out the following evening, she had been dazzled.

Everything had happened so quickly – they were engaged before she had time to discover that Edward's world was not the Utopia she had expected. Now it was beginning to dawn on her that he went to the opera to meet the right people in the bar, his yacht was merely a status symbol and he went to dinner parties not for deep intellectual conversations but because he liked eating.

'I've tried so hard to make it work,' she thought miserably as she looked at him lying there beside her. 'But how can I ever tell him it's all over? He really does love me in his own way. It's not his fault I'm some kind of freak who only feels safe on my own.'

Cautiously she slid out of bed and tiptoed across to the window. The silvery light shone down on to the little table where she had arranged the bunch of violets she had picked in the woods. How she had enjoyed sketching them – until Edward had arrived.

If only he could have left her in peace, just for today. She had tried to explain, but he had stopped her with some joke about her 'Spiritual Quest' not being much fun for him.

"I've heard of a new little place down at Rye, and I've booked a table.''

He had looked so happy as she surveyed him across the escalopes of veal, telling the usual jokes and then laughing so loudly people looked round crossly from other tables. Trying to explain their wedding must be cancelled would have felt like telling a child Christmas was banned for ever. Somehow she simply could not do it.

'I should never have let it all go so far,' she told herself as she looked out of the window. 'Poor old Edward, it's not fair on him to go on pretending like this.' On the far side of the road Miss Rosedale's tangled garden looked mysterious in the moonlight. It was sad not to see the usual chink of light showing between her 'blackout' curtains. Had *she* minded being single all her ninety-four years, Emmie wondered? She might even have been happy. Perhaps after all, it was not so unnatural to enjoy being alone.

"What are you doing, padding round in the dark?" came Edward's voice testily. "You know I can't sleep when you don't come to bed." He sounded like a husband already. 'Tomorrow I'll tell him,' Emmie promised herself and slid back under the covers.

EASTER MONDAY

But Emmie did not have time to tell Edward the next morning. He was eating her stale cornflakes when a frantic phone call from her boss had sent her dashing to the studio for a rush job which took the rest of the weekend. Edward had looked furious as she left him sitting there, like a dog deprived of its bone, and that 'serious talk' was still hanging over her head.

4.15 pm

The hospital corridors were deserted on Bank Holiday Monday. 'I must be mad,' she thought, as she peered nervously through the glass door of ward number nine. 'I hate hospitals.' Yet she had not been able to stop herself from thinking of the battered old lady from Number Sixteen. On the way home from the studio she had spent far too much on the present she was now clutching, but somehow she could never resist flowers.

"Who do you want?" enquired a tired but efficient voice behind her, just as she was planning to run away.

"Miss Rosedale," answered Emmie nervously as she turned to the nurse who looked as tired and efficient as her voice.

"Fourth bed on the left." There was no escape now, the nurse was holding open the swing-doors and Emmie knew she must walk between the two long rows of beds looking for someone she had never even met.

The memory of the bloody 'corpse' stretched flat on

47

the Turkish carpet was still so fresh in Emmie's mind, that she was totally unprepared to meet the person who was propped up in that fourth bed on the left. Certainly the face was grotesquely bruised and swollen, but the dark eyes that gazed out between the bandages were very much alive.

"I've brought you some flowers," Emmie stammered as she hovered awkwardly by the bed. Two tears oozed down the puffy cheeks but Emmie knew instinctively that they were tears of pleasure. The old lady sat with the vivid arrangement in her trembling hands gazing in silent appreciation.

"You love flowers too, then." Emmie watched in satisfaction as a wobbly old finger touched the perfect petals.

"I have always done so, but I never thought I would ever see such lovely specimens again, not in this life anyway." Her face was too stiff to smile, but her eyes most certainly did. "I used to grow lots of flowers in my garden once, you know. Who did you say you were, dear?"

"I came after you were attacked."

"Are you the nice milk-lady? The sister says that you saved my life."

"No, I just helped her a bit. I live opposite you, at Number Fifteen. I'm their lodger." Miss Rosedale looked at her more closely.

"Oh yes, of course. I always watch for you in the mornings, going off to work. Thank you, dear, you are much too kind."

"Have they caught your attackers yet?" asked Emmie to cover her embarrassment.

Miss Rosedale's eyes gleamed.

"Such a nice policeman keeps on coming to ask me questions. They were only young, you know. I've taught hundreds of naughty boys like that in my time, but the police make it all feel like an Agatha Christie novel. I love a good detective story."

"I like her books, too. Come to think of it, you remind me of Miss Marple."

"Oh my dear, I'm not nearly clever enough," but under the bruises Miss Rosedale's cheeks flushed pink with pleasure.

"What will you do now? Surely you won't want to go home alone after this?" Emmie wondered vaguely why it mattered to her so much.

"Of course I shall go home! I was born in that house and I intend to die there. One must never allow naughty boys to win."

"Wouldn't you feel a little nervous there alone now?"

"I have always relished my own company."

"So have I, as a matter of fact."

"You are still single then, dear?" Emmie glanced ruefully at Edward's diamond ring and said,

"I'm beginning to think I'll never cope with marriage." She was amazed at herself, talking like that to a stranger.

"You be an individual and enjoy it, dear. But if you do wish to remain single, you must find yourself a permanent home. You girls float about in suitcases, but you need physical roots, a place of your own to love."

"You look a bit tired now," said Emmie gently, trying not to think how impossible it would be to raise a mortgage on her salary. "Why not close your eyes and have a little snooze."

"Thank you, dear, come again, won't you? An independent spirit is a rare treasure." Her wobbly old voice trailed away and her sparrow eyes closed at last. Ten minutes later when the nurse approached the bed, Emmie had gone, but Miss Rosedale was still cradling her flowers as she slept.

As Emmie walked home from the hospital the spring sunshine was painting Laburnum Terrace in unexpected shades of pink and gold. The park, rolling away beyond the iron railings, looked like fairyland with its lacy blossom and clumps of rippling daffodils. It was not the usual dull municipal park – all symmetrical flower-beds and straight paths – acres of grassland and noble trees provided a perfect frame for the vast lake which was the pride of Welbridge. 'I belong here,' she thought as she experienced one of those rare moments of pure joy. Miss Rosedale had talked about the need for a home and physical roots. She did not have to find them through Edward, she had a home here already.

So many people seemed to be out in the road after the long winter hibernation by fire and television. Emmie, who had hardly even noticed them before and certainly did not know their names, felt a sudden rush of affection towards them now. She nodded to Nigel as he sat on his wall rocking to and fro like a happy Humpty Dumpty, and smiled at Rebecca and Amy who were earnestly planting seeds in the tiny garden opposite. As she passed Number Thirteen, Gordon Grazier was cleaning his car and Matt and Ann jogged towards her through the park gates, their clothes dark with sweat. 'People enjoy a bank-holiday in some odd ways,' thought Emmie.

For her it had not exactly been a rest, but it had been peaceful working alone, for once, in the studio. She smiled with satisfaction as she pictured the visuals she had completed before she left for the hospital. The client was trying to sell portable plastic cabins to the Bedouins in the hope that they would throw away their time-honoured tents and buy thousands of his orange monstrosities. He had sent photos of them to go into the expensive glossy brochure that was Emmie's brief. The shots, however, had been done in a lush Sussex field which would hardly make his desert customers feel at home. Emmie's brilliance with the air-brush had transformed English grass and trees into a barren rock-strewn wasteland that would have suited Lawrence of Arabia.

Yes, it had worked and she smiled as she hastily dodged Sharon's bicycle. She had done some nice little colour-wash illustrations too and dotted them round the type. The finished effect was definitely pleasing.

Of course, now it was done she felt completely drained

and yearned for the comfort of her flat. She would have liked to take a snack and a novel to bed with a hot-water bottle, but Edward's parents had asked them for dinner. A royal summons. It would be a five-course banquet instead of baked beans on a tray and Emmie sighed. She was going to have to tell Edward tonight. Glancing at her watch, she realised he would be here in an hour, and she simply must wash her hair.

As she pushed open the wrought-iron gate of Number Fifteen she stiffened. Graham was cutting the grass, his juggernaut head thrust forward, his shoulders stiff and aggressive. He obliterated the blades of new green grass just as he probably mowed down his firm's competitors. Could she slip up the path while his back was turned? No, he had seen her and the engine of the mower died to an ominous silence. Across the desecrated lawn he strode, purpose in every step. Emmie could smell trouble and her heart sank. Had she left her radio on all day again, or perhaps the kitchen sink had overflowed and ruined the ceiling below.

"Ah! Emily." He was the only person who called her by her full name, and it always unnerved her. "Look, we've come to a decision, I'm afraid we need the flat for Hazel's aunt from Australia. She's coming to stay." His words sounded smooth and well-rehearsed and suddenly Emmie felt like a wild animal whose territory was under threat.

"So you want to turn me out?"

"Well, we do rather feel you've taken advantage of us. The flat was let to you as a single person, we never imagined your boyfriend would move in as well."

Emmie flushed. When she was angry she was so dramatically beautiful that even Graham, the cool company solicitor, blinked at the effect. 'Giving her the push was Hazel's silly idea,' he thought with sudden regret, but he never went back on a decision.

"Edward only comes at weekends – sometimes," rapped out Emmie furiously, her blue eyes flashing dangerously like metal in a microwave oven.

"Yes, but weekends are when we like our peace and quiet. Two people make much more noise than one you know."

Emmie's mind was beginning to take in the full significance of what Graham was saying. The secure base of her life was rocking under her feet. Her little flat, the park, even Laburnum Terrace itself and all its funny, nameless people were all being torn away from her. So she swallowed her pride and changed tactics.

"If I said Edward would never come here again, would you still want me to leave?" With half of her mind she congratulated herself for thinking of such a good way to extricate herself from Edward.

"Charity begins at home," replied Graham coldly.

'I bet Hazel's aunt's wealthy,' thought Emmie miserably. Charity, at home or abroad, was not a quality Graham and Hazel possessed unless there was a financial reward.

"I'm sorry," he continued, "but our decision is final."

'That was a very costly bath I took on Good Friday,' thought Emmie bitterly as she turned her back and marched towards the house. 'Perhaps I'd better give in and marry Edward after all.' Anything would be better than paying through the nose for some depressing place in the soulless end of Welbridge.

Edward's Porsche purred its way out of town. Only ten miles of country roads separated him from one of his mother's excellent dinners – Edward was hungry. He glanced at Emmie with approval . . . she always dressed so immaculately. The typical scruffy artist would never have done for him. She seemed a bit quiet, though, and he hoped she was not going to be in one of her difficult moods tonight. His mother had gone to such a lot of trouble over this meal and she wanted to discuss the wedding.

Of course, marriage had never bothered him much. It was Mother who thought he should settle down now he was thirty-five and it was she who held the purse-strings in the Soames family. Perhaps Emmie was not quite the type Mother would have chosen, but she was certainly the most attractive girl Edward had ever met. She'd be fine once she was weaned away from that ridiculous job and Mother would soon help her with the vital things like how to manage a dinner party.

'I can't face "Mother" tonight,' Emmie was thinking as she sat beside him. 'I never know what to say to her.' Through her lashes she took a furtive peep at Edward. Most girls would have been so proud of him – well-bred face, the physique of a rugger player and a suit which looked as if it had been made in molten worsted and poured over him. Yet even after months of searching, she had failed to find the real person behind the attractive mask. Perhaps there was no one there to find.

She closed her eyes to shut out the road which led inevitably to the imposing house where his parents lived. She knew they did not approve of her, however hard she tried. 'I'll never fit into their Fortnum and Mason jelly mould,' she thought.

"I've got an ulterior motive for tonight." Edward was beginning to feel neglected by her silence. "Mother's heard on the grapevine that there's a super Queen Anne house coming on the market, on the far side of our village green. We could have a look at the outside tonight if you like."

Emmie felt cornered. The thought of gazing across neatly-cut grass at her mother-in-law's house for the rest of her life did not appeal to her in the slightest.

"I know it's a bit far from the station for me," he continued, "but it would be so nice for you to be near Mother. She'll soon show you the ropes, introduce you to all the right people." Emmie shuddered as she pictured the coffee mornings, committee meetings and vicarage fêtes. She took a deep breath and said nervously:

"Edward, I don't think I'm quite ready for marriage yet. My job's so absorbing."

"You could put all that creative energy into getting the house and garden nice," he suggested.

"And when I'd finished, what would I do then?"

"Have a baby?"

"But I can't stand babies." Glancing at her stiff, set face he swung the car sharply to the side of the road and switched off the engine.

"What's wrong with you?" he asked crossly.

"That's the question I keep asking myself."

"You've been so odd lately."

Edward was irritated. She had spoilt his weekend by going into work, now she had no right to ruin this evening as well.

"Edward, I'm dreadfully sorry, but I don't think I'll ever want to get married." She had not meant to blurt it out baldly like that, and she hated herself as she watched his florid face turn white.

"We don't need to tie ourselves down officially," he said quickly. "I'm quite happy to go on as we are now."

"That would only confuse the issue," she said, frowning in agitation. "You see, I know there's something I'm meant to find, but I haven't found it with you."

"Oh, for goodness' sake grow up and start living in the real world!" Edward sounded exasperated.

"But what is the real world?" murmured Emmie.

"Look here, it's after eight now and it's just not right to keep Mother waiting when she's laid on the cordon-bleu stuff. You're only tired, a good meal will soon sort you out."

"Edward, I mean it. I'm sorry, I've been dreadfully unfair to you."

"Too right you have!" From the day of his birth he had always had what he wanted, when he wanted it, and a nursery temper-tantrum was beginning to threaten his public-school manners.

"I just couldn't eat anything tonight, please take me home – right *now*."

"But whatever is Mother going to say?"

"If you don't take me, I'll have to walk." She pushed open the car door while Edward glared at her furiously.

"Alight then! Walk home, silly bitch!" he snarled. "You ought to become a nun!"

Pulling the door closed he accelerated into the road spraying Emmie's white tights with a speckled pattern of exhaust fumes and mud. She'd soon see sense, he thought grimly, but in the meantime, Mother's delicious meal must not be kept waiting any longer.

An owl hooted in the darkening woods that flanked the road and as Edward's engine died away the silence engulfed Emmie eerily. She loved walking, but not in stiletto heels and a tighter than tight skirt. Eight miles lay between her and Welbridge and suddenly she panicked. Here she was, on a dark, lonely road and . . . 'ouch!' Violently her heel caught in a drainage grating sending her plunging forward. Her hands and knees burned as they grazed the loose granite chippings and an even sharper pain seared her ankle as her foot was wrenched from its shoe. She found herself borrowing some expletives from Bea's vocabulary as she struggled painfully to her feet.

A car was coming up behind her now, its lights pierced the dusk, deforming the tree-trunks in the wood. Was it Edward coming back to find her? It did not sound like his smooth expensive engine. Headlights were picking out her long slim legs. Suppose . . .? Nasty newspaper reports flashed into her mind and the bloody, battered face of Miss Rosedale appeared before her. The car slowed ominously and travelled along behind her. Eyes seemed to be boring holes in her back as she limped painfully along in her uneven shoes. I hope he gets it over with quickly, she thought wildly, I'll just go limp like a sack of potatoes, I won't fight.

The car pulled ahead of her and finally stopped. The nearside door opened, blocking her path by the side of the road. Should she spring into the bramble-filled ditch, or try to run back the way she had come? As she stood, paralysed like a rabbit confronting a weasel, a voice from the car called,

"Can I give you a lift?" Not only did it sound pleasant, it was also female. On the back seat she saw a carrycot and beside it a small goblin figure slumped over its seatbelt — fast asleep.

"I'm Kim Patterson from Number Four, you live up the other end of the Terrace, don't you?"

Emmie climbed thankfully into the battered estate car. "I'm terribly glad to see you," she said, and wondered why her laugh sounded like an agitated hyena.

"Did your car break down?" asked Kim as she drove off.

"No," replied Emmie with another hyena impersonation, "I had a major row with my fiancé."

"I am sorry," said Kim, glancing at her quickly. "You look as if you've fallen over. Is that blood on your skirt?"

"Oh I'm all right." There was that high-pitched giggle again. 'Take a grip,' she told herself firmly. 'Act normally, don't let yourself crack. Edward will get over this one day.'

"I've often seen you on your way into the park with all your kids," she managed finally. "Where are all the rest of the tribe this evening, then?"

"Oh, I've had a lovely day with my mum in Brighton, just with Johnnie and the baby. It's so nice for her to enjoy them peacefully without being organised all day long by the girls. You know what little girls are like." Emmie did not, but she was trying hard to make conversation.

"Do you like being a mother?"

"Sometimes, in the holidays anyway, when David's at home. During the term I often wish profoundly I was back in the classroom. I used to teach English to A-level and I didn't know I was born! I've always admired that gorgeous car your fiancé drives. I envied you your freedom, driving away in that. I hope this row isn't too final?"

That was Emmie's undoing, the hysteria erupted violently. Tears positively spurted from her eyes and she hated herself for the noise she could not stop making.

56

Johnnie woke up and began to scream in the back and soon the baby joined in the chorus.

"Come on, old thing," said Kim, looking at Emmie anxiously, "it can't be that bad. You're just cold and shaken. I'm going to take you back home with me and make you a nice cup of tea."

"But I couldn't," protested Emmie, shrinking back as usual into her shell. "Your family . . ."

"Laburnum Terrace people *are* my family." Kim did not realise how tactless she was being.

"But I'm not . . . that's just it . . ." A new and larger wave of emotion engulfed Emmie without warning. "They gave me the push this evening." She had not allowed her mind to take in the fact that she would soon be homeless. The hurdle of Edward and his parents had to be faced first. Now the full realisation washed over her and she fumbled in her bag for yet another handful of tissues. No home, no future, no roots.

"Come on," said Kim firmly. "Let's get you back in the warm."

David had removed the fireguard and built up the fire with a fresh load of apple logs. The flickering flame-light darted round the mellow pine panelling and made the copper on the dresser, dusty though it was, gleam in a friendly way. Emmie was dimly aware that they had done something clever with their kitchen and dining-room, knocking them into one big family space where everything seemed to happen. Johnnie had been popped into his pyjamas by the fire and finally tucked away in his cot upstairs. The girls had been duly read to, kissed and sent off to their domain, while Kim fed the baby in the rocking-chair. She looked like a study of motherhood from an old Dutch oil painting.

As she lay on the sofa, bandaged and wrapped in a rug, Emmie felt sleepy, cared for and suddenly safe. What was it about this room? There was a kind of peace here. Was it the Mendelssohn which lapped like a gentle sea on a hot day? No, she had that record at home and it had never done this much for her before. The hiss and sigh of the fire, or the fact that these two were so obviously happy and did not mind sharing their lives with each other? Perhaps that was it. Would she have had this feeling if she had married Edward? No, Edward would never sit by the fire toasting hot-cross-buns, he would be out in the hall ringing some 'good contact' to fix a business lunch.

Other people had never mattered very much to Emmie, she did not really need them, but she found herself liking these two for some reason she could not explain. Kim's face in the firelight had a strangely restless quality, but David looked completely content. Emmie smiled secretly when she thought how Edward's well-heeled world would shudder at the thought of four children crammed into a terraced house – living on a primary teacher's salary. Perhaps these two had discovered the elusive, 'thing' she was always trying to grasp.

Much later, as she hobbled home, she realised a car was parked at the far end of the Terrace and it was a Porsche. Edward's face confronted her furiously and broke the spell of that firelit kitchen.

"It's no good following me about, I've made my decision," she said firmly when she was level with the car, and she slipped off his ring and passed it to him through the window. His loud and slightly inebriated response interested Gordon Grazier hugely as he dutifully put the milk bottles out on the doorstep of Number Thirteen.

'Life in this road's even better than the telly these days,' he thought as he watched Edward's tail-lights disappear round the corner.

FRIDAY APRIL 19TH

On the following Friday morning, Emmie was late for work. "You've never been late before," snapped the boss.

"I didn't sleep," she said dully. "Then at five I dropped off like a stone."

"You must know how pushed we are just now, it's most inconsiderate of you."

"But we're always pushed," said Emmie wearily and went on into the studio, bracing herself for the inevitable cacophony of sound.

The radio, as usual, was on at full volume, but above it Bea and Pat were having a major row across their drawing-boards. It was a frequent occurrence, but that morning their voices did something most unpleasant to Emmie's headache.

The whine of the vacuum-cleaner capped the pyramid of noise and made Emmie wish profoundly that she had stayed in bed. Joyce, the boss's secretary, was fastidious to the point of obsession. She never trusted the nocturnal cleaner, and as soon as she saw a pile of clippings and snippings gathering under someone's chair, she and the vacuum-cleaner pounced on them like superefficient birds of prey.

"I can't live in a mess." She said it so often Bea promised to have the phrase inscribed on her tombstone.

"You look awful, girl," said Bea, breaking off in the middle of her argument. "Look here, it's time you pulled yourself together and stopped mooning after that ghastly man. You're well rid of him."

59

Life was so uncomplicated for Bea – all black and white. Men were black and women were white, and Emmie was whiter than white. "Come and share my flat, girl," she had said eagerly on Tuesday morning. The idea had so revolted Emmie she had to bolt herself in the loo for ten minutes to recover.

Pat, seeing his chance to escape from Bea's bullying, disappeared into the darkroom and for the rest of the morning only a series of grunts and snorts indicated that he was still there.

Joyce finally switched off the cleaner and sniffed disapprovingly. "I think you want your brains examined," she said to Emmie. "Giving up a gorgeous, rich young man like that. You could have been married and out of here by the summer holidays." Being 'out of here' was an exceedingly desirable prospect for Emmie at that moment, but would it have been fair to use Edward as a ticket to freedom? Her emotions had been vacillating so violently all the week she was not sure if she agreed with Bea or with Joyce and she heartily wished they would both mind their own business.

She sat down at her drawing-board and tried to marshal yesterday's scattered ideas, but all creativity seemed to have dried inside her like a well in drought. All she could think of was Edward. She had hurt him, and she minded about that. 'But I didn't just want him to love my body,' she thought as she fiddled aimlessly with her set square. 'I wanted him to love all of me.' If her relationships were always going to end in pain like this, she would be very careful never to make any more in the future.

By lunch-time Bea's shrill whistle, Pat's grunts and Joyce's disapproving sniffs were making her feel like a carrot rubbed against a grater.

"I've got to go home," she told the boss firmly.

"Home?" he replied incredulously. "But it's only two o'clock."

"I did work all the weekend, remember," said Emmie

tartly, "and landed us that Saudi contract. If I stay here any longer I'll kill someone."

"Artistic temperament," she heard Joyce say as she slammed the office door. "They're all the same."

'What shall I do now?' wondered Emmie as the afternoon and evening stretched out like a long road before her. Edward always used to take her out to dinner on a Friday night. She was relieved to have made the break at last, but without him she was left with a vacuum she did not know how to fill. The shock of losing her home had left her with no desire to do anything whatsoever.

Why she began to drift in the direction of the hospital she could never understand. Was it simply that she needed an excuse to buy that bunch of tulips she could see through the flower-shop window, or had the old lady from the crumbling ruin some kind of hidden magnetism?

However, it was a rather different Miss Rosedale who greeted her from the fourth bed on the left. She looked older somehow, and crushed. Even the sight of the flowers did not quite bring the gleam back to her eyes.

"A young girl came here the other day," she told Emmie. "A social worker she *said* she was, but she didn't look old enough to be out of school to me. She said they will never allow me to go home again."

"That's terrible," said Emmie with far more sympathy than she would have had a week before. "What do they suggest you do?"

"Sell my house so I can afford to live in a hotel. Hundreds of pounds a week to be squashed up in a crowded roost with rows of other old hens."

"I suppose they're afraid of you being alone."

"But I love being alone, I always have."

"What about the stairs, though?"

"I've lived on the ground floor since this arthritis developed."

"Couldn't you find someone to live with you – a companion-help?" suggested Emmie doubtfully.

61

"I don't want to be saddled with some silly female twenty-four hours a day. I need my solitude."

"I know what you mean," said Emmie with feeling, and thought, 'She's so like me, I'd simply hate to be forced to live with crowds of strangers. It must be horrid being old and having no choice.'

There was a long silence, then Miss Rosedale put on her glasses and subjected Emmie to a penetrating stare. When she spoke again her voice had altered completely.

"Something has happened since you came here before."

"I've lost my home too," Emmie admitted shakily, and heard herself telling this incredible person the whole story.

"We're in the same hole together, you and I," said Miss Rosedale, and she gave Emmie's hand a squeeze of real old-fashioned compassion.

"Go back and take a walk round the lake," she suggested. "After a difficult day in the classroom I always found the park restored my sense of proportion. And another thing, you must stop calling me Miss Rosedale, my friends have always called me Rosie. The only trouble is," she added sadly as a nurse thrust a thermometer under her tongue, "so few of them are left alive now to call me anything at all."

As Emmie turned into Laburnum Terrace and picked her way carefully round the skipping game Rebecca was organising, she wondered if it could only be a week ago that she had felt so settled and safe here. She paused by her garden gate – a cup of tea would have been nice, but noticing Hazel stabbing viciously at the flower-beds with a fork, she hastily decided to take Miss Rosedale's advice and go into the park.

Somehow, however, it did not look like *her* park at that time of the day. She knew it well in the early mornings with its joggers and dog-walkers and in the evening with its young couples and slumbering tramps, but to find it dotted with mothers and small children gave it an entirely different atmosphere. 'Will I mind when I'm old,' she thought as she flopped down on a seat by the lake, 'if I never have any children of my own?'

Behind her, approaching at high speed, came a rumbling sound. Swinging round she saw Kim galloping down the path behind a large pram. A delighted Johnnie bounced about on top of the sleeping baby while Rebecca shepherded Amy along behind. 'Oh no,' thought Emmie, wishing she was invisible. She felt so raw and vulnerable the very last thing she wanted was to have to make conversation – even with someone she liked as much as Kim. However, the cavalcade was making straight towards her, there was no escape.

"I saw you going by our window," puffed Kim, "so I ran out to see how you are."

'How am I,' thought Emmie and deliberately closed her mind to the bleakness of the answer.

"I had an idea this morning," continued Kim enthusiastically, as she handed the girls a bag of stale bread for the ducks and clipped Johnnie firmly on to his reins. "That policeman came round asking more questions and he said that they won't let poor old Miss Rosedale out of hospital unless she has someone living in with her. What's to stop you from doing that?"

"What?" exclaimed Emmie, horrified. "Swap my dear little flat for a crumbling old ruin like that? I do a high-pressure job you know, twenty hours a day sometimes, I can't run round after an old lady all night as well." She stopped abruptly and bit her lip. 'Now I've blown it!' she told herself furiously. 'Just when we were beginning to get on so well.' "Sorry," she mumbled. "Miss Rosedale's terribly sweet and all that, but I'd be a hopeless nurse, and that house is full of cobwebs and creepy-crawlies. I'd hate that."

"No, it's my fault," said Kim smiling ruefully. "I'm always having stupid ideas and blurting them out. It's my 'mother hen instinct' I suppose. I just thought it would be a good way of solving two problems at once.

I ought to remember people hate being organised. There must be heaps of lovely flats in Welbridge," she added brightly to hide her embarrassment.

"I've seen five this week already," said Emmie, and her shoulders sagged miserably. "They were either quite ghastly or far too expensive. But something's bound to come up one day," she added. The glib words covered the doubt in her mind, but they did not deceive Kim, who opened her mouth to say something more, but managed to shut it again firmly. An awkward little silence hung between them on the park-bench until it was broken violently.

"It's not fair," shrieked Amy from the water's edge. "Rebecca won't give me any duck bread!" Before Kim could respond Johnnie had fallen flat on his face in a muddy puddle and the baby had been sick over the side of the pram.

'I can't think how she copes,' thought Emmie as she realised thankfully that motherhood was certainly a joy she could willingly live without.

"Oh look, here comes Ann Coley from Number Five," said Kim as she calmly produced a wad of paper hankies and dealt with her two protesting sons. Emmie watched a figure in a track suit bound towards them round the lake, with the effortless strides of an athlete. "Have you met Ann yet?" continued Kim. "She and Matt live opposite to us. Surely you must have noticed them jogging in the early mornings. They're health and fitness mad, you know. Both in training for the London Marathon next weekend. They teach at the school where I used to work before I had the kids. What wouldn't I give to be able to run like that," she added with a sigh. "I've put on so much weight since I stopped teaching."

"You're not fat, Mummy," said Rebecca over her shoulder as she gave up the bag of bread to mollify her small sister. "You're nice and soft and lumpy."

"Lumpy in the wrong places," replied Kim with a sigh. 'I don't usually like people who chatter all the time,' thought Emmie, but there was something oddly soothing about Kim, and she could feel herself relaxing in spite of the noise created by the children and quantities of greedy ducks.

"I'll give Ann a shout when she gets nearer," Kim continued, "then I can introduce you."

Emmie smiled, but inwardly she groaned. 'I don't want to get to know half the road just when I'm going to have to leave them all,' she thought. However, when Ann arrived she obviously did not wish to be sociable either.

"Can't stop for long," she panted, pulling the sweat band from her forehead, "or I'll seize up."

"Ann and Matt are trying to raise money for a new sports hall, at Welbridge Comprehensive," explained Kim. "Have you got lots of sponsors lined up, Ann?"

"It's incredible," replied Ann – still running on the spot. "We've got simply masses. The faster we go the more money we'll raise. It could be thousands if all goes well."

"Can't you sit down, just for a moment," pleaded Kim, "all that bouncing up and down makes me feel giddy. I wanted to ask you if you know of a good slimming diet." Ann continued to jog vigorously while she eyed Kim critically.

"You could certainly do with one," she said. "But you're going to have to exercise as well."

"Chance would be a fine thing, with four kids," protested Kim laughing.

Johnnie had fallen in the mud again, and Emmie was beginning to feel that her job, even with all its pressures, seemed infinitely preferable to life as a Welbridge housewife. 'At least I haven't entirely wasted this afternoon,' she thought. 'I've managed to discover that marriage is certainly not for me.'

"I think I ought to go home and start packing up my flat," she said, standing up hastily, but at that moment through the park gates bounded Boris. Claire usually found a chink between her hairdressing appointments in which to give her German shepherd dog a run, and Jasmine had been driving everyone up the walls of the salon all the school holidays.

Boris liked stale crusts very much indeed and he galloped towards the two little girls by the water's edge with his ears pricked eagerly. Amy screamed and backed nearer to the lake.

"Bad dog, down," admonished Rebecca coolly. She would not have been afraid even if Boris had been a lion. Unfortunately, it was Amy who was now holding the brown-paper bag which was the sole object of Boris's interest.

Death by drowning seemed a soft option to someone as terrified of dogs as Amy had always been, so she did not fall into the lake, she jumped.

Pandemonium broke loose on the bank. Jasmine screamed. Boris barked and the ducks quacked in protest. Kim and Ann waded into the lake while Rebecca, level-headed as ever, ran for the lifebelt. Amy was soon hauled out, black with slimy mud and bedraggled as a chicken in a thunderstorm. Kim, who was as wet as Amy, carried her back to the seat and cradled her in her arms.

"Poor little mite," she said apologetically, "she seems to be scared of everything."

"I hate Boris," sobbed Amy.

"She hates all dogs actually," Rebecca explained to Claire, anxious as usual that no one's feelings should be hurt. Ann Coley had no such scruples as she shivered in her dripping track suit.

"You shouldn't keep a great fierce Alsatian like that in a town," she shouted at Claire. "It barks half the night and drives my husband mad. In my opinion dogs are a complete nuisance."

'Goodness,' thought Emmie, 'did I really come out here looking for peace? The studio is a positive haven after this place.'

Claire was standing motionless in the centre of a crowd of interested mothers and children who had gathered by the lake to watch the drama. As usual Claire was cast as the villain of the piece. She knew the people in Laburnum Terrace were beginning to dislike her, but she threw back her elegant dark head and glared at them all defiantly. In the old days their opinions mattered tremendously, but now she had Roger and the Group for her security, surely she could afford to alienate a few boring little people sometimes. She was almost enjoying herself, but Jasmine stood beside her mother, stiff with anxiety and shame.

"You should keep your dog on a lead when kiddies are playing," remarked a large woman reproachfully.

"My dog has just as much right here as any of your children," snapped Claire.

"I've never trusted Alsatians," persisted Ann. She was seldom angry — she left all that to Matt — but for some unexplainable reason she had never liked her next-door neighbour, Claire, and she liked her dog even less.

Kim wrenched her attention away from Amy at last and realised an ugly scene was developing.

"It's all right, Claire," she smiled reassuringly. "It wasn't Boris who pushed Amy into the water, she really did jump in herself. She's always been a bit silly about dogs, you know. There's no harm done that a hot bath won't cure."

Claire's tense face relaxed and a tinge of colour seeped back into Jasmine's pale cheeks.

"He only wanted to be friends, Amy," explained Kim as she wrapped her up in a blanket from the pram and nestled her in beside the baby. "Come on, let's get you home in the warm."

Emmie walked up the hill with the dripping procession and then waved them good-bye at the park-gates as they plodded home up the Terrace.

"Nice woman — that Kim Patterson," said a voice at her elbow. It was the large lady who seemed to look permanently reproachful. "You need good neighbours like her in this life, don't you?"

67

"Yes," muttered Emmie miserably. "I do."

6pm

By the time St Mark's church clock had struck six, the tangled emotions of the day were beginning to defeat Emmie. Dismantling her home made the central pillar of security rock badly and every drawer or cupboard she opened seemed to contain something which reminded her of Edward. Holiday photos – theatre programmes – the card he had sent her when they got engaged. When she finally discovered a pair of his pyjamas she burst into tears and slumped down on the cluttered bed.

"Visitor for you, Emily." Hazel's clipped voice from below jerked her back to the present. 'Visitor! but I'm in such a mess. Suppose it's Edward?' But a young woman with a large briefcase marched confidently into the room.

"I am the hospital social worker," she said, rather as someone might announce that they were the Astronomer Royal. "I've just been to see a Miss Rosedale." Emmie knew at once why Rosie had disliked this young woman and she did not offer to put on the kettle.

"We are all rather concerned about her discharge. She really cannot be allowed to continue to live alone."

"I fail to see what business that is of mine – or yours for that matter," said Emmie crisply. "She says she can cope on her own, and she wants to go on doing just that. If she kills herself in the attempt, it's hardly going to be a premature death – she is over ninety after all."

The social worker looked at Emmie with dislike and then rustled her papers officiously. "She refuses to have a companion, though I believe she could afford one easily, but she does consent to a lodger. She is offering *you* the entire upstairs of her house, free of any charge, simply in exchange for being up there at night. One of the bedrooms was made into a kitchen during the war so you would be entirely independent. She assures me she will make no demands on you. We will arrange for a home help for her and meals on wheels.'' Her voice droned on while Emmie still sat on the edge of the bed clutching Edward's pyjamas.

"You can't be serious," she said at last. "That place is filthy! Taking a bunch of flowers to an old lady in hospital is one thing, but actually living with her in squalor is quite another. I can't stand spiders.''

"Miss Rosedale has given me permission to send in a firm of industrial cleaners to 'blitz' the entire building at her expense.''

Emmie made no response, and her visitor began to look annoyed. "I think you've landed on your feet, Miss Dawson," she finished by way of a goad.

Emmie looked up at her coldly. "And would you spend every night answering bells, heating cups of milk and emptying commodes?''

"Frankly, yes, because the money I could save living without rent and heating bills would either go towards a future mortgage or pay for some exotic holidays. Personally I'd jump at the offer.''

"Perhaps I'm not as mercenary as that?'' countered Emmie, nettled.

"Well, you may prefer to think of the good turn you would be doing the old lady.''

'A hair-shirt,' thought Emmie absently looking down at Edward's crumpled pyjamas. 'I suppose I ought to do penance really, after the mean way I played Edward along.' Was this part of her spiritual quest? Kim had seemed to think it would be the right thing to do. 'But I'm not like Kim,' argued the other side of Emmie. 'I can't live with people, I need space – a quiet, clean little pad all to myself.'

She got up slowly and walked across to the window. How she would miss that park. The upper bay window of the house across the road would command a magnificent view of the lake . . . what a sitting-room it would make . . . there would be a beautiful bedroom, too, and perhaps even a further room with big windows where she could paint. With a shudder she remembered the flat she had looked at the evening before with its uninterrupted view of the old gasworks. 'I couldn't live without the park,' she realised suddenly. Perhaps she had no alternative but to accept this extraordinary offer.

"I'll give it a month," she said slowly, "but if I find I'm expected to do *anything* whatsoever for the old girl, that's it! I've got a career to build, you know."

"Very well," said the social worker crisply. "We need her bed by next weekend, so could you move in by then?"

"I must be mad," muttered Emmie.

"I'm sure you won't regret it," said the social worker, pleased to be able to close her file so quickly.

'And I'm quite sure I will,' thought Emmie as she watched her visitor mincing away down the stairs.

SUNDAY APRIL 28TH

An atmosphere of excitement pervaded Laburnum Terrace that morning.

"Today's the big day, then," said Gordon Grazier as he polished the windscreen of his car outside Number Thirteen.

"Hope they make it," replied the paper-boy.

When the inhabitants of the Terrace had opened their local papers the faces of Matt and Ann Coley had smiled up at them from the front page.

"Running in the London Marathon!" snorted Alison from the doorstep. "Whatever next?"

"Just look at that," Tom Savery was saying in the house opposite. "Those two live in our road!" He waved at the picture with a fork laden with bacon and egg. The Savery family enjoyed their Sunday morning breakfast.

"I saw them setting off for London at six this morning," said his daughter Sharon with a knowing smile. "They went on a coach with Welbridge Athletic Club written on it. Everyone else cheered them when they climbed on board." Her father eyed her with dislike.

"You see too much for a ten-year-old," he said as he patted the magnificent beer gut beneath his overstretched T-shirt. "You shouldn't keep poking your nose into other people's business."

"Why shouldn't I? You do," retorted Sharon rudely. Tom ignored her.

"Listen to what this paper says, Angela." He began to read aloud slowly and laboriously, but his wife never took her eyes from the television screen.

71

Mattthew and Ann Coley (32) of Number Five, Laburnum Terrace, will be the stars of Welbridge on Sunday when they run in the London Marathon. They are raising money for a new sports hall at Welbridge comprehensive school where they both teach physical education. "Sponsors have poured in from all over the district," said Matthew Coley to our reporter this week. "Each mile we run brings hundreds of pounds to the school." If the couple succeed, the new sports facilities will be ready next year.

"I'll be at that school by then, so I'll be able to tell everyone they're friends of ours," said Sharon, smug in the anticipation of future notoriety.

"They've got to run twenty-six miles first, against the clock," growled Tom, "and their sort would never be friends of mine."

"Wake up, Ron!" said Babs, sitting up in bed in her council flat on the Charbury Estate. Sunday was the only morning free of her milk-float, and reading the local paper the big treat of the week. "There's a picture of two of my people in here:

GOOD LUCK MATT AND ANN

that's what the headline says. They live in my favourite Terrace – two blue-topped skimmed, a couple of plain yoghurts and fresh orange juice. Same every morning. I always knew they'd look like that!" Ron groaned, the only way he ever escaped his wife's constant talking was to go to sleep.

"I'm sure they're the two we saw on the Downs back on Good Friday. Look, Ron." He sat up sleepily and took the paper.

"I'd know that girl's shape anywhere," he said with such satisfaction that Babs felt obliged to cuff his ear for him.

* * *

As nine thirty approached the excitement was still mounting. People had laughed at Matt and Ann as they pounded off through the park-gates into the damp darkness of the winter mornings. Now they were crouched over their television screens convinced their suddenly illustrious neighbours would appear at any minute.

"Turn the sound up, dear," shouted Mrs Macaulay in the little shop on the corner. She and her husband made their meagre living by keeping their business open from early in the morning until late at night and their shop had long been the local gathering centre. They always did particularly well on a Sunday morning. People with bad memories or unexpected guests dashed in to replenish their larders or fetch the Sunday papers. However, this morning they all seemed determined to linger in the shop, their eyes fixed on the television set in the corner. Mrs Macaulay flitted about among them like an overweight butterfly with two heavily bandaged legs. "Great day for the Terrace this," she announced to each new customer and flashed her one remaining yellow tooth.

*   *   *

"I'll stay in this morning and mind the baby and Johnnie," said David Patterson with suspicious generosity. "You have a morning off and take the girls to church for a change."

"But I always go at night." Kim loved her peaceful, pottering Sunday mornings. "I know!" she added as light dawned, "you want to watch the Marathon." David chuckled as he heaved his two sons on to his lap and pressed the knob of the television with his big toe.

*   *   *

At Number Thirteen Clancy was also endeavouring to avoid church.

"Please, Auntie Alison, must I go with you today?"

"Of course you must. We always go to the ten o'clock service." Alison sounded shocked.

"But everyone from school will be watching the

73

Marathon," continued Clancy wistfully. In the two weeks that she had been in Laburnum Terrace she had never once opposed Alison's wishes even in the most tiny detail and Gordon looked up from his grapefruit uneasily.

"Mrs Coley's my form teacher," Clancy was twisting her delicate little bird claw hands in a way which made his heart lurch in sympathy. "She teaches us netball, too, she's ever so nice."

"Let her stay this once," pleaded Gordon, surprising himself. His bid failed, he could see that by Alison's righteous expression, so he tried another tack. "It's a very important thing for the school. They stand to raise thousands of pounds. The teachers might think you weren't much of a foster mother, not letting her watch." That worked far better, she hesitated just long enough to keep them in suspense and then smiled graciously and gave in.

"They're off!" said the television commentator as Alison was adjusting her Sunday hat and matching face. "The great throng of runners surge forward, and this year's London Marathon is under way."

"Come along, Amanda dear," said Alison with exaggerated affection. "We have our duty to do."

Two minutes later when the front door closed, the knob on the television went click, consigning the 'surging throng' to blank darkness. Clancy had never had any intention of watching any boring old race.

As she opened the door into her own domain she experienced the usual rush of pleasure. The pretty curtains, soft carpet and a real duvet, only in her daydreams had she ever had a bedroom like this. It made her feel like a film star as she looked at herself in the dressing-table mirror. No baby brother bawled for her attention here, and no greasy washing-up awaited her in Mum's sordid kitchen. Her clever plan had won her all this luxury – even the bedside lamp worked now. Last evening she had been experimenting with hairstyles when Uncle Gordon had crept in holding a screwdriver.

74

She had watched him in the mirror as he worked on the lamp-switch and thought how different he was from Kevin. On a Saturday evening like this her stepfather would have been slumped by the telly, surrounded by empty beer cans. This man was small, quiet, kind – everything that Kevin was not.

"There's a girl in our office," Uncle Gordon had said in his funny way, "she's selling a portable television. I was wondering if you would like me to get it for you?" Her own telly! The sheer joy of it! She could watch what she liked without Auntie Alison or Amanda switching over to something boring on BBC 2. She wished now that she had thanked him properly, she did not realise that Gordon had lain awake half the previous night savouring the memory of her flushed face and ecstatic eyes.

'But will Auntie Alison let me have it,' thought Clancy, now in the cold light of day. Gordon was asking himself exactly the same question in church as he knelt holding his prayer-book upside down. He would just have to buy it, fix it and tell her later. In his agitation he said "Amen" very loudly in quite the wrong place.

* * *

Back in Number Four David was leaning forward, taking in every detail of the race avidly. The baby was fast asleep and Johnnie had long since wriggled to the floor. He never sat still, but ran continuously from morning till night. "Like a mechanical toy with a never-ending battery," was how Kim described him. David, however, was too engrossed to notice Johnnie. He was sure he had seen Matt – running like something from a Greek legend. 'Go on man!' he urged – wordlessly as usual. 'Go for it.'

"Door," announced Johnnie, pointing to the back door. David had been conscious of a distant knocking for some time, but he had supposed it was only his son's toy hammer. 'No one ever comes to the back door,' he thought with a frown, 'too many dustbins to negotiate.' But there it was again, faint but persistent. Someone was out there.

75

Reluctantly he put the heavy baby in the carrycot and slid back the door-catch. He had to look a very long way down to find his diminutive visitor. As he squatted to her level he could see Jasmine had been crying. Could she possibly be even thinner than she had been two weeks ago? They looked at each other across the barrier of shyness, both wanting to say so much, but neither knowing how to begin. It was so easy to talk to kids in the classroom, so why did he have this stupid problem everywhere else?

As if to apologise for his inadequacy he took both her cold hands in his and as that warm, safe feeling flooded her whole body once again, Jasmine broke the silence in a sudden rush.

"I came to ask if you'd mind me," she gasped.

"We don't mind you one bit," replied David quite misunderstanding her question.

"No, mind me . . . after school . . . Saturdays and that," corrected Jasmine. "I used to go to Sharon's, but Mummy's cross with her now and school starts tomorrow and I hate it at the salon − and could I start today − now please − Mummy will pay . . . " She was forced to stop at last in order to gasp for breath, and she stood looking hopefully up at him.

"Did Mummy send you over here to ask all that?" David sounded puzzled.

"Oh no," replied Jasmine hastily, "that's why I had to come in the dustbin way. But you see she said she . . . doesn't want me. She said . . . " What Claire had actually said was too painful to recount so Jasmine dissolved into tears instead. Mummy's face had really looked like a proper witch that morning and her words had felt like physical blows. She'd have to find herself somewhere safe if Mummy felt like that. This man was kind. His face always looked as if something nice was about to happen.

'We can't possibly take on another child,' David was thinking. 'Kim's stretched to her limit already, and I see quite enough of other people's children in the classroom all day . . . ' But Jasmine's tears were splashing down on his hands now, reminding him of the odd feeling he had experienced at Camber. Standing on the shore on Good Friday as he held her hand he had felt strongly that he was being told to take care of this child. He had supposed it was only his imagination, but had it been?

"Look," he said awkwardly, "I'll have to talk the minding bit over with my wife, but you can certainly stay with us today. Probably Mummy wants a bit of peace, doesn't she? That was quite a party she had over there last night!"

Actually it had been like a French farce. He had to smile as he remembered it. He and Kim had given up the attempt to sleep and simply enjoyed the performance from their bedroom window. The strangest looking people in the oddest clothes had started to converge on Laburnum Terrace shortly before nine, and by the time Sharon's parents had returned from a day by the sea Claire's numerous visitors had left them no space for their car. (The unforgivable sin in Laburnum Terrace.) The Saverys had seized the chance to continue their quarrel with Claire and they seized it very loudly indeed. Alison returning from a missionary evening in the church hall had joined the fray on Claire's front doorstep, until Boris the dog had appeared and scared her off down the Terrace.

"We don't like hippies round here," she shouted as she banged her front door. But still more people continued to cram themselves into Claire's house. The heat they generated forced her to open all the windows, allowing the babble of conversation and discordant jangle of folk guitars to shatter the genteel respectability of the cul-de-sac still further.

"This isn't good enough," Mr Macaulay's voice had boomed from above the shop somewhere near midnight. "We've got to be up at five to sort the papers."

"And our little Sharon needs her sleep," added Tom Savery, standing in the middle of the road in the huge marquee that served him as a dressing-gown.

"We've got a Marathon to run tomorrow," Matt had bellowed out of his bedroom window just as the police arrived. They had been summoned by Alison, on behalf of Gordon. Someone had grazed the side of his beloved car and Alison, concerned for once with his welfare, demanded retribution.

"Yes," said David with a crooked smile, "I expect your mummy *would* like some peace today. Let's go and ask her if you can stay, then you'll have to help me cook the lunch. We're going to have roast beef and Yorkshire puddings, that's if we don't burn them." Jasmine loved real meat and her tears stopped as if by magic.

*   *   *

Even if Claire had still possessed a television, she would definitely not have been watching the Marathon – there were far too many things on her mind for that. She was standing at the kitchen sink, attacking an apparently summitless mountain of washing-up. The mess that had greeted her when she had crawled downstairs that morning had turned her wine-soured stomach. In the old pre-Roger days, friends usually helped clear up a bit after a party, but you couldn't really blame the Group – their minds were occupied with the deeper issues of life.

Of course Jasmine had only been trying to help when she dropped the tray of glasses, but the accident had snapped something inside Claire. She hadn't meant to say all that, but after having the child underfoot all through the school holidays, who could blame her? Claire pulled a fresh, dry tea-cloth from the drawer and started on another batch of dripping glasses. Jasmine had become so odd recently, always standing about on one leg in doorways. Why couldn't she . . . play or something? And why didn't she like Roger?

"I never wanted a child in the first place." She shouldn't have said that to Jasmine, but it was true. As she ran more hot water into the sink she watched an empty food carton bobbing about among the frothy soap bubbles. It made her think of a boat, free to sail away on

78

a voyage of discovery wherever the restless wind would take it. That's what her life could be now if only Jasmine was not there, mooring her securely to the shore of ordinary things.

The kettle was boiling and she made herself a mug of peppermint tea, cupping it in her slender hands as she sat at her pine kitchen table. It had been such a strange evening. So different from the parties she and Michael used to give in the old days before Roger. Ideas had positively reverberated round her little house, everything from herbalism to Moral Disarmament, the occult dimension to holistic therapies.

But something had jarred and she couldn't think what it was. Probably it was only that silly fuss with the neighbours. Mindless fools – blind to the realities of life, worshipping their telly gods and flashy cars. Were they so bound by their silly little Terrace they had no cosmic consciousness at all? Claire's hands on the mug were shaking. 'All the same,' she told herself soberly, 'last night wouldn't do her business any good. She must start being more careful. Until she'd learnt enough about psychic healing she was dependent on the shop for a livelihood. Women were very odd about their hair-dressers and there were plenty of other salons in town.

Actually it wasn't only the neighbours. She had to admit she had felt slightly puzzled by Roger. He was always saying she had potential, but how could she learn all he knew if they never had time together – alone. Last night he'd hardly spoken to her; he loved being at the centre of the stage and it infuriated her to see people clustering round him. The fact that the 'people' were mostly women and nearly all of them younger than she was did nothing to improve her temper. She needed to be with him today, and if there was no Jasmine she could be over at his cottage in half an hour.

"Mummy! Mummy!"

"Now what?" Claire's head was aching.

"Mummy, Mr Patterson's here." Mr Patterson? Claire

pulled the name out of her mind and slotted the person in behind it. 'Nice looking – slight, with a beard and hair that curled delightfully into his neck.' She smiled and hurriedly took off her apron.

'I quite fancy him,' she thought as she looked at David standing on her doorstep. 'What's his wife like?' she rummaged through her memory. 'Dumpy little creature, crawling with kids, hair that never took a perm. No problems there.'

'She could be dangerous,' thought David uneasily.

'He's dangerous,' thought Claire suddenly puzzled. 'His aura won't mix with mine. Why?'

"Yes, certainly you can go, Jasmine," she replied when David finally managed to voice his request.

"Thank you!" squealed Jasmine to both adults at once, and even her mother's promise to bring over her nut roast for lunch could not steal her joy as she walked back over the road holding David's hand tightly.

"I say," said Claire, running after them on an impulse. "I suppose your wife wouldn't like a little job, would she?" David looked confused; what possible use could an English graduate be in a hairdresser's shop? "I need a minder for Jasmine, I'll pay the going rate," she added as David hesitated. He looked down into Jasmine's face of mute appeal and felt the urgent pressure of her little hand. "I'll get my wife to pop over and talk it over with you," he said, and turned abruptly away.

'You'll "pop over" yourself one of these days,' thought Claire, and as she closed her front door she looked like a cream-laden cat.

*   *   *

"A bag of chocolate toffees and a tin of coke, please, Mrs Macaulay," said Sharon with a sickly-sweet smile. The cluttered interior of the corner shop was so crowded by this time that she had been forced to slither her diminutive body in sideways. Mrs Macaulay served her without once taking her eyes off the television screen.

"Look!" she shouted suddenly. "There she is now!"

80

Every head in the crowded shop turned as the whole screen was completely filled with Ann's face.

"Come on, Mrs Coley!" shouted Sharon, making use of the absorbing situation to slip several bars of chocolate secretly up the sleeve of her jumper.

Nigel, who spent a great deal of his time in Macaulay's, jigged up and down with enjoyment. He had no idea why everyone was excited, but he liked people to be happy.

"She's lurching about a bit," said Mrs Macaulay doubtfully. "She looks . . . ill somehow."

"She's only pulling that face because she knows the cameras are on her," said Sharon precociously. "All teachers are show-offs."

"She's probably drugged, these athletes often are," shrugged Hazel Tilson as she picked up the *Sunday Times* and walked out of the shop.

"Everyone else seems to be passing her now, leaving her behind." Sharon sounded so pleased that Mrs Macaulay sucked her tooth disapprovingly. "She can't be as good as she's cracked up to be," added Sharon with malicious satisfaction. "And now look! She's gone and fallen over!"

"Oh dear," came the commentator's voice, "someone's down, right in the middle of the pack . . . yes, and . . . oh dear, dear, dear, it's caused havoc. Runners are going over like nine-pins, this is really terrible!"

"She's fouled the whole thing up," remarked Mr Macaulay, his head protruded from his lair in the stockroom behind the shop. "I never saw such a mess!"

"That'll take her down a peg or two," muttered Sharon.

"She didn't trip," said Mrs Macaulay with a puzzled frown, "she sort of . . . keeled over. Now why should a healthy young girl do a thing like that?"

* * *

David and Jasmine arrived back in front of the television just in time to see Ann's dramatic fall.

"That school really needed a sports hall so badly,"

81

remarked David sadly. "Poor girl, she'll feel terrible letting the kids down like that."

* * *

Miss Rosedale, sitting up in bed in what had once been her parents' dining-room, switched off the television by remote control. The scene that had made Sharon laugh caused Rosie to feel more like crying. 'I do hope no one is badly hurt,' she thought as she closed her eyes. The silence of the house was blissful after the constant activities of the hospital ward, but it was good to know that nice young girl was upstairs somewhere, unpacking her possessions. 'I must keep out of her way,' thought Rosie for the hundredth time. 'Let her feel she is quite alone here. No contact or I'll lose her.' Once again she thought about the threadbare carpets and ragged curtains that had been new when her mother was a bride. 'I wonder if she would allow me to buy her new ones? Perhaps not yet. She must never feel beholden to me, forced to stay here out of gratitude.'

Upstairs Emmie looked round the antiquated kitchen that had delighted the evacuee mothers fifty years before. The ridiculous cooker and ancient fridge should really have been in a museum, but at least the place was clean, thanks to the Busy Bee Cleaning Company. She had also slept well last night in the great mahogany bed where Miss Rosedale had been born.

'I mustn't let myself get too friendly,' she thought, 'or start calling out "hello" or "I'm off now" when I go in and out. She's very sweet, but I can't have her taking up my time, I'll only survive here if I live an entirely separate life.'

She walked into her new sitting-room and felt again that tingle of joy. The large bay window did indeed look out over the park and Emmie sat down on the faded window-seat and savoured the view. It was certainly a beautiful room and its collection of dainty Victoriana would have turned any antique dealer sick with envy.

The irritating words of the hospital social worker floated back to Emmie's mind, "I think you've landed on your feet, Miss Dawson.'' Maybe, after all, she was right, and Emmie realised with a shock that she had not thought about Edward once all the weekend.

She put on the television just as Ann's face filled the screen.

'That's the sports fanatic from Number Five,' she thought. 'Oh dear, she's fallen over, how embarrassing.'

* * *

It was Sharon who had seen the Coleys leave the Terrace that morning, and Sharon who witnessed their return. But no coach full of cheering supporters transporting them this time, it had returned without them hours before.

'Must have come home by train,' thought Sharon, surprised.

''We saw you on telly,'' she said as they rounded the corner from Bakers Hill, but Matt and Ann did not want to notice her. 'I bet you've had a row,' she thought maliciously. 'She's been crying and he's cross as a bear.'

''So you weren't hurt then,'' she said, barring their way with her bicycle.

''She only tripped.'' Matt spat the words out through clenched teeth.

''How many more times must I tell you, *I did not trip.*'' Ann sounded near to tears again. ''I suddenly couldn't feel my legs.''

''You must be getting neurotic.'' Matt pushed open their garden gate so roughly it nearly parted with its hinges.

''Did *you* manage to raise lots of money then, Mr Coley?'' persisted Sharon. Matt stopped on the doorstep and threw down his leather sports bag viciously.

''No I did not! Someone from our club told me she'd been rushed to hospital, so I dropped out myself – like a fool. When I got there, she was perfectly all right. I was headed for a personal best, too.''

''So won't there be a sports hall when I come next term?'' The only answer Sharon received was the violent slamming of the Coleys' front door.

TUESDAY MAY 14TH

5.15pm

Kim sat in the doctor's waiting-room, wrestling with her youngest offspring.

"For goodness' sake sit still," she said crossly. "You're supposed to be ill." Why was it that children always perked up as soon as you got them within spitting distance of the surgery? At least it was a relief to sit down, while David coped at home with the hassle of tea-time. Kim sighed, having five children was quite an undertaking. It wasn't that Jasmine actually made more work, but adding an extra child seemed to have upset the family's natural structure. Rebecca was so busy organising her new friend that Amy was left bored and grizzling.

"Why do we have to get involved?" she had demanded when David had first suggested they have Jasmine.

He had merely given her one of his disarming smiles and replied, "Because we're a long time dead." Well they *would* be dead soon, if Johnnie and the baby didn't give them a decent night's sleep!

"Hello Ann," she said as the waiting-room door opened. Ann did not seem to hear, she simply gave her name to the receptionist and came over to sit down.

"Hi." Kim tried again. This time Ann nodded, but she still did not smile. The radiant health that Kim had always envied in the staffroom at Welbridge Comprehensive was gone – Ann looked white, and there were dark smudges under her eyes. 'What on earth's the matter with her?'

84

thought Kim. 'She looks dreadful. It's odd how you can work with someone for years and live right opposite to them, but never really know them at all. I suppose in our Terrace we all exist in separate little bubbles, somehow.'

"I've been waiting ages," she said brightly. "There's only Dr Macdermott on today." Ann still made no attempt at conversation. She was looking down at the baby kicking happily on Kim's lap.

"He isn't really ill," Kim continued, "just a bit off-colour." Slowly Ann reached out a finger which was seized eagerly in two fat fists.

"What perfect little fingers," she said at last. Kim noticed the hungry look in her eyes and smiled with relief. 'She's only pregnant after all, and here's me thinking she was ill!'

"Would you like to hold him?" she asked out loud. Ann's eyes glistened suspiciously as she looked up, but she shook her head.

"I'd better not, I keep dropping things these days."

"Go on," said Kim. "You'll need the practice." And she firmly transferred the heavy baby to Ann's lap.

"Been feeling sick, have you?" she asked sympathetically.

"Yes," replied Ann, vaguely, her attention still riveted on the baby.

"It does pass," said Kim as the receptionist called her name at last.

Kim's sojourn in the consulting-room was as brief as she had guessed it would be. "Always better to make sure," she said as she strapped the baby back in his pram.

"Mrs Coley?" said the receptionist, with a suppressed yawn. "Go in now, please."

"Well?" Doctor Macdermott's day had been extremely long and the night that preceded it had been extremely short. He was badly in need of his supper and he could not remember having seen this patient before in his life.

"I've been feeling a bit odd," began Ann. "I ran in the London Marathon last month and fell over . . ."

85

"You sporting types!" exclaimed the corpulent doctor testily, "you cost the NHS a fortune." Ann swallowed hard and gripped the arms of her chair.

"At the hospital I was told to come and see you. I've put it off for three weeks hoping . . . but things are getting worse."

"What things?" said the doctor.

"Lots of things. I'm always falling over and my hands won't grip properly. Then there's my eyes."

"Double vision?"

"No, just sort of blurred."

"Pins and needles?" snapped the doctor.

"Why yes," said Ann, "but the giddiness is the worst thing."

"Well, let's have a look at you." Doctor Macdermott stood up wearily. What had he done to deserve one of these this late in the day?

"You look marvellously healthy to me," he said five minutes later as she climbed off his couch. "Nothing much seems to be wrong. We'll just get some tests done to make sure." Ann sank back into her chair with a sigh of relief. "You mean I'm imagining it all."

"Probably. You work at Welbridge Comprehensive don't you, out on the Charbury estate? That's a very tough school, you're probably suffering from stress."

"I don't want my husband to know – about the tests I mean," said Ann quickly. "He doesn't even know I'm here, that's why I came now – he teaches athletics after school on a Tuesday."

"Why don't you want him to know?"

"If I was ill, I'd lose him," replied Ann quietly. "He can't cope with sick people and I couldn't cope without him."

It seemed like a long way up Bakers Hill that evening. 'It's all in the mind,' Ann told herself firmly as the whirling rush-hour traffic caused her head to spin violently.

Recent rain had polished the red brick pavements of Laburnum Terrace and caused the low garden walls to glisten in the sunshine, but Ann noticed nothing except Matt's long legs sprawling reproachfully on the front doorstep of Number Five. He had obviously forgotten his doorkey and was sitting on his sports bag, waiting for her. She had exactly twenty seconds to invent a good excuse for her absence.

She had hardly reached the garden gate however, before he bounded up and hugged her. A show of affection like that was so uncharacteristic it slightly unnerved Ann.

"It's wonderful!" he said as he swept her in through the door. "I couldn't think where you were, but Kim from over the road told me all about it. She was the very first to congratulate me!" He patted her on the shoulder sheepishly and added, "Sorry I got so uptight about all your aches and pains and the Marathon too, this explains it all."

Ann was completely mystified. Matt usually reacted to illness with complete contempt.

"I read an article the other day all about teaching babies to swim from birth, speeds up their muscular development. We'll have the fittest baby in Welbridge!"

For a moment Ann stood gazing at him mutely, then slowly she sank down on the bottom step of the stairs.

"Matt," she said, "I'm not pregnant." There was a long silence and then he said, "What is it then?" in a flat voice, quite unlike his own.

"The doctor says it's probably only tension."

Matt's jaw relaxed. "Oh, that's all right then. A few good long runs will soon cure that. We'll go out after supper." He pushed past her on his way to the shower, but Ann stayed where she was, huddled on the bottom step of the stairs gazing hopelessly into space.

SUNDAY MAY 19TH

12.30pm

"Well!" said Alison, managing to put such a complexity of feeling into the word that Gordon winced. "Well! I really cannot imagine what the church-wardens were thinking of – and as for the Bishop!"

"You liked this chap all right when he came to preach a while back." Gordon could not think why he was risking his neck to support the new vicar. What did it matter to him anyway?

"That was natural." Alison had switched to her pious voice. "We all felt sorry for him – losing his wife and being left with two small children to bring up on his own. But I'm afraid we allowed sympathy to cloud our better judgment. He's obviously been foisted on St Mark's simply because the Bishop didn't know where else to put him!"

Gordon wished Alison would hurry with the lunch, he wanted to be off to his allotment. The beans needed a heck of a lot of water at the moment. Today, however, her usual culinary expertise seemed to be buried under righteous indignation and the custard boiled all over the stove.

"There, now look what you've made me do!" she snorted as she dabbed at the sticky black mess. "Whatever is our poor old vicar going to say when I write to inform him about what that young man said – on his first Sunday, too! Implying you can't get to heaven by doing good. I ask you!"

"I *think* he was only trying to explain the reason for crucifixion," said Gordon timidly. He had always thought that if heaven was going to be full of millions of Alisons who'd earned the right to be there, he'd sooner go to the other place. The new vicar's pronouncement had encouraged him greatly, but to hide the fact he became very busy looking for white-fly on Alison's begonia.

"I didn't ask your opinion," she said witheringly. "It's me who's on the parochial church council remember. And I'll thank you to stop messing about with my house plants. The next thing will be guitars and drums instead of the organ, but he'll have me to reckon with first!" The expression on her face caused Gordon to flee from the kitchen. He pitied this poor young man profoundly, but he took comfort from the fact that if Alison did not do something soon, she'd lose her begonia.

6.40

The evening congregation at St Mark's was never more than a scattered handful who spaced themselves as far apart as possible. Alison was there of course and Amanda, sitting dutifully in the choir. Gordon had recently taken to staying at home in the evenings.

"It's not right to leave Clancy all alone," he would say over Sunday tea. Alison disapproved of his renegade behaviour, but she would have been positively outraged had she known about the packets of sweets they devoured as they watched television together. No one was allowed to eat or drink on Alison's velvet three-piece suite.

Mrs Macaulay from the corner shop always came in the evening, too, but she was so tired at the end of a busy week she invariably fell fast asleep, her one yellow tooth protruding from her open mouth.

Just as the organ was subsiding after the wheezing efforts of the first hymn, Kim slid into the back row.

'Late *again*,' thought Alison. 'Why these young mothers cannot organise themselves these days I do not know.'

The perspiration was pouring off Kim's forehead and trickling down her shiny nose. She hated the scramble of getting ready to come out; the baby never wanted to take his feed; Johnnie would be awkward in the bath; and Amy clung like a frantic koala bear. 'I don't know why I bother really,' she thought wearily. 'This church isn't worth the hassle.' For nine long years she had put up with that old man with the face and voice of a well-bred goat. He would bleat for exactly twenty minutes without saying anything whatsoever. Would this new vicar be any better? David had seemed very excited when he had come home this morning, but as usual he would not be drawn into any comment.

As the Reverend Richard Reynolds stood up, she thought he must be the tallest man she had ever seen. 'But he was certainly in the back row when good looks were given out,' she added. 'Only a rugger player could possibly have acquired a nose like that.' Yet there was something about the way he conducted the service that reminded her of how she used to feel about church, long ago. It had not always seemed a useless waste of time, in fact it had been a delight at St Peter's.

She tried to concentrate on the present proceedings, but these days her mind would flit about aimlessly. It seemed to be taking her back to university days where she and David had fallen in love at St Peter's, in the third pew from the back. Yes, her faith had been exciting then, and she had been so sure their lives would be used in some great venture. What had gone wrong? Was it simply the fatigue of living with four small children that had drained away her spiritual energy? No, the rot had set in before Rebecca was even born.

As the feeble voices of the congregation laboured through the second hymn, Kim's wayward mind took her into a sparsely-furnished room and she saw herself sitting

90

stiffly on an upright chair facing a row of soberly-dressed people across a polished table.

"Why do you feel called to mission in Africa, Mrs Patterson?" asked the lady in the feathered hat. Her answer had blazed with enthusiasm, and she had felt convinced that the committee would be delighted to accept the services of an English graduate married to a trained primary-school teacher.

But the missionary society had sent a polite letter refusing the offer of their lives. Yes, that was when things began to go wrong inside. It was not the committee who had refused them, she felt it was God Himself. When they were sick of applying to other societies he had shunted them off into the siding of St Mark's and left them to rust in Laburnum Terrace.

"May the words of my mouth and the meditation of all our hearts . . ." The congregation was settling back into their pews now, preparing to sit out the sermon. Alison had her notebook ready for she needed to have written evidence of her concern before the next council meeting. Mrs Macaulay was already snoring and old Mrs Galbraith's hearing-aid whined as she switched it off.

However, by the time the sermon was two minutes old, Kim felt she was beginning a ride on a roller-coaster.

"Wow!" was her irreverent reaction. God was real to the rugged mountain of a man in the pulpit. He was talking about a friend and completely failing to deliver an academic lecture.

The evening was hot and airless as Kim walked slowly home. The sermon which had moved her so deeply had not brought her peace. In fact she felt her long-buried frustration boiling to the surface dangerously. She had seen a fire burning in the new vicar's eyes which once had burned in her own − the ashes tasted bitter.

"I would have given my life for you in Africa!" she said as she shook a mental fist at the Almighty. "But I suppose," she added with a sigh, "it was David's fault really. If only he could communicate – had a bit more drive – we'd be out there by now, instead of buried here under a pile of dirty diapers.''

The kitchen mess hit Kim between the eyes as she walked in, but what was the point of clearing it all up, it would be just as bad by tomorrow morning. Upstairs Johnnie was bawling loudly in his cot, and Amy had obviously failed to settle either, because she could hear David reading her a story. 'I'm a prisoner,' she thought, 'in a sweet little antique rabbit-hutch.'

She boiled the kettle and thought about the wide expanses of Africa as she scooped coffee into two mugs. ''Blast my diet,'' she said crossly, and cutting a huge slab of chocolate cake she took a tray out into the red-bricked yard they called the garden.

'Well? Did you like him?' David did not actually ask the question, but his face did.

''He was terrific,'' she answered morosely. ''He'll sort St Mark's out all right. After the service you should have heard Mrs Macaulay and that ghastly woman from Number Thirteen!''

''If he tries to move too fast he'll stir up a hornet's nest.''

''That's just typical of you,'' exploded Kim. ''You're so like Amy, frightened of anything new or exciting.'' David looked at her, stung by the lash of unexpected anger.

''You haven't got any ambition at all. I don't suppose you'll ever get round to applying for that headship on the Charbury Estate, will you?''

''I like teaching too much to be an administrator.''

''But you could have so much influence. I'm stuck here with the kids, but at least you could get on and do something worthwhile, instead of always plodding along in the background.'' David turned to inspect the flowers in the old kitchen sink they called the flower-bed. He was hurt and angry, too, but he did not want Kim to see that. He hated it when she shouted like this.

"David, don't you want to *do* something with your life?" Kim's voice was shaking now and she was very close to tears. "What do you suppose life's all about anyway?"

"You shouldn't be mean to him like that!" said a voice from the alley. They both looked up startled. Over the back fence a face, framed by sandy hair, was glaring at them. "He's the best teacher I've ever had and *everyone* at our school thinks he's lovely."

"Sharon! Whatever are you doing there?" Kim sounded furious.

"Standing on a dustbin," she replied sulkily. At that moment, Amy ran out of the kitchen door clutching her teddy and sucking her thumb. She must have been listening too, because she dived straight for David's legs.

"Don't be horrid to my nice daddy," she sobbed. Suddenly Kim began to laugh.

"I don't stand a chance against all your supporters," she said. David hugged her with his free arm and smiled over her head at Sharon. "It's tough living with a saint who won't even give me a good argument," said Kim as she kissed him.

MONDAY MAY 20TH

The washing-machine broke down the next day and flooded the kitchen floor. Johnnie powdered his bedroom with a three-pound bag of self-raising flour and Amy whined until Kim's patience snapped.

"If I have to stay cooped up in this house a minute longer I'll commit mass infanticide," she yelled. She could pop in and see a friend, but which of them could tolerate an explosion like Johnnie tearing their tidy house to bits? They all seemed to have nice little girls who sat playing with their dolls all morning. When black smoke began to pour from the back of the vacuum-cleaner, Kim burst into tears.

"That does it!" she shouted, just as David's doorkey turned in the lock. He had dashed home during break to collect the track suit he had forgotten.

"Take the whole lot of them into the park for the rest of the day," he suggested.

"How can I?" sniffed Kim. "Just look at the mess everywhere."

"I'll help you tonight. The monsters'll be fine in the park."

'He may be infuriating, but he's usually right,' thought Kim two hours later. 'There must be some kind of magic in this place. I can never remember all three of them sleeping at the same moment.' Splashing in the paddling pool and then a walk up the steep rhododendron path had tired Johnnie and Amy out. They were now both stretched out on the rug where they had eaten their picnic lunch. Kim leaned her back against the trunk of a beech tree and sighed with relief as the scent of the bluebells wafted around her. At last she had time to think.

Welbridge sprawled across the hill on the far side of the lake and she could see right up Laburnum Terrace from here. Somehow, viewed from this distance, it did not look like the prison it had felt that morning.

Up the winding path a man was toiling, wheeling a sleeping child in a stroller. 'Now where have I seen him before?' mused Kim absently – then she remembered. The new vicar! He recognised her at once and came across the turf towards her.

In Kim's mind, vicars spent their time preparing sermons or visiting the sick. It seemed odd to find one in the park wearing a T-shirt.

"Shush," she warned, standing up hurriedly, "let's let the 'sleeping dogs lie.' " He took out a hankie and mopped his broad forehead.

"It's hot work up that hill," he whispered obediently. "Mind if I sit down for a minute?" She nodded politely and watched him deposit all six foot five inches of himself in the shade.

"We met in church last night, didn't we? I'm afraid I'm not too good at putting a name to a face." Kim smiled and introduced herself.

"This is Jess," he said, indicating the sleeping child, who looked as diminutive as her father was enormous. "Pippa's eight and she's just settling into the primary school on Bakers Hill."

"That's where my husband works," said Kim. "However do you cope with them both?"

"My mother's staying with us for a while." He sounded rather bleak, and Kim hurriedly changed the subject.

"Whatever made you choose St Mark's? It's really rather ghastly, isn't it?"

"The building or the people?" He looked amused.

95

"Both, to be honest. But I must say I enjoyed your sermon last night."

"You didn't look as if you did." He was obviously the outspoken type – Kim liked that.

"I suppose it's just that I'm a bit peeved with God, actually," she said and then stopped. She was always blurting things out and shocking people, but he still seemed to be smiling.

"How come?" he said. She found herself wanting to tell him, but could she really talk to a complete stranger about something so personal? As she looked at him – sitting there chewing a piece of grass and twinkling at her – she discovered that she could – it was his own fault for looking so interested!

"You see, before we came here, I wanted to go abroad and turn the world upside down for God. But He didn't seem to want my help after all."

Richard said nothing, he sat looking across the valley at Laburnum Terrace. It looked solid and unchangeable, sleeping in the midday sun. "I suppose it must be tougher being a missionary in a gossipy little road like that," he said at last.

"But I'm *not* a missionary, that's the whole point. I'm only a housewife."

"But don't you think we're all missionaries wherever God puts us?" Kim looked at him hard, she was beginning to revise her first favourable impressions.

"What do you expect me to do? Stand on a soapbox in the middle of the road? If people want to find God, they can jolly well come to church, it's only at the bottom of Bakers Hill."

"But they hardly ever find faith, unless they see it working in someone else." Kim still looked ruffled and he added apologetically, "I don't mean we have to preach. Surely it's the way we relate to people that shows them what we believe?"

"Johnnie doesn't leave me much time to relate to anyone these days!" said Kim with feeling. "Laburnum

Terrace will just have to wait until the kids are all at school," she laughed as she added, "after all, I've got a whole lifetime ahead of me." His face flickered with pain, and she stopped smiling abruptly.

"Oh I am sorry," she said, embarrassed. It couldn't be more than eight months since his wife had been killed. Why did she always have to put her great foot in it?

"That's all right," he said with a quick smile. "I'm afraid I'm still a bit raw under the surface. I suppose we all tend to feel we're immortal, but I've discovered that bereavement shakes all that a bit."

This conversation was becoming a little too serious for Kim and she was quite relieved when Johnnie terminated it by waking up and pulling Amy's hair until she screamed.

SATURDAY MAY 25TH

7.45am

When the milk-float reached the park railings Babs was
so surprised she could hardly climb out.

"There's been a ruddy miracle," she said reverently.
Yesterday the garden around Number Sixteen had
resembled the wilderness which enveloped the Sleeping
Beauty's castle. Today the raging weeds and brambles
had been wiped clean away, revealing neatly-dug flower-
beds and the grass where, a century ago, the Rosedales
had played croquet.

"Hello." A disembodied voice assailing her from
behind the wall caused Babs's memory clock to spin
backwards over the years quite alarmingly. But there
were no sweetpeas this time, and it was Emmie kneeling
there.

"You nearly gave me an 'eart attack. I didn't expect
to see anyone gardening this early in the morning,"
gasped Babs. "You never shifted all this lot of mess in
twenty-four hours, did you?"

"Goodness no," laughed Emmie, "Miss Rosedale had
a firm of landscape gardeners here all day with all their
marvellous machinery. I just wanted to get some bedding
plants in before it gets too hot. I'm going to fill this garden
so full of flowers you'll hardly be able to wade up to the
front door with the milk."

"Shall you grow sweetpeas?" asked Babs.

"Masses!"

"There you are at last!" Alison's voice from the far side

of the road startled Babs out of her nostalgia. "You've
been two hours late all this week."

"It's not my fault if they go and reorganise my round,"
retorted Babs, and was secretly pleased to note that
'Number Thirteen' looked exactly as she had always
imagined she would. She handed Alison her milk and
turned pointedly back to Emmie.

"You've moved in, then, to look after the old lady?"

"Oh no! I'm only the lodger; we hardly ever see each
other. Oh dear," she added, "Hazel must be having one
of her famous do's tonight." A large van rumbled up the
Terrace and edged its way in beside the milk-float.
"Marquees and awnings for all occasions," announced
large red letters.

"Must be a *big* do." Babs was consulting her order-
book, "She wants ten pints of double cream!"

She was about to climb back on her float when Emmie
said, "I suppose you wouldn't pop in for a moment. I
have a feeling Miss Rosedale would love to be able to
thank you for Good Friday."

"We can't wake the old lady," protested Babs, turning
a modest pink.

"She's been awake for ages. I heard her radio at crack
of dawn."

"You've done wonders in here, too," remarked Babs
as she stomped across the hall to become re-acquainted
with the stag's head. Even his antlers seemed to have
been polished. Thanks to the weekly visits of Busy Bees
Ltd, the whole house smelt of beeswax and pot-pourri,
and Babs sniffed approvingly.

"This is our milk-lady, Rosie, the one who found you
that morning," explained Emmie, after tapping on the
door of the old dining-room where Rosie now slept.

When she remembered the last visit to this house, it
was extremely difficult for Babs to recognise the old lady
who sat up in bed in her pretty pink bed-jacket. But the
smile was the one she had remembered down the years.

'That girl may only be the lodger,' she thought as she

walked slowly back to her float ten minutes later, but she's certainly made things feel a bit better round here.'

10.30

Gordon was spending a happy morning hoeing among his lines of new seedlings. It was going to be a good year for carrots. Behind him a shadow moved and he jumped guiltily.

"Clancy, what are you doing up here?"

"I came to see where you go when you want to escape."

"That's not very nice," chided Gordon without conviction. "Is she being a bit . . . you know?" Clancy nodded, wondering how she was going to survive a whole half-term week shut up in the house with Alison.

"Well, this is my estate then," said Gordon with the sweeping gesture of a landed gentleman. "I'll see if I can find you an early strawberry."

"Is that your little shed?" asked Clancy when her mouth was full. "Can I look inside?" Gordon hesitated, no one else had ever gone in there. "Please," her black eyes twinkled at him like the bird he had once saved from the ginger cat.

"All right then, but you won't tell . . . anyone."

"I never tell her anything," replied Clancy with perfect truth.

"It's got a carpet and all," she exclaimed, looking round with admiration. "Curtains, too." Her quick eye took in the armchair, camping stove and stack of beer cans. Gordon tried to hide the pipe Alison banned from the Terrace, but he was just too late.

"All you need's a telly, then you could move in," said Clancy wistfully. Gordon, who often dreamed of doing just that, only smiled.

"Would you ever let me come up here – to do my

100

homework like? It would be easier to concentrate on my own." She never did any homework on principle, but a key to this shed and the privacy it offered would be very useful.

"Grazier! Are you in there?" A harsh, rasping voice interrupted Gordon's reply.

"Ah, George," he said nervously. "Fancy seeing you."

"Fancy my foot," said the burly man in the doorway. "My allotment's next to yours after all. And that's why I've got a bone to pick with you." He was backing Gordon and Clancy up against the wall. "Someone's just told me you did a bit of weedkilling last evening."

"Yes." Gordon's voice resembled the squeak of a cornered mouse. "I sprayed over my edges that's all."

"I suppose it didn't occur to you to notice which way the wind was blowing?" continued the bullying voice. "Right across my patch!" Clancy's presence lent Gordon a helping of courage which surprised him.

"Well, you seem to have plenty of thistles to kill," he said breathlessly.

George glared at him in outraged surprise and his reply reminded Clancy of her stepfather at his worst, and reminded Gordon of Alison at hers.

"What a mean man," she whispered when George had gone off to complain to the chairman of the Allotment Holders' Association. "Is he always like that?"

Gordon was trying in vain to disguise the way his body was shaking. "It's like this," he explained. "In the autumn we have a bit of a show. There's a silver cup for the best collection of seven different vegetables. Everyone wants to win that one and George usually does, but last year I just managed to beat him and he's been sore about it ever since."

"You'll beat him again this year, too," said Clancy, pushing Gordon down into his armchair and handing him his pipe and a can of beer. "I'll come up here and cast spells on your veggies till they grow enormous." Gordon smiled fondly at her.

101

"All right," he said, "you and I'll share my hideaway. But we won't tell Al . . . I mean anyone, will we?"

7pm

Hazel Tilson looked magnificent as she walked down the elegant staircase of Number Fifteen. The pure silk two-piece had been an excellent investment and that woman, Claire from the salon round the corner, always did her hair so well. Hazel needed to look magnificent, it was all part of the mask she put on deliberately before a party and as she went on duty in the hospital. Inwardly she was not the cool, confident career woman she appeared on the outside, that was merely a part she had been rehearsing most of her life.

"How do I look?" she asked Graham.

"Perfect – as usual," he replied morosely as he poured her a gin and tonic without looking up. "I wish we didn't have to keep giving these wretched do's. What's the point?"

"What's the point?" snapped Hazel. "We've got to make connections, that's the point."

"Why? I've already got where I want to be."

"Well, I haven't! Not yet. So I still need the 'right people' to get me there." She patted her glossy red hair and frowned at herself in the mirror. Behind her the house positively blazed with light, the caterers flitted about putting the finishing touches to the buffet, and the lavish flower arrangements were exactly as she had ordered. Yet tonight that mask of confidence seemed oddly elusive, she felt nervous and defeated. 'I'm being stupid,' she told herself firmly. Tonight's guest list was most pleasing – she had managed to land some very big fish indeed. It was just bad luck that this stupid bug should hit her at the wrong time. She ought to have thrown it off by now, a week was too long to feel as nauseous as this. At least her reflection looked all right. She'd managed to cover that peaky look with make-up.

"We ought to move out into the country," growled Graham. "Put down some roots. Then perhaps I could relax when I'm at home from London."

"Yes, a house in the country would be better," agreed Hazel absently. "It's ridiculous making guests park on Bakers Hill and then traipse down this scruffy little Terrace."

"At least they've done something to that garbage dump of a garden over the road. It used to be such a mess – let the whole road down."

"Emily's doing, no doubt," said Hazel, wondering if the gin had been a mistake, her stomach seemed to be quarrelling with it violently. "Little gold-digger," she added acidly. "She gets ditched by the rich boyfriend, so she promptly finds herself a wealthy old lady with no one else to leave it all to."

"At least she's not still cluttering us up over here," said Graham without being able to keep the regret out of his voice.

The first guests rang the doorbell at exactly seven twenty. 'The boring ones always come early,' thought Hazel as she saw Dr Macdermott and his wife Jane on the doorstep. What a frump she looked these days. Jane had been the first person she had met that autumn day when they had both arrived at Oxford. How she had envied Jane then – sleek and fresh from her expensive boarding-school. *She* would never have to work for connections to get where she wanted to go in life. She already had them without effort – uncles, cousins and the brothers of school friends – ready-made strings waiting to be pulled. Hazel had soon realised that life would never be easy like that for her. All she had behind her were her comprehensive school and her parents' council flat. Yet life had not conformed to what had seemed an inevitable pattern. The roles were reversed now, she was sleek and elegant and Jane looked like a down-trodden nobody. What a waste of a promising career, tethering herself to a dull doctor who wanted a big family.

"Jane, you look divine," she said.

The party was as successful as Hazel's parties always were.

"Scrumptious food, darling, and having the bar out there in that baby marquee is pure genius," said Jane Macdermott, as she wondered acidly how ostentatious people could get.

By ten o'clock Hazel had mingled with most people, but the room was swirling round her alarmingly. 'Where the hell is Graham?' she thought furiously, 'I might have guessed, propping up the bar, talking shop with his senior partner.' Even in a paisley cravat and blazer Graham still contrived to look like a London solicitor. 'I'd better go and dislodge him,' she thought grimly as she wove her way into the marquee, but a hand on her arm delayed her.

"Can you spare me a minute?" said a voice behind her.

"The request of my Big White Chief is a command," she said archly, while she wondered what the silly old fool wanted now.

In the garden they found two white wrought-iron chairs with a view of the lake, and Hazel thankfully sat down. This was not the moment to vomit she told her stomach firmly.

"I've decided to retire," began the senior pathologist. "We're buying a little place in Tuscany. I've always felt I was grooming you for my job. Have you ever thought about it?"

"Well no," said Hazel, who seldom thought of anything else. Welbridge General was one of the most influential of provincial hospitals and the pathology department was revered throughout the medical profession. She wanted that job more than she wanted anything else in life.

"I shall be recommending you most highly, but it's not

going to be all that easy," he continued. "Some of the committee have their own candidate lined up already. You know what these Masons are."

'I'll bring them round,' thought Hazel. 'Graham wouldn't care, even if I have to sleep with every one of them, not when he knows what my salary would be.'

"At least you've managed to get most of them here tonight," Dr Squirry continued, looking back approvingly into the crowded drawing-room. "But there is one other problem."

"What's that?" asked Hazel sharply.

"The chairman, Clarence Cromway, has a positive 'thing' against appointing a woman with a family, and frankly the responsibilities of the job are so great the two simply wouldn't mix. It's a shame you haven't got all that kind of thing out of the way by now. Or perhaps you're not planning to have children?"

Hazel paused. Of course they wanted a family. Graham was always talking about 'his son'. Someone to take fishing, follow him to his old school and even take his place in the firm. But Squirry was watching her narrowly from under his shaggy eyebrows and she realised that the way she responded now could alter the rest of her life.

"We decided against children years ago," she said lightly. "You can tell the chairman I'm a dedicated career woman."

"Are you feeling all right, Hazel?" he asked suddenly. "You look quite pale."

"Perfectly," she replied crisply as she fought a fresh wave of nausea. "Red-heads always look like ghosts in the moonlight; surely a man of your experience must have discovered that?" She reached the downstairs cloakroom only just in time, and swore at herself furiously. "This must be some kind of food poisoning." She could never remember feeling quite as frightful as this before.

It was while she was on her way to be charming to the hospital administrator that Jane Macdermott fainted. One minute she was talking to the headmaster of Welbridge Comprehensive and the next she was lying like a corpse on the Chinese rug at his feet.

"Oh, dear," he said, "is there a doctor here?"

"At least twenty of us," said Hazel crossly. Trust Jane to create a drama. "If you'll just give me a hand, we'll get her up to my bedroom. Graham? Where on earth has he got to now?"

"Sorry, darling," mumbled Jane when she found herself in Hazel's reproduction four-poster bed. "Don't fuss, I'm only pregnant. Standing around always makes me dreadfully sick and giddy."

"Not again," said Hazel caustically.

"But we always wanted four." Jane sounded nettled. "If you two don't get going soon, it'll be too late."

St Mark's clock had struck two before the last guests departed.

"Super do, absolutely marvellous," they called loudly as they walked away past Alison's house next door.

"She'll complain in the morning," sighed Graham as he sank into bed. He was asleep instantly, but Hazel lay beside him stiff with suppressed shock.

"Don't fuss, I'm only pregnant." Jane's words had tolled in her mind like a funeral bell for hours, but she had refused to take notice of them. "Standing about always makes me feel sick and giddy."

"Oh no!" Hazel put her arms over her face as if to ward off a blow. "It can't be." She'd had to stop taking the pill last year, after that wretched thrombosis, but surely they'd been careful. With devastating clarity she realised she had every single symptom in the text-book. Why hadn't she realised it before?

As she lay there in the dark, she saw herself during the next few vital months trying to woo the hard-nosed male-dominated management committee wearing a pair of maternity dungarees.

BANK HOLIDAY MONDAY MAY 27TH

'It feels like taking off my dirty working overall and putting on an entirely new personality,' thought Claire as she began the long descent to Mill Cottage. It was always like that when she came to see Roger. Welbridge and its commuter trains, bustling shops and nosy neighbours were left behind. Ahead, down in the valley where the world of commerce had never penetrated, lay silence.

Rain fought her windscreen wipers and washed the colour out of the last of the primroses which grew on the high banks of the lane. 'It's an outrage when it rains in May,' she thought indignantly and wondered how the Pattersons and Jasmine were surviving on Camber Sands. 'They'll probably come back early,' she thought gloomily. Down below she could see smoke curling from Roger's chimney, and she smiled. He'd be sitting in his armchair beside the fire like a sleepy tabby-cat. The ordinary concerns of life such as going to work and making money never worried Roger. He didn't have to think about mortgages, staff problems and new ballet shoes.

But he was not beside his fire when she parked by the stream at the bottom of the hill. He was standing motionless gazing across the old millpond, with a sack protecting his head and shoulders from the rain. 'He looks like a crazy old monk in wellington boots,' thought Claire affectionately, as she came over to stand beside him.

The mill-wheel was silent, it had not turned for sixty

years, and the water, splashing through the ancient brick conduit, was soothing and eternal. A line of plump, white ducks sailed across the grey, rain-pitted water and the stillness of the place began to work its usual spell. 'If only I lived somewhere like this,' she thought, 'what a different person I could be.'

Another, smaller cottage stood by the mill – it looked empty behind its leaded panes. Claire looked at it curiously through the rain and realised it was exactly the kind of place she dreamed about frequently these days. 'What heaven to come home here after a long day's work and lie in bed listening to the water splashing endlessly under the window.' It had a little garden, too, she could grow herbs, start living a real life at last.

She glanced sideways at Roger's impassive face. He had become the hub of her world. Her feeling for him was quite untinged by desire; Roger was sexless and she had found that distinctly restful – at first. Now she was beginning to want more than that. An invisible veil seemed to separate them and even though it was so nebulous she could never break it down.

"Is something wrong?" she asked after five minutes and when the rain began to trickle down her neck. Sometimes his inscrutability irritated her.

Roger pulled himself out of his abstraction with a visible effort. "You're wet, my dear," he said. "Let's go inside."

"I brought the books back," she said when they were settled by the fire. "I've got lots of questions. I've written them all down." She fumbled in her handbag, and then stopped. "Something *is* wrong," she said again.

"No, no, my dear," he replied, sipping his rosehip tea as if it had been vintage brandy.

"Look, Roger, I don't seem to be getting on very fast, do I?" The pragmatic temperament she had been stifling for months was beginning to demand expression. "I hardly ever have time with you alone like this, and when I do, you're all . . . distracted."

"My dear, you must not treat this quest for knowledge like a crash course in beauty therapy. Take your time."

"But I always feel you're communicating with someone else, even when we're alone. It's unnerving."

"We are never alone, my dear. There are always the sympathisers."

"Sympathisers?"

"So many people come here to me because medical science has failed them. I could never find my way to their pain without the sympathisers – people who have suffered in a previous life."

"There's so much I don't understand," said Claire uneasily. "I just wish you could realise how hard it is for me to be two people. Living out here you wouldn't know how different life is in Welbridge. I wish I could get right away. Who owns that empty cottage, the one next door?"

"My mother," replied Roger from the depths of his armchair. "I was thinking about her when you found me by the pond. Missing her."

"Is she . . .?"

"She's very well, for a woman of eighty-five. She lives in a nursing home in Welbridge. The cottage is too damp for her arthritis."

"I'm sorry," said Claire. "But all the same, it does seem a pity to leave it empty. I suppose you wouldn't consider letting it to me? I could rent out my own house in Laburnum Terrace to pay you." Her mind was racing ahead so fast, she was almost planning the curtains. "We could be together often then. I could learn so much faster."

For a long time Roger surveyed her over the rim of his earthenware mug, then he said, "No" with chilling finality.

"But why don't you want me here?" Claire was stunned; surely they had something going for them on a spiritual level at least.

He leaned forward and took her hands in his. "There

109

are two reasons why I say no. One is the child. I need complete silence in which to work.''

''But Jasmine's terribly quiet,'' protested Claire.

''Children grow into teenagers and teenagers have radios and boyfriends.'' Claire bit her lip. Always Jasmine – the millstone round her neck.

''The other reason is that I need you in Welbridge.''

''What?''

''If we both lived here away from the world how would we ever contact the people who need help?''

''But surely you don't expect me to go on living in a little cul-de-sac for ever and boring myself to tears in the salon?''

''It is in the cul-de-sacs and salons of this world that the people are found.''

''But I'm fed up with being a beautician – preening the peacocks all day long. The young girls remind me of what I once was, and the older women force me to realise what I'm soon going to be.''

''They need you, my dear. They bring you their inadequacies, their insecurity – trusting you to make them feel good again. A hairdresser has a unique relationship with her clients. Through your hands you will feel your way to their pain and recognise those who would be psychically susceptible to my healing touch.''

''And then bring them out here to you I suppose,'' said Claire crisply. ''Like chickens to be plucked.''

''Claire!'' He sounded hurt. ''One day you won't *need* to bring them to me, you will be able to help them yourself.''

''How far away is your 'one day'?''

''When you receive your spirit guides.''

''Oh, no thank you very much.'' Claire stood up with such force her milking-stool fell over and rolled across the red-brick floor. ''I never bargained on becoming a medium. You simply said I had a natural touch.''

''So you have, my dear,'' soothed Roger, pulling her down on the arm of his chair. ''But we are nothing of ourselves. The dead can do so much for the living, those of us with the right gifts can channel their energy.''

''Are you really telling me that you heal through people who've died?'' quavered Claire.

''You know already that I use many methods of healing, herbs, crystals, the touch of my hands, but always I am guided. They are only shadows – there to help us.''

Claire was silent for a long time, looking into the weird caverns formed by the glowing logs on the fire. Roger's words seemed to dance in the flames, 'there is always a cost.'

''I've run my own business successfully for twenty years now,'' she said at last. ''I don't want to hand over my independence and find I'm being controlled by some supernatural force.''

''That is why I say 'one day'. You are not ready yet to face your own need.''

His strange, pale eyes seemed to fill the universe as he leaned forward and put his hands on her shoulders. As his unearthly strength poured into her, she began to feel mean and base for allowing herself to be irritated by someone as special as Roger.

FRIDAY MAY 31ST

Hazel sat in the deserted salon swathed in a black gown. Behind her stood Claire, silently blow-drying her hair. This regular, evening appointment after work was most convenient, and it was more restful to have her hair done when there was no one else milling about the shop.

She closed her eyes wearily. What a week it had been. Thank goodness for a hairdresser who did not chatter endlessly about holiday plans or pop music.

The buzz of the dryer died behind her now, and she felt Claire's hands on her head. A strange sensation of warmth flooded through her and she began to feel drowsy and strangely relaxed.

"Whatever are you up to?" she asked suddenly and her eyes flew open like a doll's.

"I'm simply trying to find what's troubling you," replied Claire calmly. "I sense that your spirit is warring against your body."

"Don't be so ridiculous!" snapped Hazel.

"I think you're pregnant, Dr Tilson – and you don't wish to be."

Hazel glared at her hairdresser's reflection in the mirror, but Claire smiled back and continued gently, "Do you want to talk about it?"

"Certainly not!" said Hazel, realising she wanted to very much indeed. The last six days had been the loneliest of her life.

"You can trust me." Hazel sat looking at Claire silently. *Could* she trust this extraordinary woman? For some unaccountable reason she felt that she could.

"I simply can't understand how you could possibly know," she said at last. "No one does, not even my husband. He'd be delighted of course, he's always wanted a family, but for me it would be curtains for the job I set my heart on years ago."

"But surely the decision is yours," said Claire. "It's not *his* body that will have to carry a child, and it's not *his* career that will be ruined by it."

Hazel chewed the end of her thumb and frowned. "I could go to a private clinic, I suppose, and tell Graham I was at some medical conference, but would it be fair, when it's his . . .?" She could not bring herself to say "baby".

"Once I was faced with exactly the same decision," said Claire softly. "I wish now that I had been brave enough to be faithful to myself, instead of letting guilt control me."

'She's right,' thought Hazel as relief swept through her. What gave Graham the right to make her a useless nonentity like Jane Macdermott? If she swung this job they could afford that house in the country he wanted so much. Children weren't everything. But in spite of those compelling dark eyes looking at her from the mirror, she still felt uneasy.

"How did you discover about this?" she asked by way of a diversion.

"I'm psychic," said Claire with a mysterious smile. "I'm studying ancient forms of medicine and the old cures that were effective long before your modern drugs and techniques were thought about."

The bell on the shop door made them both jump. Kim was standing on the threshold with the baby on her hip and Jasmine clutching her hand.

"We were getting rather concerned," she began. "It's a bit late you know. Had you forgotten David and I are going out?"

"My fault," said Hazel, pulling off her gown. "I kept her talking."

113

"I hope your party went well on Saturday," Kim remarked. "Those floodlights and the marquee made the Terrace look very festive." But Hazel was not listening, she was staring at the baby with the same fixed expression that Kim had seen on Ann's face a little while before. She too reached out a finger to be grasped and sucked with relish.

"What incredible hands babies have," she said softly, and Claire looked up sharply from the till. Behind her smiling mask, Hazel was thinking how many dead babies she must have seen, flat and white on the slab in her mortuary, but this one was so wonderfully alive. How could she possibly contemplate . . .? Abruptly she turned to fumble on the rail for her jacket. Claire must not see her face until she had it back under her control. No! She wasn't going to let herself get sentimental. She would merely be dislodging a cluster of alien cells which threatened to destroy her life as surely as if they had been cancerous. Claire was perfectly right, she must be brave enough to put the more important things first in life.

FRIDAY JULY 26TH

By six o'clock the holiday spirit was bubbling in Laburnum Terrace like an irrepressible mountain spring.

"No more school for six whole weeks," breathed Rebecca. "It feels like always."

Nigel sat on his garden wall in the dusty evening heat. He liked to watch everyone coming home from work — but really he was only waiting for one particular person.

A London train had just rumbled into the station, disgorging its load of brief-case bearers to walk in a weary wave up Bakers Hill. Graham Tilson was among them and, as he turned into the Terrace, he looked a trifle less sleek than usual, for London had been stifling and his expensive suit was badly crumpled.

Graham ignored Nigel. He was looking straight past him to where Tom Savery was trying to pack a mound of holiday equipment into his rusty old car.

"Come on, Daddy, or we'll miss the ferry-boat," said Sharon, carrying out yet another bag to add to the load.

"Women!" muttered Tom. "We're only going for a fortnight."

"I always wonder why men get so bad-tempered packing cars," said his wife, as she appeared with a large picnic box. 'That's what Hazel always says,' thought Graham, and in spite of his fatigue he smiled as he encountered Tom's look of exasperation. However, the thought of Hazel soon extinguished his amusement. She had been so odd lately, sharp and scratchy like a cat, and she was thinner than ever. Probably the strain of trying to land this new job — she needed the holiday in Turkey.

Gordon was next along the road. He usually stopped to speak to Nigel on his way home from his office round the corner. However, his attention was also distracted by the sight of Tom, trying vainly to close the trunk of his car. This time next week that would be his unhappy lot. They were off on the annual penance to Eastbourne to stay with Auntie Madge.

"We can't afford to pay out on holidays." Alison said the same thing every year. "Not with Amanda's education to pay for." Gordon was not sure that she was worth the sacrifice.

At least Eastbourne would be more fun with Clancy there this year. He could show her Beachy Head and the lighthouse. He had stood up there last summer and wished he dared jump the four hundred feet into the sea. Funny, he hadn't felt that bad once since she'd come.

"Daddy, Daddy, have you remembered?" David Patterson had hardly turned the corner before three small girls hurled themselves upon him. "There, Jasmine," said Rebecca, "I told you he always brings us ice-creams on the last day of school. Oh Daddy!" she added reproachfully as she peered into his brown-paper bag. "You forgot Mummy's on a diet – she really mustn't have one, you know." David smiled as his oldest daughter ran across the road to present the offending ice-cream to Nigel. She was so like her mother.

He sat down on the wall to enjoy his ice-cream beside Amy, but as usual Jasmine squeezed her way in between them.

"This time next week we'll be in our caravan," said Rebecca as the Saverys' overloaded car lurched past them with Sharon waving triumphantly out of the back.

"Everyone's going away," said Jasmine tragically. "Except me."

Ann and Matt were next. Nigel smiled hopefully even though they had never acknowledged his existence. Handicaps of any kind revolted them both. Today, however, Ann stopped.

"Hello," she tried tentatively.

"Hello," he parroted.

"Are you going away on holiday soon?" Ann did not realise that her question would baffle Nigel completely and she turned pink with embarrassment when he stared at her blankly. He knew he was going tomorrow in a coach to Bournemouth with the others from the day centre, and he tried hard to snatch the words out of his mind. When he failed to do so, he giggled happily instead. Nothing ever worried Nigel, and Ann turned away hurriedly.

"Handicapped people are really better off in homes," remarked Matt as he pushed open their gate. "Come on," he added impatiently. "We've got to make the big decision this evening. Are we going to do it North to South or South to North?" Walking the Pennine Way was his next great physical challenge. "After supper we'll spread out the maps and decide." Silently Ann began to put away the shopping. Her face was very white.

"Matt, I'm not coming," she said as he pulled their walking boots out of the broom cupboard. There was a stunned silence while he gazed at her uncomprehendingly. "I just don't feel up to it," she finished miserably.

"But you know all this silly business is in your head. It would do you nothing but good to walk two hundred and fifty miles – blow your cobwebs away."

In Ann's handbag lay a letter from a London hospital asking her to come into their neurology department for a week of tests on Monday, the fifth of August. "I'll probably go up to London and stay with Mum on Monday week," she said dully. "I'd only hold you up the way I feel at the moment, and everyone says the Pennine Way is much more of a challenge if you do it solo."

Long ago Matt had learnt to hide fear behind a mask of anger. "Your trouble is you've let yourself get flabby, that's why you're feeling so weak these days." He was snarling like Boris, the next-door dog.

"Matt . . . please, let's have supper and then look at the maps."

"We've always done things together," barked Matt. "You've changed completely recently."

"I know," said Ann, trying to keep the anguish out of her voice. "But I can't help it, so couldn't you love me anyway?"

"You're impossible. I'm going round to the Prince Albert. I don't want any supper after all."

"I'll come, too."

"No. If you're so fond of your own company, then give me space to enjoy mine."

By seven thirty Nigel was still waiting, licking the silver paper of the ice-cream Rebecca had given him.

"Wish you'd come on in for your tea, love," said his elderly mother from the doorway behind him. As she spoke the paper dropped from his hands and his whole body stiffened with excitement. Round the corner came Emmie; his vigil was over. He knew she would not speak, she never did, but sometimes she smiled. Since Good Friday, Emmie had become the centre of Nigel's world. His mind may have been that of a child, but he had a soul and with it he loved Emmie – devotedly.

The pressure in the studio had been enormous recently and the day had resembled a nightmare, but as she left Bakers Hill behind her the tension began to recede a little. How she loved this funny little Terrace, it gave her fresh delight every day of her life. Each tiny front garden seemed to reflect its owner's character. At Number Four an extravagant profusion of colour frothed out of tubs and cascaded from the window-boxes. 'All eager and impulsive, like Kim,' thought Emmie affectionately. Claire had transformed her low stone wall into a herb garden. Out of small pockets of soil sprouted parsley, clumps of chives and pink-leaved thyme. Alison's garden was stark in comparison. Well-swept concrete encasing a few sensible shrubs that never dropped their leaves.

It was Hazel's 'estate', however, which always seemed to Emmie to be the most revealing. French marigolds and red alyssum stood in straight rows like rigid soldiers on parade. Emmie winced. 'She can't make the natural world do as it's told like that,' she thought.

It was good to have neighbours to observe from a distance, so long as they never encroached on her personal space. Kim was the only person with whom she had any kind of relationship. They often seemed to bump into each other in the park. 'I don't really like bustling people like that,' thought Emmie, 'but there's something about her that always makes me feel safe.'

As she pushed open her garden gate, she sighed – this was home. Colour was everywhere, and Babs's sweetpeas surged their way up the trellis on the south wall. The French windows that had once been obscured by brambles stood open and Rosie waved happily from her chair. The old lady did not ask trying questions about the day or make irritating comments on how tired Emmie looked – just a smile and a wave of acknowledgment.

The smell of fresh paint greeted her as she walked up the stairs to her domain. New carpets, curtains and matching wallpaper, not to mention the beautiful fitted kitchen.

"You mustn't spend all this money on me," Emmie had admonished Miss Rosedale.

"It all came from the insurance, after the burglary, dear," Rosie had replied. When Emmie had continued to look doubtful she had hurriedly added, "If you ever had to leave, I would never find anyone else willing to put up with all that shabbiness. Then those horrid doctors would force me into a home. I am indebted to you for choosing and planning it all – I could never have managed without you."

Emmie smiled to herself. It was rare to find someone who did you a massive favour and then pretended you were actually doing one for them!

'I wish I could think of some way of saying "thank

119

you," ' she thought as she put the kettle on. 'Without getting involved, of course,' she added quickly.

It was past eight o'clock and David with his sleeves rolled up was still working his way through the kitchen midden while Kim fed the baby in her rocking-chair.

"Roll on next week," said Kim with a yawn. "I can't wait to flop out on all those golden Cornish sands. Hope this weather holds. I saw Sharon's parents trying to pack their car and they've only got one child. How on earth are we going to manage with four?"

"I was wondering . . ." began David slowly, "about Jasmine." Kim looked up sharply.

"What about Jasmine? Surely you're not suggesting we take her as well?"

"I hate leaving her behind."

"But she operates like a cuckoo in the nest; she simply won't share you with the others," protested Kim.

"She'll settle down when she knows she can trust us," said David, and hurriedly turned back to the sink as Jasmine appeared in the doorway – looking like a pale ghost.

"Mummy's home," she said tensely.

Kim looked at her small, white face and wondered why she always seemed to shrink when Claire arrived. David was always so maddeningly right! They couldn't condemn Jasmine to two stuffy weeks cooped up in the salon. She put the baby down on the hearth-rug and hugged Jasmine. Her body felt so stiff and fragile it ought to have been labelled 'breakable'.

"See you in the morning, love," she whispered into the wispy brown hair, "God bless you tonight."

"He can't," said Jasmine flatly. "He doesn't live in our house."

"Why do you suppose she thinks that?" said Kim, when Jasmine had trailed away in Claire's wake.

David said nothing.

"All right, you old softie, we'll squeeze her in somehow. I must be mad," she added ruefully. "I need

120

a holiday away from my *own* children, let alone other people's."

"You know you always start missing them horribly even after you've only been away for an hour."

"Yes, I know I do, and I expect if we left Jasmine behind I'd worry about her all the time, too. What a frustrating thing motherhood is," she said, and laughed. "It's an absolutely ghastly job, but you're stuck with it for life because you have the misfortune to love your kids! We're saddled with Jasmine now for exactly the same reason," she added softly as she remembered that brittle little body in her arms. "You'd better pop over and see Claire about it this evening."

David was frowning as he slowly dried his hands. How could he ever explain to Kim that the thought of 'popping over' to see Claire disturbed him profoundly.

Claire had also sensed the holiday spirit in the Terrace and it irritated her. During the day, she must have dispatched at least twenty twittering clients to exotic sun-drenched beaches only to ruin the hairstyles she had worked so hard to create. How long was it since *she'd* had a holiday she wondered as she climbed out of the bath. She was tired of being hard-up and overworked. 'I'm also tired of being celibate,' she admitted as she wrapped herself in her cotton dressing-gown. It would be nice to be wined and dined and then loved passionately – just for one night.

She looked at herself in the mirror as she brushed out her hair and let it cascade down her slim shoulders. Surely she was still beautiful, all she needed was a man to tell her so. Roger only ever noticed her soul.

She was thinking of David when she put off Jasmine's bedside light at about nine thirty and went downstairs. Every time she called at the Pattersons' house to collect Jasmine she was aware of him. He never spoke, but he had a courteous way of standing up and smiling when she came in, making her feel like a lady. The image of his perfectly structured face often wafted about in her mind. Claire loved physical perfection.

121

When the doorbell rang and she saw him standing on her step, she smiled. 'I always knew he'd come one day,' she said to herself.

"I'm just brewing a pot of camomile tea," she said. "Come in and have a cup. It's so soothing after a long day." David followed her silently and then sat watching her glide about the kitchen − graceful as a cat. The room was lit only by sweet-smelling candles and the bowl of roses and lavender on the table completed the old-fashioned bouquet. 'Funny how much younger people look by candle-light,' he thought absently. He had only just discovered something that Claire had known for years.

"I hope you haven't come over to tell me you're fed up with Jasmine," she said as she poured out the tea.

"We're going away next week," said David, "renting a caravan for a fortnight."

"Oh, how awkward," exclaimed Claire. It was her policy to make her employees feel guilty about taking their annual leave. 'And that's all he is,' she thought as she looked at him in the winking flame-light, 'just my employee − I could make him do anything I want − take him away from that funny little wife, spoil his peace of mind when he kneels in his church.' A whisper of doubt echoed in her mind, 'But I'm forty-five now,and he can't be much more than thirty.'

"We wondered if you would like us to take Jasmine with us," said David, sipping the revolting tea with a valiant impersonation of pleasure. Two weeks of freedom shimmered before Claire like a heat haze. She could see Roger every evening.

"Well, that would be kind," she said. "I can never take time off, you see, being the boss. But why? What makes you offer me this?" she added with quick suspicion. David hesitated. He could not possibly tell her the reason so he simply smiled, just as he always did in difficult situations.

"Well, you're welcome to her," said Claire with a

shrug. "She's always pestering me for a holiday. You look as if you could do with one yourself," she added and standing up she came gracefully behind the Windsor armchair where he sat. "I sense that you have pain in your neck and shoulders," she continued softly. "I'm doing a course on alternative medicine – will you let me see if I can feel what's causing you the trouble? You look so tired."

Her cool sweet-smelling hands began to move over his neck and he sat very still. Yes, he was tired. The fatigue of a whole school year weighed him down. After all, she was just a lonely woman, crying out for a bit of neighbourly friendship, and whatever she was doing to him, it was rather nice.

'He's mine now,' thought Claire, and smiled like a satisfied Mona Lisa.

'Why did she ever frighten me so much?' wondered David dreamily as the music and the scent of the candles merged with the pleasant sensation of Claire's hands. Then, quite suddenly, he knew.

As he stood up, he took hold of her slender wrists and forced her hands away from his body. Anticipating ecstasy, Claire smiled up into his face – but she saw only revulsion in his eyes.

"I should go home to my wife now," he said, struggling to maintain his habitual good manners, and he left her standing in the middle of her kitchen.

"Ten years ago I would have had him crawling for me by now," she spat as the front door closed behind him. But as the anger died away she knew it was not her fading looks which had put David out of her reach. "He really wanted me just then," she whispered, as she snuffed out the candles, "but there's some kind of power which controls that man, and I don't understand what it is."

SUNDAY AUGUST 4TH

2.15pm

Laburnum Terrace resembled a ghost town as it lay quivering in the afternoon heat.

"Bliss," said Emmie, peeling off her gardening gloves and flopping down on the lawn beside Rosie's deckchair. "I wish they'd all stay away on holiday permanently, it's so lovely and peaceful without them."

"The botanical name 'Laburnum' means deserted," said Rosie, "so our Terrace is aptly named today."

" 'Deserted Terrace,' " murmured Emmie. "I don't suppose we should like it to stay like this for ever."

Rosie looked down at her anxiously, in her opinion the girl was looking peaky.

"Are you not planning a little break yourself, dear?" she asked gently. Emmie sighed and looked up into the limitless blue sky where a silver Boeing 747 climbed steeply after taking off from Gatwick Airport. She wondered about its exotic destination.

"We're frantic at the studio," she replied regretfully. "The work would pile up and drown me if I left it now."

Rosie said, "How well the sweetpeas are doing," but she thought, 'This child will have a breakdown if she goes on pushing herself like this.'

The tide was in at Eastbourne. Gordon hated the mounds of grey pebbles. They hurt his feet even through the soles of his sandals. Alison and Aunt Madge seemed to have settled down in their deckchairs at last. They were always

124

convinced that another spot would suit them better than the one where Gordon had just deposited their flock of baskets and carrier bags.

He glanced cautiously at Alison, who was sitting bolt upright wearing her hat. She did not approve of going on the beach on a Sunday, but it was really too hot to do anything else. Obviously the hat was to ease her conscience. He sank gingerly into his own hired chair. He could never forget the agony he had experienced one year when the wretched thing had collapsed, plummeting his skinny posterior on to those cursed pebbles.

Carefully he knotted his hankie at its four corners and placed it over his bald patch.

"This is the life," he said jovially, as he yearned for the privacy of his allotment.

"Wherever *is* that child? She can't *still* be changing?" said Alison testily. Clancy was not docile like Amanda, she needed watching. All that fuss last night when they were unpacking. Stupid child leaving behind that perfectly sensible school bathing-suit, and how ridiculous of Gordon sneaking off with her to buy a new one.

"Hope she bought something sensible," she said to Aunt Madge, but Clancy had not. As she picked her way over the pebbles towards them, Gordon said, "Oh dear!" and pushed his sunglasses up to the top of his head.

"Well really!" said Alison. "This is all your fault, Gordon. Clancy, how could you? You know what I think about bikinis. You could at least have got a bigger size."

"But this was the cheapest, Auntie Alison," said Clancy innocently.

"I should think it was," boomed Auntie Madge. "There's so little material in it I wonder they had the gall to charge you at all."

It was a difficult afternoon. Alison was definitely not talking to Gordon and he was struggling with a crushing sense of loss. Clancy was no longer a little girl in need of his protection.

* * *

125

"Come on Jasmine," shouted Rebecca as she raced across the vast expanse of Cornish sand. "We're going to be late!"

Jasmine was completely mystified, but she always followed Rebecca wherever she went. After the picnic lunch the Pattersons had said they were all going to church, but they did not seem to be heading in the direction of a gloomy building like St Mark's with a steeple on the top. Ahead, in the dunes was a large group of children surrounding a man who stood on a mound of sand. Rebecca must – for once – be wrong, but when she glanced over her shoulder she could see the rest of the Pattersons following behind in various stages of undress.

"It was great last year at the beach church," puffed Rebecca. "They told us lots of stories about Jesus. You're going to love this!"

Jesus to Jasmine was an enigma. A baby in a stable at Christmas-time who seemed to grow with such remarkable speed that by Easter he was a man they killed on a cross. It seemed an oddly short life for someone who was so important in the Patterson household. They were always asking his help or thanking him for something. To Jasmine it seemed strange to be friends like that, with someone who was dead.

She had asked Rebecca about that when they were going to sleep in the caravan last night.

"*Everyone* knows Jesus didn't stay dead," she had replied. "He's just invisible now, that's all. People couldn't possibly kill him properly, because he's really God – dressed up as a man."

As Jasmine pattered over the sand she was still feeling puzzled, but one thing she knew for certain – when she was with the Pattersons she felt completely safe.

In Turkey it was decidedly hotter than Eastbourne – or Cornwall. Not the smallest breeze stirred the palm trees by the hotel swimming-pool. Hazel sipped her Martini as she lounged under the brightly coloured sun-shade. She was bored. There were no interesting people around this year and she really ought to be back at Welbridge General while opinions were still malleable. She needed to show them that old Squirry was not the only pathologist in the place. If only she could sleep at night.

"Let's go down to the beach," suggested Graham hopefully.

"All that expanse of white sand gives me headaches," replied Hazel with a yawn. "Holidays are so pointless now it's not sensible to get a suntan."

"What the hell's the matter with you?" blazed Graham. "This holiday's costing us an arm and a leg. You never used to be like this."

"Like what?" demanded Hazel, quite unconscious of the interested stares of the German family at the next table.

"All aches and pains," snapped Graham without lowering his voice.

"Kinder! Kommt mit!" said the Teutonic mother hen next-door as she ushered her children tactfully towards the swimming-pool while her blond giant of a husband hastily brought up the rear. Squeals of excitement sound the same in any language and Graham stood watching all four of them bobbing about in the sparkling water. "That's what's wrong with us," he said morosely. "We're not a family."

"And just how much more do you want out of me?" Hazel sat bolt upright, her lethargy forgotten. "I sweat and slave to bring in a large salary and I'm twisting myself in knots to land an even bigger one. I couldn't do that if my life was littered with squawking kids at this stage."

"But you're thirty-six," said Graham bitterly. "It's time you stopped pushing and thrusting and started enjoying life."

Hazel felt her fragile confidence beginning to slide. Apart from herself, Graham was the only person in the world who mattered to her.

"I can't stop until I get there," she said with a valiant attempt at a smile.

"What do you mean by 'getting there'?" demanded Graham. "I know you. As soon as you think you're 'there' you'll push the finishing tape further up the track. You'll never be satisfied."

"It's my life we're talking about." She was endeavouring to sound like Claire now. "I've got to be true to myself and I'm going to get that job whatever the cost."

"Well I hope you enjoy it," muttered Graham. "Because I might not be around much longer. I can't stand the pace."

Hazel's cool confidence had slithered again and she reached out for Graham's hand almost nervously. "Look, I'm sorry," she said. "If I don't get the job, we'll have six children and live happily ever after. I promise."

"And if you *do* get it?" said Graham wearily.

"We'll still live happily ever after, but that way we'll do it in luxury!"

FRIDAY AUGUST 9TH

2.15pm

'It always seems to be raining up here on the Pennines,' thought Matt as his boots pounded the black sheep-track across the moor. 'But I bet Ann's sweltering back in Bromley with her wretched mother.' Desolate hills surrounded him for miles in all directions, and it surprised him to find just how much he missed her.

'Wish I could give her a ring,' he thought as he hitched up his backpack morosely. 'But even if I managed to find a phone box, I still couldn't talk to her.' It had always irritated him that Ann's mother refused to have a telephone.

A fresh squall of rain stung his lean face and blurred the plastic cover which held his map. He'd be lost soon if he wasn't careful. 'I wonder why she wouldn't come.'

It was after he had slipped over in the peat mud that the thought came to him. 'Suppose she's not at her mother's? Suppose she's with someone else?' Was that why she'd been so touchy recently?

''Well, two can play at that game,'' he told a startled sheep which limped out of his path on two lame legs.

'Suppose he meets up with someone else?' Ann was thinking as she lay in her hospital bed. For five terrible days the relentless sun had glared at her through the enormous glass windows, while London roared continuously about its business. She would have given anything she possessed to be on the moors with the wind blowing through her hair, and Matt lecturing her about the science of physical fitness.

She had never been in hospital before, and for the first two days she felt she had coped rather well. The brain scans and X-rays were painless and the electrical tests were only mildly unpleasant. Then came the mylogram – that was devastating. Ann could not remember ever being so frightened. The headache which followed lasted two days and reduced her to lying motionless like a corpse. The other five girls in the ward all had boyfriends or husbands who visited them in the evenings while she lay there missing Matt until the hurt was worse than the headache.

Her only comfort was that he was not actually there. She suspected he would make a terrible hospital visitor.

She liked the young math teacher in the next bed, but after the girl was told she had a brain tumour Ann found herself unable to sleep during the long, dimly-lit nights. 'That's what's wrong with me too,' she thought as she pictured herself coming out of surgery speechless and paralysed. Before the tea arrived at six in the morning she had already convinced herself she had lost Matt for good.

The ward 'know all' was a woman in a wheel-chair who had been there so many times she could cap any tale of woe with a worse one of her own.

"Friday's the day, if you're in here for tests," she had told Ann. "The big chief comes with all his attendants and they have you in sister's office for the verdict." From then on the minutes dragged by as Ann waited.

Her legs would hardly take her into the sister's room when the moment finally arrived. The ominous sight of the consultant neurologist sitting behind the desk like a presiding god, flanked by six students in white, did nothing to allay her fears.

"Well now, Mrs Coley," he began breezily. "We've given you a pretty rough week I'm afraid. I hope you've forgiven us." The students laughed as if on cue, but

Ann did not join them. The man reminded her of a fat bullfrog.

"Look, do you have to tell my husband what you've discovered?" she asked abruptly.

"We'll be sending a full report to your doctor, he'll deal with everything like that for you. But there doesn't really seem too much to worry about."

"You mean I *haven't* got a brain tumour?"

"Absolutely no trace of a tumour at all. I think if you take life quietly for a bit, try and avoid any stress, you'll do fine."

Ann looked into his bland face so intently that the rest of the world seemed to disappear. 'So it *was* all in my mind after all,' she thought. 'If this was a film, violins would be playing in the background now!'

"Go along and talk it all through with your doctor," said one of the students as he hastily shooed her from the room.

'I won't bother,' thought Ann as she reeled along the corridor. 'I've had enough of doctors to last me a lifetime.' The nightmare was behind her, she could start to live again.

SUNDAY AUGUST 11TH

3pm

Perhaps the National Trust garden at Sissinghurst was not the best place for a wheel-chair whose driver needed L-plates. The paths were delightfully uneven and impeded by clumps of encroaching flowers. Yet, if Emmie's novice efforts jarred Rosie's arthritic spine the old lady gave no indication of it, she was far too busy enjoying herself.

The inspiration for this outing had come to Emmie in a flash, over her drawing-board. Bea had launched into one of her endless stories about the day she had borrowed a wheel-chair from the Red Cross to take her auntie to Brighton. Emmie, who was pasting up a brochure about a stately home and garden, put down her scalpel and said, "Why not?"

"Why not what?" said Bea crossly. "You haven't been listening to a word I've said."

"Yes I have and I'm off to ring the Red Cross."

However, the chair she had borrowed for the day appeared to have egg-shaped wheels, and by three o'clock Emmie was cursing Bea and her auntie. Surely there must have been an easier way of saying 'thank you' to Rosie, she thought as she mopped her forehead.

"Sorry about the irritating squeak," she panted.

"What squeak, dear?" replied Rosie vaguely as she gasped with delight at yet another vista. "Vita Sackville-West must have been a genius to create all this. I visited her here once you know. She used to sit up there in that

132

Elizabethan tower, right in the middle of her garden, writing books."

"Lucky her," said Emmie.

Every corner they turned seemed to plunge Rosie into fresh exclamations of delight until they reached the White Garden. There were no more words to communicate her joy then, so they sat in the arbour in silence for a whole hour.

Over by the tower Edward was wondering why he had let himself be bullied into boredom like this. Mother had said Jo-Ellen should see a real English garden before she went back to the States, but Jo-Ellen did not look as if she was enjoying it much either. However, she had the North American's inbred compulsion to 'do' every available place of interest and she had come complete with the standard equipment − a camera, guide-book, plastic mac and trainers.

"Cute little place," she drawled as she tipped back her green plastic sun-visor and looked up at Vita's tower. "But fancy the family all living in separate little houses all round the garden. Not very together were they?"

"Good British sense," yawned Edward. "Like public schools and the London club."

"Oh you and your British sense of humour," purred Jo-Ellen playfully. Was it only six weeks since they had met, he wondered? Mother wanted him to marry Jo-Ellen and he probably would. After all, her father was chairman of Health Care USA − their parent company. Edward's career would rocket to the stars before he came home from his honeymoon. She wasn't bad-looking either in a chunky kind of way − what else could a man want? Emmie perhaps? He followed Jo-Ellen's cart-horse legs up the spiral staircase in the tower and tried not to remember the delicate beauty of Emmie's fragile body.

"This is the room where she used to write," breathed Jo-Ellen reverently. She had never even heard of Vita Sackville-West until fifteen minutes ago. Painstakingly she went through the relevant pages from the guide-

133

book, while a crowd of exasperated tourists thickened on the stairs behind them. Jo-Ellen never noticed the frustrations of others; her father had always paid people to wait for her.

Suddenly Edward discovered that he was angry. So angry he had to grip the rails which kept the public out of Vita's lair. If ever he saw Emmie again he would make her sorry for landing him with Jo-Ellen for the rest of his life. No one had ever left him before − he was the one who did the leaving, when it suited him.

"I think we should go now," he said shakily. "Mother said you'd love something called the White Garden."

It was cool in the arbour. For some strange reason Emmie found herself thinking of Edward and she smiled grimly when she realised how much he would hate being in a paradise like this.

Beside her, Rosie's sharp black eyes took in every detail of the beauty around her. 'She's loving all this,' thought Emmie and realised to her surprise that for the first time in her life, she was actually enjoying living with another human being. 'Everyone else in my world constantly makes demands so I back off fast. Rosie simply enjoys whatever I'm prepared to give − even when that's nothing at all.' She closed her eyes sleepily and added, 'Perhaps that's because she doesn't depend on me for her happiness.'

Edward and Jo-Ellen 'did' the White Garden so quickly they were round it before Emmie opened her eyes again. Rosie noticed them, however, and her lips twitched slightly in amusement as she thought, 'What a pompous young man.'

In the National Trust gift-shop Emmie and Rosie bought a tea-cloth to commemorate the day, and several plants from the nursery next-door.

"Now, dear, I want to give you a little treat," said Rosie, waving towards the oast-house which had been converted into a tea-room. "I'm just beginning to feel a little dry."

They sat over their scones and jam in the comfortable silence which characterised their relationship. After her second cup of tea Emmie said: "If we could get a nice modern wheel-chair with *round* wheels, we could explore more of these famous gardens."

"My dear, I could not possibly put you to the trouble!" exclaimed Rosie. Emmie buttered her scone slowly. This was just the kind of thing she had told that social worker she was not prepared to do. Yet she found herself saying, "But you know so much about flowers, I really enjoyed today."

"Surely you have a family you like to visit at weekends?"

"No, there's no one. Well . . . my mother is still alive, but . . ." Emmie looked across the tea-table and wondered if she dared tell Rosie that her mother was in a long-stay mental hospital? She had certainly never confessed that to Edward's mother.

"She went mad when I was four." There, the phantom which had haunted her all her life was out of its cupboard at last − Emmie waited tensely for the reaction, but Rosie simply said, "Tell me about her."

"She lost a baby boy and it broke her inner mechanism like a clockwork toy without a key. I do go to see her sometimes, but she never knows who I am. She sits in a National Health Service armchair gazing at the wall."

"How did your father manage?"

"He didn't. He was in the army, you see. Always moving. He left me with his aunt in Bromley. She was just settling into a comfortable retirement full of bridge and gentle rounds of golf when I arrived on her doorstep. She never even pretended to be pleased. You must think I'm riddled with self-pity, but actually I had just the kind of childhood I wanted. Auntie was good about buying me art materials; they kept me quiet while she played bridge. I was always perfectly happy when I was alone painting."

"Then why did you not become a straight artist?" A

135

shadow crossed Emmie's face. Rosie was too perceptive. She saw herself back in the careers room at school, facing Auntie furiously across the gap between their moulded plastic chairs, saying furiously, "But I don't want to be a graphic designer."

"But your aunt has a point," the careers teacher had said. "Graphic design is much more secure than illustrating."

"I couldn't sponge on Auntie while I got established," the grown-up Emmie explained to Rosie. "Do have another cup of tea." She never felt safe when conversations became personal. She picked up the teapot, it was round and fat with a spout which seemed to smile. It reminded her of another teapot stacked far back on a dusty shelf in her memory. She frowned as she tried to push the past away, but the beauty of the garden was making her vulnerable.

It was her first term at school. She could see herself sucking the end of her blonde plait as she sat at the low table. As usual she was alone, divorced from the tight friendship groups that were already forming in the infant classroom. In front of every child was a lump of grey squelchy clay and Miss Thundersley was saying:

"Now, children, I want you to make a present for someone who loves you very much."

"Mine's going to be for my mum . . . my nan . . . my granddad . . ." the excited response echoed round the classroom, leaving Emmie feeling hollow. 'Who loves me very much? Mummy? Daddy? no, they both went away. Auntie? No, she is always cross.'

As the other children made lopsided ash-trays and deformed dogs, Emmie had poured her five-year-old soul into the creation of a teapot. Fat and round, with a spout which positively smiled.

The following week she had painted it in delicate eggshell blue and covered it with clusters of tiny yellow flowers.

"It looks like real china now, doesn't it?" she said with

136

deep satisfaction when the final, but messy, varnishing stage was over. Miss Thundersley had sat down suddenly beside her on the small infant-sized chair and said quietly,

"This is the finest thing I have ever seen in a reception class. Emily, you have made 'A thing of beauty which is a joy for ever.' "

"Eat your tea," Auntie had snapped the following day. "Your father's coming home – and about time too." Emmie had stopped eating her tea at once, simply because her tummy had closed its 'mouth' tightly. She hoped her daddy would love her like next-door Kate's daddy loved her. He used to throw her up in the air when he came back from London at night and kiss her hundreds of times. At school, when you wanted someone to like you, you gave them something – sweets perhaps, or a toy smuggled from home. What could she give Daddy? Of course, the little blue teapot.

She had been standing in the draughty hallway for ages clutching it tightly when his heavy footsteps approached the door. He had not kissed her or thrown her up to the ceiling, in fact he did not even seem to see her standing there in the dismal shadows cast by Auntie's forty-watt bulb.

"How's she been behaving?" was all he said.

"All right – sometimes," was Auntie's ominous reply.

"Give your father a kiss, child." Emmie held out the teapot instead.

"What on earth's this?" he had said absently as he struggled out of his stiff khaki greatcoat.

"I made it at school."

"Typical!" said Auntie. "They don't seem to do anything but play these days! How's she ever going to get a decent job? I can't go on supporting her for ever you know."

When Emmie had come downstairs in the morning, her father had gone. The little teapot had been left behind on the sideboard. Rejected. Slowly and deliberately she dropped it on to the red quarry tiles of the dining-room floor and then ground it to eggshell blue powder with the heel of her outdoor shoe. Auntie had slapped her legs until they hurt like nettle-stings. 'It doesn't matter if nobody loves me,' she had thought as she swept up the remains of her 'thing of beauty'. 'I don't need people. I'll make beautiful things all my life – just for me.'

"Are you feeling all right, dear?" asked Rosie anxiously, and Emmie forced herself to make conversation.

"I want to pick your brains, Rosie," she said. "Tell me, how have you managed to live a single life with such success? What's your secret?"

Rosie surveyed Emmie speculatively. She was wondering if the girl wanted a serious answer or just a flippant retort. She decided after a further sip of china tea that she probably wanted both.

"First, buy a dog," she said decisively. "A very big one." Emmie burst into a peal of laughter that caused a ripple of smiles all over the oast-house.

"Why?" she demanded.

"For the sake of safety, when you go out into the park or woods on your own."

"Well, dogs are out," said Emmie firmly. "Just think what a puppy would do to our new carpets. What's next?"

"Underwear." Rosie lowered her voice discreetly. "Always use the prettiest and most luxurious you can afford."

"Why?" (Rosie really was the most enjoyable person she had ever encountered.)

"Because it will make you *feel* feminine and attractive, and that's very important," whispered Rosie with a modest blush. "I've already told you that you must have a home of your own. So we move to what I have found to be the most important thing of all. Make God your companion and friend."

The laughter drained slowly from Emmie's face and she leaned across the table stiff with interest.

"You've never talked to me about God before."

"You never asked me." Emmie was silent for some time and then she shrugged.

"That one's out, too — for me anyway. I don't think God would want to be my friend. I'm too selfish."

"Are you?"

"Well, to be honest, I don't feel exactly proud of the way I treated Edward. I used him — to prove to myself that I wasn't a freak who can't get close to people. When I discovered I actually am a freak — I dropped him. The whole thing still bothers me a lot and makes me feel terrible. So you see why God wouldn't approve of me."

"I have always found he is amazingly forgiving when we go to him and ask," said Rosie gently.

'But if I did go to him, would he really want me?' thought Emmie as she remembered standing in Auntie's dark hall, hoping fervently that 'Daddy' would love her. If her own father had rejected her overture of love, would God treat her any differently? She doubted it.

"Surely, using God like a companion would simply be escaping the responsibilities of a human relationship?" It sounded silly as she said it, but she felt she must fill the silence with something.

"The spiritual dimension of life is not a second best or a substitute for the real thing." Rosie was choosing her words with meticulous care. "It is far more satisfying than the physical world and infinitely more lasting. Yet some people live their whole lives through and never discover that it exists."

"I've always been looking for something — real — like that, something beyond . . ." said Emmie slowly. "Edward used to call it my spiritual quest." As she mentioned Edward's name she froze like a video halted by the pause-button. Rosie, following her startled gaze, saw the 'pompous young man' she had seen in the White Garden.

"Edward," whispered Emmie.

"Emmie!" exclaimed Edward.

"D'you think they serve drinkable coffee in a place like this?" drawled Jo-Ellen. "Or do we only get to have British tea round here?"

Edward gulped and remembered that Mother had brought him up to be meticulously polite on all occasions – particularly difficult ones. He cleared his throat and made the introductions.

"Glad to have you know me," gushed Jo-Ellen with forced enthusiasm. She positively loathed thin girls with small bones and delicate features.

"Oh good," said the genteel but commanding voice of the café manageress. "You all know each other, so you won't mind sharing a table." All four of them minded intensely, but they could do nothing but smile weakly.

While Jo-Ellen held forth exhaustively on the subject of Vita Sackville-West, Emmie took a cautious peep at Edward. 'Poor old thing. He looks thinner and he's being so sweet to Rosie.' Edward, struggling to maintain his polite veneer, was thinking, 'How magnificent she looks beside Jo-Ellen. I could throttle her for doing this to me.' Suddenly the desire to hurt became stronger than all Mother's precepts and he broke rudely into Jo-Ellen's monologue on British tea and American coffee.

"So you're still working on that spiritual quest then, Emmie?"

"Whatever do you mean?"

"Well, Miss Rosedale here has been telling me how much you do for her. Good works in order to redeem your soul I suppose." Emmie blushed.

"Miss Rosedale is my landlady." She sounded like an offended duchess. "She also happens to be my friend. We share a common interest in botany."

"And in acquiring expensive antiques, so they tell me at the Prince Albert," said Edward with heavy meaning.

Rosie could not understand why Emmie looked so embarrassed and she made matters worse by saying, "I have no family and very few friends left alive, so Miss Dawson's kindness to me has changed my life."

Jo-Ellen was as thick-skinned as she was thick-bodied, but even she sensed the thunder-storm which was reverberating round the tea-table. This skinny girl was obviously an ex-girlfriend.

"Absolutely thrilled to have met you both!" She jerked to her feet scattering pamphlets and guidebooks across the floor. "But we must be getting along now. Eddy's mom will be expecting us back home. Eddy, I'm just going to the bathroom." Rosie watched her disappear and then looked speculatively at Edward, who was standing morosely at the cashier's till.

"I think I will pop off myself for a few minutes," she whispered to Emmie. "But I shall be back for a final cup of that excellent Earl Grey."

She struggled out of her wheel-chair with the aid of two sticks and tottered away after Jo-Ellen. Emmie knew an offer of help would only offend her so she sat waiting for Edward. She knew he would come, just as Rosie had done.

"Found a clever way of getting rich without the bother of being married, have you?" he said morosely as he slumped down in his chair. "Swapped me for a rich old 'sugar mummy' who'll die soon and leave you the lot. Your trouble is you never think of anything but the best interests of Miss Emily Jane Dawson."

"How rich is Jo-Ellen may I ask?" said Emmie evenly.

"Fabulously. You did me a good turn there, I assure you. We're about to announce our engagement."

"Congratulations," said Emmie crisply, but Edward did not seem to hear; he was staring out of the window.

"Emmie," he said in a very different tone, "I need you. Can't we meet somewhere – we must talk." He swallowed hard and loosened his cravat.

"Edward, I can't," said Emmie firmly.

"Eddeeeee," drawled Jo-Ellen's reproachful voice from the door. Without a word he stormed off in the direction of the carpark, his shoulders squared like a charging bull. He was dangerous when he was thwarted.

8.45

The afternoon had been pleasantly warm, but by evening
the atmosphere was sultry and oppressive. The
conflicting emotions of the day had left Emmie seriously
shaken. Restlessly she prowled about her flat from one
graciously proportioned room to the next. There was
something about Rosie and her simple appreciation of
beauty that made Emmie feel tainted.

'Edward's right,' she thought. 'I did come here for what
I could get out of it for myself. I do use Rosie, just like I
used him. I'd better leave now before she begins to need
me, because as soon as I start feeling trapped I'll just walk
out and let her down. I always do that to people.' She
stopped and looked at her reflection in her oval mirror.

'You're trash, Emily Dawson!' she told herself. 'You've
always been a selfish cow! Poor old Edward, he obviously
still loves you, perhaps you should marry him after all.
Spend your life trying to make him happy instead of only
ever thinking of what *you* want.' As she flopped down on
her bed she added, 'Maybe you reach the end of a spiritual
quest only when you start living for someone else.'

9.20

Rosie was watching the end of the news in bed when she
heard Emmie bang out of the front door. 'She always goes
to the park when she's upset,' she thought anxiously.
'It's nearly dark, too. I do wish she had a dog.'

The coach from Bournemouth had deposited Nigel at
the end of the Terrace at seven thirty that evening. Mrs
Mills from the day centre had walked him down the road
to Number Three where his mother welcomed him like
the prodigal son. She had missed him profoundly during
his two-week holiday.

''He's brought you a present,'' said Mrs Mills, giving
Nigel an encouraging prod.

"Present," he repeated happily, and as Mrs Mills hurried back to her waiting charges he slowly undid the catches of his battered brown suitcase.

"*Two* sticks of rock candy," said his mother with exaggerated gratitude. "*Thank* you, dear." The beaming smile faded from Nigel's peeling red face and he shuffled his shoes miserably.

"Oh, I see, only one is for me," said Mrs Jardine, who could read his every gesture. "The other one was for somebody else."

"Somebody else." Nigel's happiness was restored as if by magic.

"I'll have a nibble after tea while we're watching the telly." But after tea Nigel did not want the television. He sat outside on the garden wall, smiling hopefully. There had been so many pretty things in the shop-windows of Bournemouth, but he had been sure Emmie would like the stick of pink rock candy more than anything else.

The streetlights were on before his patience was rewarded. Looking down the Terrace he saw Emmie emerge from her garden in the twilight and disappear through the park-gates. Nigel had never been out alone at night in his life, but a new adult power was driving him and he shambled after her eagerly.

'That's funny,' thought Sharon, who was busy unpacking her holiday souvenirs. She opened her bedroom window and leaned out dangerously far. 'Why would that Nigel be following Emmie Dawson into the park?'

It was difficult to see and Nigel's legs never went quite where he wanted them to go. Someone stepped out from the shadows by the park-gates and pushed past him rudely, but he kept on doggedly. People had been overtaking Nigel like that all his life – it never bothered him.

Emmie was walking quickly, her whole body felt taut and stiff and she knew the only way she would ever sleep was by expending this restless energy. The lake was a still sheet of glass, and among the shadowy beech trees on the hill an owl hooted plaintively. She first became aware of the quiet footsteps behind her when she was climbing the winding rhododendron walk and she cursed herself for being an idiot. She would have been safer if she'd stayed out in the open. She stopped and the quiet footsteps stopped too. She walked more quickly and so did they. She took the right fork. They followed. Her chest felt as if it would burst open and her hands were cold and clammy. Why ever hadn't she brought her pocket alarm? 'I ought to scream,' she thought, but she had never done so in her life and did not know how to begin. She stopped again, just to make sure she was not imagining it all, but this time the footsteps came on, light and fast like a tiger preparing to spring. 'Pray!' she told herself and found she was reaching out wordlessly to the God whom Rosie seemed to trust so completely.

"Hello Emmie."

"It was only you!" She swirled round furiously to confront Edward. "How dare you scare me half to death."

"You always loved this silly park. I thought you might find it romantic if I surprised you here." He was mocking her and his breath smelt of garlic and whisky.

"Edward, I've already told you . . ." He kissed her so harshly her lips were bruised against her teeth.

"I thought you were going to marry Jo-Ellen," she gasped furiously.

"Yes I am, but come on Emmie, you owe me one more night first − you cost me a fortune." His voice was as thick as treacle.

"That's all you ever wanted from me!" stormed Emmie, as she tried to push him away. "And just now I was feeling so sorry for you I forgot what you're really like."

"I'll make you sorry you said that!" he snarled as he backed her up against a pine tree with brutal force.

"Sorry you said that . . ." The disembodied voice came

144

eerily from the gloom behind them. Edward spun round, startled.

"Go away you idiot," he said when he recognised Nigel standing in the moonlight. "She's a friend of mine."

"She's a friend of mine," parroted Nigel, and turned obediently to go away. He always did as he was told.

Emmie tried to run after him, but Edward was too quick for her. He jerked her round and began to fumble with her blouse.

Emmie had always prided herself on her fingernails, long, sharp and purely decorative on most occasions. That night they came into their own as she dug them into Edward's fleshy cheeks with quite remarkable strength.

"Little wild cat! You're incapable of loving anyone," he spluttered and hit her violently across the face. She gasped and cried out indignantly. Nigel, shambling disconsolately down the path, suddenly halted in his tracks. An appeal in words would have meant nothing to him, but the sound of Emmie's startled cry told him that this man was hurting his special friend and galvanised him into action.

He could not even say her name, but at that moment he would willingly have died for her. Snarling like a vengeful lion he lunged at Edward brandishing the Bournemouth rock candy above his head. The unfortunate Mr Soames of Health Care International had no means of knowing that this murderous looking weapon was only made of pink sugar.

"You're mad," he gasped. "You're dangerous!" He bolted down the rhododendron walk, not slackening his pace until he reached his Porsche, parked discreetly in Albert Gardens.

Huddled on a pile of brittle brown leaves, Emmie was sobbing. Edward was filthy, but what he'd said about her was right. She was actually just as disabled as this boy who stood looking down at her.

Nigel knew that she was sad, but he also knew he had

145

something that would make her happy again. Squatting beside her he finally presented her with the gift that had absorbed his entire thinking for days. Emmie looked down at the sticky mess in her hand and felt too dazed to say more than "Thank you very much."

"Thank you very much," repeated Nigel, beaming with delight.

"Will you help me to get home?" she asked shakily.

"Help me get home."

There was something pure and wholesome about his gentle sympathy, which contrasted starkly with Edward's bestiality. The fear began to recede a little and as they staggered home together across the park the lights from Number Sixteen streamed out to welcome them. Emmie could see Rosie waiting anxiously for her at the French windows.

"I thought there'd been a murder," said the crestfallen Sharon from her vantage point by the park-gates. "A man came running by so fast he nearly knocked me over. I thought he was a policeman." Emmie ignored her.

"Sorry I worried you, Rosie," she said as she dragged herself up the garden path leaning heavily on Nigel's willing arm. When she saw the genuine love on the old face she knew she would never be able to leave her now, whatever people like Edward thought about her motives. "I think your God sent along one of his angels to look after me."

"Angel . . . look after me," repeated Nigel over and over again, as he ambled away down the Terrace.

The only thing that comforted Emmie, during that long sleepless night, was the thought of Edward trying to explain his shredded face to 'Mother' and Jo-Ellen.

WEDNESDAY AUGUST 21ST

11.30am

For once the studio was as silent as a crypt. Bea was not whistling and Pat, closeted in the darkroom, was obviously too upset even to grunt. Through the open office door Joyce's back was stiff as her fingers pecked the typewriter like a disapproving hen. It was hard to believe only twenty-four hours had elapsed since the boss had delivered his blow.

Emmie sat at her drawing-board trying to prevent her shaking fingers from being trimmed by the razor-sharp scalpel. Ever since that night in the park she had been struggling to live only on the outside, afraid to face her inner thoughts and feelings in case they erupted and immobilised her completely. Yesterday when the boss had called them all into his office, the molten mass of emotional lava had come dangerously near to the surface.

"You all know that Welbridge is now considered the UK capital for graphic design," he had begun grandly. He had just returned from a conference on the Isle of Wight, so really they all ought to have been prepared for something like this. "We want to be out there in front of the pack. Therefore . . ."

'Here it comes,' they had all thought (or anyway they told each other later that's what they had thought).

"We must modernise the way we work, computerise everything. The bank has offered a substantial loan and all the new equipment will arrive next week, complete with a technician who will train you all in its use."

147

A ghastly hush had descended on the room, broken finally by a despairing grunt from Pat.

"A page-maker would save such a lot of mess," said Joyce brightly. "No more pasting up and fiddling about."

"But we like 'fiddling' and making messes," said Bea defiantly.

"Then perhaps you'd better move to a more old-fashioned firm." The boss looked like a belligerent orang-utan. "Well, Emmie? What would be your reactions to a computer paint-box?"

Emmie had been forcing herself to have no reactions at all; she was too afraid of them. She had never really liked typography and had only joined the firm because the boss always said he wanted to expand the illustration side of the work. Now all she had to look forward to was scratching on a tablet in black and white and then pressing keys to put colour on a screen. No more loving a design into life through her paint-brush or pens.

All that had been yesterday and the idea was still just as unbearable now. She held her throbbing head as it dawned on her that for a long time she had been driving herself by will-power alone. Suddenly she could go no further.

"Haven't you got that scamp finished yet, Emmie?" The boss materialised behind her left elbow. "You don't appear to have done *anything* all day."

Emmie heard his voice receding into the background as the room began to sway and shiver around her. She was going to be sick, but her legs were too weak to carry her to the loo, she was falling . . . falling.

4pm

"Do you often faint like that, Miss Dawson?" asked Doctor Macdermott, swivelling gently from side to side in his surgery chair. He approved of Emmie because Rosie was his favourite patient. He knew that this wisp of a

148

girl had done more for the old lady than anything he could have prescribed.

"No, I never have before, but I've been feeling terrible recently. Awful headaches and I never seem to stop shaking."

"Can you think why that is?" asked the doctor blandly.

"Well, I suppose I've been overworking for a long time really, but it's got lots worse since a man attacked me in the park. I suppose fainting today was just delayed shock."

"He raped you?"

"No, but it made me feel dreadful . . . sort of dirty all the time," she added dissolving into ridiculous tears. "I keep having baths, but somehow I never feel clean. I can't work either, and my boss is getting . . . I just can't cope with anything or anyone."

Jim Macdermott handed a wad of tissue across his desk and said sympathetically, "It must be a bit of a strain living with an old lady."

"Oh no! That's worked out marvellously. But before I met her I broke off an engagement. I still don't know quite who I really am. I feel lost. Drifting."

"Have you been on holiday yet this summer?"

"No. We're too busy at work."

He stood up decisively.

"You are to take one month off and do nothing but eat, sleep and exactly what you enjoy doing most."

"Oh, but I couldn't. My boss . . . the new computers . . ."

"You will do as I say, Miss Dawson. I'll give you a certificate and a prescription, then you're going home to bed."

SATURDAY AUGUST 24TH

12 noon

Emmie was awake, but she would not admit it. If she woke
she would have to get up and start living again. She could
not face that. She must have been lying here for days now.
The doctor had said these pills would make her sleep and
he was dead right. Wild dreams had attacked her like flocks
of aggressive ravens – she had constantly been running
away from Edward, Great Aunt Jane or the boss. "I don't
want anybody in my world!" She could remember
screaming that so loudly once she had woken herself up.
   Dimly she could remember Rosie's home-help putting
glasses of cool fruit juice or warm milk on the table beside
her bed, but the days were mostly a blur.
   Somewhere behind the curtains a fly was buzzing
against the glass. The irritating sound was pulling her back
into the world again, reminding her that the room was
unbearably hot. Unwillingly she slid out of bed and
pushed open the sash-cord window. It was every bit as hot
and airless outside in the brown-scorched park.
   'What am I going to do with myself for a whole month,'
she thought wearily. Her legs felt like a mixture of cotton-
wool and jelly, and the face that gazed back at her from the
mirror looked ghostly. 'If I could only get out into the
woods, but . . .' Since that experience in the rhododendron walk she had not dared to go for a walk on her
own. Edward had robbed her of the solitary places where
her soul might have mended.
   "I'm going mad like my mother," she told the fly that
still basked lazily on the hot glass. "She must have been

150

about my age when it happened to her." She huddled down in her armchair and pulled her dressing-gown round her for protection.

"Are you awake yet?" It was Kim's voice outside her bedroom door. "Do you mind if I pop in?"

'Yes I do mind,' thought Emmie defensively, but the door had opened before she could say so.

"Oh good, you're up," Kim exclaimed, adding doubtfully, "but you still look rough!" She was carrying a tray laden with little foil-wrapped containers. "Rosie and I were getting a bit worried about you. It must be four days since you ate anything, so I've brought you some lunch and one or two bits and pieces for your fridge."

Emmie did not know what to say, no one had ever done anything like this for her before in her life.

"It's terribly kind of you," she said doubtfully, "but why should you bother?"

"Oh, you'd do the same for me," said Kim shyly. Emmie was sure such an idea would never occur to her.

"I didn't realise you knew Rosie," she said as Kim put the tray down beside her chair.

"She's always sitting out in the garden now you've made it nice again for her. We chat every time I go by with the kids. She's lovely, isn't she?"

"Look, I'm not sure if I'm going to manage to eat anything," said Emmie nervously as Kim began unwrapping the meal.

"You'll probably feel more like it later on then. I'll leave it in your kitchen." To Emmie's relief she did not look at all offended. "I must go now, I've abandoned the pram in the garden."

She was running downstairs before Emmie could thank her.

4.15pm

The day seemed like a year and her room like a prison. At

151

last she put on some clothes and went down to the garden, but as she opened the front door she saw Rosie sitting on the seat in the shade of the apple tree. She wanted to slide back nervously again – into solitude, but the old lady had seen her and waved.

As Emmie walked over towards her she could not help thinking Rosie looked like an illustration from a Victorian children's book, sitting with her white hair piled up on top of her head. 'She's so pretty, I really must paint her sometime,' she thought absently.

"I've been so vexed with myself, dear, not being able to climb the stairs to see how you are," said Rosie as Emmie sat down next to her.

"I'm much better since I ate that feast Kim brought along for me," replied Emmie. "She thought of so many tempting little things, I've got enough to keep me going for a week." They reverted to their usual silence and watched the life of the Terrace go by their front gate. Kim, on her way from the park, waved as she passed with the children. "I just can't understand her or David either," said Emmie thoughtfully. "Have *you* any idea what makes those two so . . . so different?"

"I imagine it must be their faith," replied Rosie simply. Emmie looked at her incredulously.

"You mean a couple of nice, sane people like them, actually go to an ugly old church like the one at the bottom of the road?"

"I used to go there too when I could walk that far." Rosie pretended to be offended.

"Well, I never!" said Emmie.

"Kim was telling me they have such a nice new vicar there now," added Rosie wistfully. "And now I am going indoors to leave you in peace."

As Emmie watched her shuffle painfully away, she told herself she would definitely paint that interesting old face one day.

SUNDAY AUGUST 25TH

9.45am

'I really *am* going mad,' Emmie told herself as she walked down Laburnum Terrace towards the clanging bells of St Mark's. 'How Bea would laugh if she could see me now.'

She had lain awake most of the previous night – thinking. Sometime about four it began to dawn on her that the three people she liked most, Rosie, Kim and David, each possessed the elusive 'thing' she herself had always wanted. 'Perhaps I might find the answer if I went to church myself,' she thought, and instantly fell asleep.

Now here she was on her way and already she wished she had stayed in bed. The hideous building loomed in front of her, reminding her of Aunt Jane's words of long ago: "A church is God's house." Emmie paused, nervously. She still had that stupid 'unclean' feeling and she was not at all sure she was ready to get too close to God just yet. Surely she couldn't barge in there, in an emotional mess like this. At Sissinghurst, Rosie had said He would help her, but was she right?

"Please," she whispered as she was passing the shop on the corner, "if you are real show me in some definite way that you don't reject me – like my father did."

'There!' she thought in surprise, 'I actually prayed!'

The vicarage stood next to the church opposite the end of the Terrace. 'What a monstrosity,' thought Emmie as she crossed Bakers Hill and walked past the laurel hedge which enclosed its untidy garden. Two little girls were

153

playing on the lawn with a hose and sprinkler and Emmie could hear their squeals and giggles above the religious tolling of the bell. They sounded so happy that she smiled in spite of her apprehension.

"Disgraceful!" said Alison's voice behind her. "On a Sunday morning, too, and they're only wearing underwear."

"We are having a heat wave," protested Gordon.

"Vicarage children should set an example. In my day children sat still right through the service – morning and evening – in their best clothes too. That grandmother of theirs has no control over them whatsoever." With a snort of disgust Alison stalked up the steps into church.

'If that's what God does to people,' thought Emmie, 'I don't think I'll get involved,' and she hastily turned round.

"Hello, are you coming to hear our new vicar?" Kim was running across the road towards her, clutching a small girl in either hand. "Johnnie's been driving me nutty this morning, so David said he'd stay home with the boys and give me a break." Emmie found herself swept along as firmly as Amy and Rebecca and before she could escape, she was handed a bulletin and settled in a pew.

"You'll like the vicar," hissed Kim. "The first time I talked to him he irritated me madly, but I'm getting rather fond of him now because he's so down to earth."

The organ blared its way through the first hymn, echoing round the Gothic arches and battering Emmie's aching head. She wondered why God should need to be worshipped by such an unpleasant noise? 'I could sidle out during a prayer – tell Kim I've got a headache. God's not here, this is just an out-of-date building.' However, she felt too weak to move, and anyway the vicar was standing up at the front now in his crazy white dressing-gown ready to open the proceedings. 'He must be the ugliest man I ever saw,' thought Emmie. Her love of symmetry was outraged by his whole appearance. His face and body looked as if they had been thrown together by an art student devoid of talent. Nothing was right except his voice which was strangely beautiful. Emmie relaxed slightly against the back of her pew.

It was during the prayers that it happened. Heads were bowed devoutly all over the church, but Emmie's eyes were open. She was watching the way the coloured sunlight filtered through the stained-glass windows and lit up the face of this odd-looking priest. It surprised her that he did not seem to find it necessary to talk to God in a strange affected voice; he spoke as if he was addressing a friend. Suddenly a slight movement caught her attention. The smaller of the children from the vicarage garden was standing in the West door. She was a tiny thing, no more than two and she had obviously fallen over because her wet knees were streaked with blood and dirt and her face was awash with tears. Somehow in her haste to elude her grandmother she had parted company with her underwear.

Her little bare feet made no sound as they ran up the aisle holding out her arms for comfort. She was naked, hurt and dirty, but what could her father possibly do about it with a service to conduct?

Suddenly Emmie knew exactly how she must feel, as she saw herself as a child again, desperately wanting her father's love and attention as she held out her teapot to him in Aunt Jane's hall. Would this child also be pushed away? It mattered so vitally to Emmie that she sat watching, stiff with tension.

The voice of the vicar never changed. The prayer continued to flow, but a smile of peculiar sweetness lit up his rugged face, giving the irregular features a beautiful new form. Emmie found herself wondering why she had ever thought he was ugly. Silently he held out his arms and sliding back into his pew he made a lap for her. Round the naked body swirled the sleeves of his flowing surplice covering her with protection and security.

Never before in the history of St Mark's had a vicar led

worship and preached a full-length sermon with a small child fast asleep in his arms. Alison was outraged, but Emmie knew she would never be the same person again. Like that child, she had come into church feeling distressed – looking for comfort and protection. Through the way the vicar had responded to his daughter, God had given her the sign for which she had asked. She knew she was accepted and loved.

The church was empty, but she was still kneeling alone in her pew. She had cried her mascara into such a mess she could not face the departing congregation.

A rustling startled her and she looked up. For a moment she actually thought she was being confronted by an angel. The sunlight still blazed through the coloured windows of the side aisle and all she could see was a silhouette in flowing white. But an extremely large and very human body sat down in the pew beside her. It was Richard Reynolds, and Emmie stiffened and backed away.

'Any moment now he'll start desiccating my soul, marching me to confession,' she thought. 'I'd better make a run for it.' But the man beside her said nothing, he just sat there quietly as if she was the only person in the world. She felt so comforted she wanted the moment never to end.

"Kim told me you haven't been well," he said gently at last. "Will you let me help you home?"

'No questions, no sermons,' thought Emmie, 'just acceptance.'

"Thank you," she said stiffly. "I do feel a bit shaky."
He pulled off his surplice and chucked it down on the pew with what Alison would have said was a shocking lack of respect. Then he almost carried Emmie home up Laburnum Terrace.

"Just look at that girl! She's after him already," said Alison acidly from the front window of Number Thirteen.

Once again Rosie was waiting anxiously for Emmie at her window, but as usual she demanded no explanations.

156

"I have some warm milk ready in a thermos," she said. "Come and have it in the drawing-room, dear. And you, young man, would you be so kind as to stay a minute or two, I may need your help getting her up the stairs. She is far from well, you know."

Emmie sank obediently into a buttoned armchair and managed *not* to mention how much she detested hot milk.

"It's Miss Rosedale, isn't it?" said Richard. "I feel bad that I haven't visited you yet. They tell me you used to be a pillar of St Mark's."

"Never a pillar — just a footstool," she said, and was rewarded by his delightful smile.

"And you must be the new vicar. I have been praying for you since you arrived. They tell me that you are on your own with a young family."

Emmie, surveying him over the rim of her cup, noticed that the smile faded.

"Yes," he replied, "two girls, eight and two. Quite a handful, but my mother is staying with us for a while." Lines of strain conveyed the impression that this was not a happy situation and Emmie looked away.

"What a magnificent piano!" He seemed to want the subject changed as much as she did. "One doesn't often see a concert grand in a private house these days."

"It was my father's pride and joy," Rosie's face was alight with pleasure. "Every morning before breakfast he used to come down here for what he called his dawn chorus. It was one of my earliest memories."

"Would you . . . allow me to try it?"

"Most certainly. I have it tuned from time to time for my father's sake."

Emmie had always loved Chopin, but she had to admit she had never heard his preludes played with such feeling.

"You missed your way in life," she said dreamily when the plaintive music died away at last. Rosie was wiping nostalgic tears with an ancient lace handkerchief.

"I'm a bit rusty I'm afraid," said Richard apologetically.

157

"You see there isn't a bearable piano in St Mark's and not even an unbearable one in the vicarage."

"You shall come here as often as you like," said Rosie. "Nothing would give me more pleasure." His sad eyes lit up instantly.

"I could pop along here when the girls are in bed sometimes," he said. "Was your father a musician, Miss Rosedale?"

"He wanted to be, but his father put him into the family building business. It was my grandfather who built this Terrace you know, the vicarage, too, and most of Bakers Hill. He chose the prime site overlooking the park for his own house – Number Fifteen, over the road there. Then he built this one for his son – my parents moved in here when they were married, more than a hundred years ago."

"I've often wondered why two such magnificent houses should be at the end of such an ordinary little Terrace," admitted Richard.

"Well, I am afraid my grandfather felt more of a person of consequence when he and his family lived in much bigger houses than their neighbours!"

The ornate clock on the marble mantelpiece struck one and Richard jumped guiltily to his feet. "My mother will be keeping lunch," he said, "and I must be disrupting yours, I'm afraid. Do you need help with the stairs, Miss Dawson?"

"Thank you, but I'll manage," said Emmie firmly.

"Well, don't forget if you ever want anything at all, I'm only at the end of your road."

"Delightful young man," said Rosie, when Richard had ambled away like a huge shaggy bear. "I do wish I could still manage the walk to church."

"I'll take you," said Emmie, "when your new wheel-chair arrives. I've decided to start going myself – I actually enjoyed it."

As she sat gazing out across the park, nibbling the

158

remains of the food Kim had brought yesterday, Emmie was conscious of a strange feeling. She was not alone. Someone was there in the room with her. It was not an eerie, unpleasant experience; in fact it was exactly the opposite. She felt surrounded by the peace she had wanted for so long.

"It's you, isn't it, God?" she whispered. She ought to resent this intrusion, but as she lay back in her chair she said, "You will stay, won't you? I never want you to go away again."

4.30pm

Ann had never given a party before. "What's the point?" protested Matt. "You know we're not the sociable kind."

"But it's not every day you do the Pennine Way," said Ann. It was so hot, not even Matt could consider doing anything more energetic than sunbathing on the hot red bricks of their tiny backyard.

"Who are you going to ask, for heaven's sake?"

"Staff from school, and the Head of course."

"I wonder you've got the nerve after taking so many days off sick last term."

"That's the other reason I want to have a party," said Ann. "To show them all I'm better." Secretly she did not *feel* better, but she was not going to tell anyone that.

"Who shall we have from the Terrace?"

"You don't want any of that lot – surely," contended Matt. "We don't even know them."

"We know Kim and David from when she worked at school."

"They're religious. Surely you don't want to get mixed up in that kind of stuff."

"Of course I don't, but Kim would be a good person to have. She always generates warmth, somehow."

"Life and soul of the party," said Matt drily, "but I've never heard her husband open his mouth."

"Well, David's a jolly good listener and that always makes people happy. Then there's Hazel and Graham from the park end."

"Snobs," said Matt dismissively.

"I'd like to ask that blonde girl who used to live with them, the one we used to see in the park."

"Why? She's odd, always mooning about on her own."

"But she's very attractive."

"Well, she doesn't do anything for me," said Matt, "but you can ask Claire from next-door if you like."

Anne paused. Claire's name was not on her list. There was something about their next-door neighbour which made Ann feel threatened.

"What about the Saverys?" she continued hurriedly.

"Never heard of them," said Matt.

"Yes you have. They're the parents of that frightful child Sharon, who's always poking round everybody's dustbins."

"I'm not having those two fat pigs in my house."

"But you could convert them to health food and jogging," giggled Ann wickedly.

"Ugh! The thought of them in track suits revolts me." Matt laughed and rolled Ann over on top of him. "You can have them if you like, but don't you dare ask that dragon Alison from Number Thirteen."

"Mrs Grazier would never come to a party," said Ann between kisses. "She's a thousand times more religious than the Pattersons."

Alison adjusted the lace table-cloth and moved the cut-glass jamjar slightly to the left. Sunday tea was a sacred institution at Number Thirteen – two kinds of cake, fresh scones and home-made meringues. Everything was ready, but Alison was upset. Gordon should be here at a time of crisis like this, not up at that wretched allotment.

For perhaps the hundredth time she opened her front door and gazed anxiously down the Terrace. Wherever could she be? Never in all her seventeen years had Amanda Grazier failed to arrive home on time. Of course, Alison was delighted that she wanted to spend so much time with her school-friend Alexia. It was rather an unorthodox home with the father abroad and the mother a barrister, but the house was vast and in the best part of Welbridge. Amanda had been there last evening and Alison had not minded when she phoned to say that she and Alexia were going to a party and could they stay the night.

"All my school-friends are going, Mum," she had said. Alison had gone to bed quite happy – Welbridge Convent only took the nicest girls from the best backgrounds. Amanda would be safe staying with well-brought-up girls like that. No, the worry had not begun until Amanda failed to return in time for church.

"She's never missed choir before," Alison had told Gordon as they were forced to leave without her.

By lunchtime she had become seriously worried, but the aupair girl who looked after Alexia had been no help at all when she spoke to her on the phone. Pretending she couldn't speak English, indeed!

Someone was walking up the alleyway beside the house. Full of hope, Alison hurried to open the back door.

"Look what we've got for you, Auntie Alison." It was only Clancy with her arms loaded with muddy vegetables.

"Never known squash like 'em," said Gordon proudly as he followed her into the kitchen, equally laden. "They're far bigger than George's."

"It's like harvest festival," said Clancy when they had deposited their muddy burdens all over her spotless work surfaces. Gordon looked hopefully at Alison, eager for praise, but she ignored him. She always wished they could buy their vegetables from Brightways, where they came scrubbed, packaged in polythene and totally slug-free.

"Put it all . . . somewhere else," she said crossly. "I can't do anything about it now – it's Sunday."

As he carried his squash down to the cellar, Gordon

161

wondered miserably if he would ever be able to achieve anything which would make Alison feel proud of him.

Sunday tea began badly. Gordon was so upset by the treatment his produce had received that he could eat nothing, and Alison took his loss of appetite as a slight to her cooking. Things might have become quite ugly had not Amanda suddenly returned.

"I've had ever such a lovely time," she said ecstatically. "They had a great big swimming-pool and I met a boy there whose father is a duke."

Gordon had the distinct impression she was lying, but Alison was instantly mollified.

"Come and have tea, my sweetie," she said fondly.

Alison sat watching Amanda eat while the stories about her high society adventures grew taller by the minute.

"Look at the time!" exclaimed Amanda at last. "I must go up and change."

"Yes," said Alison, affectionately, "we mustn't be late for church, must we?"

"Oh, actually Mum, I'm going out again with Alexia. I'm a bit tired of church really. I don't think I'll be going any more. Can you tell them I won't be at choir practices?"

"Not go to church?" said Alison, stunned. "But what will people think?"

'What people "think" is all that matters,' thought Gordon cynically as his daughter ran upstairs.

"Pheeeew!" whistled Clancy.

"Don't be rude," snapped Alison.

The silence thickened uncomfortably. "This is not like her," said Alison at last. "She's a sweet, spiritually-minded child."

"It's that snob school that's done it," remarked Gordon unhelpfully.

"No it is not!" replied Alison indignantly. "I'll tell you whose fault it is. It's *his*."

"Whose?" Gordon wondered vaguely if she was blaming the Almighty.

162

"The vicar's. Changing all our church traditions. No wonder my Amanda can't stand it. She's much too sensitive for a bulldozer like him."

"I rather like the way he does things," admitted Gordon when Alison had taken herself off to the kitchen to wash up like the overworked martyr that she was. "I can't think why people are getting themselves so worked up about this poor young chap."

"Don't worry, Uncle Gordon," said Clancy soothingly. "There's a thriller on the telly tonight." As she came over to him and put her arms round his neck, he found there were tears in his eyes. Amanda had never done a thing like that. Alison was never one for showing affection. Seventeen years ago when Amanda was born he had hoped things might be different with a little girl of his very own to love, but she had been her mother's child right from the very beginning. Not only had she refused his love, but she had stolen from him the last remnants of Alison's attention and affection.

He hugged Clancy and pulled her down on to his knee. She was still only a little girl; he must go on believing that, in spite of her bikini.

"You said she wouldn't be pleased about all those lovely things you grew her," she said. "Never mind, she'll have to be proud when you win the silver cup again."

"She won't be. She'll only grumble about having to clean it. So long as you're proud, that's all that matters."

"I will be," said Clancy and patted the bald patch on top of his head.

MONDAY AUGUST 27TH

10.15am

At the precise moment when the 'Accursed Monsters', as Bea called the new computers, were arriving at the studio, Emmie's Fiesta nosed its way out of Welbridge and headed towards the South Downs. The hatchback was filled with the feather-light wheel-chair which had been delivered that morning, and on the back seat was a basket containing some of Mrs Macaulay's delicious sandwiches.

There was more purpose in the 'jaunt' than just a picnic lunch, however. Rosie's shaky fingers held a page she had carefully cut from the local paper and her 'sparrow' eyes sparkled with excitement.

RUNSTAN THE SUSSEX ANSWER TO BATTERSEA
DOGS HOME

read the headline. The previous evening Emmie had been feeling completely trapped as she sat in the garden watching the sun setting over the park. She would have given anything for a long walk on her own.

Rosie, sitting quietly beside her, had suddenly produced this clipping and handed it to her without a word.

"Surely you're not suggesting . . .?" Emmie had protested.

"A dog is such a comfort on a country walk," Rosie had said. "I was never without one in the old days."

"You never give up, do you?" Emmie had laughed,

and she finally conceded that something large and fierce could be her passport to freedom.

Runstan was now their destination.

The new wheel-chair swished noiselessly along between the rows of wire-runs and spotless kennels, while a lady whose face resembled a wrinkled russet apple pointed out the inmates of the 'Sussex answer to Battersea Dogs' Home'. Superfluous puppies, ancient dogs with white whiskers and cats of doubtful ancestry, mongrels that yapped and spaniels that whined.

"Oh dear," said Rosie at last, "I really don't think after all . . ." At the end of the 'ward round' in the very last run – Gwyllum was waiting for them, gazing nobly out through the wire netting. He knew they had come for him, and they knew it, too, the moment they both saw him.

"This is Gwyllum," said the russet apple, "he's a Newfoundland."

"He must be the biggest dog I ever saw," said Emmie weakly. "He'll never fit on the back seat of the car."

"Of course he will," said Rosie briskly. "He'd fit into a matchbox if you asked him to. You can tell by his eyes."

"His family emigrated and simply could not afford to take him too," said their guide. "He costs a bundle to feed I'm afraid."

"We have both had unfortunate experiences," explained Rosie, "which could have been avoided had Gwyllum been with us. We will not begrudge him his food."

2pm

There was hardly a breeze on the Downs that day. Emmie had driven up the same tiny lane that Matt and Ann had taken on Good Friday morning. The primroses and violets on the banks had given way to honeysuckle and white convolvulus, but the skylark was still singing when they reached the top.

Rosie sat in her new wheel-chair and feasted her eyes on the view like someone who has been shut up for a long time in a dungeon. The little church bell which had set Ann thinking, chimed twice in the distance.

Emmie had spread a rug on the ground and was sitting gingerly on one corner while Gwyllum occupied the rest; he looked as if picnics were pleasures he had enjoyed all his life.

"He's so enormous," she said doubtfully. Rosie offered Gwyllum the end of her ham sandwich and he ate it with the dignified manners of a perfect gentleman.

"I hope he won't frighten the milk-lady," said Emmie.

"He wouldn't dream of it. You can tell by his eyes."

Emmie sat gazing into the hazy-blue distance which contained Welbridge. "How ever do you survive, shut up in the house all the time?" she said.

"There is always something lovely to enjoy in every day if you look for it," replied Rosie. "Music, books, radio – the television takes me all over the world, you know. Then, of course, there are the people."

"People?" said Emmie.

"I sit at my window and watch everyone who goes by in the Terrace. When you still lived at Number Fifteen I prayed for you every day when I saw you."

"I never knew anyone ever prayed for me," said Emmie softly. They finished the thermos of tea in companionable silence and then drifted happily in their own thoughts. They were an unlikely looking trio; two sharply-contrasting women and a huge shaggy dog.

"I brought something I rather wanted you to see." Rosie was rummaging in her battered old canvas bag. Emmie looked up in surprise, they so seldom broke silences that something important must be happening.

"It is a book I once wrote for children," continued Rosie as she produced a hard-cover notebook full of water-colour sketches and a younger Miss Rosedale's handwriting.

"This is your house!" exclaimed Emmie – the picture

on the first page caught her attention instantly. "And this is you – but who's this funny little girl?"

"I shall never forget her. It must have been thirty years ago. I was gardening one afternoon and there she was with her fat pink cheeks pressed against the iron bars of the gate. It was the flowers she was looking at, I never saw such a look of ecstasy on a child's face." Emmie had begun to skim politely through the book, but soon she found she was completely absorbed as she fell under its delightful spell. 'This is buried treasure,' said the professional inside her. The water-colours had an old-fashioned, faded charm even though they were obviously the work of an amateur whose draughtsmanship left a lot to be desired. It was the atmosphere they portrayed that was so arresting.

The story was simple and clear and Emmie realised it had the quality that would hang in the mind of a child for ever. When she had finished she went back to the beginning and read it all over again. It was a sweet story of a Victorian child who lived in a basement by the station. Her longing for flowers led her into a deep friendship with a lonely old lady who lived next to the park. The book had an unexpected ending and Emmie breathed a sigh of satisfaction. She knew quality when she saw it.

"Did you ever send it to a publisher?" she asked.

"Oh no, my artwork was not up to scratch. I have been waiting ever since to find a really good illustrator who loves flowers as much as I do."

"The publisher would probably have done that for you," said Emmie. "I have an art-college friend who works for MacDillan's Educational and I know she'd jump at this. It's the kind of thing which could become a classic. Did the little girl really come into your garden like she does in the book?" She looked again at the wistful little face in the picture.

"Sadly no. Her mother used to drag her by on the other side of the road, screaming. Perhaps she thought I was

167

an oddity. Anyway, I was never allowed to speak to her again. So I wrote the story as it might have been. I've prayed for that little girl ever since – all I know about her is that her name was Babs.''

"Pity I'm only trained in graphic design. I've always wanted to illustrate a book.''

"But you paint exquisitely,'' said Rosie hopefully.

"I suppose I could have a go. It would give me something to do this month.'' She returned to the book with a sense of growing excitement. She would base her work on Rosie's own style and allow the book to be a Victorian period piece. What joy to paint and paint and not feel she was wasting time! After all, the doctor had told her to do what she enjoyed most.

She became conscious of Rosie watching her intently. 'This book means a lot more to her than she'll ever admit. Perhaps I could make it a "thing of beauty" – just for her. My way of saying sorry I've been such a leech.'

"I think we should make for home soon,'' she said, closing the book carefully. ''I must buy some paints and then turn the spare room into a studio.''

As they drove home with Gwyllum looking regal but squashed on the back seat, Rosie sighed with satisfaction.

"I must talk to Mr Ponsonby about changing my will,'' she said. Emmie shot her a horrified look as she recalled Edward's cruel words. 'If she tries to buy my friendship, she'll spoil everything,' she thought.

"Most impressive – that Runstan place,'' continued Rosie. ''There ought to be far more sanctuaries like that. Yes, I must certainly talk to Mr Ponsonby without delay.'' Emmie experienced a curious sense of relief as she drove down the winding hill. 'That's one in the eye to Edward,' she thought happily.

SATURDAY AUGUST 31ST

7.30am

"Do you know what I'm going to be?" Rebecca Patterson had been waiting for Babs to arrive in the Terrace for at least half an hour and her chest was positively heaving with pride.

"A good little girl, I should hope," replied Babs as she checked the order for Number Four. Rebecca ignored this typically grown-up remark.

"An artist's model!"

"Are you now?" said Babs, looking somewhat startled.

"Miss Rosedale's written a book. Miss Dawson's drawing pictures of me to go in it – and her new dog. He likes being a model, too. Miss Rosedale says you can tell by his eyes. I've got to dress up as a Victorian girl. Mummy's making me a long dress. Soon I'll be in all the book shops."

"Well, aren't you lucky?" said Babs as soon as Rebecca's excitement left her the opportunity. "No one ever put me in a book."

Rebecca's face clouded with sympathy. "I could ask Miss Dawson to squeeze you in too."

"Don't worry, luvvy," smiled Babs. "I'm far too fat to be squeezed into anything these days." She went off up the Terrace laughing. Books, indeed, whatever would her old lady be up to next?

10.30

"I can't think why you bought so much," complained Matt, as they battled up Bakers Hill, heavily loaded with Brightways shopping bags. "I thought we weren't having eats."

"We must have appetizers to go with the drinks," snapped Ann. She was so tired she wished she had never thought of this party. Why did Matt have to argue over every little detail? Surely he could see she was doing all this in order to prove his pet theory that the body can be made to do as it's told?

"Blast!" she said, stopping short in the middle of the pavement.

"Now what?"

"I forgot the matches for the candles." She was close to tears.

"Well if you think I'm going to stand at the check-out for another half-hour . . ."

"No, we'll pop into Macaulay's, it won't take a minute." But it seemed that the corner shop was as crowded as Brightways that morning.

"Hello," said Kim, smiling over the head of the baby on her hip. "We're so looking forward to this evening. Well I am – David's a shy old stick."

Hazel was paying her paper bill. "Been buying the party booze?" she asked with a forced smile.

"Yes," replied Ann, and wished Hazel would stop staring as she fumbled awkwardly with her purse. This clumsiness was bad enough without other people noticing it.

Had she been able to erase one clip from the film of her life, Ann would certainly have chosen the one which followed. It seemed to her that the whole Terrace was watching as, without warning, she fell backwards right into one of Mrs Macaulay's elaborate tower-block displays. Tins, bottles and packets of cereal crashed down with her, and over went the stand of paperbacks. As it fell it demolished yet another construction of chocolate-boxes – the chaos was incredible.

"Well really!" exclaimed Mrs Macaulay indignantly.

"Are you all right under all that?" asked Kim anxiously.

"I just came over giddy," said Ann, too shaken to move.

"Like the Marathon all over again, I suppose," snarled Matt. Hazel loosened the top button of Ann's shirt. "Who's your GP?" she asked without the slightest display of emotion.

"Dr Macdermott."

"I'll give him a ring when I get home – get him to pop round."

"No!" said Ann. "I'm going back to school on Tuesday. I'll be perfectly all right again by then." Hazel stood looking down at her speculatively. 'All the same,' she thought, 'I'll give Jim a ring and find out what's up with her. Not that it's hard to guess.' "I take it this evening's off, Matt?" she added, trying to keep the pleased note out of her voice.

"Oh yes, of course," he said morosely. "I'll ring all the others." Was there no end to Ann's bizarre attention-seeking devices? Really! His patience was fast running out.

8.15pm

'Thank goodness the Coleys cancelled their wretched party,' thought Claire as she tipped the sprouted mung beans into the sieve and rinsed them. She was tired. The salon was hectic these days, since Roger had it refurbished.

"We want to attract the right kind of people," he had said. Well, they were doing that all right! Being tired was worth it when the takings were as high as they had been today. The place looked so different with rainbows and triangles covering the walls – they set off the

171

arrangement of crystals in the window so nicely. All those new herbal beauty products and natural health cures were also bringing in customers by the shoal.

"I'm not hungry, Mummy," said Jasmine. "I had an extra big tea at the Pattersons."

"Chips and fish fingers, no doubt," said Claire crisply.

"But they're nice."

"If you don't want to eat, why are you still hanging round looking at me?" said Claire irritably. "Go and do something."

"I wanted to ask you if . . ." began Jasmine tensely. "Would you like not to have to take me to Roger's on Sundays? I hate sitting outside his house in the car all day, it's so boring."

"But I spend the earth on stuff to keep you amused."

"The Pattersons said I could stay with them."

"Oh yes, and charge me for another whole day I suppose!"

"They said you wouldn't have to pay on Sundays." Jasmine was standing on one leg now in her anxiety. Uncle David had also said she must tell her mother the whole truth. "I want to start going to church with them, it was such fun on holiday." She was hopping about now, like an agitated stork as she looked up into Claire's face, striving to read her reaction. "Jesus *isn't* dead, Mummy, *really*, he's not. He lives with the Pattersons and looks after them all the time."

'Those Pattersons are brainwashing her,' thought Claire.

"Jesus has been dead for two thousand years," she said coldly. "He was a guru who paid the price for being too outspoken."

"What's a guru?"

"A good man − like Roger."

"Oh no! Jesus isn't a bit like Roger!" Claire mixed the bean sprouts with the salad in her wooden bowl. Her mouth was set in a hard, thin line. She felt trapped now. Of course she didn't want the Pattersons indoctrinating

Jasmine, but a few Sundays without her would be very helpful just now. Roger was being a bit distant these days and he frequently rang at the last minute to put off her visits. Perhaps it was Jasmine's presence which was irritating him. She never would stay in the car, but kept traipsing into the loo and disturbing their concentration. 'I need Roger's undivided attention if I'm ever going to learn enough to pull myself out of this dreary Terrace,' she thought. And, of course, that meant she also needed the Pattersons.

"I'll go over later and see if they really mean it," she said wearily.

"Someone's at the door, Mummy," said Jasmine and Claire's fatigue vanished.

"Go to bed, then, and give me some peace," she said quickly. She hoped it would be Roger, but it was only Hazel standing on the step.

"Graham's gone up to the golf-club for a drink," she said brightly, "so I thought I'd just slip along and say hello. Shame about the party."

For Hazel to 'slip along to say hello' to a mere hairdresser was so unlikely that Claire almost smiled as she led the way up the hallway to her kitchen.

"I've got a pot of apricot tea brewing," she said.

"Actually, I'm in a bit of a hole," said Hazel as she tried to sip the strange concoction without a grimace. "I've just had a phone call, right out of the blue, asking us to a very important lunch party tomorrow. It was Clarence Cromway actually, the chairman of the hospital management committee. It's crucial that I make a good impression on him, but my hair's an absolute ruin these days. Must be that wretched sun in Turkey. It might look better if it was cut really short, but I need it done by tomorrow. I was just wondering if . . .?"

Claire glanced at the preparations for her meal. Did this woman not realise she had been doing people's hair for the last thirteen hours without a lunch break? Really! Then she paused. Hazel looked oddly shrunken and the

173

suntan accentuated her wrinkles. 'Perhaps she wants more than a hair-do,' she thought.

"All right, come upstairs and we'll see what we can do."

Claire had always loved her bedroom – it was beautiful and she was not ashamed to take anyone there, but Hazel looked round and said patronisingly, "You must find it terribly hard to manage in such a small house."

The remark revealed something to Claire. She wanted to get 'into' this healing business not just for adventure or even money, but because she wanted power over arrogant, successful women like this.

"How have you been feeling since June?" she asked when her scissors were snipping the wet red hair.

"Oh fine. No emotional after-effects." Hazel's words were bright and staccato, sharp as gunfire. "The holiday was a flop, though. Graham and I don't seem to be hitting it off at present. I'm a bit under par physically. Can't sleep. Ghastly headaches. It's the strain of working towards this new job."

"Are you sure it is only that?" said Claire gently. "Don't forget there's still a lot of guilt generated by pseudo-religious conditioning."

Hazel laughed rudely. "You amateur psychologists! I suppose you think I'm in a depression caused by doing my husband out of his precious son? Well, I can assure you I'm not the sort who whimpers emotionally for months after a termination. No, everything's going to be fine when I swing this job."

"The lunch tomorrow," said Claire. "It matters to you?"

"It's probably as important as the interview. Everything depends on this one man now, so I've simply got to slay him."

"Be careful," said Claire suddenly. "Your tactics are wrong, Dr Tilson. Concentrate your efforts on this man's wife, she is your route to success." Hazel was stunned. How could she even know Clarence Cromway had a wife.

She hadn't mentioned her. Her scalp began to prickle as she realised she had dismissed the chairman's wife as an insignificant little *hausfrau*. If she really did wield the power behind the throne, she might have blown everything tomorrow by antagonising her.

"You and your ESP," she said with a nervous little laugh, but Claire could see in the mirror that she was impressed and she had to turn away to hide her smile. She hoped Hazel would never discover she had been doing Mrs Clarence Cromway's hair every Thursday morning for the last five years.

SATURDAY SEPTEMBER 21ST

"That's the last page finished," said Emmie as she put down her paint-brush. The shadows lay long on the velvet grass in the park. It had been another golden day, like all the others in September. To Emmie they had seemed like precious amber beads on a chain.

'I'll remember this month as the happiest time of my whole life,' she thought. 'But it's gone too fast.'

All round the make-shift studio were propped the finished illustrations for the book. It had been a struggle to get Rebecca right, but she was very pleased with the pictures of Rosie. She lifted one up and studied it closely.

"Old age doesn't need to be ugly," she told Gwyllum. "It can be very beautiful. I hope I can help the children who read the book to see that." Gwyllum merely thumped his tail on the carpet. Emmie had sat at the table in the window from sunrise until dusk every day while he lay dozing on the floor at her feet. "I just can't think how I managed it all in the time," she continued, "but the silence in the house made working so easy."

As she had painted the intricate details of the flowers and trees which were a feature of the book, she felt a strange identity with the person who had created such beauty. She knew now that at the end of her spiritual quest, God had been waiting for her and He was not simply a vague 'feeling', but a person who was very real indeed. She had wanted this book to be a way of saying "thank you" to Rosie, but it had also become an offering to God Himself.

She stood up stiffly and yawned. "I've got to go back

to work on Monday, Gwyllum," she said. "But how on earth am I going to bear typography now I know for certain I can illustrate?"

She only had to have the manuscript typed and then she could send it up to MacDillan's with her illustrations attached, but an idea had been forming in her mind for some days. The graphic designer in her wanted to stroll into the publishers and present them with finished perfection – a portfolio of visuals. She could see in her mind the way she wanted the text to be laid out on the pages, merging subtly with the pictures. If she had the manuscript typeset, all she would need were a few nights alone with the camera, processor and waxer in the studio. But dare she?

FRIDAY SEPTEMBER 27TH

5am

"I've done it!" said Emmie – weary but happy. It was weird being alone here in the studio at this odd time of the morning, and she was glad of Gwyllum's company. She'd had to spend several hours each night here alone like this, but it had been worth it. There lay the finished book, ring-bound neatly and looking as lovely as it had done in her imagination. Rosie was going to love it!

She sat on at her drawing-board while a strange feeling of sadness assailed her. The whole experience had been so lovely, but now it was all over. Nothing lay ahead but the misery of life with the 'accursed monsters'. Emmie's first week back at work had been ghastly.

"Well, you're here early." Emmie jumped violently. The boss's voice behind her sounded ominous.

"I might say the same of you," she said nervously.

"Bea told me she thought you'd been unofficially using the processor after hours, so I thought I'd better investigate."

Emmie felt she had been stabbed in the back by an old friend, but she knew Bea had never really forgiven her for living with Rosie and not sharing her flat.

"What are you working on?" His voice was icy. Emmie had pushed the book under some papers, but the messy evidence of her night's work littered the entire studio.

"Let me see," he insisted. "A book? So that fainting act was simply put on so you could give time to a private

178

client, eh? And then you have the cheek to use my equipment to finish it off.''

''The doctor said I should do something I enjoy,'' said Emmie defensively.

''I think you'd better consider your employment here terminated.'' The words were cold, hard and as final as a gravestone.

''No, please . . . I really am sorry.'' Emmie's security was rocking dangerously. If she left after an incident like this, how would she ever find another job? The world of graphic design was small and tight-knit. ''It was just something I was doing for my landlady.'' The boss was glancing through the pages of Rosie's book as she spoke and he looked up with a sneer.

''Do you think I can't spot quality when I see it? Don't be ridiculous, Emily, this book's a winner. Your kind of flair's redundant here now. I was going to give you the shove this evening actually. I need someone who really understands these new techniques and you must admit you're hopeless. I've got a real whiz-kid starting on Monday.'' Emmie looked so stricken that he added more kindly, ''You're obviously a brilliant illustrator, why don't you go freelance?''

''No capital,'' said Emmie with bitter finality.

''Well that's your problem. Now if you wouldn't mind leaving, I'd like to get home to bed for a couple of hours more sleep. And I won't say 'see you later','' he added unkindly as he hustled Emmie towards the door.

St Mark's clock was chiming seven, but Emmie still sat alone in the garden with Gwyllum beside her. She had flopped down on the seat under the apple tree after their long trudge home from the studio. She hadn't even mustered the energy to climb the stairs and make a cup of tea. 'Whatever am I going to do now?' she thought for the hundredth time. It was another perfect morning, but the birds need not have bothered to sing as far as she was concerned.

179

Suddenly Gwyllum stood up, his tail waving a welcome. Emmie looked over her shoulder to see Rosie shuffling painfully towards her across the lake of dew. Panic flooded her. She knew without doubt this upright old lady would not approve of her nocturnal use of the studio. All at once she was back facing Aunt Jane and scouring her mind for the best lie to tell. Create a diversion, that policy had always worked best.

"I've got something for you," she said. Rosie lowered herself on to the seat and opened the Brightways shopping bag which contained the finished book.

"Exquisite!" She looked like a child examining a long-awaited birthday present. "It is just how I always hoped it would be."

"I had it processed professionally to impress the publishers." It wasn't exactly a lie, but somehow it made Emmie feel uncomfortable. Rosie did not appear to hear, she was far too busy gazing at each page and exclaiming over every perfect detail.

"It is beautiful," she said softly at last. Emmie had imagined this scene so many times, but for some reason it seemed spoilt.

"There is something I want to say, dear," began Rosie while she sat cradling the book as if it had been a precious newborn baby. "I have been very anxious about you this week, since you returned to work. Already you are looking pinched and strained again." Emmie felt as if an oily paint-rag had become lodged in her throat. Rosie was always so perceptive. "I feel that your studio job is not good for you, and I wondered if I could make you a little business proposition."

Emmie gazed at her. This was not at all what she had expected her to say. "Could we not turn that spare room upstairs into a permanent studio and found a firm of our own?"

"But, Rosie, I'd need a processor and all kinds of other expensive equipment and materials."

"My grandfather left me very well endowed and I can

afford to be a little adventurous with my capital. Please give me the pleasure of being your partner in this venture.''

Freedom! The chance to work *alone* on the projects she enjoyed doing most. Everything in Emmie was screaming, 'yes, yes, yes!' But could she use Rosie like this?

''I couldn't let you do that for me,'' she replied huskily.

''I would not be doing it for you, dear, but entirely for myself. Mr Ponsonby tells me I ought to rearrange some investments.''

''But it could take ages before I made a profit.''

''I intend to live at least another ten years – I can wait for our ship to come in.'' Emmie still looked doubtful and Rosie could see that her bid was failing, so she quickly played her trump card. ''There is another reason for my offer,'' she continued more diffidently. ''Doctor Macdermott was here yesterday. He says he is worried about me being alone all day – he would keep talking about homes again. If you were upstairs working he might give me my freedom for a little longer.''

Emmie sat perfectly still for some time. She still could not hear the birds singing.

''Something has happened to worry you, dear?'' said Rosie gently. ''Since yesterday evening.''

''Yes, but how ever did you know?''

''One cannot be a headmistress for thirty years, without learning to know when a person is holding something back.''

''Yes, I'm sorry, I did tell you a bit of a whopper just now. I didn't *have* the book processed, I've been doing it myself at night, and I got caught.'' Out poured the whole story, while Rosie sat listening in thoughtful silence.

''It wasn't fair of the boss to do a thing like that,'' Emmie finished indignantly. Rosie reached out shyly and took her hand.

''I am deeply touched that you should have done all

181

this for me, particularly when it has cost you so dear, but should you not have asked your boss first before using his equipment?"

"I knew that's what you'd say! But he'd never have let me. Everyone does things like that these days, Rosie. You're just old-fashioned," she added affectionately.

"So is God." The smile vanished instantly from Emmie's face.

"You think I've been dishonest, don't you? Does that mean He'll ditch me because I've upset Him?"

"Certainly not! He promised He would never leave you. However, human beings like us are always getting ourselves into muddles, but His forgiveness is never more than a whisper away."

Emmie sat looking out across the park thoughtfully. At last she said, "I'd better go for a walk and get this straightened out with Him, hadn't I?"

"When you come back, will you allow me to give you some breakfast, dear? Boiled eggs and brown toast — a feast to celebrate our new business venture."

"Thank you," said Emmie softly. "Thank you for *everything.*"

WEDNESDAY OCTOBER 2ND

5.15pm

"That was a very nice piece they wrote about you in the local paper Dr Tilson, I must say." Alison was brushing the immaculate concrete of her front garden when Hazel hurried by and for once she was smiling. "Congratulations!"

Hazel swore silently. She only had half an hour to get round Brightways – and now she would have to stop and chat. It simply was not worth snubbing a neighbour who could make life as unpleasant as Alison frequently did.

"I suppose you'll be moving into something much grander now you've got yourself this wonderful new job up at the hospital."

"Probably," said Hazel vaguely and glanced at her watch. She was about to launch into an excuse for her haste, when she realised Alison was no longer smiling. In fact she seemed to have forgotten she was addressing the youngest senior pathologist Welbridge had ever appointed. Her face had frozen into an expression of outrage as she stared over Hazel's left shoulder.

"Just look at her!" Alison, tight-lipped with righteous indignation, was pointing at Ann who lurched unsteadily through the park-gates. "Sometimes she is so far under the influence of drink she can hardly walk straight and she's actually a teacher at our Clancy's school! It's an absolute disgrace. I'm really going to have to complain to the headmaster."

"Complaining seems to be a hobby of yours," said Hazel, who had long endured Alison's tirades about bonfires, noise and 'alien' cars parked in the road. Suddenly she was unable to stand this woman a minute longer.

"Perhaps you would be wiser to get your facts straight, before you poke your nose into other people's business. Ann Coley is *not* an alcoholic; she happens to have multiple sclerosis." The effect of her crisp words upon Alison was most satisfactory. Yet as her mouth opened and closed like a goldfish, Hazel recalled with a twist of compunction her telephone conversation with Jim Macdermott on the day Ann cancelled her party.

"We haven't given her the diagnosis yet," he had said, "but I know you'll be discreet."

"Look here, Mrs Grazier," said Hazel hurriedly, "I think I may have betrayed a professional confidence. Dr Macdermott doesn't want Ann to know what's the matter with her just yet, so you won't tell anyone, will you?"

"Won't breathe a word," said Alison earnestly. "Poor thing and so young, too. She'll be in a wheel-chair soon I suppose."

"She may never need one," said Hazel crossly. "Now if you'll excuse me, I've to shop for a dinner-party." She hurried away leaving Alison gazing after her. 'I must inform them about this at the prayer-meeting tonight,' thought Alison. 'They'll certainly want to lift her up.'

Hazel went on down the road seething with rage. 'Stupid woman! What had she ever achieved in her life apart from producing a clone as obnoxious as herself? All the same, she mustn't let a silly little incident like that spoil her evening. She deserved her celebration after months of pulling strings, "hacking" as they had called it at Oxford. Now she was at the top of her chosen tree and life was going to be wonderful!'

She was passing Claire's house now and she quickened her pace uneasily. She would like to change her hairdresser, but Claire knew too much about her. 'If I

184

cross her, she could bust up my marriage,' thought Hazel with a nervous flick of her red hair. How could Claire possibly have known what a vast influence that quiet little woman Mrs Cromway had on her husband? Without that insight she would have played her cards completely the wrong way and probably lost the game.

As she hurried down the hill past the salon she wondered why, even though she had everything she had ever wanted, she still felt flat? 'It must be living in that boring little terrace, full of busybodies like that Grazier woman,' she thought as she stopped outside the estate agents. Perhaps the time really had come to move out of town to something more spacious.

THURSDAY OCTOBER 3RD

4.30pm

Ann had been painfully conscious of Alison's muttered condemnation of the previous day. She heard a lot of remarks like that at school these days. It was not proving easy to supervise games from the side-lines or face crowded classrooms which spun like dizzy whirlpools. Still it had been a triumph to get back to school all this term. She'd feel better in a few weeks – that's what Matt said, anyway. As she opened her front door, she was yearning for a nice cup of tea before he followed her home from school. But there were no tea-bags left in the caddy. 'Blast!'

The walk down to Brightways was out of the question after a long day at work, so Macaulay's it must be, even though she had vowed never to darken its doors again after the embarrassing demolition incident. She needed that tea, so she would simply have to swallow her pride.

A pram was parked outside the shop when she arrived and its occupant was protesting loudly. Ann's shaky hand was on the door when it was opened from inside by Kim. She looked like a tired version of the Pied Piper, surrounded by so many children.

"Pocket-money day," she said apologetically. "Terrible for their teeth, but marvellously soothing for my nerves. I haven't seen you lately, how are you?"

Ann wanted to shout 'I feel ghastly; if I can't pull myself together soon, I'll slit my throat.' Instead she smiled mechanically and said, "Fine thanks, and you?"

"You don't look fine," said Kim doubtfully.

"Well actually I . . ." began Ann, but Amy was grizzling as she pulled at Kim's skirt, Jasmine and Rebecca argued over a bag of sweets and Johnnie dropped his red lolly and bellowed with grief.

"Sorry," said Kim, "I'd better go. See you sometime."

'I wish I didn't have to rush,' she thought sadly as she shepherded her unruly flock towards home. 'I know she was trying to say something important. If only I had more time these days.'

'She couldn't care less,' thought Ann bitterly, as she watched the procession straggling away. 'No one really cares about how other people feel.'

"Will that be all, luv?" said Mrs Macaulay with an unusually motherly note in her voice. "I was so sorry to hear about you at the prayer-meeting."

"Hear about what?" said Ann absently as she stuffed her tea into the pockets of her duffel coat.

"About . . . you know . . ." Ann stared blankly at Mrs Macaulay's yellow tooth. "About you having multiple sclerosis and all. Mrs Grazier had it from Dr Tilson. I am sorry."

Ann weaved an erratic path down Bakers Hill. In her mind she saw thousands of pieces of jigsaw puzzle muddled together in a heap. They meant nothing until two magic words had caused them to gather together and form themselves into a picture stark in its clarity. Multiple sclerosis were those two words.

Perhaps she had always known subconsciously that they were the key to her mental chaos. How dare those doctors deceive her like this? Ann realised she had never been more angry in her life.

"I want to see Dr Macdermott," she told the receptionist firmly.

"What time is your appointment?"

"I haven't one, but I'm going to see him all the same."

A woman emerged from the 'holy of holies' and before the astonished receptionist could call the name of the next patient, Ann was through the door and glaring at the doctor across his littered desk. She did not sit down.

"Why didn't you tell me? Why leave me to discover through street gossip?"

"Ah!" Enlightenment replaced the bewildered expression on Jim Macdermott's face. "It's Mrs Coley, isn't it?"

He leaned back in his swivel-chair, swaying gently from left to right.

"Don't keep doing that," snapped Ann. "It makes me dizzy when people sway about. I suppose that's just one of the symptoms of MS." Her tone was dark with bitterness.

"I cannot imagine how you came to discover your diagnosis, but I'm extremely sorry . . ."

"Two months ago that man in London told me I was imagining all this," cut in Ann. "Left me to think I was going nutty."

"I am sure if you think carefully you will realise you misunderstood what the consultant said." Ann frowned. "It's terribly easy to get the wrong end of the stick." He had regained his smooth bedside manner now, and Ann thought he sounded as if he was addressing a backward child. "We don't like to burden MS patients with a diagnosis too soon. You see it's a very capricious disease and many people only have a few symptoms which then disappear – maybe for years. Instead of worrying about the future they can live normal, happy lives, and it's sometimes kinder to keep them in ignorance."

"But my symptoms haven't gone away, they're getting much worse and you had no right to leave me in the dark."

"Sometimes MS does advance rapidly, but at any moment you could go into remission. Why see yourself in a wheel-chair before . . .?"

"My husband must never know about this." Ann had to sit down now as the terrifying ramifications of this nightmare began to dawn upon her.

"I think he should, Mrs Coley. You need someone to stand beside you in this." He was swaying again, but he checked himself quickly.

"Stand beside me?" sneered Ann. "Fat chance!"

"Perhaps you misjudge him? I'll pop round and have a little chat with him sometime." The doctor stood up and glanced at his watch. "Go home and rest," he said blandly. "If you take this term off, who knows after Christmas you may be in perfect health." As he opened the door for her he added, "Do come in again, I'm always here to help."

"Help?" said Ann as she looked at him amazed. She had a crippling disease which would probably kill her eventually and there was absolutely nothing this highly-trained professional could do about it. The occupants of the crowded waiting-room gazed at her in astonishment as she said through clenched teeth, "Go to hell!"

FRIDAY OCTOBER 4TH

11.15am

Claire was busy with a perm when the woman walked
into the shop.

"I want an appointment with Claire," she said firmly
to the new receptionist. "No one else will do."

Claire surveyed the stranger as she stood impatiently
tapping her car keys on the glass top of the desk. Her
coat was expensive and the shoes had the handmade
look.

"Excuse me a moment," she murmured to her client
and reached the desk just as Di was saying, "Claire's
booked up completely today."

"I was just going to take my lunch-break," she purred,
"but I'd be happy to fit you in, Mrs . . . did you say
Babbington Brown? Would you like to come through and
I'll get one of my *senior* girls to shampoo you." There was
something about this woman which gave Claire an odd
feeling of destiny.

"What do you want done?" she asked when her new
client was settled in the chair with her wet head wrapped
in a towelling turban.

"Actually I have my hair done in London most weeks,"
was the reply. "I have a very good little girl in Harrods."

"So you only need a blow-dry. Would you like a cup
of coffee?" Claire was trying hard to cover her growing
dislike with a heavy veneer of charm.

"As a matter of fact a friend gave me your name." Mrs
Babbington Brown had dropped her voice so low that

190

Claire had to bend down to hear her. "As I say, I don't really need a hair-do, but six months ago I had a car crash. Wrote off my husband's Jaguar. I've been in quite ghastly agony ever since, whiplash of course. Been to two men in Harley Street, both useless. My friend told me you're a . . . healer?" She whispered the word as she glanced furtively round the salon.

Claire smiled mysteriously into the mirror. Roger would soon have this one eating out of his hand – he'd charge her the earth but he'd almost certainly make her feel better. He really was a master-craftsman and it was no wonder he never had to worry about money. She remembered how willingly she had parted with her grandmother's diamond brooch; rich women like Mrs Babbington Brown would give far more than that for their health. 'But is it fair that I should work my guts out here in the shop to feed him with clients when I get nothing out of it for myself?'

She put her long slim hands on Mrs Babbington Brown's scraggy neck. "Let me try and feel my way to this pain," she murmured softly. She tried to clear her mind of everything, just as Roger had taught her, but as she stood there in the crowded salon, all she could think of was the tranquillity of his room by the millpond. It was so easy for him to work, nestled there in 'the other world'. All the uneasy feelings she had been smothering for weeks forced themselves into her mind and she realised she must face the fact that Roger was definitely irritating her. Only last night she had gone out there to confront him unexpectedly. The hunter's moon had created a silver path across the millpond and a fox had barked in the silent woods behind the empty shell of his mother's cottage. She could have been so happy there.

Roger had not been alone when she rapped on the ancient oak of his front door. Two girls she had met at Group gatherings were sitting at his feet, gazing up at him adoringly. Was he teaching them the art of psychic healing as well? 'Perhaps I'm just one of many spiders who spin his webs,' she had thought bitterly.

Of course, those doubts had vanished as he sat holding her hand in the firelight when the other two had gone. Everything was always all right when she was with him; the niggles only began when she was back in Welbridge.

"I feel such a warmth . . ." sighed Mrs Babbington Brown, her voice made Claire feel like an actress, day dreaming on stage and forgetting her cue.

"I think you should see a friend of mine," she said. "He has far more experience than I have."

"Oh no, my husband would never countenance me going to a *male* healer, and I don't think I'd like it myself. I know *you* could help me."

"I am terribly booked up," said Claire, playing for time. "People come to me from all over the country."

"I wouldn't mind paying . . . extra . . .?" Mrs Babbington Brown was pleading for help, 'and I must know once and for all, whether I really do have the touch or if Roger's simply been using me as his decoy,' she thought decisively.

"As a matter of fact, I am unexpectedly free this Saturday evening," she said. "I'll give you my home address."

SATURDAY OCTOBER 5TH

9.15pm

'Well, here goes,' thought Claire as she lit the joss-sticks and arranged a bowl of roses on the table. She looked anxiously round her kitchen – mellow pine, old copper saucepans and bunches of dried herbs. Yes the atmosphere was right, it was as near to the 'other world' as anyone could get in Laburnum Terrace.

She put a carefully chosen selection of dried herbs in the teapot and set it to brew. Now for some music. That Irish harpist would be just right.

She was thinking of Roger as she checked her appearance in the hall mirror. He often knew what she was thinking, but what if his power of telepathy extended as far as Welbridge? How would he feel about what she was going to do? At least she was satisfied with her reflection; it resembled a portrait of an Edwardian lady. That lacy blouse and the cameo brooch created just the right impression. 'But what if I can't do it after all?'

''It really is so good of you to fit me in,'' said Mrs Babbington Brown as she settled into the Windsor armchair. It occurred to Claire that she would never have used a deferential tone like that to her 'little hairdresser' in Harrods.

Half an hour later the music, herbal tea and Claire's soothing voice had begun to work their spell and Mrs Babbington Brown looked suitably relaxed as Claire moved behind her chair, ready to begin the treatment. She had felt all the evening that she was simply playing a part in some amateur theatrical, but that feeling changed completely as her hands began to move. Something came stealthily up behind her, more of a feeling than a shadow. Someone put invisible hands over her hands and she knew they wanted to think through her mind. "When you receive your spirit guides," Roger's words came back to her like an echo. Was that happening now? She wanted to fight, to refuse this monstrous invasion of her privacy, but she longed for power and perhaps this was the only way to gain it. "There is always a cost." Roger had said that too. Her attention was forced away from the struggle in her own mind by what was happening to her hands. A strange warmth was passing through them, and she felt her client's muscles relax beneath her touch. 'I can do it,' she thought exultantly.

"I will need to see you regularly for a while," she said later, and when Mrs Babbington Brown produced her cheque-book, she named a daring figure for her evening's work.

"Thank you, I'm more than grateful," murmured Mrs Babbington Brown as she slid into her Saab.

'I don't need Roger,' thought Claire, closing her front door with a satisfied smile. 'I can manage on my own.' But as she went to bed, someone walked upstairs behind her. She looked over her shoulder, but of course there was nobody there.

SATURDAY OCTOBER 26TH

8am

"Heaven will be like this, Gwyllum," whispered Emmie as she stood gazing across the park. The early morning light certainly lent the scene an unearthly quality and down in the valley a fluffy white shroud of mist covered the lake. The sun was rising behind her and catching the tops of the beech trees on the hill, burnishing their autumn colours until she had to bite her lip with sheer joy.

The park railings were festooned with cobwebs. Emmie had always hated spiders, but as the sun touched the dew on their fragile threads, each tiny drop twinkled at her. 'Just like deceptive diamonds,' she told herself.

"I can't think why everyone stays in bed on a morning like this, Gwyllum, but I'm glad they do, so we can have it all to ourselves."

Gwyllum did not enjoy looking at views, he preferred to explore them, and he raced away down the hill leaving a trail of footprints across the sparkling grass. As Emmie followed him she wished there was some way of freezing mornings like this – to preserve them for ever.

At last they reached one of her favourite spots – a tiny peninsula jutting out into the lake, covered with Scotch firs. They always reminded Emmie of little girls clinging together, afraid to get their feet wet.

Much to Gwyllum's disgust she sat down with her back against a pink trunk to watch a heron fishing earnestly in the shallows. She had always enjoyed beauty, but since her spirit had come alive, it seemed as if her body and mind experienced everything with a greater intensity.

Yes, life seemed very good. During the last few days two firms had given her briefs and MacDillan's had been so delighted with the children's book they had asked her to illustrate another on seashore creatures. The new business venture looked as if it was actually going to work.

As she sat there, positively basking in happiness, she gradually became aware that another human being was sharing her private world. She could hardly be nervous with Gwyllum sprawled on the pine-needles beside her, she merely felt annoyed.

As she looked round, she saw someone sitting on the far side of the peninsular. The 'intruder' was Richard. He was gazing down the length of the misty lake, and she could read grief in every curve of his body and line of his face. Beside him stood a stroller containing his small daughter wrapped like a cocoon against the chilly dampness of the morning.

Emmie remained motionless, considering how best to escape without attracting his attention. It would be unthinkable to intrude on his misery, particularly when she was feeling so happy herself. It was unusual to see him looking like that. Most of the time he seemed so cheerful and he had a way of throwing back his head and laughing — like a small boy delighted with a new joke. Yet she was beginning to recognise a different, sadder side to the vicar and she dreaded the evenings when he came to play Rosie's piano. She could hear the muffled music rising through the floor-boards, and felt the anguish which poured out through his fingers. She usually found herself wishing he would take his melancholia somewhere else.

Stealthily she began to creep back towards the path, but Gwyllum was not so reserved. He bounded towards Richard, recognising a friend. Unlike his mistress he always dashed downstairs to listen to Richard playing Chopin.

"He likes music," Rosie would always say, "you can tell by his eyes."

"Gwyllum, come back!" whispered Emmie urgently, but it was too late. Richard looked round and the wintry expression was banished by his smile.

"Hello," he said, untangling his lengthy legs and banging his head on an overhanging branch as he stood up. 'It must be tricky being that tall,' thought Emmie.

"I didn't mean to disturb you," she said shyly.

"Sometimes it's good to be disturbed." He was making a valiant effort to banish his gloom. "Jess and I both woke up early, so we came out to give my mother some peace. Isn't it all lovely? Somehow it's a comfort just sitting and looking."

"Yes, I love every inch of this park," agreed Emmie, and wished her voice did not always sound so odd and jerky when she tried to communicate with other people.

"If you're going to walk Gwyllum, do you mind if we join you?" he asked. Emmie *did* mind, she much preferred to walk alone, but it would have sounded rude to say so.

"I hear from Rosie that the book has been accepted by MacDillan's," he said as they started up the path. "She showed me their letter. The paper almost smouldered with the warmth of their comments."

"Oh well, that must be because I've got a friend working there," said Emmie blushing.

"I hear they want to make a big publicity thing out of it," he brushed away her modesty with a wave of his gigantic hand.

ELDERLY AUTHOR IN CRUMBLING RUIN, DISCOVERED BY YOUNG ARTIST

"What a headline! That should get you on the TV chat-shows, surely?"

"I'm afraid Rosie got a bit carried away when MacDillan's publicity man came down the other day."

"But surely a bit of media interest won't do your new business partnership any harm."

"They want Rosie to write a sequel," said Emmie, "and she's already working on it, bless her. Fancy embarking on a new career at ninety-four!"

"She tells me she owes all that to you," Richard smiled down at her from his lofty height. "She never stops telling me how much you've done for her, Emmie."

"She's done infinitely more for me. She's helped me discover my faith. I've been searching for so long you know. I used to call it my spiritual quest." She stopped, suddenly feeling very silly, but like Kim before her, she discovered that Richard had a way of looking so interested it made it easy to talk to him. "I'm only fumbling my way along still," she continued shyly, "but I just feel knocked out by the fact that God actually loves me!"

"Yes," he said quietly. "I don't know how I would have managed these last few months if I hadn't been sure of that." He cleared his throat and went on quickly, "I was hoping to start some discussion groups at St Mark's this autumn, but I seem to have trodden on so many corns recently, I think I'd better lie low for a while." Emmie smiled.

"Yes, I heard from Kim that Alison Grazier is getting up a petition against you for the bishop!"

"Poor old Alison," sighed Richard, "I'm sure my wife would have been able to charm her — and the organist, too!"

"It must be hard coping without her," said Emmie softly, and then felt furious with herself for being so personal. 'I really am useless at conversation,' she thought, and Richard's silence only added to her discomfort.

"It's a year ago today that she . . ." When he finally spoke his voice cracked suspiciously and by this time Emmie was so embarrassed she wished she could run away. Then she remembered how he had stayed quietly beside her that day in church when she had felt so utterly wretched. Just the fact that he was there had comforted her, perhaps she could do the same for him by listening now.

"She was driving Pippa to Brownies," he continued. "They were late. Grace was always late for everything, bless her. Pippa was urging her on, and I think they must have been going too fast – but the other car was certainly driven by a maniac. There was absolutely no escape, the road had high banks. Grace must have realised it was going to be a head-on crash, so she slewed the wheel round to the left so she would take the full impact herself. Her body protected Pippa completely and she hardly had a scratch when they pulled her out, but . . . Grace . . . died instantly."

"She must have loved Pippa very much." The remark sounded fatuous to Emmie as soon as she had made it, but somehow it seemed to comfort Richard. He almost smiled.

"Yes, it is quite extraordinary – to love that much. You know, the way Grace died has really helped me to appreciate what Christ did for us on the cross." He blew his nose. "I am sorry," he said. "They say vicars aren't supposed to have feelings, but I don't seem to manage mine very well."

They were back at the park-gates by now, and he stood still, looking down at her apologetically.

"Thanks," he said huskily, and turning abruptly he walked away up the Terrace.

10

Emmie was hot in spite of the crisp morning air. 'Poor old Richard,' she kept thinking as she attacked the autumn leaves which had scattered themselves across the lawn. 'No wonder he takes it out on Rosie's piano.' She thought of the great gloomy vicarage at the end of the road and shuddered. 'But he's bound to marry again,' she told herself firmly. 'A man with a smile like that must have loads of girls running after him. He'll choose someone motherly who'll fatten him up on her nice home-made cakes.' With this comforting thought she tried to dismiss him from her mind.

She was soon so absorbed in her sweeping that it was quite a time before she became aware that someone was watching her from the garden gate. She would not allow herself to look round, she liked to feel she was invisible in her garden. When quiet footsteps began to approach over the grass behind her she felt annoyed. A large hand firmly took hold of the rake and pulled it out of her grasp. She swung round to confront Nigel. His smile was so broad she found herself having to return it.

"You did give me a fright," she said breathlessly, as he began to lunge at the golden leaves.

"Give me fright," he repeated.

"You want to help me?" she said.

"Want to help me," he beamed.

1pm

"Whatever am I going to do, Rosie?" said Emmie three hours later as they stood watching him from the kitchen door. "He's been a marvellous help all morning, but I can't take advantage of him like this."

"He has enjoyed himself hugely," replied Rosie. "I think we should reward him with a feast. Will you allow me to treat us all to one of those Chinese take-away meals you say are so nice?"

"Ask him in for lunch, you mean?" It never occurred to Emmie to have visitors.

"Why not? We need someone strong to help put the garden to bed for the winter. And like all human beings he needs to be needed."

3.30

The bright autumn sunshine did not seem to penetrate the front windows of Number Five. Ann lay on the sitting-room sofa and pulled the rug up to her chin. The sports programme flickered on the television screen but she was too tired even to watch.

The front door banged and Matt, lathered in sweat from his run, staggered into the room.

"Still laid out?" he gasped. "I hope you've done your exercises." On the coffee-table were piled numerous books on multiple sclerosis and Matt had read every single one of them meticulously. Pulling on his tracksuit he fetched a bottle of orange juice from the fridge and threw himself down in a chair.

"I just can't think why you sit about looking so sorry for yourself," he said. "This is the biggest challenge we've ever had."

"Not one of those books says there's a cure."

"We'll be the ones to discover it." Matt's eyes glistened with enthusiasm. "I'm convinced we can crack the disease by a blend of diet, rest and a carefully-planned exercise programme. There must be a way to train the mind to form new pathways through the nervous system and bypass damaged areas. When we've discovered the MS secret I'll write a book about it." Ann glanced at the heap on the coffee-table and felt there had been too many written already. "It's your attitude that's wrong," said Matt exasperated. "Come on, get up off your backside and start fighting this thing. You're in control of your body remember, your body's not in control of you." Ann rolled obediently off the sofa, and took up her position on the floor for the routine Matt had devised for her. She felt as if she was made of soft sponges, but she must make herself believe in him. Matt was always right. It was only this suffocating exhaustion which made fighting so hard.

5.30

The sunset looked magnificent behind the beech trees in the park. "If I painted all that glorious colour, people would think I was exaggerating," sighed Emmie.

They were standing in the garden by the bonfire which had taken Nigel all day to build. His face positively beamed with pride as the flames leapt and danced.

"There is nothing so therapeutic as a bonfire," said Rosie from her perch on an ancient stump.

"Or a whole day in the garden," put in Emmie. "This crumpet's nearly ready," she said, holding it out towards the blaze on the end of a long stick. Her cheeks were red with a combination of heat and happiness.

Kim looked round at all three of them and smiled – they looked so happy together. She and Rebecca had been delivering parish magazines when they had been called over to admire the fire. Nigel had insisted on rolling up a log to make a seat for her and covered it with his jacket.

It was always fun to escape along here for a few minutes while David coped at home, and Rebecca had been Rosie's devoted slave ever since September when they were models together. Rosie had the unusual quality of always appearing to be the same age as the person she was with at the time.

"This is great," said Kim as she tackled her rubbery crumpet. "The soot brings out the flavour!"

"Gwyllum would like one too," said Rosie.

"You can tell by his eyes, I suppose," said Emmie with a chuckle. "I thought I'd say it before you did this time, Rosie!"

"Well you can tell," protested Rosie. "He will also enjoy the fire in the drawing-room this evening. We are lighting it for the first time in years, Kim," she added happily. "Emmie and I are each in the middle of very good books – I only hope we shall stay awake to read them after all this fresh air." Kim smiled as she thought of the piles of ironing which awaited her at home. 'It's strange,' she thought, 'we all live in the same road, yet we operate at such a different pace.' She had forgotten what it felt like to spend a whole day doing what she liked and she hadn't opened a book in weeks. Every single five minutes counted as she hurtled through days of continuous activity. The nights were not much better – neither of the boys appeared to need sleep and Amy's asthma had been very bad recently.

"Sometimes I really envy you your single, child-free lives," she said wistfully.

"Two old maids living happily ever after," said Emmie and smiled as she went off to help Nigel collect another barrow-load of burnable rubbish from Rosie's garden shed.

"She's so different these days," said Kim. "When I think of how strained and nervous she used to be, it hardly seems possible."

Rosie nodded. "Yes," she said softly, "it has been most enjoyable observing a miracle."

"She's come alive on the inside somehow, hasn't she?" continued Kim, thoughtfully. "That's happening to me, too, at the moment. You know, before Richard came to St Mark's I'd just about given up my faith altogether. All the same, Emmie does make me feel a bit left behind," she added ruefully. "I suppose that's because she has time to wander round the park praying for hours while I have to make do with chatting to the Almighty while I clean the bath!"

"Don't be so hard on yourself, dear. Emmie is a true contemplative, but you are a woman of action – God needs both kinds." She accepted the crumpet Rebecca had toasted for her and continued, "It would be very dull for Him if we were all exactly the same."

"I suppose you're right," said Kim and smiled as Nigel and Emmie came staggering back round the corner with the barrow piled high.

"We should have saved that stuff to burn at Guy Fawkes," said Rebecca sadly.

"We'll have another fire then," said Emmie.

"Another fire then!" repeated Nigel happily. He had soot all over his face from the many crumpets he had devoured and his smile was almost as warm as the fire itself.

"How is that poor girl who lives opposite you, Kim – the one who has developed multiple sclerosis?" asked Rosie.

The smile died away from Kim's face. "It's so sad," she said. "Ann was always bouncing with health when we worked together. Being fit matters so much to her." Suddenly she remembered the expression of longing on Ann's face as she had looked at the baby that day in the doctor's surgery. 'And I've got *four* children,' she thought guiltily. 'And I really love being a mother in spite of all the hard work. I ought to be shot at dawn for grumbling!' Out loud she said, "I keep popping over to see her, but she won't open the door to anyone."

"She probably needs space," said Emmie with feeling. Kim looked at her in amazement – she found Emmie so difficult to understand sometimes.

"If something like that happened to me, I'd need clouds of support from all directions. We can't just leave her stuck in there alone, she must think we don't even care. I've asked Richard to go and see her. I'm sure they'll let *him* in."

"Excuse me," said an irate voice from the dusk behind them. They all turned from the warmth of the fire and encountered Alison, muffled in a grey scarf and looking cold.

"The smoke from your fire is blowing right into my house," she said accusingly. "It's most inconsiderate."

"Would you like a crumpet, Mrs Grazier?" asked Rebecca. Alison ignored her. "Can I have a word with you, Miss Dawson, in private?" Emmie followed her reluctantly towards the gate.

"I couldn't help noticing the way you are befriending

that boy Nigel," she began. "I think it's only right to offer you a word of warning."

"Oh?" said Emmie coolly.

"It's best not to get too involved with these handicapped people. It might not be safe . . . when you're on your own."

"I believe we're all handicapped in this road, by something or someone." Emmie's voice shared the nip that was in the autumn air. "I think Nigel is less handicapped than most of the rest of us."

"And that girl's actually asked to be confirmed!" snorted Alison when she reached the safety of her kitchen. Gordon hid behind his newspaper, but she continued, "At least our Amanda hasn't got a head full of silly ideas like that."

6.30

Richard walked down Laburnum Terrace feeling miserable. He was always painfully shy when it came to visiting. He took a deep breath, murmured a fervent prayer and pushed open the garden gate of Number Five.

Matt answered the door in his dressing-gown, his hair still wet from his shower. He was not pleased to see a visitor on his doorstep, particularly one in a dog-collar.

"Yes?"

"I wondered if I might see your wife for a few moments."

"I don't think she wants to see anyone – always says she's too tired." Matt sounded exasperated. "Ann," he shouted over his shoulder, "do you feel like a visit from the vicar?"

"No," was the flat reply from the front room.

"See what I mean?" shrugged Matt.

"I was just wondering if there were any little practical things the church could do to help make things easier?

Shopping, cooking, that kind of thing?" Matt glared at him.

"We're managing perfectly all right on our own, thanks."

"And tell him he can stop his prayer-meeting gossiping about me," shouted Ann.

"Oh-oh," murmured Richard miserably as the door shut in his face. Claire was just coming out of the house next-door with Boris and she smiled. 'Serves him right for interfering,' she thought grimly. Kim had also watched the scene as she and Rebecca walked Nigel home to Number Three. When Richard turned round she noticed his face in the streetlights and she stopped and gave his hand an impulsive squeeze.

"It must be terribly hard, sometimes, being a vicar," she whispered.

SUNDAY OCTOBER 27TH

4.30pm

"Evenings are closing in now," remarked Gordon. "Still, it's cosy enough in here," he added as he puffed at his pipe. "That old heater soon gets up a jolly good fug."

Clancy could not hear him. Her ears were filled with the earphones of her cassette player and she had the volume turned up full. Gordon smiled at her affectionately; she was enjoying that tape she'd wheedled out of him yesterday. He loved treating her to the little things she fancied. Alison would be horrified, of course, if she ever discovered how much money he was spending on her sweets, magazines and music.

They had tacitly agreed to allow Alison to think she spent her free time with her cross-eyed friend Tracy. Alison had not objected to the thought of Clancy digging beside Gordon in the summer, but it would never do for her to discover what a haven the shed had become. The camping-lamp spluttered companionably and Gordon helped himself to another beer. Pity they'd soon have to go home and face Sunday tea.

On the wall above his head was pinned the front page of the local paper, dated September 13th. Clancy liked to look at Gordon's picture proudly displaying his prize-winning vegetables and holding the silver cup for 'going best in show'. The face of the runner-up was somewhat blurred, but George's expression of fury was satisfying to imagine.

"I wonder if he really will get even with you like he said," asked Clancy, pulling off her earphones.

"Who?" asked Gordon blankly.

"That horrible George man."

Gordon shifted uneasily in his deckchair. There seemed so many worrying things on his mind these days. George's threats were at the bottom of the heap.

Alison was making everyone's life a misery over this new vicar. She seldom stopped talking about him these days.

"I do so dislike the way he prays," she had said at breakfast only that morning. "It's not reverent to talk to God as if he lived next-door. And fancy making people laugh like that when he preaches." However, the vicar's worst crime seemed to be the introduction of modern hymns and songs.

"They mightn't be quite so bad if he didn't encourage the young people to accompany them with their guitars."

"I think he's trying to make the services more fun," Gordon had ventured.

"Services aren't supposed to be fun." The very idea had put Alison clean off her apple-pie. "I can't find any mention of guitars in *my* Bible."

"I don't think the Bible mentions organs either." He had regretted that remark almost at once. It wasn't worth arguing with Alison, not when her best friend was the organist.

"The bishop ought to do something," she had said. "He's attracting crowds of most undesirable people; and don't you say the church council ought to be pleased to see the pews filled at last. St Mark's has always prided itself on being the most respectable church in Welbridge."

'And the dullest,' Gordon had told himself.

"Do you know what happened when I arrived for the service last Sunday evening? Three . . . creatures . . . with spiked hair were sitting in *my* regular pew. I had to speak quite sharply to them before they would move."

She had a way of tucking in her chin and pursing her

208

lips which made Gordon fear the intensity of his own irritation. Perhaps these constant tirades would not have upset him if he had not become secretly rather fond of the Reverend Richard Reynolds.

Of course, this morning had changed all that. He shuddered at the memory and looked across at Clancy deep in her glossy magazine.

As usual she had been sitting in the pew beside him. He loved the trusting way she snuggled up close. She made him forget he was only five foot three, bald and fifty; she made him feel big and protective.

The sermon began and, as usual, he began to slide off into his fantasy world – but this morning, for some reason, the vicar's words would keep penetrating his concentration.

"We pride ourselves on being upright members of this church. Yet it says here in Matthew five that simply to *imagine* ourselves committing adultery or killing someone is as bad in God's eyes as the actual sin. Many of us live secret inner lives which no one knows anything about, yet God sees everything that goes on in our minds."

Gordon had winced and turned up the collar of his brown raincoat. He had always seen the Creator as a mixture of his mother and Alison, both of whom saw it as their life's mission to crush him. Since this new man had arrived he'd begun to hope that perhaps he had been mistaken – God did not altogether despise him, but his hopes had been damned by those words.

The vicar had gone on to say something about a thought not being a sin unless we welcome it, but living with Alison forced him to indulge in so many bizarre thoughts he did not feel reassured in the slightest. In fact, he had begun to be angry. This young chap was going too far. Alison said his ideas were heretical – perhaps she was right. After all she *was* on the church council.

Gordon was often angry under his acquiescent surface, but just for once, instead of smothering his feelings, he allowed them to goad him into action. He'd have a few

209

words with the fellow, he told himself. Take him down a peg or two.

Now that so many people were thronging St Mark's it was hard to get a word alone with the vicar as he shook hands at the door. However, Alison's irate conversation with the organist was so lengthy, that Gordon was able to hang around long enough to gain his private interview.

"I didn't think much of the sermon this morning, Vicar," he began, trying to sound like Alison. "Your standards are just too high. If God judges us for our thoughts there's no hope for any of us." 'Not even Alison,' he added under his breath.

The young man had looked suitably upset, and even tried to say something about the crucifixion being the answer to all the things we're ashamed of, but he hadn't waited to listen.

'I'm *not* ashamed of just thinking,' he had argued with himself as he hurried home across Bakers Hill. 'I never *do* anything wrong, so I'm not hurting anyone.'

"Did Amanda come up here to your shed, when she was little?" Clancy's voice jerked Gordon back to the present and he jumped nervously.

"Never been up here in her life," he replied. "She's Alison's daughter."

"You mean you're not her dad?" asked Clancy, sounding mildly interested.

"Course I am, what I mean is, Auntie Alison can't share her. She's worshipped Amanda ever since the day she was born – reckons the sun rises and sets on her alone."

"Well, she's not the angel she looks," said Clancy with satisfaction. "She's picked up a fella. Goes to pubs with him every evening."

"Amanda would never go into a pub," said Gordon horrified, "she isn't old enough."

Clancy had been waiting for months to see the smug Amanda shot down, but it had been Sharon, the Sherlock Holmes of Laburnum Terrace, who had provided the ammunition.

210

"Sharon says her dad's often seen them."

"Why doesn't she bring him home? We wouldn't object to a nice steady young man." Gordon was looking perplexed now.

"She'd never let Auntie Alison see this one." Clancy giggled; she was enjoying herself. "He's got long tangled-up hair and a stubbly face and he wears jumble-sale clothes – all dirty. Sharon's dad says he's a junkie."

"Are you sure about all this?" Gordon wondered if it could be some kind of a nightmare.

"Sharon's seen him, too. Where do you suppose Amanda goes of an evening and at weekends?" she added triumphantly.

"Round to Alexia's house, of course," answered Gordon. "They help each other with their homework."

"She's no more there than I'm at Tracy's, but of course that stuck-up Alexia would swear blind she was if you tackled her, so would the crazy au pair. Amanda's a right crafty one."

Gordon did not know whether to be more upset by his daughter's deception or Clancy's startling transformation from innocence to a woman of the world.

"I don't like you talking like that," he said stiffly.

"You learn all kinds of things living at the Charbury estate," said Clancy.

"You never talk about how it was up there." Gordon badly needed to change the subject, and he also realised there was a lot about Clancy that he simply did not know.

"I liked it until I was fourteen, then *he* came along – Kevin I mean. Mum worked at the pub and I had the place to myself. Then Mum started going with Kevin and when she got pregnant he moved in. I hated him." Clancy's small pussy-cat face clouded at the memory and Gordon's heart lurched in sympathy. "Always drinking, shouting, hitting. When Mum had the baby I was expected to mind it all evening 'cos she still kept on her job. Kevin wouldn't lift a finger. It bawled and bawled, I couldn't stand it there after that."

211

"I'm sorry," Gordon's voice croaked with emotion.
"That's why I like living with you," she added artlessly
as she curled up like a warm kitten on his lap.

"Was it when your mum was out working that he . . .
interfered with you?" Gordon stopped as Clancy looked
up into his face sharply.

"I'm not talking about any of that – ever," she said.
It would never do for him to know how cleverly she had
extricated herself from her home, it suited her very nicely
to have Gordon thinking she was just a sweet little girl.

WEDNESDAY NOVEMBER 6TH

9pm

Emmie sat curled in her armchair trying to read. Outside, the November fog hung like a damp blanket over the Terrace, muffling the streetlamps and smothering the chimney-pots. She had worked hard all day in her studio next-door and now she was tired. Below, in the drawing-room, Richard was positively punishing Rosie's piano as his huge hands crashed out chords from the more savage of Beethoven's sonatas. It was anger and not misery that was pouring from his soul that night. Earlier in the evening a deputation of some of the more long-standing members of St Mark's had faced him over his study desk. They could not have looked more threatening if they had been carrying machine-guns.

"We don't like these new services," Alison, who was their spokeswoman, had said. "They're bringing so many new people to St Mark's we don't know who half of them are! And as for these new family communions – they're going to have to stop."

"But why?" he had protested. "It's lovely to see so many children enjoying themselves."

"Well, for one thing they make so much noise and, besides, it's obvious you don't have to clean the church on a Monday! The pews are covered in sticky fingermarks."

How he had missed Grace. She would have had them eating home-made shortbread out of her hand.

"Surely we ought to be pleased that we are having a wider appeal in the community." He had been in serious danger of losing his temper by then.

"If people want that kind of thing they can go elsewhere," Alison had replied. "St Mark's is *our* church."

He had managed to show them all out before he exploded, but Alison's parting shot on the doorstep had almost proved too much for him.

"We on the church council intend to do something about you." He played a final cadence with such force the whole piano vibrated. The anger was dissipated at last, but it left him feeling empty inside. As he sat there motionless, this vacuum began to fill with the all too familiar black fluid called grief. He must fight it! Be positive. Think of something for which he could thank God.

Yes, he was grateful for this room and the freedom of this house. His mother did her best, but she would peck at him continuously like an agitated little sparrow. Rosie always met him at the door, showed him into the drawing-room and then went to bed. He could stay here undisturbed for as long as he liked; privacy was a priceless gift, but he didn't want to be here on his own, he wanted Grace.

Hastily he began to shuffle through the music on the stand; he must force himself to go on playing. It was the only way he could survive the evening.

As the more sombre music began to float upstairs Emmie finally threw down her book. It was unnerving, having to overhear pain like this. She went down and tapped on Rosie's bedroom door.

"I fancy some hot chocolate. Would you like some, too?" she whispered as she popped her head inside. Ten minutes later she was sitting by Rosie's bed with a tray containing two mugs and a plate of biscuits.

"A midnight feast," said Rosie, but she glanced anxiously up at Emmie. Something had been troubling her recently.

"Richard's really going through the mill in there tonight, isn't he?" sighed Emmie uneasily. "Makes me feel low, too. Rosie, would you mind if I asked you something?"

'I rather hoped you might,' thought Rosie, but she did not say it.

"The Saturday before last, I met him in the park and he told me about his wife's accident. Ever since I've had this nasty feeling. Rosie, I'm scared my faith just wouldn't be strong enough to cope with a tragedy like that. Has yours ever wobbled?"

Rosie disliked talking about personal things, but she knew this must be important to Emmie because direct questions were not a usual part of their relationship.

"I was going to be married once," she said slowly. "Just before the wedding he was killed in a climbing accident and for several years I simply could not go to church at all. It seemed impossible for a God of love to allow the life of such a remarkable man to be lost. Then the war came and everyone else seemed to be suffering as well. I was sitting here in this very room one night, during an air-raid. I ought to have gone out to the shelter in the garden, but preserving myself seemed rather pointless just then.

"I put off the lights and opened the blackouts. I could see fires all round the park and the bombs were falling so unfairly on Welbridge, hitting some houses and missing others. I suddenly realised that if this life was all we had, then it would be grossly unfair. Some people suffer so much, others seem to get off almost scot-free. My dear, I am sorry, I'm finding all this very hard to put into words – it meant so much to me at the time."

"Please try, Rosie, I must sort this out."

"Well, as I stood by the window, I suddenly knew that the whole crux of the Christian faith is that life on this planet is not our only existence, just a brief prelude. Over the years since, I have come to realise that Christ warned us we should have trouble in this life, but He promised He had prepared a permanent home for us where we can be happy with Him for ever."

"Yes, but Rosie, just listen to Richard in there. However short this life may be, it can still hurt horribly. Why does God allow that?"

"I've lived for nearly a century, and I still do not know the answer to that. Perhaps none of us ever will – in this life anyway. However, I do know God made the world perfect, but human beings chose to spoil it and that is what brought suffering into the universe."

"Yes, but how can God just stand by and watch?"

"But he does not just 'stand by', dear. He cares intensely. He loves us so much that He was willing to become human himself and suffer too.

"The thing which helped me *most* that night was realising Christ had gone right through His suffering, so He knew exactly how I was feeling, but He came out safely on the far side. That is what gave me back my hope."

"Richard said something a bit like that had helped him, too," said Emmie softly.

"Listen, dear, he's playing me my favourite hymn. He always finishes the evening like that."

'Well, at least he's finishing,' thought Emmie, relieved. In the next room, Richard was singing the words of Rosie's hymn quietly to himself as he played:

> Jesus lover of my soul
> Let me to thy bosom fly . . .
> Hide me, oh my saviour hide,
> Till the storms of life be past . . .

All at once, he was no longer performing for Rosie, these words were for him. He was thinking of a letter which had arrived on the day of Grace's funeral. It had read:

> There is no getting over grief. You have to get into it, but there waiting for you in the very centre you will discover the Man of Sorrows himself.

When he finally walked home up the Terrace, he actually found he was humming.

216

THURSDAY DECEMBER 12TH

8pm

"We are interrupting our programmes with an urgent news flash. Severe gales, with winds up to force ten, are hitting the South of England . . ."

"We don't need you to tell us that!" growled Tom Savery, glaring at the face on the TV screen which had disrupted his film.

"The police are urging people to stay indoors . . ."

"Come on back in here, young Sharon," he shouted.

"But, Dad," she protested from the front doorstep. "I don't want to miss all the fun!"

The wind was hurling itself across the park, flinging trees to the ground and ripping the flimsy roof from the park-keeper's shed. Slates whirled around Laburnum Terrace like boomerangs and the bus shelter on Bakers Hill did a belly-roll right over the laurel hedge on to the vicarage lawn.

"It's God's judgment on a wicked town," said Alison with satisfaction.

"The rain's supposed to fall on the righteous as well as the ungodly," said Gordon. "So you'd better watch out yourself."

"At least Amanda's safely at Alexia's house," continued Alison, ignoring his silly remark. "She'll probably ring and say she's going to stay the night, she often seems to do that these days." Gordon glanced furtively at Clancy and thought that she winked at him.

8.15

Emmie sat hunched miserably over her drawing-board surrounded by pictures of shells, crabs and starfish. She needed to work late – the deadline for her seashore book was only a week away – but every time she heard a crash out there in the darkness, she winced. She knew every tree in the park intimately and she felt as if old friends were dying violent deaths which no power could prevent.

Downstairs Rosie lay listening to Richard playing the piano through the wall. Far from being alarmed by the storm she was actually smiling.

"He's getting over it at last," she told herself. There had definitely been a new lightness about Richard's playing during the last five weeks. She closed her eyes, and continued to pray for him.

Number Fifteen, on the opposite side of the road, was lit by only one table-lamp. The house had an empty, dead feeling about it. Graham was slumped in an armchair with a half-empty bottle of whisky beside him. Of course it was stupid to drink that much on an empty stomach, he knew that, but what else was he supposed to do, when life was so intolerable?

He had arrived home an hour ago, tired, cold and wet, only to be greeted by a brisk note from Hazel.

"Back about ten, dig yourself something from the freezer." What sort of a life was this, he asked himself as he poured another lavish dose of Scotch? Where was it she'd said she was going today? Lecturing at Sussex University?

On his lap, and over the floor at his feet lay estate agents' particulars. They had been scouring the countryside for weeks, but the final choice was proving awkward because they both wanted something so different. He picked up a sheet headed "The Willows", and studied the photo closely. This was his first choice. "Modern single-storey residence commanding magnificent views." But, oh no,

218

Hazel wanted Gresham Manor – large, pretentious and hopelessly costly to run. Graham sighed. Why couldn't they just stay here, and save all the hassle?

"Hazel ought to settle down and enjoy what she's got – stop chasing the moon." He spoke out loud and wondered why his voice sounded so strange. This new job wasn't doing her any good at all – must be too much for her. He'd discovered a bottle of tranquillisers in the bathroom cabinet. How much longer was this blasted lecture going to take?

8.30

The wind and rain shook Hazel's BMW as if it had been an old tin can and she swore at it viciously. She was lost and she might as well admit it. She should never have tried Graham's famous shortcut. This ruddy lane seemed to be taking her down into a deep valley and its high banks gave her claustrophobia. At the very bottom lay an old millpond, but tonight its traditionally calm water was chopped and churned by the wind.

"Haven't they heard of signposts in these parts yet?" she fumed. Three lanes led away from the pond, but which one would take her home? The place had an ancient, brooding atmosphere which was alien to her scientific world.

A man was standing outside an old cottage. He wore a sack over his head and he reminded Hazel of a garden gnome as she pressed the button which lowered her window.

"Which way to Welbridge?" she bawled into the teeth of the gale. Roger turned and looked at her.

"The middle lane," he said. "But, my dear, I must warn you, you are in grave danger, the road runs through woodland at the top of the hill."

"Well there's not a lot I can do about that," she replied crossly.

219

"You are welcome to stay in my cottage."

"No thanks!" She hurriedly raised her window. 'Dirty old man,' she thought as she drove up the hill. All the same, the incident had ruffled her. Something about his voice reminded her oddly of Claire.

She snapped on Radio Four and heard a blind woman describing her childbirth experiences. Hazel swore and changed channels hastily. This was the week when her own baby would have been born and she did not wish to be reminded of that.

The full ferocity of the wind lashed her when she reached the top of the hill, and there ahead were those wretched woods. Great beech trees towered on either side of her like angry giants in a battle. Through the streaming windscreen she could see their branches slashing and lunging at one another while their trunks swayed and shuddered in agony. With a crash she could hear even above the roar of the wind, the huge limb of a wounded tree blew across the road ahead of her. She swerved to avoid it, skidded round in a haemorrhage of mud from the bank and finally stopped.

"That was close!" she gasped and swore loudly. What had that odd little man said, "My dear, I must warn you, you are in grave danger . . ." Had his words held some kind of sinister threat? She dismissed the silly notion from her mind. Now the road was blocked, she would have to go back and find another way to Welbridge through more open country. As she slammed into gear she saw the great beech begin to move and she froze. It lent heavily towards the road, ripping apart the earth at its feet. She sat watching mesmerised as it crashed past its companions, wrenching at their branches as it fell. When the great corpse finally came to rest across the road, it lay just short of the hood of her car and she realised she was trapped.

Hazel, who had spent her life trying to control everything and everyone in her environment, had never felt quite so helpless.

"I must get out of here – fast," she said, fumbling for the door handle. Then she realised she would be in far more danger outside the car, and anyway there was nowhere to run for help, except back down to that odd little man at the mill. "No way!" She would just have to sit and wait for the police to come to the rescue, but in the meantime how many more trees were likely to fall? The thought made her shiver and she fumbled in the glove compartment in search of a packet of cigarettes. She'd managed to give up, but fortunately Graham had not – there were even some matches. Her hand was shaking ridiculously as she opened the box. Suppose that tree had fallen in her direction? She had performed post-mortems on crushed skulls, but the idea of someone doing one on hers was not pleasant. What an odd thing death was. You spent your life working and striving, and then suddenly . . . curtains! She gripped the steering-wheel as she wondered what Graham would do if she were dead. Probably he would be relieved. He could marry a dull little woman like Jane Macdermott and have his precious son. The son who might have been born today. Someone else would take over her department and in a few months people wouldn't even remember her name. "What a pointless waste of effort life is," she muttered as she lit a second cigarette from the stub end of the first. Did it make any real difference whether you died before you were even born, or laboured on through a lifetime, sweating, straining, striving? Death came to everyone in the end whatever they had or had not achieved. So why bother?

"Shut up!" said Hazel suddenly. She had always seen herself as two distinct people, the one others admired and the shrinking, vulnerable little person tucked away behind the mask. If she was not careful this weak side of herself was going to take over.

"That's quite enough from you!" She sounded as if she were addressing squeamish medical students. "Most women who have terminations feel depressed afterwards, it's purely hormonal. Think positively, Hazel Tilson. The tree didn't fall on you, you're probably only halfway through your life and the best is yet to come."

221

A strange tranquillity settled upon Hazel as she sat there smoking. Outside the wind raged unabated, but the car formed a cocoon in which she could stop and think for the first time in months.

She was on to her fourth cigarette when she realised why she had been feeling so depressed since she swung the new job. It wasn't the termination at all. ''Your trouble is you don't have a goal to aim at any more,'' she told herself. Yes, that was it. Why had she been stupid enough to think a department of Welbridge General was the top of the world? She must start 'hacking' towards a London hospital appointment. ''Take life in both hands, Hazel Tilson,'' she told herself, ''and shake it into submission. Get yourself out of that stuffy little ghetto of a terrace. Make an offer on Gresham Manor in the morning. Damn Graham and his endless procrastinations!'' She tossed the butt of her cigarette out of the window and twisted the ignition key. You only had one life and it wasn't a waste if you knew where you wanted to go.

With new determination she swung the car round and used the power of its engine to shunt out of her path the branch which had fallen first. Then she put her foot down hard against the carpet and drove towards Welbridge.

8.45

Back in Laburnum Terrace David Patterson was sitting on the sofa by a roaring fire, surrounded by piles of exercise-books. Kim was ironing. The softly-lit room made her feel safe and protected, while beyond her front door the wind played havoc with the town.

''It's nearly Christmas,'' she remarked. ''Wherever has this year gone? I was listening to you reading *The Lion, the Witch and the Wardrobe* to the girls this evening. You know, where it says, it was 'always winter but never Christmas'.'' David did not look up, she always talked when he wanted to concentrate, so he had trained himself not to hear her.

"That's how I was beginning to feel inside," she continued dreamily, "until Richard came to St Mark's. All frozen up and wintry. Now I feel I'm coming alive – like springtime. I actually look forward to going to church these days!" She switched off the iron, removed the exercise-books from the sofa and sat down very close to him. "You're not listening to a word I'm saying, but I love you all the same." David smiled and closed the book, for he might as well give up trying to work. Anyway, there was something he wanted to talk over with Kim.

"I'm worried about Jasmine," he began, as he put his arm round her shoulders. She frowned thoughtfully.

"I know what you mean," she said slowly. "She was looking so much better in the summer, but now she's got that wispy furtive look back again."

"She's frightened," said David thoughtfully. "When I'd finished reading to them this evening she told me a tale about feeling there was someone upstairs in her mother's bedroom. Someone evil whom no one can see. All imaginary of course, but Jasmine is usually such a truthful child."

"Perhaps she's trying to get attention. Hoped you might start a ghost hunt, perhaps. It's your own fault for reading her stories about witches in wardrobes."

"She told me she thinks Claire's a witch."

"Well there you are, kids'll say anything for attention. Claire's a funny old stick, with all her ideas about food and Old Mother Earth, but she's only an ordinary hairdresser really."

"I don't know," said David slowly. "All those people who've started visiting her in the evenings recently, why do you suppose they come?"

"To have their hair done, of course," said Kim, blankly. "Why else?"

"But why not go to the salon – it's only round the corner? Jasmine says they come to Claire for healing."

"Well, there's nothing wrong in that, surely," said Kim.

"Yes there is. There are lots of these so-called faith

healers about and they can land people in all kinds of psychological trouble, even lead them into the occult."

"Come on, David!" laughed Kim. "All that kind of thing's faked."

"It's not, you know. Look, if God gives His servants the power to heal in order to help people to believe in His power, then Satan's bound to try and do the same thing."

"But David, you don't really think Claire . . . not in Laburnum Terrace of all places?" He said nothing. For some reason he was remembering the little waves sliding over the mud flats at Camber. Jasmine had been his responsibility ever since. But however was he going to help her with something like this?

9

Graham Tilson was sound asleep in his chair when the crash woke him. The whole house seemed to rattle on its foundations. For a moment he could not think where he was. Someone was hammering on the front door. He didn't want visitors, he told himself, as he staggered out into the hall. He must look a mess with his shirt undone and his tie hanging loose. And of all people it had to be the vicar! Odd time to call, probably wanted money – they usually did.

"I saw it fall, I was over at Number Sixteen," said Richard. "Is anyone hurt up there?"

"Up where?" said Graham stupidly. "Been ashleep ol' boy."

"You've got a great big plane tree through your roof."

Just then the whole of Welbridge was sentenced to darkness.

"Power cut," said Richard. "Got a flashlight?" Graham hadn't, but he did remember the candles on the dining-room table. His cigarette-lighter shook about in the oddest way as he tried to light them.

224

"We'd better go up and see the damage," said Richard.
"The whole house could be in danger."

"Shouldn't shink so, ol' boy," said Graham and burped.
Richard was halfway upstairs already. The rooms where
Emmie had lived were filled with rubble and plaster-dust
and branches were sticking through the ceiling of her
sitting-room.

"How very odd," said Graham, blinking like an owl in
the gloom.

"I've got a large waterproof groundsheet at home," said
Richard. "I'll dash and get it. At least it'll save your carpets
and the ceilings underneath. Do you think you could ring
999 while I've gone?" Graham honestly meant to, but
somehow it slipped his mind.

9.05

Claire had not expected her client to come on such a
tempestuous evening. The appointment was for ten, and
just after the electricity failed she looked out at the storm
and wondered if it was worth bothering to go through her
preparation routine for him. She decided it was. He had
not been before and if he did manage to arrive she must
make a good impression.

As she lit the aromatic candles she recalled the last two
extraordinary months. Mrs Babbington Brown had proved
to be a most influential lady. Her voice echoed round every
coffee morning and drinks party in Welbridge.

"My dear, I've found an absolutely marvellous woman
– a healer, she's completely cured me and now she's
helping me lose masses of weight. You simply must try
her."

Her friends and acquaintances came hurrying to
Laburnum Terrace in their big, expensive cars and
suddenly Claire was fashionable. Her evenings had
become as fully booked as her days in the salon and they
were infinitely more profitable. If things went on like this

she would be able to afford a boarding-school for Jasmine in the new year. Life ahead looked good at last.

She began to think of Roger as she brewed the herbal tea. She had been deliberately vague about Mrs Babbington Brown and her followers because she did not want him to feel hurt as he slid into her past. 'He helped me through an identity crisis,' she thought, 'but I'm over that now, back on my own two feet, relying on myself again.' She brushed aside the memory of the shadow who stood behind her when she worked. He didn't count. It was not his power which healed people but *her* ability to harness his power.

She savoured the sweet taste of success as she sat down in her chair by the kitchen table and began to 'centre' herself. As she breathed deeply, she relaxed and, holding out her hands, she welcomed her spirit guide.

9.30

Someone was coming out of the front door as Hazel swung the BMW into the driveway. Whatever was the vicar doing here at this time of night?

"Ah I'm so glad you're home. I'm afraid your husband isn't too . . ."

"If he's boozing again I can't see it's any business of yours," snapped Hazel. She was far too shaken to take a lecture on temperance.

"No, of course it's not," said Richard apologetically. "It's just that your house has been damaged by the storm. A tree through the roof." Hazel almost bumped into Graham in the darkness of the hall.

"What's he on about?" she demanded.

"I rang 999 just now," continued Richard from behind her, "but they said they were inundated with calls of a similar nature. They suggest you sleep downstairs tonight. It might be safer."

"Hole in the roof," nodded Graham. "He's covered

everything up with blue stuff. Very good chap, been a great help.''

"That's obviously more than you've been!" spat Hazel. "I suppose you're too far gone to realise what this means. We won't be able to put the house on the market for months now, not till we've got the blasted roof rebuilt. We'll still be stuck in this dump at Easter!" She fumbled in her bag.

"Put this in your church fund," she said, handing a ten-pound note to Richard, as if he had been a taxi-driver.

He stood looking down at it, struggling with himself, then he looked at Hazel and smiled. "Thank you," he said gently. "But you know, Dr Tilson, money isn't everything."

"Isn't it?" said Hazel coldly. "You could have fooled me."

9.40

"Goodness, you look half drowned!" Kim was laughing as she opened the front door and illuminated Richard's face with a flashlight. "Come in and get warm."

"I'm most terribly sorry to call so late," he apologised, "but I saw your candles moving around and I remembered I needed to ask David something."

"This isn't the time of year to go swimming in the lake, you know," said Kim. "You look as if you could do with a hot chocolate. I've just managed to warm some milk on the embers of the fire. However did you get so wet and dirty?"

"The Tilsons at Number Fifteen copped a tree through their roof. I've been helping him mop up."

"I hope Emmie and Rosie are all right," said Kim anxiously.

"I checked and there are no big trees near enough to do them any damage. The vicarage is all right too, but we do seem to have acquired a bus shelter on our lawn!" He was trying valiantly to fold his extreme length into a bean-bag chair. When he was finally settled he added, "I really came to ask if you could organise the carol singing this year, David. It seems Alison usually does, but . . ."

"Say no more," smiled David. "I'd love to."

Kim came over and sat down in her rocking-chair. Richard looked dog-tired, but when something was on her mind, she could never manage to leave it there.

"We were just talking about our neighbour over the road," she said. "Her little girl thinks she's a witch, and she does seem to be into some kind of psychic healing business. Jasmine's frightened by a feeling of evil in the house." Richard looked startled. "Yes, it's ridiculous, I know," continued Kim with an unsteady laugh. "We're just prejudiced because she's into all this New Age stuff. I don't believe in it really."

"I do," said Richard. "The trouble with most Christians is that they don't realise the New Age is dangerous."

"But surely it's only lots of different organisations combining to stop the world from being polluted." Kim was looking worried.

"Yes it's that all right, but it's a whole lot more, and on the outside it looks great. They're beginning to work towards a single world-wide state which will enforce peace and fair deals for all through a universal monetary system. Individually, many New Agers are good people, trying to work for peace. They don't object to religion, but the one thing which characterises them all is their disregard for Christ as God and the reason for His cross. We Christians are just waking up to the fact that the powers of darkness are using this movement to work against us. They want to make Christ-centred religion seem old-fashioned. The church is in great danger, but we're so busy with our petty politics and squabbles we can't see what's coming to us."

"Well, Claire over the road isn't into high-powered stuff like that, she's simply out for number one."

"But that's the great doctrine of the New Age — self-fulfilment. In many ways it's more sinister than Com-

228

munism, because it's actually more appealing to the baser side of human nature.''

"You've left me behind I'm afraid,'' said Kim. "But what about Jasmine's fears about Claire being a witch?''

"The occult fringe of the New Age is becoming increasingly powerful.''

"Richard, your clothes are steaming,'' said Kim. "You must be wet to the skin.''

"You always change the subject when you're out of your depth,'' put in David.

"Well, I don't want to get mixed up in anything nasty like this,'' replied Kim.

"But we must fight the darkness,'' said Richard gently, "not sit in our churches feeling cosy.''

"So what are we supposed to do? Drown Claire in the lake as a witch?'' Kim was laughing to cover her uneasiness.

"We have only two weapons, but they are the most powerful in the world – love and prayer. I think the three of us should make a pact to pray for Jasmine and her mum.''

"But Richard, have a heart! Where am I going to find the time?'' He had to laugh at her horrified expression.

"I only meant we could shoot up a sentence every time we pass her house or the salon, and get together like this for a few minutes whenever we can.'' Kim relaxed.

"Well that's all right,'' she said, and David added his agreement with a smile.

10.30

At the precise moment when the three of them made their pact, Claire was also kneeling in her kitchen, while her hands gently caressed the feet of her new client. He was a young man who had sustained serious leg injuries in a helicopter crash. He had a wonderfully bright aura, and not only was he psychically receptive, but he was also extremely attractive. The unseen hands were over hers and she was floating in that vast expanse where there were no horizons.

"You feel pain in your feet," her voice seemed to come from a long distance, "but the trouble is really caused by trapped nerves in your ankles. We must concentrate on them."

Suddenly it was as if the hands had been forcibly pulled away from hers and she was dragged backwards into jagged reality. She paused, closed her eyes again and breathed very deeply. She must compose herself. But the power which had been flowing freely through her like an electric current had stopped abruptly as if it had been switched off at the mains. 'Concentrate,' she told herself, 'you're probably tired.' She tried to send her mind reaching out into space, searching for help. Yet somehow her thought-patterns seemed as if they were being jammed by some kind of interference. Was it the client's fault? He had seemed so co-operative at first. She tried again, but without the extra hands she knew it was useless.

"I'm sorry," she said at last, "I think that is as far as I can go tonight. Perhaps the storm is interfering with the atmospheric conditions." The client looked annoyed. "I'm terribly sorry," she continued, "you will forgive me, won't you?" Few men had ever been able to resist that particular expression on Claire's face.

"Perhaps I could stay a while and . . . talk?" he suggested.

Claire smiled. "That would be delightful," she said archly. "Give your wife a ring and tell her the roads are too dangerous to drive home tonight."

"Mummy, can I come down and stay with you?" came Jasmine's inevitable voice from the stairs. "I'm frightened."

'Typical,' thought Claire grimly. 'Boarding-school's the only answer.'

SUNDAY DECEMBER 2ND

10am

"Amanda? Come down, my sweetie, your breakfast is getting cold," called Alison. "I worry about that poor child," she continued as she made Amanda a nice fresh pot of tea. "She's been so stressed recently by these exams."

"She's changed a lot," admitted Gordon, "but I wouldn't say it's exams that bother her."

"All that make-up and the funny clothes she wears," said Alison with a vague wave of disapproval. "It's such a pity they don't insist on school uniform in the upper sixth. It's the other girls who are pressuring her, I'm sure of it."

"She ought to have left school in the summer," said Gordon doggedly. "All the teachers said she'd never pass her A-levels."

"They're completely wrong. It should be obvious to them that Amanda is a girl of outstanding ability. She'll prove it when the results come out. Just look how hard she works every evening round at Alexia's house."

Gordon swallowed his last mouthful of toast with difficulty. In his pocket the letter felt like lead. It had arrived several days ago, addressed to Mr and Mrs Grazier. It had the school's crest on the envelope so he had presumed it to be yet another bill, and opened it. Actually it had been written personally by the headmistress. Apparently Amanda was hardly ever at school these days, and seemed to be doing not one stroke of work. He had replied at once, of course, promising to "give the girl a jolly good telling-off". That was his honest intention. He knew as a father he ought to confront her face to face, but Amanda's face reminded him too forcibly of her mother's – and courage failed him.

His discreet enquiries had proved Clancy to be perfectly right. Amanda was spending all her spare time with a young man of no fixed address who had been in trouble with the police on more than one occasion. The barman at a run-down pub on the Charbury estate told Gordon he even suspected the lad of pushing drugs. 'Best leave well alone,' he had decided as he picked the Brussels sprouts from his allotment. 'She'll grow out of it in time.'

Outside in the Terrace, Christmas trees winked festively at each other from the front windows of the houses, and jagged frost sparkled from the tops of the garden walls. As Kim flew out of her gate, she nearly collided with Tom Savery's protruding stomach as he and Angela strolled along to buy their Sunday papers.

"Whatever would we all do without Macaulay's?" laughed Kim after they had exchanged seasonal greetings. "I've run right out of coffee this morning." When they all reached the shop door, they were confronted by the large poster which Richard had stuck there the previous day.

CAROLS BY CANDLELIGHT AT ST MARK'S CHURCH

"Are you coming tonight?" asked Kim. "We're taking all the kids – Sharon might enjoy it, too."

"Actually," said Angela hastily, "there are some rather good things on telly this evening, being near Christmas, you know."

"Another time perhaps," said Tom dismissively.

"Yes, of course," said Kim, smiling brightly to cover her embarrassment. "There's always another time."

* * *

"I'm quite sure Amanda won't want to miss church tonight," Alison was saying back at Number Thirteen. "The carol service was always her favourite – not of course that we'll be allowed to do it the traditional way this year." Her voice was heavy with sarcasm and her chin was tucked in tightly with disapproval. "That vicar's got a lot to answer for. At least I've informed the bishop." She made a few minute adjustments to Amanda's place at the table and added, "I think I'd better pop up and see if she's all right. I'll scoot young Clancy out of bed at the same time. That child's getting lazier every day."

Gordon sat gazing at nothing as he listened to Alison's feet pounding over the bedroom floor above his head. Then there was silence.

'Must be sitting on the bed chatting,' he thought bleakly as he poured himself a cup of tea from Amanda's freshly-made pot. Alison never chatted like that to him.

Clancy, her hair tousled with sleep, slid into the room. Gordon could not help thinking she looked unusually furtive.

"Auntie won't be long," he said, "she's just gone to find Amanda."

"She won't," said Clancy, stuffing her mouth full of cornflakes. "Won't find her, I mean. She's gone for good this time."

"What do you mean?" Gordon stood up so quickly his chair rocked on its back legs.

"She's left a note," continued Clancy. "I saw it on her bed just now. A man came for her about six this morning. I saw him out in the road."

Gordon ran halfway upstairs and then paused; Alison was blocking his way, looking down at him with a face as white as Amanda's old choir robe.

"She's gone," she said in a terrible voice.

"I know, Clancy told me."

"Clancy!" She nearly toppled him off balance as she thrust him from her descending path.

233

"You *knew* about this, Clancy?" Alison's voice was shrill.

"Known she was a bad 'un for months." Alison had never hit anyone in her life, although she had come close to it with the vicar on several occasions, but she slapped Clancy's cheek with a ferocity which surprised even herself.

"You horrible old cow," sobbed Clancy, running into Gordon's arms for protection. "It's not me that's bad."

"Amanda isn't bad!" shouted Alison. "She's been kidnapped."

"That's not what her note says," retorted Clancy. Alison made a grab at her, but found Gordon's meagre body in her way.

"And how long have *you* known about all this, Gordon?" she demanded, diverting her wrath on to him. His fingers tightened on Clancy's hand in a dumb appeal.

"I only told him a minute ago." Clancy's voice was muffled by the jacket of Gordon's Sunday suit.

"Well, don't just stand there encouraging the silly girl. Ring the police," said Alison with something resembling a sob in her voice.

"Let me see the note first," pleaded Gordon miserably. She handed it over without a word and then became unnecessarily busy in the larder. He read it through misty glasses.

I'm fed up with being the little social butterfly you've forced me to be. I've found a real man and we're leaving this dump of a town. Don't worry about me and don't look for me. I'll get in touch when I'm ready.

"She didn't even say 'Dear Mum,' or 'lots of love'," said a shaky voice from among the shelves of tinned fruit.

"It's no good ringing the police; she's nearly eighteen now, they wouldn't want to know." Gordon dis-entangled himself from Clancy and squeezed into the larder. "She'll come back, old girl," he said, putting a tentative hand on his wife's shoulder.

"When she's pregnant," said Alison bitterly.

"Or hooked on drugs," added Clancy tactlessly.

"After all the sacrifices I've made for her,"said Alison, sitting down in Amanda's place at the table and looking suddenly old. "When I think how I even took a part-time job to send her to that school." Gordon did not mention that *he* had earned most of the money, nor did he say, "I told you so." Alison looked so crushed he did not even think of saying it.

"You did your best for her, old girl," he said instead, and found he had his arm around her shoulder.

"I worshipped the ground she walked on," said Alison as the tears rolled slowly down her face. Gordon could never remember seeing her cry before. "How could she turn round and do this to me, when I loved her so much?"

'Perhaps you can love a person too much,' thought Gordon as he looked uneasily across the room at Clancy.

CHRISTMAS

Rosie opened her eyes slowly and smiled. Papa was playing carols on the piano; he always woke the household on Christmas morning like that. Slowly she realised Papa had been dead for sixty years, the music must be imaginary. She struggled up on her pillows, hampered by her stiff and painful joints as the nostalgic tears rolled down her wrinkled cheeks. Christmas allowed memories to escape which usually stayed tucked neatly away in their pigeon-holes.

The door opened and Emmie came in carrying a tea-tray decorated with sprigs of holly and ivy.

"Happy Christmas, Rosie darling," she said affectionately. "I've brought you tea in bed as a treat. Oh, but you mustn't cry," she added in dismay.

"I thought it was Papa next-door," said Rosie, embarrassed. "Foolish of me, but surely I can hear someone playing?"

"It's only my prezzy to you," replied Emmie. "It's a portable stereo. I've got lots of tapes, too, all the things you love – Mozart, Chopin and the *Moonlight Sonata*."

"My dear, you should not spoil me like this," said Rosie, but her smile was restored.

Rosie's present for Emmie was a set of such ravishing underwear that she could do nothing but sit and gaze. "However did you get hold of all this?" she demanded at last.

"Kim was my accomplice," admitted Rosie. "I could hardly entrust poor Mr Ponsonby with such a delicate task."

Emmie laughed and said, ''Will you let me cook your Christmas dinner? I've got two nice chicken breasts.'' Rosie looked nervously over her glasses.

''Emmie,'' she began, ''I do hope you are not going to be vexed, but I have booked us a table at the Welbridge Hotel. Their Christmas menu looks delicious.''

''Why should I mind about a treat like that?'' Rosie, however, was still looking guilty.

''In the old days it was always a tradition in this house to ask the vicar and all his family to Christmas dinner.''

''Oh, Rosie, you haven't!'' exclaimed Emmie.

''Well, dear, how else will that poor man have a decent meal? His mother is so frail these days.''

''But I don't want people like Alison Grazier or even Kim thinking I'm setting my cap at the vicar! I'm going to stay single because I enjoy it.''

''I understand that, dear,'' said Rosie meekly, ''but do try and be nice to him – just for today. He is such a very kind man.''

Claire stayed in bed throughout Christmas. She always did. The activity in the salon increased throughout December until it reached a final frenzied crescendo late on Christmas Eve. She was so exhausted she was thankful to allow Jasmine to spend her time over the road with the Pattersons. ''If only I could sleep!'' she muttered as she tossed about. She had seen no more clients at home since the night of the storm. People seemed to forget their aches and pains and weight problems over the festive season, but no doubt they would come flooding back in the bleak anticlimax of January. She really must try and rest before then and regain her lost spiritual energy. This odd malaise which had gripped her since the night of the storm seemed to be getting worse.

Jasmine stood alone in the church. The noisy congregation had surged rapidly away to enjoy their Christmas dinners and the Pattersons must have forgotten her. She was glad; she wanted to be alone when she looked at the little crib scene by the font. The painted figures seemed so real, lit by the flickering candles.

"I wish I knew what you were really like," she whispered. Slowly she reached out and lifted the manger.

"I don't like babies," she continued as she examined its tiny occupant. The smallest Patterson was a noisy person who dribbled. She put the manger down again hurriedly. No, Jesus would be a grown-up man, he'd have a beard and a very smiley face. In fact he'd look exactly like Uncle David. Yes, that's who Jesus was like.

"There you are! We were halfway home without you." David did not sound cross, even though he had left Kim seething on Bakers Hill. He crouched down to Jasmine's level and put an arm round her stiff little body. She did not look like a happy, excited child on Christmas morning. If only he could see behind her rigid defence and discover why she was so afraid. They stayed quietly like that for so long that he was sure Kim would divorce him when he finally arrived home.

"Mummy thinks Christmas is silly." At least Jasmine was talking at last. "She says we should call it Yuletide."

"But we call it *Christ*mas because that's when Jesus Christ came down to earth." He was not sure she was listening. "He came to keep us safe from everything that's bad and frightening in the world." Still no response. Jasmine simply gazed woodenly at the manger.

"If ever you were frightened of anything, His name is so powerful, you only have to say it – Jesus – and believe in it, and nothing can harm you. It's like putting on invisible armour every time you're scared." She looked round at that.

"Even witchy things and nasty feelings you can't see?"

"Specially things like that."

"Even in my bed at night?"

"Specially then. He'll stay with you all the time if you ask Him."

"What if Mummy sends me to boarding-school?" His arm tightened around her.

"Nothing and no one will ever be able to take you away from Him if you ask Him to stay with you." There was another long silence, but David was good at silences. Then she put her hand in his and smiled for the first time in weeks.

"Let's go home, then," she said. "I like turkey."

'I wonder,' thought Kim, 'why visitors always insist on standing right in the middle of the kitchen and talking while you try and dish up a meal?'

"Mummy, I've put twelve glasses on the table," said Rebecca. "Can I make little red fans to go in them?"

"Well you could, if I hadn't lost the paper-napkins."

"They're in the fridge," replied Rebecca.

"Well! I wonder whatever possessed me to put them in there?" Perhaps it was something to do with the five o'clock start they'd had that morning, when the Christmas stockings had been discovered.

The sink was filling with saucepans now, and she would really have liked David's help, but he was by the fire, deep in conversation with her mother. Well, her mother was talking – David just put in a nod or a smile at the right places. He was deliberately keeping her from joining the other visitors in their maddening positions – right between the stove and the sink. Bless him! She felt mean now when she remembered how she'd bitten his head off for disappearing like that after church. At least Jasmine looked happier now, but it would have been nice for the kid if Claire had let herself come over here for the day.

"Mummy, I don't think we'll ever be able to squeeze this many people in," called Rebecca from the dining-table, and Kim hurried over to help. It was a difficult journey, she had to step over Nigel on the way. He was lying full length on the carpet, his tongue between his teeth in order to aid concentration. Beside him squatted

Johnnie, gazing at his hero who was laying out a complicated arrangement of toy cars. They often played like that on the floor for hours, communicating with each other continuously, but without the use of a single word. It would be hard to say which of them was the more content.

"David!" shouted Kim suddenly. "The tree, look out!" Of course they were proud that the baby could now pull himself up to a standing position, but it was just unfortunate that he would practise his new skill on the Christmas tree. She turned her back on the chaos of scattered decorations and fused fairy lights and went back to the stove – something was hissing ominously.

"My Nigel loves children," said his mother fondly. She was standing right in the middle of the kitchen, just where Kim needed to be. "You and Miss Dawson make him feel so appreciated. No one else ever has."

"But he's such a help amusing the children," panted Kim, "and Emmie couldn't manage that garden without him."

"It's the future that really worries me," continued Mrs Jardine. "You see I'm seventy-three now and if anything should ever happen to me . . . poor Nigel, those institutions are such horrid places."

It seemed to Kim a strange time and place to talk about something which obviously was such a major concern. She looked helplessly at Mrs Jardine and could not fail to see the stark fear in her eyes.

"Oh well," she said brightly as she bent down to check the roast potatoes, "don't worry, it may never happen." It sounded an inane thing to say, but really it was all she could manage at a time like this.

"But you can't help worrying, can you, Mrs Galbraith? Over the future I mean," continued Mrs Jardine. Old Mrs Galbraith eyed her coldly. Her large body was completely blocking Kim's kitchen-sink. "Christmas makes everything feel worse, don't you think?"

"What was that?" said Mrs Galbraith, who had been

deaf for years. "Christmas did you say? Yes, very nice, very nice indeed."

'If these two don't clear out of my way,' thought Kim as she straightened up from her squat by the oven, 'I'll never manage to bring this wretched meal to birth!' Across the room she caught David's eye and over the bobbing heads they found themselves smiling at each other.

Number Fifteen was also pulsating with festivity and so many cars were parked at the far end of the Terrace that Alison phoned the police. They failed to respond to her complaint.

"You'll all have to come to dinner at Gresham Manor next year," said Hazel as she looked round her crowded dining-table. "Let's drink to the future." As they raised their glasses she felt distinctly optimistic. They had managed to jump the queue at the best building firm in town, and the work on the roof had already begun. The estate agent assured them 'everyone' wanted to buy a house with a view of the park, so it looked as if they would be safely away from here by Easter after all.

"How are you these days, Ann?" she asked as the babble of conversation recommenced around the Regency table. Ann and Matt Coley were dreadful bores, but she felt she owed them this, after spilling their beans to that Grazier woman.

"She's much better," said Matt before his wife could answer. "Actually I've devised a most successful all-round regime for MS patients. I'd love to talk it over with you."

"Sometime perhaps, but I never talk shop at home," said Hazel firmly. "Did I hear you say you're going back to school in the new year, Ann?" Again Matt answered for her.

"She's going to teach geography after half-term."

"You're obviously over the emotional trauma, then." Hazel continued to address her remarks pointedly to Ann, and at last she was rewarded by an answer.

241

"You have to fight problems, don't you?" Ann sounded as if she was quoting someone else, and all the time she was speaking, her eyes kept straying to her husband's face for his approval.

"Yes, we can pull ourselves out of anything by the bootlaces when we have to," she said as she leaned back in her rosewood chair and sipped her drink. She'd been doing it all her life, she told herself with satisfaction. "A successful new year for all of us," she said, and raised her glass again. Matt and Ann smiled at each other as they drank the toast.

It was a bleak festivity next-door at Number Thirteen. For a while after Amanda's departure, Gordon had nursed a crazy hope that without her, Alison might turn to him for comfort. The hope was definitely dead by the end of Christmas. After her one moment of weakness, Alison channelled her grief and disappointment into feats of incredible activity.

"I shall pour myself out for the parish," she declared as she took hampers of goodies to everyone on her list of 'shut-ins'. She did not, however, visit Miss Rosedale. "I know when I'm not appreciated," she said with a sniff. Gordon doubted it.

Before the cat had eaten the last dregs of the turkey she began to redecorate the sitting-room, and there was no sloping off to the allotment to escape her paint-brushes and wallpaper glue. She found strings of little jobs to keep them both occupied continuously.

Clancy began to look rebellious. 'If she gets fed up and goes off, too, she might as well take the sunshine with her, as far as I'm concerned,' Gordon thought miserably as he rehung the curtains.

FRIDAY FEBRUARY 28TH

Clancy often wondered why she did it. She later concluded it must have been boredom. The two months since Christmas had been long, grey and cold, and Clancy yearned for sunshine like a tabby-cat.

"I'm fed up," she said. Tracy peered at her slightly accusingly through the thick lenses of her glasses. They were smoking on the wall behind the school tennis-courts, keeping out of Mr Coley's way. He could get very upset about cigarettes could Mr Coley.

"What you fed up *for*, anyway?"

"So'd you be if you had to live with an old bag like her," replied Clancy broodingly. "I thought it'd get better when Miss Toffee Nose left home, but she's worse. Kicks up if I'm even five minutes late home."

"Lend me that new Danny Man tape your Uncle Gordon got you on Saturday, Clance."

"You're always pestering for something." Of course she knew she'd have to hand it over; she needed to keep Tracy sweet. The alibi for her frequent absences from home depended on her. It was just too bad that the only friend she had was so completely boring. When she'd lived up on the estate she'd had lots of mates, but they dropped her when she moved to the stuck-up end of town. Said her clothes were snobby and she talked all posh. That was Auntie Alison's fault, trying to make her sound as if she had a plum in her mouth!

She was getting sick of Gordon, too, now. Always looking at her, like she was some kind of angel. Expecting her to spend all her free time with him instead of up at the shops. Really, life with the Graziers was worse than a prison. Would Mrs Gray move her to a new foster-home if she asked? Never! Auntie Alison had her well and truly charmed.

"I've had Laburnum Terrace up to here."

"You don't know when you're well off. I wish I had an 'Uncle' who'd buy me anything I fancied. He spoils you rotten."

It was then that it happened. Clancy really only meant to shake Tracy a little. She looked so smug sitting there.

"He *has* to buy me things, to keep me quiet," she said significantly.

"Quiet about what?" Tracy still did not look interested.

"All the things he does to me up at his shed."

The previous evening she had watched an absorbing late night film on the television in her bedroom. The plot about the foster father who molested his teenage charge had totally fired her imagination.

Tracy's eyes were satisfactorily round by the time Clancy had told her story. "You poor thing," said Tracy, at last. "Why don't you tell?"

"That's why." Clancy hitched up her skirt to reveal some magnificent bruises.

"You told me this morning you fell downstairs," Tracy sounded suddenly suspicious.

"I had to, didn't I? He may be small, but he's vicious. So don't you dare open your mouth," she added uneasily. "Or he'd murder me for sure."

"Course I won't," promised Tracy, but she could hardly wait to catch her bus after school. It would be quite safe just to tell Fiona.

SATURDAY FEBRUARY 29TH

It snowed heavily all that Friday night and when the sun came out in the morning, Laburnum Terrace looked like fairyland.

"Come on! We're off to have a snowball fight," shouted Rebecca. Sharon eyed the procession which was passing her house uncertainly. David, assisted by Nigel, was pulling a red plastic toboggan on which sat Johnnie. They were followed by a hoard of local children, and Sharon would have liked to join them, but she was not sure, now she was at the comprehensive, whether she was supposed to be a child or an adult. She wished she had a dad like Mr Patterson, who made life fun.

The excited squeals which accompanied the sledge as it hurtled down the slope towards the frozen lake soon brought Alison to her front door.

"David Patterson ought to know better than to let that Nigel Jardine get so worked up," she said disapprovingly.

"But he's enjoying it just as much as the children," said Gordon, peering over her shoulder.

"That's just it. He's twenty-eight, but he never grew up." Gordon watched Nigel rolling down the snowy hillside, revelling in the wonder of it all. He envied him – lingering for ever in the world of childhood; growing up had never made *him* happy like that.

"You're terribly late this morning," said Alison severely as Babs slithered up the pavement towards her. "We had to have tinned milk on our cornflakes."

Babs was incensed, but before she could express her

feelings with adequate venom, Gordon had taken his wife's place on the doorstep.

"She's been a bit . . . you know . . . lately . . ." he whispered vaguely. "Must be her age." Actually the last two months had been almost unendurable for Gordon.

"Isn't it all lovely, Babs?" shouted Sharon, forgetting for a moment that she was a grown-up. Babs, who had been out in the slippery cold since four that morning, did not look particularly enthusiastic, but she had always liked Sharon – they shared a common interest in local gossip.

"Mrs Coley's come back to school again this week," announced Sharon importantly.

"Thought she was a goner," replied Babs, "disabled for life."

"She can't teach PE any more and she walks like a wobbly jelly on two sticks."

"You didn't ought to laugh," chided Babs as she carried the order for Number Fifteen up the drive. "I see it's sold then," she added, nodding towards the agent's board which felt to Hazel like a ticket to freedom.

"Yes, they're moving to a posh house in the country."

"And what else's been going on?"

"Little Amy Patterson had such bad asthma on Tuesday night she had to go to hospital to have oxygen. And I think the vicar fancies Emmie Dawson. He's always visiting the old lady next-door to us, but I reckon it's not *her* he goes to see."

Babs was outraged. "You shouldn't say such things about a vicar," she said. Just at that moment Emmie and Gwyllum came out of their front gate. Emmie was wearing a periwinkle-blue scarf which brought out the colour of her eyes and she looked so attractive that Babs had to admit she could hardly blame the vicar.

"Talk of the devil," she said, as she noticed Richard sliding down the middle of the road with his two little daughters.

"Hang on a minute, Emmie," he called, but she was

246

pretending not to notice him as she hurried away across the virgin expanse of undented snow.

"She doesn't seem to fancy *him*," said Sharon precociously.

"I should think not, indeed," snorted Babs. As she slid her milk truck out into the salty slush of Bakers Hill she added to herself, "Marriage isn't all it's cracked up to be; she's got her head screwed on, she has."

Richard sighed as he watched Emmie retreating into the distance.

"Come on, Daddy," shouted Pippa, "you promised we'd make a snowman."

"We'll make a snow-giant," he replied, pulling his attention back to his daughters with difficulty. "Let's build him down by the lake. Up you come, Jess, I'll give you a piggyback."

Of course Emmie was no more important than any of his other parishioners, he told himself firmly as he plodded down the hill through the snow. It was just that he knew how much she would appreciate a morning like this when every twig and branch sparkled with a coating of silver and white. There were so few people with whom one could share the joy of things like that. She was such an unusual girl, he mused, and her enthusiasm for her new faith was refreshing to a jaded old professional like himself. Whenever he climbed into the pulpit these days, he raked the pews for her face, simply because he so much enjoyed watching her expression as she grasped the things he was trying to say. She even laughed at his jokes. All the same, he must be careful. Sometimes a vague romantic attachment could develop as part of the natural grieving process – and that could be most embarrassing for a busy clergyman.

"Hurry up, Daddy!" called Pippa impatiently. "The lake's frozen stiff."

The snow worried Claire; it could ruin everything. She peered through the steamy windows of the salon looking

247

for signs of a thaw. Today was Roger's birthday. Of course she had been invited to the party, along with everyone else in the Group, and go she must. She'd been trying to see him alone ever since Christmas, but he was always, "madly busy, my dear."

Something was going badly wrong and only Roger could help, but for some reason he seemed to be avoiding her. At least the party would give her an excuse to get into the mill-house, but the hill down to it could be a sheet of ice by tonight.

The day dragged by interminably. The bad weather caused so many cancellations she went home at lunchtime and lay down on her bed. She didn't even have the energy to take Boris into the park. Tonight wasn't going to be easy with Jasmine. Kim was being awkward about having her since that whining brat of hers had an asthma attack. She had been reduced to asking Clancy from Number Thirteen to baby-sit, but her appalling foster-mother wouldn't let her stay past midnight. Well, she had no intention of being back by then. Alison Grazier would simply have to like it or lump it.

Claire closed her eyes and tried to remember her relaxation technique; she must do something for her body, it felt sore and stiff with tension. However, her mind refused the instruction to think of smooth black velvet and insisted on nagging her instead.

Why was Roger being so elusive? Had he found out about all the success she'd had before Christmas? No, surely he was above petty emotions like jealousy? She pulled the duvet higher up round her chin; it was cold since she had discovered central heating caused pollution. Sooner or later she was just going to have to admit to Roger that she was in serious trouble. Her power was gone.

She still saw patients, of course, and advised them about diet and natural remedies, but when she began to work on them, she felt as if she was groping in the dark, with no additional 'hands' to assist her.

"Hands", the word made her huddle farther under her

covers. Claire was beginning to be afraid. She was never alone these days; there was always someone standing behind her as she worked in the salon and waiting in the kitchen when she arrived home. Sometimes up here in her bedroom she seemed to see the hands that used to help her, but they were against her now. They clenched into threatening fists or pointed in accusation. She knew she had angered her spirit guides, but why? What had she done?

Roger would know, if only she could reach him through the snow.

In the end she left her car in the beech-woods at the top of the hill where the road had been gritted and she walked the two miles down into the dell in the glittering starlight. She was glad she had taken Boris with her. Plenty of people had already arrived at the mill; the front porch was littered with boots and the noise was deafening after the stillness outside.

They were all there, saying the same old things: Pete with his pendulum, Alan talking about the global village and Eve lamenting over baby seals. She tied Boris's lead to the knob at the bottom of the stairs and craning her neck she looked for Roger.

"Come on in, my dear," he said, hurrying towards her, "have some brandy, it'll warm you up."

"Happy birthday," she murmured.

"Thank you, my dear. I only have a birthday every four years, that's what keeps me so young." He laughed as he took her coat, but Claire felt that his eyes were not kind towards her. She began to feel uneasy.

New arrivals claimed his attention and she drifted towards the ingle-nook where it had all begun. She had travelled a long way since that day two summers ago, but she was not sure now if the journey had been worth the effort. When she had come here first she had a safe little business, a nice house and ordinary friends. She turned her back on the babbling crowd – they had never really accepted her into their strange abstract world, and

249

the high ideals they preached so loudly did not always match the way they lived. She was beginning to wonder if behind all their talk of life forces and ancient arts there did not lie something sinister. 'I don't fit in anywhere now,' she thought, and the damp, snow-sodden logs hissed at her in agreement.

"Roger, could I have a word with you?" He had come over to stand beside her, and the brass buttons on his green velvet waistcoat winked quite kindly in the firelight.

"I felt you had something you wanted to tell me. Let's go out and look at the stars, it's so terribly hot in here, don't you think?"

Claire didn't think it was, but she needed Roger more than she had ever needed him before. The millpond was a frozen sheet of glass in the bright moonlight, but there was still a trickle of water splashing down the old brick conduit. Beneath her boots the snow crunched like white sugar icing and she shivered. Roger, however, seemed oblivious of the cold beneath his comforting layers of fat, and he puffed at his cigar contentedly as he looked out across the glistening ice. Boris scented rabbits in the distance and he was off over the white fields like a swift shadow.

"Have you ever had the experience of being blocked . . . blocked in your work?" Claire began. She was very much aware that her allowance of time with him would be short.

He said nothing, so she continued. "For weeks now I can't seem to focus. I've lost my spiritual energy somehow."

"I've missed you," he said.

"It was you who wouldn't see *me*," she reminded him.

"Before that." So he had minded her absence after all. "It has only come to my notice gradually just how many people you have been seeing." In the starlight his face looked benign. Was she merely imagining the threat she had seen in his eyes? She looked at him more closely, and then suddenly she gripped the frosted fence in surprise.

"Was it you? Have you been . . . hindering me because I wasn't bringing you clients any more?"

"You overestimate my powers, my dear, you always did."

"But I'm being stopped in some way. Is this some kind of a curse you've put on me?" Her voice was rising shrilly now and somewhere a duck woke and protested loudly. Faraway on the hillside Boris pricked up his ears and galloped back to her rescue.

"You have hurt me by your deception, my dear, but you must not also misjudge me. I am your creator, remember. Why should I destroy you? I did however warn you that you were not yet ready to work without my support. Perhaps your lack of experience is to blame? We will see clients together again from now on. You don't have to fear *me*, I am your only friend."

Claire looked at him uncertainly. It was so difficult to know what he was thinking behind that pleasant mask. Gently he took her hand,

"Will you let me see if the answer to your problem lies in the future and not the past?" he said as he gently pulled off her glove. The moonlight, reflected on the snow, lent a sharp clarity to the scene and she watched his face anxiously. She wanted to trust him – if only she could be sure . . .

He was silent for a long time gazing down at her palm. The silence was intense, broken only by the water, splash, splash, splashing in the conduit. Then he stiffened and drew a quick, startled breath. As he hastily released her hand Claire sensed danger like an animal approaching a trap.

"Forgive me, my dear, it's extremely foolish of me to attempt to read a hand in a poor light. One can so easily be deceived by shadows."

"You saw something, didn't you? What did you see?" Claire was very frightened now and, inside her head, someone laughed mockingly. "If something terrible is going to happen to me, I want to know." Boris growled his support.

251

"I think we should go back to the others, my dear," he said quickly, but Claire was becoming angry. Had he really seen something in her future, or was he frightening her as a form of punishment?

"We're not going anywhere until you stop these ridiculous threats and stupid mysteries." Boris was barking now.

"Do tie that dog up. I never have trusted Alsatians."

"Not till you tell me what's going wrong in my life," said Claire in a low, shaky voice.

"I'm afraid I can't do that. Sometimes one sees things that one must never disclose."

"I hate you, vile little man!" Something had snapped inside Claire. "I'm not afraid of you or anything you can do to me. You can drown yourself in that pond for all I care. Come on, Boris."

She turned and began to run over the crackling snow and away up the hill.

"Be careful, my dear," he called sadly. His voice sounded as if he pitied her, but she ignored it.

'I'll never come here again,' she promised herself. It was always like this. All her life she had kept on reaching out restlessly for different things, longing for solid reality on which to build her life. Over and over again she had grabbed at something, only to be disillusioned when she discovered it had no more substance than a spider's web. Roger and his strange world had proved to be just as unsatisfactory as everything else.

'This is all I've got left now,' she thought as she finally drove into Laburnum Terrace. All right, so Alison might complain on her front doorstep and Sharon might spy through her back window, but that little Victorian villa was safe, solid and permanent.

As she climbed out of her car, she looked up above the slate roofs and chimneys. An aircraft from Gatwick travelled across the sky overhead, its lights resembling a clutch of shooting stars in slow motion.

FRIDAY MARCH 6TH

An epidemic of flu began to scythe down the inhabitants of Welbridge as soon as the snow thawed.

"It's like the Black Death," said Richard. "We'll be asked to put crosses on the doors soon."

"Going down like bowling pins, they are," agreed Mrs Macaulay happily – she was doing a roaring trade in aspirin and throat lozenges.

"Glad someone's pleased," added Gordon as he scuttled out of the shop, clutching his medical supplies. Clancy had been very poorly all week, and he had never known Alison take to her bed before. She lay up there, managing her household by remote control, and made him feel like a hamster running in a wheel of perpetual activity. He wouldn't have minded quite so much if he had not taken this week off specially to work on his allotment.

Clancy, back at school for the first time after her flu, was finding the morning most strange. People actually noticed her for the first time in her life. Wherever she went she was followed by sympathetic glances, girls who were usually catty smiled at her and complete strangers offered her sweets.

She did not realise that during her four days of absence she had become a celebrity.

Unfortunately, Tracy's friend Fiona was an accomplished gossip and with Clancy safely banished by flu, she had been able to 'leak' her startling story with liberal dashes of artistic licence. As the week went on the news was whispered in every changing-room and corridor in Welbridge Comprehensive and the details grew more lurid every time they were described.

"She's off school because she's covered with bruises." That was the final touch which made a heroine out of the nondescript fourth-year no one had ever noticed before.

Of course, Mrs Pembroke, the chairman of the PTA, was bound to hear about it before long. She always knew everything that happened in the school. Her daughter, Amelia, was a sheltered child who had never been allowed to watch television. Learning the harsher facts of life in the playground had upset her so much she was ill in bed by that Friday morning.

"How dreadful!" exclaimed her mother, when she had finally bludgeoned the story out of a tearful Amelia. "I must tell the headmaster at once."

"Oh no!" she shrieked – stricken with remorse. "Poor Clancy will be beaten dreadfully if that terrible man discovers she's told."

"Then I must move fast," said her mother and reached for the telephone.

12.30pm

When Clancy was summoned to the headmaster's office, she wondered if perhaps everyone had been nice to her because they knew she was about to be expelled. But whatever was she supposed to have done?

"Come in," said the head when she knocked on his door. He was a small fussy man who was despised by his staff and pupils alike. Clancy's heart sank when she saw that the senior mistress, Miss Hayward, was also in the room. At least *she* was a force to be reckoned with. 'I'm dead meat now,' thought Clancy.

"I hope you would always look on me as a friend," began the head. Clancy had never looked on him as anything but an enemy, so she said nothing.

"I would like to feel you could tell me anything." The

only thing Clancy had ever wanted to tell him was that his breath smelled.

"You live with some people called Grazier, don't you?" put in Miss Hayward. So that was it. Auntie Alison had complained about her. She'd threatened to do it enough times.

"How do you get on with . . . er . . . Mr Grazier?" asked the head, but Miss Hayward was becoming irritated by his pussyfooting approach.

"We know what he's been doing to you," she said briskly, and put what she hoped was a friendly arm round the girl's shoulders. Clancy stiffened. She'd kill Tracy for this!

"You can trust us," murmured the head.

Behind her wooden expression Clancy's brain was leaping in all directions at once. Of course! That's why everyone wanted to be her friend. They were sorry for her. If she went back on her story now, she'd look such a fool she'd never live it down. She could say Tracy invented it all, but then she'd lose the only friend she had.

There must be a way of making this thing work for her. Being a tragic heroine was certainly bringing her popularity at long last, and having these two so nice to her might also make life round here much more pleasant.

"Tell us all about it, Clancy," said Miss Hayward, patting her arm gently.

When the story was finally told, she couldn't help thinking how well she did it. Of course, she had given this performance before – when Kevin was cast as the villain, but she'd had hours of late-night TV to feed her imagination since then. She really sounded like a professional actress now and it was gratifying to have such a distinguished audience hanging on her every word. She even managed to finish her speech by dissolving into a dramatic flood of tears.

"He made me promise never to tell. He said it was our secret." The sobs sounded convincing.

"Don't worry, Clancy," said Miss Hayward, "the social workers will find you a nice new home. You'll never have to go back there again."

A new home . . . no more Auntie Alison! But that meant no more Uncle Gordon either. 'He *was* rather sweet,' she thought sadly. 'But he would keep treating me like a little kid.'

"We're going to have to ring the police now, and Mrs Gray, your social worker." Miss Hayward's voice cut into her thoughts. "They'll all be very understanding, but they will want you to see a doctor." Clancy hesitated. She had got away with the medical examination last time, because from the age of thirteen, she had not been the little innocent she appeared. So it would probably be all right this time too.

As she sipped the hot sweet tea from the cups reserved for visiting VIPs she never ever considered what her moment of glory might actually do to Gordon.

2.35

Tracy was in tears when it was her turn to sit in the headmaster's office later in the afternoon. A WPC in a checked hat sat next to her, smiling professional encouragement.

"Clancy told me I had to say she was with me up at our house, if anyone wanted to know where she was," she explained with a sniff.

"And where was she when she was supposed to be with you?" asked the policewoman kindly.

"In that shed . . . with . . . him," faltered Tracy. "Weekends and evenings, too, when it wasn't cold. He kept giving her sweets and tapes to give to me, so I'd say the right thing if anyone ever asked me."

"And did anyone ever ask you – Mrs Grazier for instance?"

"No, 'cos we haven't got a phone, have we?"

256

4

Sharon, trailing home from school with a bag full of homework, pricked up her foxy ears when she noticed a police-car parked outside Number Thirteen. Out came Mr Grazier and was bundled into the back seat by two large policemen.

"Wow!" breathed Sharon. She could hardly wait to tell Babs about this in the morning.

10.30

Alison sat alone on her velvet sofa staring into space. She was wearing her dressing-gown, and she still felt ill with the flu. Gordon had been at the police-station for hours now, and she knew she ought to get herself back into bed, but somehow she could not make the decision to take herself there. She had always prided herself on knowing exactly what everyone else should do in all situations, and she had never hesitated to tell them so. Now in her own trouble she did not have the least idea what to do next.

SATURDAY MARCH 7TH

10am

"Excuse me, sir," said PC Blackett as the newly-turned clay clogged his polished boots. How could anyone voluntarily spend their spare time up here on this draughty vegetable patch? George looked round cautiously, and leaned on his fork.

"If it's about that parking ticket . . ."

"No, sir, I just wanted to ask you a few questions about a Mr Gordon Grazier. Do you happen to know him?"

"Know him?" snorted George. 'That's his patch next to mine. More's the pity."

"And is that his shed, sir?"

"Holiday home more like," answered George sourly. "The allotment holders' committee ought to put a stop to all the goings-on in there."

"What kind of 'goings-on' would that be, sir?" asked Blackett innocently.

"He practically lives in it."

"On his own?"

"No, that wretched child's always about. They ought to ban kids up here, treading all over the seedlings. Here, what's all this in aid of anyway?" His small, crafty eyes looked suspicious.

"Have you ever observed Mr Grazier behaving towards the girl in . . . an improper manner?"

George almost laughed in derision. "What? Little Gordon Grazier . . .?" Then he paused. Suppose

258

something fishy had been going on? It *had* crossed his mind a few times.

George pulled a pouch from his pocket and began to roll himself a cigarette. He wouldn't tell any whoppers, of course, but making a lot out of a little could embarrass Gordon a bit. He'd been wanting to do that for a long time.

"Well, seeing you mention it," he began, "I often seen her sitting on his lap like, but I don't know what they get up to when they draw them fancy curtains of an evening."

PC Blackett disliked this kind of case. Kids deserved better than they received these days. Right back last Easter he'd had Gordon Grazier labelled as a weirdo.

"It's more like a blooming hotel in that shed," finished George when he had 'recalled' as much as he could.

"Would you be willing to testify in the Magistrate's Court on Monday morning?" George hesitated. He'd not bargained on going that far, but in for a penny in for a pound, and that silver cup might even return to its rightful place on his mantelpiece this year, if Gordon was upset during this vital planting season.

"Will they put him inside?" he asked hopefully.

"If the case goes on to the Crown Court, who knows?" said the young policeman as he wrote busily in his little notebook. George whistled.

As PC Blackett tackled his cod and chips in the canteen later that morning he was frowning. Grazier was clearly some kind of a pervert, that was obvious. He'd dealt with many in his time, but this one was different. His initial reaction to the allegations had been odd somehow. Most people denied everything, got all steamed up and even abusive. This little man couldn't have been more upset if they'd gone to tell him his next of kin had been killed. All he would say was, "I loved her so much. I had this coming to me." Of course he'd denied the charges later, said he'd never done anything wrong, but they all did that. Even Sergeant Tomkins hadn't been able to get

259

anything more out of him in the chargeroom last night. A nutter that's what he was – he could get five years for this. All the same, if they didn't get some very definite medical evidence their case probably would never stand up in the Crown Court.

TUESDAY MARCH 10TH

The flu was still raging and by Tuesday almost every house in Laburnum Terrace had been affected. Dr Macdermott dived in and out of his car wearing a hunted expression as he wondered if his visiting list could possibly grow any longer. Since Jane's latest baby had been born at Christmas he had forgotten what sleep felt like and he was beginning to hope he could catch the flu himself. At least it would give him a rest.

The epidemic did not, however, affect Hazel and Graham – they were off skiing in Val d'Isere.

"It's all right for some," remarked Kim enviously as she stood outside Number Fifteen, surrounded by children.

"What did you say?" demanded old Mrs Galbraith, fiddling with her hearing-aid. "Were you talking about that Gordon Grazier?" she added as she eyed the tightly-closed curtains of the next-door house. They had been like that for days now.

"I don't believe a word of it," Kim yelled indignantly into her ear. "That Clancy's a minx. I've taught girls like her."

"I've *never* trusted that little man," replied Mrs Galbraith, who had failed to hear a single word.

Kim tried a safer subject. "Awful weather! Makes you wonder if Laburnum Terrace will ever see another summer."

"Yes, Laburnum Terrace of all places! Terrible to think of that kind of thing going on here."

Kim gave up and trudged on through the park-gates.

261

She knew she would regret this outing, the cold wind always made Amy wheeze and Johnnie was beginning to whine already. He hated walking.

In the distance she could see Emmie and Gwyllum coming up the hill towards them from the lake, and Amy's hand clutched her mother's coat for protection. She still hated dogs.

"Hi," said Emmie, when she reached the slow cavalcade. 'She always looks so lovely,' thought Kim despairingly. 'It's the clever colours she wears and that fragile Dresden china look.' Kim knew from her mirror that her own face was having one of its bad days and something had gone dreadfully wrong with her hair.

"Your tribe haven't caught the bug yet, then?"

"No, apart from Amy, we're a healthy lot," answered Kim, denying the fact, even to herself, that her whole body ached ominously and her throat felt full of sharp pins.

Johnnie was crying in earnest now and Kim scooped him up on to her hip and steered the pram with the other hand. Emmie did not offer to push. 'She never thinks of practical things like that,' thought Kim.

"I suppose you've been on one of your lovely long prayer walks," she said, trying hard to keep a sour note out of her voice. "You ought to have been a nun."

"A nun? Oh, no, I'd hate to be part of a community. I need freedom to be alone, and just be me."

Kim stopped so abruptly in the middle of the path that Amy blundered into her legs and fell over. She began to cry, too. Irritation was boiling up inside Kim, and before she could stop herself she said:

"You live in an ivory tower, don't you? Other people simply don't exist." With a wailing child on each hip she had to shout to make herself heard and Emmie looked startled. Kim bit her lip. 'There goes another friendship,' she told herself. 'Why can't I keep my big tactless mouth shut?'

"Do you really think I'm selfish?" asked Emmie in a small tight voice.

Kim swallowed hard and tried to backtrack. "Not really. Look at all you do for Rosie."

"I don't do much for her," confessed Emmie. "I'm positively snowed under with work now and we both live very separate lives you know. But we prefer it that way."

"Oh look, Emmie, I'm sorry. I've just been feeling so low recently I'm always taking on far too much and then feel sorry for myself when I'm tired. Sometimes I feel like giving up and reading a book in bed all day long!"

"Don't do that, old thing; half Laburnum Terrace depends on you," replied Emmie with a shy little smile. "Remember what you did for me when I was ill?"

They were walking back out of the park-gates by now; the expedition had been as abortive as Kim had feared it would be. She was bent almost double with the effort of pushing both boys in the pram while she piggybacked the wheezing Amy. As Emmie waved good-bye and hurried across her garden, Kim smiled affectionately after her. 'It wouldn't occur to her that I've still got to toil all the way up Bakers Hill with this lot to collect the girls from school,' she thought. 'I suppose it would never even occur to someone like her to offer to fetch them for me.'

Emmie, still smarting from Kim's lecture, decided she had better look in on Rosie before she went back upstairs to work.

"Darling, whatever's the matter?" she exclaimed. Rosie was huddled in bed, wrapped in two rugs and a shawl, but she was still shivering violently. "You've caught this ghastly flu. I ought to have checked on you this morning."

"Nonsense. I'm perfectly all right," croaked Rosie. "My home-help fetched me some cough mixture from the chemist."

Emmie looked at her closely. "I don't think you are all right," she said. "Why didn't the stupid woman phone the doctor?"

"Because I would not allow it. That man has an unholy desire to push people into hospital for no reason at all."

She began to cough painfully and Emmie hurried towards the telephone in the hall. Kim was right; she *was* selfish! She had neglected Rosie shamefully.

Doctor Macdermott groaned. He had only just returned to the warmth of his surgery after his long round of visits, but a call to visit Miss Rosedale was so rare that it must be serious.

"You seem to have developed a bit of a chest infection, Rosie," he said half an hour later as he pulled the stethoscope from his ears. "Complication of flu."

"Pooh," said Rosie scornfully. "We teachers are immune to these silly bugs."

"I've written her up for some antibiotics, but you'll have to give her lots of warm drinks and see she keeps sitting upright in bed," he told Emmie.

"Are you sure you can cope, Miss Dawson?" he added when Rosie's door was safely closed. "You don't exactly look like the Florence Nightingale type, and I'm afraid she's going to need a lot of care."

Emmie paused. She had never nursed anyone in her life and the very idea would have revolted her a few months ago. There were heaps of private nursing homes up at the top of Bakers Hill. They'd look after her so much better . . . but Rosie loved her own home.

"I'll give it a whirl, Doctor," she said.

"Ring me if you're worried," he shouted from the garden gate. He liked that young woman more every time he saw her.

4.15pm

Gordon sat huddled in his shed, gazing at a pile of *Honey Girl* magazines. A bitter March wind licked like a whiplash round his wooden shelter and cut him cruelly through its cracks. There didn't seem much point in lighting the heater – just for one. He heard the knocking, but he made no response.

"You in there, Mr Grazier?" It was the voice of the chairman of the allotment holders' association. 'Funny,' thought Gordon vaguely, 'I've known Jim since we were at school together; what's he want to go calling me Mr Grazier for all of a sudden?'

"He's in there all right," came George's voice. "Look, the padlock's undone." They were standing round him now. Four of them, all his friends, but they were not smiling. 'This is just a bad dream,' thought Gordon. 'You don't have to be polite to people in dreams, you just let it all happen round you.'

"We've come to say the committee feel it's best if you don't come up here any more," said Jim miserably. "They . . . we feel you've let the association down badly."

"The whole of Welbridge is sniggering at us," put in George. "We don't want your sort here."

"I'll pack up then," said Gordon mechanically. He always made things easy for people. "I'm sorry," he added from force of habit. They seemed to be saying a great many more things, but he didn't listen. They didn't want him, that was all that mattered.

It was the same wherever he went these days. The office had suspended him on full pay and when he'd gone into Macaulay's to buy tobacco for his pipe, she'd asked him to take his custom elsewhere. Net curtains quivered every time he walked up the Terrace and old Mrs Galbraith, deadheading her winter pansies, had deliberately turned her back. Pity all this couldn't have been kept quiet – for Alison's sake, but George happened to be Mrs Macaulay's cousin. No doubt she would be handing out the gossip with every paper she sold.

"I wouldn't mind taking over this shed myself, and your plot," George was saying. Gordon bit on his empty pipe and made himself go on thinking about Laburnum Terrace.

Alison was taking all this very hard. She sat all day on the sofa muttering, "What will people think?" She

265

wouldn't speak to him and even refused to cook his meals. After years of verbal abuse, her silence troubled him, and the sight of her sitting there immobile and disorientated was most unnerving.

'Poor old girl,' he thought, 'she's just had too much, what with Amanda going and now this. I've always known only two things mattered to Alison – her girl and her reputation.' He had robbed her of neither, but she *thought* he had, so it came to the same thing.

"I'll move my stuff out then," he said to the four unfriendly backs as they disappeared out of the door. No one said good-bye.

Slowly he fumbled in the pocket of his jacket and producing a small key he undid the wooden chest in the corner. Inside was a shotgun. He loaded it and then sat down again with it laid across his knees. He'd been thinking about this since the Magistrates Court yesterday. It was the best way really. Make things easier for Alison; the least he could do.

They were back again. He could hear the knocking and he felt vaguely irritated. Couldn't he even have privacy for this last job? The small door of the shed was completely filled by a very large body. Richard had to bend his head and edge himself in sideways.

"I hoped I might find you here," he said quietly. "I've been looking all over for you since Sunday."

"Come to tell me not to show my face in St Mark's, I suppose," said Gordon with neither self-pity nor bitterness. "I won't, I promise."

"That's the very last thing I've come to say." Richard glanced at the gun, but he merely sat down in Clancy's old chair and crossed his legs. "Just thought I'd come and keep you company," he said. "We don't need to talk."

It occurred to Gordon that this was the first human being who had spoken kindly to him since the police-car drew up outside Number Thirteen five days ago. His throat felt as if he had swallowed one of his own turnips

266

and he tugged at his dirty shirt collar. Alison had refused to wash for him either.

"I loved the girl, you know," he said abruptly. "I've never loved anyone else but her. We had such fun up here together. I never did the things the police say I did, but I did them all in my head so that makes me just as guilty as if I had."

"Does it?" said Richard.

"Said so yourself, back in October. Preached a sermon about thinking things being as bad as doing them. We went to Eastbourne last summer and it all started then – when Clancy wore a bikini. I knew after your sermon that I was doing wrong, letting all that happen in my mind, but I couldn't stop. That's why God's down on me like a ton of bricks. I expect I'll go to prison, but what does it matter – now she's gone." Gordon's voice sounded completely without hope as he added, "I really thought she loved me, too, in her funny little way. I deserve everything I'll get, you know."

Richard was silent for a long time, then he said, "I can remember that day on the church steps too, Gordon. You said, 'If God even judges us for our thoughts, there's no hope for any of us.' I suppose you felt God's standards are too high."

"So they are!"

"But you're forgetting what I said next. We're *none* of us good enough to come close to God, that's why Jesus let Himself be nailed to a cross and killed. He was being punished for the things we do wrong – so we wouldn't have to get what we deserve. We can be free of all our mistakes, just by asking for His forgiveness."

"I dunno about that," said Gordon cautiously. "It doesn't seem right, letting someone else . . . do it for you."

"That's just pride talking." Gordon was wearing the mulish expression which always enraged Alison.

"You know," said Richard thoughtfully, "Jesus went through sheer agony on that cross for us. It's a terrible

267

thing to reject love like that." Gordon looked at him sharply.

"I'll have to think about it," he said.

"Well, that's a decision only you can make, but don't wait too long. Time's short," he added, eyeing the rifle. "Suppose I give you until Easter and then we'll talk again?"

"I'm not sure I'll still be around by Easter," said Gordon.

"Going to shoot some rabbits?" asked Richard casually.

"I keep it here for that. They're a pest in the spring. But I wasn't thinking of rabbits."

"Wouldn't that be running away? You've always struck me as rather a brave man, having to put up with . . . er . . . so much." Gordon looked at him in surprise. No one had ever called him brave before.

"I might like to do some shooting myself," said Richard. "I suppose you wouldn't lend me the gun – just until after Easter?" Gordon almost looked relieved as he handed it over.

"Come on, I'm going to take you home to the vicarage; you look as if you haven't had a decent tea for a week."

WEDNESDAY MARCH 11TH

When Kim woke up next morning, she felt as if she had been nailed to the bed, and David was being violently sick in the loo.

"I'm going to die," he said as he slumped back down beside her.

"Men!" groaned Kim. "You're terrible when you're ill." She heaved her hot and protesting body out of bed – someone had to see to the kids.

Both the boys were giggling gleefully in their cots like two wicked monkeys behind bars, but when she looked into the girls' room Rebecca said, "My tummy hurts, Mummy, and Amy's been sick all over her duvet."

'I'll have to get Mum to come over,' thought Kim desperately.

By eight o'clock Amy was in the middle of another attack of asthma and the doorbell was ringing loudly. Kim left her with Rebecca and staggered downstairs.

"I'm terribly sorry, Claire," she said, clutching the front door for support. "I can't possibly have Jasmine today."

"But I'm frantically short-staffed, thanks to this flu. I really can't cope with her in the salon," protested Claire. Kim looked at her annoyed expression through a hot and painful haze.

"I'm sorry," she said. "I've just got to go back to bed," and she shut the door on Claire's astonished face.

"It's all very well," she said as she flopped back beside David with Amy in her arms. "You do your best for people, but they just stamp all over you."

David blew his nose like a full fanfare of trumpets. The noise did nothing for Kim's headache.

269

12 noon

Richard was deep in thought as he walked up the Terrace. He had just dropped some shopping off for Emmie at Number Sixteen, and he had been surprised and secretly pleased to see how well she was caring for Rosie.

"She's such a good patient I can't trust her to ring her bell when she needs something," Emmie had told him. "So I've brought my work down here. I can do it beside her." For two such solitary people they looked remarkably companionable.

So it was not his concern for Rosie which was making Richard frown his way along the pavement; the church council were complaining about his sermons and he was worried about his mother. Doctor Macdermott had diagnosed angina.

"It simply isn't fair of you, Richard," his sister had said on the phone last night. "You're letting her do far too much."

"But I can't possibly stop her," he had protested.

"She ought to be back in her snug little bungalow in Worthing, not running your parish. If you can't cope with being a vicar, you ought to go back to teaching."

"Sisters!" thought Richard. But perhaps she was right. Was St Mark's just too tough for him? All the wrangling and arguments left him little time or joy for his daughters.

He was feeling so lonely he decided to call on Kim as he was passing Number Four, but it was her mother who opened the door.

"They're all tucked up in bed," she said severely. "But seeing as it's you, I'll let you go up. I hope you won't catch it yourself."

"Vicars and doctors never do," replied Richard wearily. Like Jim Macdermott he was beginning to think that a bout of flu would provide heaven-sent peace.

As he entered the bedroom he longed to say, 'Look you two, I'm fed up with this parish; I can't cope with my kids and my mother's cracking up.' Instead he heard himself sounding exactly like a clergyman visiting the sick.

"Well, well, well . . ." he began and then stopped abruptly. Kim was sitting up in bed crying.

"Mum's been on at us ever since she arrived," she sniffed. "Says I've been doing too much having Jasmine. I'm beginning to think she's right too. Claire was so rude this morning."

David heaved himself up in the bed, and blew his nose violently. Kim winced. "If you keep doing that I'll hit you," she said crossly. "You know, Richard," she added, "the people in this Terrace can be so irritating! I'm just not a saint like you." Richard smiled at her ruefully.

"But I'm not a saint either." He walked over to the window. As he looked out at the road his broad shoulders drooped; these two were both feeling so ill he could not tell them he felt discouraged, too, or admit he was even toying with the thought of giving up his church altogether. He pulled aside the net curtain and looked across the road at Claire's house. It was so ordinary, just like all the rest, yet as he gazed at it, he suddenly realised something.

"That's it!" he said, whirling round with a new surge of energy. "What a fool I've been not to realise it before!"

"Richard, are you feeling all right?" inquired Kim.

"Remember the three of us made a pact to pray for Claire, back in November?"

"Well, I don't think our prayers have done her any good, if anything she's worse than before."

"Yes, but we don't know what's going on inside her head, do we? No wonder the powers of darkness are trying to stop us praying. They want to make us all so discouraged and sorry for ourselves we give up. Well, I'll be blowed if I'm going to be run out of town like this! We ought to be glad. Our prayers are obviously being answered."

David and Kim lay in bed staring at him in amazement, and then a slow smile spread over David's face.

271

2.30pm

Doctor Macdermott sat down on the end of Matt's and Ann's bed. He could have done without a case like this today.

"I'm afraid this kind of thing does happen," he began.

"But I was doing so well." Ann was almost hysterical. She had got out of bed that morning to discover her legs no longer worked at all.

"What went wrong?" demanded Matt. He had been so worried about his wife he had taken a day off school. "She'd got herself back to work, did her exercises and stuck to the diet."

"MS often relapses after an infection," said the doctor. "I expect you had this flu bug, Mrs Coley?"

"Only mildly. I was getting better."

"Look, I admire the way you and your husband have been fighting this thing, but sometimes with MS you can fight too hard. A more peaceful, accepting approach is often better." Matt snorted.

"You're not suggesting we sit down under this thing?" he demanded.

"Certainly not, but perhaps she's been trying to push herself too hard. Meditation or some kind of a religious faith might have a better effect."

"For goodness' sake!" Matt was incensed.

"I want her to have complete bed-rest for at least two weeks and I'll send the district nurse in at once to fix up a catheter. She'll visit you each day. Rest, mind," he added firmly as he went out of the door. Ann lay back against her pillows and turned her face to the wall.

10.45

Ann pulled herself up in bed with difficulty and looked out between the curtains. They had always had their bed right under the window so they could sleep with the maximum amount of fresh air. As the curtain dropped round her shoulders, she remembered a dream she'd had last Easter – velvet folds had wrapped round her like this, separating her from Matt.

"How much longer is he going to be?" she thought miserably.

"Just going for a quick drink at the Prince Albert." He had said that hours ago and she'd known he meant to stay there until he was well and truly plastered. His great regime had failed; the disease had beaten them both after all. She had never known him quite so down, but, of course, he would soon recover, his life would begin to happen in other places and with other people. She would cease to matter to him as she sat here with nothing better to do but watch the comings and goings in the road outside.

'It's all right for them,' she thought, as she looked at all the warm, dimly-lit windows of her neighbours. They could go on living their happy, well-organised little lives, doing the things they enjoyed, going where they wanted to go. They had a future ahead of them, while she faced nothing but a blank.

THURSDAY MARCH 12TH

5pm

Emmie put down her paint-brush and sighed with satisfaction. She had worked all day at the table in the bay window of Rosie's bedroom, but now the light was fading rapidly. Outside, the spring flowers they had planned together so carefully positively glowed in the pale evening sunshine.

"I think we'll have a nice cup of China tea, now," she said, as she rearranged Rosie's pillows and smoothed her sheets. "But first I'm going to fetch a bowl of water and give you a little wash." Later, as she was boiling the kettle in the old-fashioned kitchen next door, she thought how oddly satisfying it was to care for the basic physical needs of another human being. During the last few days she had done things for Rosie which would once have been repugnant to her. 'P'raps that's why women can leave interesting careers to look after babies,' she thought. 'You can probably do all kinds of things when you really love the person.'

"It's just as well we got all those press and radio interviews out of the way before you caught this bug," she said as she handed Rosie a delicate Crown Derby cup. "At least you can lie there knowing that you're a 'newly discovered author', whose book is being launched in grand style."

"We've had fun together, you and me," said Rosie.

"Not so much of the 'had'," said Emmie. "We've still got the sequel to work on, remember? Shall we have Babs looking a bit older in this book, do you think?"

Rosie put down her cup – she was really too weary to hold it. All day she had felt her strength draining slowly away. She was not afraid of what that might mean – she had been forced to wait longer than most people for the joy of meeting her God. However, as she had watched Emmie working away in the window she felt worried about her.

"You know, I am not sure you ought to remain single, after all, dear," she said diffidently.

"But I love being on my own and you've always enjoyed it, too, surely?"

"It all depends on your reasons for wishing to remain single." Emmie was silent for some time as she examined a minute blemish on her thumbnail.

"The other day Kim practically told me I was selfish. I've been thinking about it ever since."

"How could you be selfish and do all this for me?" Rosie sounded quite ruffled.

"I know what she was trying to say – I love being with you, but other people really don't exist in my little world at all."

"I think perhaps Kim could be right there," nodded Rosie.

"It's just that I always seem to muck up my relationships, so I decided it would be less painful if I didn't try to make any at all. It wasn't difficult with you – or God. Somehow I felt you both accepted me for what I am. With other people, I'm always scared that I won't live up to what they expect of me."

Suddenly she was back in Aunt Jane's dining-room, with that angry face looming over her. Under her foot were the crushed remains of her special 'thing of beauty', which her father did not seem to want. That was the moment when she had decided that loving was too risky.

Rosie was fighting a dark pall of fatigue now, but she made herself say, "So, because you are afraid of being hurt, you keep everyone at a distance. That, Emily, is not

275

at all how God behaves. When I am gone, be single if you wish, but do not be solitary. There is a difference.'' She closed her eyes, but beside her Emmie looked alarmed.

"Don't you dare talk about going!'' cried Emmie. ''I can't bear it. You're all I've got. Come on, I'm going to cook you a nice piece of fish for your supper.''

Rosie was now too tired to fancy anything whatsoever, but she smiled gratefully as she closed her eyes.

As Emmie went into the kitchen, Richard was just pushing open the garden gate. He glanced over his shoulder to see if Alison was watching from her window, but her curtains were still tightly closed. He sighed, poor old Alison. She would usually have been so quick to 'inform' him that there were dozens of sick old ladies in the parish, but Miss Rosedale was the only one he visited every day. She would have been quite right to challenge him, too – he was honest enough to admit that he came to this house far more often than he should.

'I'm going to have to face up to this, one day soon,' he told himself as he walked across the lawn. Emmie seemed to be spending a disturbing amount of time hanging round in his thoughts these days and he found himself tripping over her at awkward moments. She was there in his study when he tried to prepare his sermons and she walked with him in the park and interrupted his brief snatches of sleep. If he saw something funny he instantly longed to share it with her and one brief conversation could make his whole day.

'I thought it was just a passing phase,' he told himself anxiously, but the idea of Emmie being only transient was now quite intolerable.

'Where's all this going to lead?' demanded his conscience relentlessly. 'She doesn't show the slightest interest in you – why should she? You must be at least ten years older than she is. It wouldn't be fair to ask her to marry you, she's a free spirit; to confine her in the constant pressure of the vicarage would be like

276

imprisoning a butterfly on a summer morning. The Alisons of this world would destroy her in a matter of hours. She'll probably marry an artist and live the creative life with him halfway up a mountain.' By the time Richard was tapping on the kitchen window he already detested that artist.

"I'm so glad you came this evening," said Emmie as she opened the back door. "I wish you would talk to Rosie for me, I'm sure she could throw this infection off if she tried a bit harder."

Richard looked down at her, and noticed that her blue eyes were misty with tears. 'She doesn't realise just how ill Rosie actually is,' he thought miserably. 'And wherever will she go if Rosie dies?' The thought of Emmie leaving Laburnum Terrace was bleak indeed.

"You do know, don't you, that I would do anything – anything whatsoever to help you," he said jerkily.

"Thank you," said Emmie. "You're a wonderful vicar, you do so much for us all." Richard sighed heavily as he followed her into the house. That was not at all the capacity in which he wanted her to think of him.

FRIDAY MARCH 13TH

8.30am

Emmie sat by Rosie's bed trying to encourage her to sip some tea from a baby's feeding-cup she had borrowed from Kim. It had been a long night, huddled in the armchair by the fire, but this morning her patient seemed even worse. Emmie had the feeling Rosie was drifting away from her like a boat without oars, leaving her alone on the shore. Desolate.

Her voice trembled suspiciously on the phone when she rang the office, and the receptionist put Miss Rosedale's card first on the doctor's visiting-list.

"I'm afraid the situation isn't too good," said Jim Macdermott as he stood in the kitchen with Emmie a little while later. "You've done a magnificent job, Miss Dawson, but I think the time has come to get her into hospital."

"Will she get better if she goes?" asked Emmie directly.

"She's ninety-four," replied the doctor uncomfortably. "I'm afraid we're going to have to face the fact that this is probably the end."

"Then she's staying here with me," said Emmie firmly.

"But, my dear girl, it's going to mean round-the-clock nursing." Her face was already white and pinched with fatigue; she had done more than enough already.

"There's a nursing agency advertising in the local paper, I'll get them to send someone at night," replied Emmie decisively. "She loves her own home and she always said she wanted to die here, and so she shall!"

Jim looked at her and smiled.

"One of the things I've always valued about Miss Rosedale is her faith," he said. "I haven't acquired it myself yet, but she always talks to me about how much she's looking forward to heaven. Perhaps it is up to us to make the journey easy for her."

"I'll do my best to see that it is," replied Emmie, and with a watery smile she went to ring the agency.

At eight o'clock that evening just before the first private nurse was due to arrive, Rosie opened her eyes and smiled at Emmie.

"Now you know God, don't ever be afraid of death," she said quite distinctly. "It's not the end, only the beginning."

She never spoke again. The nurse called Emmie early the next morning.

"She's going, I'm afraid, pet," she said briskly.

Emmie, in her dressing-gown, sat close to the bed, holding Rosie's hand. She had been so afraid of this moment, but now the whole room was flooded with a supernatural peace and she felt she was being comforted profoundly.

Rosie's breathing was intermittent and she appeared to be asleep. Then, suddenly, someone seemed to be coming in through the door behind Emmie. She swung round to look and saw no one, but Rosie opened her eyes and smiled an ecstatic welcome.

"I never knew death could be beautiful like that," said Emmie, half an hour later when Richard arrived. "She lifted up both hands just as if an old friend had come to take her on an exciting journey they'd been planning for years. She looked so wonderfully pleased, I can't be sad for *her*, but life's going to be so empty for me now she's gone." Her voice trailed away and cut deeply into Richard's newly healed scars. He knew from bitter experience exactly how she was feeling.

"Let me help you through all this," he said gently, and he put his arms around her. Emmie stood there motionless. She did not even attempt to push him away. The feel of his body so close to hers made everything that had ever happened between her and Edward seem like a mockery of the real thing. In that moment she knew for certain that she was not some kind of emotionally stunted freak – she would be able to love someone one day, and the experience, when it came, would be wonderful. 'Of course Richard's only trying to comfort me as a friend,' she thought hastily. 'He would never look at anyone like me – not after Grace.'

"Cup of tea, vicar?" said the nurse tactlessly. "Sugar and milk?"

SUNDAY MARCH 15TH

8.30pm

Claire sat slumped in her front room – it had been a dismal Sunday. The house was a dump, and the salon paperwork mounted up alarmingly, but she had no energy for anything these days. She had tried to put the clocks back and rediscover the person she had been before she met Roger, but she had found time does not travel backwards.

"You still don't fit in anywhere," mocked the voices in her head. *"You're losing your grip – heading for a breakdown."*

"Why don't you leave me alone? Let me go back to being ordinary?" she demanded. Day and night they taunted her until her head ached continuously.

"Something terrible is going to happen. Roger saw it in your palm." Claire almost wished that it would; anything was better than this agonising uncertainty.

For some odd reason she found herself thinking back to Friday afternoon, when the vicar had come shambling into the salon. He reminded her of a great embarrassed bear as he asked if Jasmine could go to tea with his daughter. She was used to men looking at her appreciatively, but he had gazed down from his incredible height as if he really cared what happened to her. She had only imagined it, of course; no one bothered what happened to Claire Lassalle any more.

'Perhaps that's what I need,' she thought. 'A new man in my life. Not a saint like David Patterson, but someone who could live dangerously.' Yes that would jerk her out of this lethargy.

It was at that significant moment that Matt Coley rang her doorbell. As she saw him standing there she felt he had been sent by the gods themselves. He was undoubtedly all man, and she wondered why she had never really noticed him before.

"I think I need your help," began Matt gruffly. "My wife . . . has . . ."

"I've known for a long time that she had MS," said Claire softly. She did not want to ask him in, the house was too messy.

"The medical profession's completely let us down. All the doctor can suggest is that she takes up religion! I've heard you're into alternative medicine and I was wondering if you'd be prepared to help her?" Claire paused. Half an hour ago she would have said "no" definitely, but it would be a shame to nip such a nice neighbourly relationship in the bud. So she snapped on the smile which had slain many a man in her time.

"Of course I can help."

"*No you can't!*" tittered the voices. "*You'll only make a fool of yourself again.*"

"How much do you charge?" asked Matt cautiously.

"Nothing at all, between *friends*." She allowed her voice to linger over the word 'friends', but he seemed not to notice. "When can you bring your wife to see me? I usually work here in my own environment." He looked annoyed.

"I can't possibly cart her down the street, trailing her catheter-bag behind her. I was hoping you'd come to us . . . now."

"So? You're the masterful type, are you?" murmured Claire. "All right, give me a moment to see if my daughter is safely asleep."

She'd wear her hair loose she decided as she hurried upstairs, and that silky Edwardian shawl. She must take some candles and joss-sticks, too, for atmosphere.

"He'll never look at you, you're far too old."

"Shut up!" she spat as she checked her make-up in the mirror.

Matt was leaning on the doorpost, with his arms folded morosely when she was ready.

"Are you sure your wife wants my help?" she enquired gently.

"Ann'll do as she's told," growled Matt.

"Yes, you really are the masterful type; I like that in a man. Come on then, Mr-next-door-neighbour, I'm all yours."

As she followed him, she noticed the easy stride of his long lean legs, but was he really the macho 'caveman' he liked to appear?

"Why are you so afraid, Matt Coley?" she asked. He stopped suddenly, with the key in the front door.

"I'm not afraid of anything whatsoever," he snapped. "It's my wife who needs the help, not me."

Ann was not pleased to see Claire. "I didn't think you'd come tonight," she said. This was just another of Matt's crazy schemes; it would be herbal concoctions and muttered chanting this time. Well, she was just too tired to play ball any more.

"People are always a little nervous at first," said Claire as she sat down by the bed.

"She's got almost no aura at all," said her voices, *"this is going to be useless."*

Claire ignored them and looked around her. The place had the cluttered appearance of a neglected sickroom. Dirty mugs littered the bedside table, dust covered every surface and a commode which did not smell too clean stood in the corner.

"Can we switch off the lights?" she said firmly. "I prefer working by candle-light."

Matt lay on the far side of the bed watching her in the flickering shadows. There was something hypnotic about her soothing voice. He closed his eyes and began to feel more relaxed than he had done for months. He admired

283

women with strong determined characters. Ann was like putty. How strange that this woman had known he was afraid.

"Don't worry, there's always hope." Someone brushed his cheek with a cool, soft hand. He looked up startled to find Claire bending over him. He must have dozed off. She smelled of fresh air and summertime. Ann smelt of urine and sweat.

"I'll see you out," he said abruptly.

"You need help just as much as your wife," she said quietly as they walked downstairs. "You're exhausted." They were standing in the passage now. It was so narrow it forced them close together. "You *are* afraid. Why don't you tell me about it?"

"I'm not much of a man for talking," said Matt awkwardly. "I prefer action myself. But you're right, I am scared. When I was a kid my gran was number one for me. But I had to watch her lying in our spare room while her body slowly decayed. Cancer − and it smelt evil. The day they finally pulled the sheet up over her face I vowed I'd never let that happen to me, I'd always keep my body fit and strong. But now it's happening to Ann, and I can't seem to stop it. If you can't help, then I'm just going to have to get her into some kind of a home." His voice grated suspiciously. "It's not that I'm heartless, but you see it's death I'm scared of; I can't face watching it happen a second time round."

"This is all being too much strain for you," Claire murmured. "If we can stabilise your psyche, you will be much more able to support your wife. Come in and see me tomorrow evening, and we'll get to work on you."

The idea appealed to Matt. "Thank you," he said.

THURSDAY MARCH 19TH

3.15pm

'Richard's doing this so well,' thought Emmie, 'it's just the kind of affair Rosie would have wanted – more like a celebration than a funeral.'

It was sad that Kim and David were still too ill to come, but she had Gwyllum there in the pew to support her. She always took him with her to church, in spite of Alison's complaints.

Glancing round, she was amazed at how many people were there: the governors of St Mark's school where Rosie had once been headmistress, a representative from MacDillan's and even a reporter from the local paper. The editor wanted to make a big feature out of the lady whose grandfather had built so much of Welbridge.

Then Emmie noticed Mr Ponsonby, and she quickly averted her eyes. He would have to wind up the estate soon, and Emmie simply could not face the dismal hunt for an apartment where Gwyllum would also be welcome. She'd have to start looking for a job too: without Rosie's financial backing she couldn't go on freelancing. As she fondled Gwyllum's ears she tried not to think about unpleasant things like that.

For the last few days she had felt herself surrounded by a protective jelly. It numbed her feelings and cushioned her from reality and whenever anything nasty threatened to penetrate – Richard appeared at her elbow. He had helped her make all the difficult arrangements and she was not sure what she would have done without

285

him. She must stay inside that jelly – at least until tomorrow.

She glanced up at him in the pulpit. He looked even bigger than ever up there, and so solid and dependable. What was he saying? The words from the Bible suddenly caught her attention.

Such is the destiny of all who forget God, so perishes the hope of the godless. What he trusts in is fragile; what he relies on is a spider's web. He leans on his web, but it gives way; he clings to it, but it does not hold.

"Miss Rosedale did not rely on a fragile spider's web, her faith was founded on a sure and certain hope . . ." His voice rang out across the church triumphantly and Emmie wished Rosie were there to enjoy it.

"Could I possibly come down with you to the house, Miss Dawson? I have a little business I need to discuss." Emmie positively glared at Mr Ponsonby as she stood at the churchyard gate shaking hands with the departing mourners. "It is important," he added pompously.

"I expect you'll have to put Number Sixteen on the market," she said as they walked down the Terrace together. "You couldn't very well fill the house with dogs, the neighbours would complain about the barking." Mr Ponsonby frowned and said he would prefer to discuss the details indoors.

'Horrid little man,' thought Emmie miserably. She showed him into the drawing-room and reluctantly went off to make him a cup of tea. When she returned with the tray he had covered the mahogany Pembroke table with papers – just as if he owned the place. 'He looks like a solicitor in an old black-and-white film, reading the will after a funeral,' she thought, and again she wished Rosie were there to share the joke.

"Miss Dawson, I wonder if you can help me," Mr Ponsonby opened the proceedings at last. "Miss Rosedale has left a sum of ten thousand pounds to – and I quote

– 'my gallant milk-lady who not only saved my life but also introduced me to Emmie.' Do you have the slightest idea who that might be?''

"Oh, yes.'' Emmie sounded pleased. "She's quite a local character. I don't know her name, but I'll find it for you.''

He bowed his head in grudging thanks and continued. "I have now to inform you that Miss Rosedale has left everything else of which she died possessed, to you.''
He allowed her time to absorb the shock and then clearing his throat he continued. "The estate consists of this property, all that it contains and some substantial investments.''

Emmie dropped her cup into the saucer with a clatter. "There must be a mistake,'' she said jerkily. "She told me she wanted to found a home for stray dogs.''

"There is no mistake, Miss Dawson, but there may, however, be an explanation. Miss Rosedale adds this proviso, and again I quote, 'You must always welcome strays to the house, including the human kind.' ''

When he finally left, Emmie stood alone in the centre of her very own drawing-room.

"You gave me my physical roots after all, Rosie,'' she whispered. "And your business venture is safe, I promise.''

Richard walked rather uncertainly down Laburnum Terrace and for once he was not praying for the occupants of each house as he passed it. He was practising his speech. He had it almost word-perfect now, but he had to admit he was as nervous as the day he'd preached his first sermon. As he pushed open the gate of Number Sixteen, he nearly collided with the sombre figure of Mr Ponsonby, but he was so preoccupied he hardly noticed him.

"Hello,'' said Emmie as she opened the front door, and gave him her fatal smile. She did not ask him in, so he would just have to try and say his piece on the doorstep.

"My mother and I were talking . . ." In his study that had felt like a good way to begin – now it sounded ridiculous. "I say, I hope that solicitor didn't bully you?" (He had strayed from his script already.)

Emmie only smiled again, and Richard decided that, as he had lost his place, he might as well go back to the beginning.

"As I was saying, mother and I were . . . You see the vicarage is a bit big for us. We don't use the top floor at all and we could easily make it into a nice big flat. You could live and work up there quite undisturbed. Plenty of light. I . . . that is mother . . . we couldn't bear to think of you having nowhere to . . ." He could hear himself drying up completely, and when Emmie took both his hands and squeezed them – he was finished.

"Richard, it's lovely of you to offer me a home, but something wonderful's happened. Everything's going to be all right, thanks to Rosie. She's left everything to me. I can stay here happily for the rest of my life. It's just what I've always wanted – space to be alone and enough capital to establish my career. It's like a fairy tale where they all live happily ever after." Richard said nothing. This fairy tale did not seem to be ending very happily for him!

"I wanted to ask you something," continued Emmie, but he hardly heard her. "I know how much you like playing the piano." That caught his attention. If she wanted him to continue his evening recitals he might at least see her sometimes. However, even that hope died when she went on to say, "I think Rosie would like you to have the piano, then you could play it in the vicarage without the bother of traipsing down here all the time."

"It was never a bother," said Richard sadly, and he had to force himself to smile as he thanked her.

FRIDAY MARCH 20TH

7.45am

The sky looked stormy and full of rain as Emmie sat on her garden wall with Gwyllum's shaggy head resting against her knee. She was waiting for Babs. As the milk-float edged its way slowly down the Terrace towards her, she was gazing at the beautiful house which now belonged to her alone. Rosie had had the outside painted a few weeks ago, and now it looked as fresh and clean as its twin over the road. She had everything she had ever wanted, but Rosie had taught her how to love another human being, and now for the first time in her life she was feeling lonely.

"Seems odd," remarked Babs when she finally alighted by the park railings, "Laburnum Terrace without the old lady. But I suppose it comes to us all in the end, we just don't like thinking about it."

"I was wondering if you'd mind coming inside for a moment?" asked Emmie shyly.

"Had another burglary?" Babs was laughing loudly at her own joke as she followed Emmie through the front door. "What's going to happen to him?" she added as she recognised the stag's head. "Got quite fond of him, I have."

"Would you like him?" Emmie sounded hopeful.

"He'd look nice on our bedroom wall," admitted Babs. "Ron would like that."

"Miss Rosedale left you something else," said Emmie. "Ten thousand pounds. All I need is your name and address for the solicitor."

289

Babs collapsed on to the Chesterfield. "I'll take our Ron on that Caribbean cruise he's always on about," she said as soon as she caught her breath. "I don't know, first a bunch of sweetpeas and now this!"

"Sweetpeas?" queried Emmie blankly as she handed Babs a piece of Rosie's headed notepaper and a pen. "Oh, so your name's Barbara, that's nice," she added a few moments later.

"Call me Babs, everyone does." 'Sweetpeas' and 'Babs' – suddenly the two things connected.

"Did you ever come to Laburnum Terrace when you were a little girl?" Emmie sounded excited.

"Course! That's when I first met the old lady."

"And she gave you some sweetpeas when you looked at her through the garden gate."

"Yes, but how did you know that?" Emmie was rummaging in a large, brown parcel which had recently arrived from MacDillan's. It contained six complementary copies of what the critics proclaimed was the children's book of the year.

"Well!" said Babs as she finally stumbled away down the path with the book under one arm and the stag's head clutched to her bosom. "Ron's never going to believe this."

'If only I could tell Rosie,' thought Emmie bleakly, 'I must ask Richard if people are allowed to know nice things like that in heaven.' As she closed her front door she realised how much she missed his frequent visits.

1.30pm

The entire Patterson family crowded into the bay window of their front room to wave as Kim's mother drove off towards Brighton. It had been a difficult ten days. Kim had developed bronchitis and David an ear infection, and while they were safely immobilised, Nan had seized her opportunity to beat the house and its occupants into shape. The children positively stood to attention, the copper shone for the first time in years and you could actually see through the windows again.

That morning David and Kim had struggled into their clothes in desperation and declared firmly that they were better.

Now, as Nan and her two yapping dogs disappeared in the lashing rain, it was impossible to say who was the more relieved, Amy or her father.

"How kind of her to stay so long," said Kim brightly.

"Yes," added David heavily.

"Let's all flop out by the fire, and perhaps by tea-time, we'll have summoned the energy to toast some crumpets."

"Nan says toasting makes a mess," said Rebecca.

"The house is so clean a few crumbs won't hurt," said Kim and added with a sigh, "the only problem's going to be finding anything in the kitchen cupboards."

She sat down on the sofa where Johnnie lay sucking his thumb. He had been the last to succumb to the flu, and as he snuggled up against her, his body felt like a hot-water bottle. Kim thought how nice he was when he was ill.

"Peace at last," sighed David from the rocking-chair. "But we couldn't have managed without her, of course," he added quickly.

"There's something lovely about being just us though, isn't there?" said Kim. Amy was sitting on David's knee, Rebecca was colouring on the hearth-rug, and the baby watched them all from behind the bars of his play-pen.

The afternoon unfolded in a gentle leisurely manner while David read aloud and the baby fell asleep in his box of toys. Kim could never remember ever sitting like this before – doing absolutely nothing. The warmth of the fire was making her drowsy when all at once she began to think about Ann.

The sight of the district nurse running in and out of the house opposite had haunted her all the previous week as she sat up in bed watching through her window. She had lain and listened to Nan downstairs organising things in her house while she felt too weak to get up and make herself a cup of tea. She had hated the feeling of helplessness it gave her, but was that how Ann felt all the time these days?

"Mummy, you're crying," said Rebecca, scattering her pencils as she threw her arms round Kim's neck.

"I'm not really, darling, it's just called 'post-flu blues'," sniffed Kim.

"What's up, old thing?" asked David anxiously, as the book slithered to the floor. "I thought we were all so happy, cuddled up in here."

"That's just it," said Kim. "We're so happy. It doesn't seem fair with Ann lying only a few metres away all on her own."

"But she won't let anyone near her," David pointed out.

"Last time I spoke to her was months ago outside Macaulay's. She looked so ill, but I had to dash off as usual and I bet she thought I didn't care. I've been wondering this week if I could take her some flowers. What do you think?"

"It'd be a drop in the ocean really," he replied, "but I suppose it might be a start."

"It would make me feel better to do something," sighed Kim as she kissed the top of Johnnie's damp head.

"I thought you said you didn't want to be a door mat," David was laughing at her now.

"Oh well, that was ten days ago, lots can happen in that time."

3.30

"Do you mind if I take in these flowers?" Kim was splashing up the garden path through the puddles just as the district nurse came bustling out of Ann's front door.

"She's so mopey she could do with a bit of company," replied the nurse. "You can carry those incontinence pads upstairs for me." Kim left them outside the bedroom door. She felt instinctively that Ann would not like her to know she needed them. She had battled her way down to the florist's in the rain and spent more than she could afford on the bunch of spring flowers, but as she put the vase down beside the bed, Ann scarcely seemed to notice them. She was gazing without any apparent interest at a portable television.

"I suppose you know by now," she said without preamble. Kim looked puzzled. "About Matt and that woman next door."

"What about them?" Kim sat down suddenly on the bed.

"He's been in there every evening this week."

"Perhaps they . . . Maybe there was nothing . . ." Kim's words petered out pathetically.

"Don't be stupid!" said Ann bitterly. "What do you suppose she does to him, cuts his hair? He *says* she's teaching him about the healing arts, so he can help me." Her mouth twisted into a thin line. "He told me yesterday he's applying to the Cheshire Home on the London Road. Says he can't hold down a job and look after me as well. But I reckon he just wants to stick me in an institution so he can enjoy himself with her." This was too much for Kim and her post-flu blues – she was crying again, but by now Ann was a long way past tears.

"I can't cope without him," she said flatly. "He's always been everything. We started going out before we went to college."

Kim sat looking at her dumbly. She simply could not think of anything to say.

"I suppose you came over here to spout religion at me," continued Ann.

"No," said Kim miserably. "I only wanted you to know I care."

"Any minute now you'll say, 'I know just how you

293

feel.' Everyone says that! But how could you possibly know?" She struggled up on to her elbow and glared at Kim aggressively. "You've got everything I want: health, kids and a husband who adores you. You could never understand."

"I know I couldn't, but I mind for you all the same," said Kim in a small voice.

"You lot are always carting off to that ghastly old church, but I can't think why you bother. How could a loving God let a thing like this happen?"

"I just don't know the answer to that," Kim admitted nervously. "But I do know for sure that he'd help you through all this if you'd let him."

"You wouldn't go on believing that if you were me," said Ann.

"I don't really know what I'd do," replied Kim. "But our vicar lost his wife about eighteen months ago. If ever you did feel like talking to someone who really understands suffering, you could always ask him to come and see you."

"I'll think about it," said Ann unenthusiastically. She looked tired and Kim realised she had better go.

"I'll come back soon," she promised as she pulled herself on to her shaky legs. Ann merely shrugged and said,

"Switch the telly off before you go."

By the time Kim had waded back home through the driving rain, her teeth were chattering with cold and she was quite exhausted. David hastily despatched the girls to play in their bedroom and sat her down by the fire again.

"Bad, was it?" he said gently.

"Terrible." Kim was beginning to feel angry as well by now. "How could Claire try to steal Ann's husband just when she needs him most?"

"Very easily," said David ruefully. He had never told Kim about that evening last July.

"Poor little Jasmine."

"I was thinking of going to fetch her in time for the crumpets – now your mum's safely away," he said. "She's been at the vicarage every day after school this week, and Richard's mother's not too well." Kim smiled. It was a long speech for him.

"I believe you miss her," she said and hugged him.

"I won't be long," he said, buttoning up his overcoat. "Get the fire nice and hot." But none of them ate crumpets that night.

4.45

Richard was playing snakes and ladders with Pippa and Jasmine in the threadbare drawing-room of the vicarage when David arrived. The lofty room was cold and dusty, but they were enjoying themselves hugely.

"Come on then, Jasmine," said David, when she had climbed her final ladder to triumph. "Let's go home."

She slid her hand happily into his as they battled down the drive behind a large umbrella. "I'm glad I'm coming back to your house," she said. "You always look after me best."

"You old creep," said David.

"Do you think Mummy really will send me to boarding-school?" She tightened her grasp on David's hand and added, "You won't let her, will you?" He looked down at her, but he never had time to reply. They had reached the kerb and it seemed as if every vehicle in Welbridge was whizzing up and down Bakers Hill that evening.

"David! You forgot Jasmine's lunch-box." Richard's voice floated through the gloom from the front door of the vicarage.

"Wait here and hold the umbrella," said David, "and don't you dare cross on your own."

Ron was driving his lorry down Bakers Hill, cursing the traffic and the weather. He was wondering what Babs had for his tea when the car swung out of Laburnum

Terrace in front of him. It was Hazel's BMW. She had arrived home from her skiing holiday that afternoon and was in a hurry to see if her department was still intact.

"Bloody fool!" yelled Ron, and swung the wheel sharply to the left. The rain was running like a river down the hill and his tyres simply could not cope. His lorry was skidding out of control as it mounted the kerb. He knew at once that he had hit something which he had failed to notice through his rain-blurred windscreen. Hazel sailed away past the salon and off down the hill. She had no idea what her moment of impatience would do to Ron and Claire.

"What's happening out there?" Claire's client was a nervous, twitchy little woman, and she was struggling to her feet in the salon before Claire's concentration had even been penetrated by the noises outside in the road.

"There's been an accident," said Michelle, wiping misty windows. "Lorry's hit someone. Do you think I ought to dial 999, Mrs Lassalle?"

"Don't bother, everyone else will," said Claire absently. "You haven't swept up yet, Michelle."

As she hustled her client under the dryer she was thinking of Matt. Would he come again this evening? She was not sure if this relationship was going to work. She always felt he was thinking about his wife when they were together. It wasn't fair on the young man, having to carry a heavy burden like that.

Someone was coming into the shop.

"So you've recovered from the flu at last then, David," she said coldly. Then she saw his face.

TUESDAY MARCH 24TH

7pm

"Roger? Where have you been? I've rung you so many times since Friday night." Claire clutched the telephone receiver for support.

"Been away, my dear. Took Mother to Bournemouth." The sound of his treacly voice brought tears of relief to Claire's eyes. Everything would be all right now.

"Roger, look, I need you. It's my little girl. She's been badly hurt. Head injuries. Can you come here at once?" She could hear her voice rising high and sharp now, as hope began to replace the despair which had gripped her over the last four days.

"My dear, be calm. Where are you?"

"Welbridge General . . . the intensive care unit. The doctors can't do a thing, she's in such a deep coma. I've been working on her night and day ever since, but I just can't seem to channel the spirits any more."

"My dear, I will come as soon as I've had my supper. All will be well."

"Damn your supper, come *now*!" Claire put down the phone in Sister's office and walked slowly back to the figure on the bed. It didn't look like Jasmine, wired to all those machines, with her head shaved and her mouth full of tubes.

"Keep talking to her," Sister had urged, but Claire feared there was no one there to listen.

"Roger's on his way, my darling," she tried uncertainly. "I know you never liked him, but he's your

297

only hope." Her only reply was the rhythmic wheeze of the life support machine and the regular bleeps from the screen which monitored Jasmine's heart. "Just hold on till Roger gets here. I know I've been a rotten mum, but I'll make it up to you, when I get you home."

Someone was walking up the ward. Someone who was not wearing a white coat or a nurse's uniform. Roger? Claire looked up hopefully, but it was only David standing at the foot of the bed.

"You!" she said indignantly. "Haven't you done her enough damage already?"

David said nothing. He just stood looking silently down at Jasmine, and then bent to pick up one of her limp hands. He had tried to see her so many times since Friday night, but this was the first time Sister had allowed him in.

"I'm desperately sorry, Claire," he said miserably. "I only left her on the kerb for a few seconds."

"I don't want you here."

"I just wanted to ask you if you would allow the vicar to come and pray for her."

"Go away," said Claire rudely. "My friend Roger will be here any moment. He'll help her. He has enormous power."

"Not so much power as Jesus Christ," said David with a gulp. "Please let us pray for her."

"That won't be necessary," said Claire hurriedly. "Now will you please leave?" David looked down at Jasmine as if she had been his own child lying there on the bed. Indeed he felt as if she was.

"If you should change your mind . . ." he said, but when he encountered Claire's expression he blundered away down the ward. He was so blinded by distress that he almost collided with a fat little man coming out of Sister's office. Everything within David recoiled as they passed one another.

"Roger!" he heard Claire exclaim behind him. In the waiting-room Richard was pacing up and down, but when the door opened he looked round hopefully.

"No good," said David, blowing his nose. "She's got one of her healers there now. We're too late."

Richard put a hand on his shoulder. "Not necessarily," he said gently. "The power of God is greater than any other power in the universe. We must keep on praying."

Roger pulled up a chair and sat down by the bed. He looked oddly out of place in this sterile modern world wearing his old waistcoat and faded velvet jacket. But to Claire at that moment he resembled an angel of light.

"This is what you saw in my hand that night, wasn't it?" she demanded without preamble. Roger nodded. It was *not* what he had seen, but it was kinder to allow her to think so.

"Don't talk now, my dear," he said softly. "Just centre yourself – so the spirits can do their work through us."

"I'm afraid it's time we cleared the ward," said Sister a full hour later. "Take her out to a meal, will you?" she said to Roger. "She'll wear herself out sitting here all the time."

The restaurant was crowded and after the hushed silence of the hospital ward Claire found the noise almost painful.

"How can you possibly think about food?" she demanded. She had watched him chewing his way through three filling vegetarian courses, while she toyed with a string of black coffees. Ever since this nightmare began, one hundred hours ago, she had longed for Roger, now he was there in front of her and the sight of him was strangely disappointing. When he had finished the last spoonful of the fruit muesli, he sat back and sipped his brandy in silence. Claire sensed he wanted to tell her something she did not wish to hear.

"My dear, the child no longer has an aura." There, he had said it at last, but as she sat gazing at him, her mind refused to receive his words. He might be a revolting little man, but of course he was going to be able to help Jasmine.

"The brain is . . . beyond our reach." Roger tried again, but there was still no response. He used a different tactic, "My dear, I've missed you. Perhaps the time has now come for you to start a new life in my mother's cottage." For some reason his words penetrated Claire's defences at last.

"Now Jasmine won't disturb you with her radios and boyfriends?" She almost shouted the words at him. "You're going to let her die, aren't you?" Her voice was shrill and people looked round inquisitively from other tables. "You've never liked her, and you've brought us both nothing but trouble!" She stood up and leaned aggressively over him. At that moment she could have throttled Roger.

The pianist on the dais struck up a medley of loud, cheerful tunes while the head waiter hurried up with another cup of coffee. Roger looked up at her helplessly and said, "My dear, you must face it. There is nothing anyone can do now."

"I don't believe you!" raged Claire, and stepped backwards with such force she sent her elegant dining-chair crashing over backwards. Interested eyes followed her as she stalked from the room, but Roger merely beckoned the waiter,

"I'll have one more glass of that excellent cognac, if you please," he said as he leant back in his chair. She would settle down in time, he told himself. The child had always been an interruption to her work.

As Claire drove back to Laburnum Terrace she knew she was going to do something she might later regret, but only Jasmine mattered now. She hammered on the door of Number Four and Kim took her straight to David and Richard who were sitting in the kitchen.

"Come on in," said David gently, "you look so tired."

"You said earlier on . . . the vicar . . . if I changed my mind." Claire was beyond sentence construction, but they understood what she was trying to say.

"We'll go back to the hospital with you at once," said Richard.

"I'm afraid it's far too late for visitors now," said the night sister severely, but when she saw Richard's collar she relented. "You'll have to be extremely quiet," she said grimly, "we do have other patients to consider."

One dim light illuminated Jasmine's bed. She looked like a corpse already lying there among the machines.

David and Richard stood on either side of her and began to pray silently, while Claire stood awkwardly at the bottom of the bed, wondering what she was supposed to do. Inside her head the spirits were raging at her, screaming abuse and disapproval.

"Claire," whispered Richard, "I feel Christ would like you to ask him to heal Jasmine. Do you think you could manage a short prayer?"

"I haven't prayed for years," protested Claire so loudly that Sister glared at her across the room.

"Jesus Christ doesn't exist!" screamed the voices. *"He's powerless, he's dead!"* Claire ignored them. Slowly she knelt down beside Richard, but the hands seemed to be round her neck like iron now, choking her and preventing the words which were trying to form. She couldn't even breathe. Vainly she struggled to free herself, but the hands grew tighter still.

"I take the authority of Jesus Christ over these spirits," came Richard's low voice beside her, and the hands were gone instantly. She could breathe again and in short jerky sentences she began to pray.

It must have been a long time that she remained kneeling beside Richard, there by the bed. A warmth and a peace she had never known before settled on her like a soft cloak.

Suddenly the bleeps on the monitor seemed to change their rhythm and Sister hurried over to the bed.

"You'll have go out to the waiting-room I'm afraid," she said briskly. "Her condition seems to be deteriorating. I'm sorry."

301

Dumbly all three crept out of the ward, exhausted and confused. Behind them a doctor and two more nurses hurried to Jasmine's bed.

"Go and sit down for while, Mrs Lassalle," said Sister as she dived for the phone on her desk. "I'll have some tea sent in."

"Don't bother," said Claire bitterly. "I'm going home. There's nothing more I can do here."

"We'll keep in touch, I promise," said Sister.

"There you see!" said Claire furiously when they reached the corridor beyond the swing-doors.

"We're going to run you home, Claire," said Richard firmly, "then David and I will go back to the church to pray for Jasmine – we'll stay there all night if necessary."

As they walked her up her garden path, David said gently, "Let me get Kim to pop over and make you a cup of tea."

"Just leave me alone," snapped Claire, and as she closed her front door the tears she had been fighting for days could not be held back any longer. She had hardly reached the sanctuary of her kitchen before Matt was tapping on the back door.

She ran into his arms. "Take me to bed," she sobbed. "I'll never make it through tonight unless you stay with me."

WEDNESDAY MARCH 25TH

7.45am

Babs was not sure if she should have come back to work this morning. She was chewing her thumb anxiously as she turned the truck into Laburnum Terrace. It was the first time she had left Ron alone since the accident. Poor old boy, even the thought of his Caribbean cruise couldn't cheer him up, not with these police charges hanging over his head.

"Well, you're up early," she said as she walked over to the Pattersons' gate with their six bottles clutched to her chest. Rebecca eyed her solemnly from her seat on the garden wall.

"I'm waiting for my daddy. He's been in church all night long, praying for Jasmine."

"Well, that's nice of him I must say," Babs thought of her Ron sitting tensely at home and she profoundly hoped the Almighty would listen.

"I think Jasmine's going to heaven."

"Gracious, we don't want that!"

"Oh, but she'd like to go. You see she's frightened of absolutely everything. Mummy says she'll grow up to be a right worry-guts. She'd be ever so much happier in heaven. Amy and me think she's lucky."

Just for once Babs was bereft of speech. She was still trying to regain her equilibrium when she reached Number Five. On the doorstep she stopped, the skimmed milk and yoghurts poised in the air. Whatever was that noise? It sounded like some sort of animal caught in a trap. Who was it who lived here? Oh yes, that nice-looking girl who ran in the London Marathon, the one who was crippled now. She bent down and pushed the letter-box flap inwards.

"Oh Gawd, not again!" Yet another body lay huddled at the bottom of the stairs. This kind of thing was becoming a habit in the road!

"You all right, luvvy?" she asked unnecessarily.

"Get my husband," moaned Ann.

"Well, I would if I knew where he was."

"He's been next door with *her* all night."

Babs stood up, seething with indignation, and caught her fingers painfully in the flap.

"Well! There's a vegan for you!" she snorted. "I'll soon sort them out for you, luvvy," she added, and stalked into the next-door garden. Poor girl, fancy leaving her alone like that!

"You two lovebirds, wake up at once," she yelled as she hammered loudly on the door. All the way up the Terrace she was pleased to see a shock wave of rippling net curtains. "Come on out of there, Mr Coley, your wife needs you."

It was Claire who opened the door in the end. Matt had deemed it more prudent to leave by the back alley and he was already bending over his wife.

"Silly bitch," he murmured miserably. She had obviously crawled out of bed looking for him, and rolled down the stairs. He rubbed her hands, and felt how cold they were.

Ten minutes later, along at Number Twelve, Sharon looked out of the window just in time to see Dr Macdermott's car swing into the Terrace. It was nice to have a bit of drama on the first day of the school holidays.

"I'm afraid we're going to have to get her into hospital, Mr Coley," said the doctor. "That arm looks fractured and she's obviously suffering from hyperthermia. She must have been lying there all night. How was it that you didn't hear her calling for help?"

304

"I sleep soundly," said Matt sullenly.

Claire, still in her dressing-gown, stood gazing after the ambulance as it drove off down Bakers Hill. It reminded her of the one which had taken Jasmine away. As she stood there gripping her front door for support she noticed two bedraggled figures coming across the road from St Mark's. Richard and David looked exhausted and they both needed a shave.

"Any news?" called Richard hopefully. As they came towards her, the concern on their tired faces suddenly made Claire feel ashamed.

Back in the house her phone was ringing. They could hear it, too, and they hurried up the path to her front door.

"This is Sister from ICU," said a crisp voice. Claire bit the insides of her cheeks until they hurt.

"I think you should come up to the ward at once, Mrs Lassalle, your daughter has just regained consciousness. She's asking for you."

3.15pm

Someone was knocking on the door again. If she took no notice they always went away. Alison sat in her darkened front room surrounded by the kind of debris which, until recently, would have horrified her. 'It's probably only that vicar again,' she thought. 'As if he could possibly help me! What does he know about suffering?'

If Gordon had died she would have been entertaining the whole district and basking in their sympathy. This was far worse for her than any bereavement, yet she could turn to no one for comfort. 'They'll all be blaming me, saying I should have been more careful! No one cares how I feel.'

Outside her front door, Kim rang once more, then sighed as she put a box of home-made Easter biscuits on the step.

MAUNDY THURSDAY
MARCH 26TH

8.30am

Tom Savery sat up in bed sipping a mug of tea. He and
Angela had taken the whole week off and had enjoyed
every minute of it. Being able to read the paper from cover
to cover like this before he got up in the morning was
very pleasant indeed.

"Terrorists are at it again," he remarked as he poked
at an obscure paragraph on the second page.

"What now?" yawned his wife. The crackling newspaper always irritated her when she wanted to sleep in.

"It says here they're threatening to hit an aircraft
somewhere in the world over Easter."

"Terrorists always say that," replied Angela. "I'm
going down to cook a bit of breakfast. Oh look," she
added as she pulled open the bedroom curtains, "there's
a removal van over the road at Number Fifteen. Those
Tilsons must be moving today."

9.30

Richard was at his desk, wrestling with his Good Friday
sermon. It simply would not take shape. At last he threw
down his pen and walked over to the window. He loved
this study of his. It was on the first floor and from here
he could see right down Laburnum Terrace.

It was a superb spring morning; flowers filled the

window-boxes with vivid colour and the sparrows chattered busily on the slate roofs. The whole scene seemed to promise a new, fresh start to life, but when he thought about some of the people who lived down there, and the problems which crushed them, he sighed. During the past year he had discovered that Christ was there in the centre of his own grief, helping him with all his uncertainty. How was he ever going to help those people to see that Christ could do the same for their pain, too?

"I've tried to tell them," he said softly, "but most of them won't listen to me. Did you die in vain for them, that first Good Friday?" Should that be the theme of his sermon tomorrow? As he picked up his pen again, he whispered, "I suppose it's not really me they're rejecting – it's you."

10

The salon was a whirl of pre-holiday activity, but for the first time ever Claire simply was not coping. Outwardly, as she drifted between her clients she merely looked dazed; inside she was terrified.

"You've got your life into such a mess, you're finished!" mocked the voices in her head. They were there all the time now, yelling silent obscenities and destroying her relentlessly.

"Are you all right, dear?" asked Mrs Cromway as Claire brushed out her tight white curls.

"No she's not all right," snarled the voices.

"I'm fine," replied Claire. "Naturally I'm still a bit worried about my daughter. They tell me at the hospital she's making a miraculous recovery, and there's no sign of brain damage, but of course she's still pretty ill."

Someone was standing behind her with their hand pressing down on her shoulder – she swung round, but no one was there.

"You might as well be dead!" they whispered.

'I need help,' she told herself. 'I wonder if that vicar . . .?'

"You're dirt! He wouldn't want you near him if he knew what you're really like."

11

"It's time we had a break," said Emmie as she looked round the chaotic room. "I'm going to toast us some hot-cross-buns and make a pot of tea." She had always known this job was going to be painful. That was why she wanted to get it out of the way before Easter. Sorting through drawers and cupboards full of Rosie's clothes and personal possessions felt like violating her privacy. She had not been able to face doing it on her own, so she had asked Nigel to come and help her. His silence was soothing and his strength was useful – when it came to humping heavy cases from the attic.

She put the tea-tray down in the middle of the pathetic piles of belongings and smiled at him. He was a good friend.

"We'll have a huge bonfire later, Nigel." She knew she was promising him his greatest treat, but his mouth was too full of currant bun to repeat what she had said.

11.30

"It's going to look lovely when it's done, darling," said Kim brightly as she walked into the bathroom carrying a mug of coffee. David, balanced precariously on the edge of the bath, was stripping the old paint from the walls. He grinned down at her affectionately. They both knew how much he detested decorating, but Nan had said the room was a positive disgrace and she was coming for lunch on Sunday.

11.40

It took Matt all the courage he had just to walk down the middle of that ward. He hadn't been able to bring himself to do it yesterday: hospitals terrified him. Ann was pretending to be asleep when he reached her bed so he sat down beside her awkwardly.

"What have you come here for then?" she said without opening her eyes.

"Just thought I'd say hello." He was trying hard to sound breezy.

" 'Sorry' might be better for starters."

"You know I'm no good at that kind of thing," he said sheepishly.

"Don't forget it's bank holiday tomorrow, so get yourself in enough food." She opened her eyes then, and looked at him sharply as she added, "Or is she going to feed you?"

"Don't be an idiot. You ought to know I'll never go near that woman again."

"But I don't know that; how would I?"

"Because I'm telling you, that's why. You know there's never really anyone else but you."

"What about when you stick me away in that home?"

"Don't be stupid. You know I won't be able to do that." He fumbled under the sheet for her hand. "We'll make a go of all this somehow," he said. "We've got to, haven't we?"

3.15pm

"Thank you, Nigel, you've been such a help." Emmie's task was nowhere near done yet, but she knew Nigel's mother had wanted him home by now. "I'd really like to give you something of Rosie's as a present."

"Present." He nodded vigorously.

"Why don't you look round and choose what you

want, Nigel?'' She was not sure if he would understand, but he jumped instantly to his feet and hurried straight over to the mantelpiece.

"Choose what . . . you want, Nigel," he repeated as he grabbed a picture in a silver frame. Emmie looked at it in surprise. It was the original of the famous self-portrait which still sold Brightways cornflakes by the bushel. Rosie had taken a fancy to it, and had it framed.

"You can't possibly want that old thing, Nigel," she protested.

". . . want that old thing, Nigel," he said firmly and cradled the picture to his chest as if it had been Emmie in person.

She tried to take it from him, but with a squeal of glee he galloped out of the house and up the Terrace to show it to his mother. He looked as proud as if he had just been given the crown jewels. Emmie stood looking after him and had to smile.

"You know, Gwyllum, I sometimes wonder how people round here can possibly call him handicapped," she said. "If finding happiness is what life's all about, then he must be the most successful person in the road." Gwyllum wagged his tail encouragingly. "You're asking for a walk, aren't you? Rosie would say 'I can tell by your eyes,' " she added sadly. "Perhaps you're right, a break would do us both good." She found her blue scarf and went out across the garden.

She stopped by the railings, uncertain which way to go. The park was lovely in all directions, but the dismal job had sapped her usual energy. For some reason she remembered Richard sitting by the lake under the Scotch firs, the day in October when he had felt so desolate. What was it he'd said? "Sometimes it's a comfort just sitting and looking." Perhaps he was right. 'That's where I'll go,' she thought.

3.30

Richard was struggling hard to regain his calm as he sat on the peninsula by the lake. He had just battled his way round Brightways with his mother's weekend shopping list while his two daughters 'helped' him to the point of exasperation. The doorbell and the phone had been ringing all day and he felt he simply could not face all the pressing needs of the parish without a few moments here in his favourite place to recharge his batteries.

Today the lake up at this end was shallow, revealing an ugly mudbank clogged with dead leaves and rotting wood. Out of the mess and decay sprang an extravagant clump of vivid yellow kingcups and he sat gazing at them in pure delight. He must tell Emmie to come here and see this.

Emmie. He sighed as he was forced to admit to himself that he had not only escaped to this place for some peace – he loved it here because it always reminded him of her.

She was crossing the peninsula before she saw Richard and she stopped short in an agony of embarrassment. It felt like watching a film and discovering suddenly that she'd seen it before. He sprang up, his face alight with pleasure, and hit his head on exactly the same branch.

"Come and enjoy it all with me for a few minutes," he pleaded, and peeled off his elderly sweater to make a cushion for her on the seat. "Just look at those kingcups! Aren't they lovely? I feel they're telling me something important, but I'm too thick to work out what it is."

"I'll come down here tomorrow and paint them," murmured Emmie. "I tried to do some violets last Good Friday but . . ." It occurred to her that Edward would never have noticed those kingcups and this time last year she was still engaged to him. "You shall have the picture when it's done. You really do seem to love this spot, don't you?"

"That's because something very special happened to

me here once . . ." He stopped in confusion and discovered he was extremely hot even without his jumper. "Oh look, Emmie, I can't go on pretending like this. Do you remember we were both out here early one morning? I looked up and saw you standing there. I've never really been the same ever since. I love you. I'm sorry, but I just can't help it."

Her blue eyes widened in surprise and she blushed. "Vicars can't say things like that," she said.

"Yes they can. I'm afraid I'm asking you to marry me," he said apologetically.

There was a stunned pause. "I couldn't, Richard," she said at length. "I'd be a terrible vicar's wife."

"But I'm not asking you because I want an unpaid curate to help me run the parish. I'm asking you because I love you so much the thought of life without you is completely intolerable."

"But what about Grace?"

"I don't love her any less, and this isn't just an imitation of the way I felt about her. This is new and quite different."

Emmie, looked away up the length of the lake. "I thought you were just being kind, helping me with the practical things when Rosie died."

"Emmie I'm crazy about you. Do you feel anything towards me in return?" His face was positively twisted with apprehension.

She looked round at him, sitting there at the far end of the seat – big, kind and utterly dependable – and she realised suddenly that she did not simply like Richard's company – she loved him, too. She remembered the feel of his arms around her on the morning of Rosie's death and the smell of his tweed jacket as it scratched against her cheek. She longed for him to hold her tightly against him again like that.

'But I can't,' she thought. The familiar panic was rising in her again. 'I mustn't let myself be committed to another relationship and then find I can't cope. It was bad enough

312

hurting Edward without doing the same thing to Richard as well. And suppose he finds out what I'm really like?' She couldn't cook, she was scared of the telephone and she might need to paint a picture when Grace's children clamoured for attention. One day she might see the kindly look in his eyes change to bewildered disappointment because he had discovered she was not the kind of person he wanted her to be. As she sat there by the water she realised with terrible clarity that she loved Richard too much to face his ultimate rejection.

"Richard," she began. "I'm . . . not . . ." and she stopped, somehow she just did not know how to say it.

"Of course you're not ready for this so soon after losing Rosie," he said full of compunction. "I'm selfish to mention it yet, but this place seems to be my undoing. All the same, please don't turn me down flat. I simply couldn't bear that. At least sleep on it, Emmie." They stood up and faced each other shyly. "Couldn't we meet here again – say tomorrow afternoon – and talk it all through?"

"Richard, I don't think a night's going to make any difference," said Emmie nervously. He took both her hands and looked down at her.

"At least I can pray that it will," he said sadly.

4.15

They parted at the gate of Number Sixteen, polite but restrained, and as he turned heavily away Richard saw Gordon sliding furtively out of his house. 'Poor chap,' he thought and tried hard to shelve his own problems. He seemed smaller than ever and the skin which covered his cheekbones appeared to have shrunk. Richard put a huge hand on his shoulder.

"Haven't seen you for days," he said. "Don't forget we've got a date tomorrow." Gordon looked up at him nervously. "You promised we'd have another talk on

Good Friday, remember. Shall I come down here in the evening?''

"Oh no! She'd never let you in. The doctor's had to give her some pills for her nerves." He looked as if he could do with some himself.

"You come up to the vicarage, then, and have some supper with me." Gordon almost allowed himself to look pleased as he sidled away into the park.

"Dirty little man," remarked Tom Savery from the far side of the road. "They oughtn't to let him loose in there with all those kids about."

"But he hasn't even been found guilty yet," said Richard indignantly.

"He has round here." Tom was standing at his gate watching two men lift his brand new-television from their van.

"Treated ourselves to a luxury model," he said proudly.

"It's got a computerised video too," added Sharon from the garden wall.

"Not going away this Easter?" asked Richard endeavouring to sound more friendly.

"Not likely, not worth the hassle, is it? Got everything we want here − brand-new telly and the wife's been down to Brightways and laid in enough grub for a siege. It doesn't take much to satisfy us." He laughed happily as he followed his shiny new god into the house.

Richard sighed and walked on slowly up the Terrace. He was so deep in his own thoughts he did not notice Matt hurrying out of Number Five.

"Excuse me." He sounded most uncomfortable. "My wife gave me a message for you when I saw her this morning."

"Ah," said Richard, yanking himself back from the shores of despair with an effort. "How is she now?"

"All right, I suppose. She said . . . .er . . . Kim Patterson told her that if ever she wanted to . . . you know . . . sort herself out a bit, she was to ask you to go and see her." He tugged awkwardly at the collar of his track suit.

"I'd be glad to," said Richard. "Shall I go now?"

"Oh no, sometime tomorrow'll do," said Matt vaguely. "She's got her mother this afternoon."

'Tomorrow,' thought Richard. 'Everything's going to happen tomorrow.'

"I'll go tomorrow then," he said, "and . . . thank you."

4.30

"He's still at it then," chuckled David as he leaned out of the bathroom window. Down below Johnnie stood at the garden gate.

"See 'moval van, see 'moval van," he chanted incessantly.

"He's been wanting to watch the Tilsons moving house all day. Come on, let's take him along there."

"What? Stand gawping at all of Hazel's possessions? I'd die of embarrassment," said Kim indignantly. Anyway she wanted David to finish the decorating. Like Mole, however, in *The Wind in the Willows*, the spring sunshine was calling David loudly and he threw down his paint-brush with an air of finality.

Ten minutes later he and Kim were standing at the park railings trying to pretend they were admiring the view. Meanwhile, Johnnie and his small brother gazed unashamedly at the removal van from the safety of the twin stroller. The little girls had been sent on ahead to buy ice-creams in the park with Nigel.

A fierce altercation was going on at the doorstep of Number Fifteen, and it took a great deal of will-power on the Pattersons' part not to turn round and enjoy it.

"What do you mean, you can't finish packing tonight? This is outrageous!" Hazel, who even on her moving day contrived to look immaculate, was standing with her hands on her elegant hips. Not a red hair was out of place, but her voice sounded like the bark of a vixen. The man who appeared to be in charge slid his cap to the back of his head for a leisurely scratch.

"We'll leave you your bedding, lady," he said soothingly. But Hazel would not be soothed. "Your firm undertook to get us to Gresham Manor by this evening. This is gross incompetence."

"Our Dave couldn't 'elp strainin' his back and young Keith didn't mean to twist his ankle. And after all's said and done, it ain't a bad house to sleep in for one more night. I'd swap it for my council flat any day." He wheezed with laughter, but Hazel did not appear to share the joke.

"Be careful with that dressing-table," she snapped at his two sweating companions.

"I can't think why she ever wanted to leave Number Fifteen," whispered Kim out of the corner of her mouth. "That house has always been the pinnacle of my dreams."

"Oh well, perhaps she fancies her Elizabethan 'cottage' with six bedrooms and a swimming-pool," grinned David as he rubbed some splashes of white paint from his nose.

"Just look at all that gorgeous furniture," sighed Kim. "Hazel's got absolutely everything – good looks, money, success. Some people seem to have life so easy, honestly it just isn't fair."

David laughed. "Oh come on, don't begrudge her that, it's all she's got."

" 'All she's got' my foot! Just think what their combined salaries must be."

"What about the 'moths and rust' then?"

"I'll remind you of that when all the kids next need new shoes," said Kim, but she could not help hugging him.

"Graham!" came Hazel's voice behind them. "This man says we'll have to spend another night in this dump of a Terrace. I simply can't stand the thought of it!"

316

"I can't think why you're getting so worked up," replied Graham grumpily. "We can't complete on this place until Tuesday and we're already bridging on Gresham Manor – all because of this 'thing' you've got about being there by Easter. Surely one more night in Laburnum Terrace won't hurt you?"

8.15

Claire was late leaving the salon and she had to dash to reach the hospital before Jasmine was settled for the night. She was driving down Bakers Hill when her tormentors began again.

"You're going to die tonight." She was still shaking when she reached the ward.

"I'll spend all day with you tomorrow, sweetheart," she whispered as she stroked her daughter's thin little face. Jasmine smiled sleepily at her. "I love you," added Claire, "always remember that . . . whatever happens."

"I'll remember, Mummy – I'll always remember."

9

Gordon lay alone in the big double bed. Alison had taken to sleeping in Amanda's old room since . . . He'd come up rather early, but what else was there to do?

'Good Friday tomorrow,' he thought. A whole year since it all began. Funny to think they wouldn't be going to church this year. Alison said she'd never show her face there again. Poor old girl. He wondered vaguely why she was not finding more comfort in God during all this trouble – after all, she'd been worshipping him long enough. But maybe it was the church and not God she'd worshipped all along.

9.15

The house felt very cold and empty when Claire opened her front door. Even Boris did not bounce up to greet her. She could go over to the Pattersons and tell them how Jasmine was that evening.

"No. No. No!" screamed the voices.

She shrugged and went into the kitchen. Matt would be all alone next-door, but she knew better than to call him. All that was definitely over. He had let her down just like all the other spiders' webs she had clutched at before.

She made herself some toast with the stale loaf in the bin, filled a hot-water bottle and climbed slowly up the stairs. Outside her bedroom she hesitated. She was dog-tired, but recently she had been afraid to be in there alone.

"You're not going to do this to me!" she said firmly, and opened the door. She undressed slowly and then sat down at her dressing-table to apply her night-cream. It was while she was brushing out her hair that she noticed Jasmine's latest school photo standing by the mirror. The little face looked up at her with an expression of complete despair.

"I've been so busy with myself these last two years, I never even noticed you looking like that," she whispered, and wondered miserably when she had last seen Jasmine really happy. "I'm sorry – but I'll make it up to you. I promise."

"No you won't, you can't, you're going to die!" They were not just voices in her head now, they filled the room, malevolent and vengeful as they closed in behind her. When she swung round to face them, the photo frame fell to the floor and the glass shattered. What was it that vicar had said in the hospital? Would it work for her now?

"I take the authority of Jesus Christ over you," she shouted. "Go away!"

Only laughter greeted her. "What's he to you?" they mocked. "You're dirt."

318

"I won't listen," she said as she slid into bed. Where was Boris hiding, she wondered. He always slept on her feet. When she called, he appeared in the doorway, whining. Putting his tail between his legs he slunk away downstairs.

"Coward!" yelled Claire, and pulled the duvet over her head.

"You'll be dead before you get up in the morning." She sat up again like a jack-in-a-box.

"I'll prove you're wrong!" she shouted, and grabbing her bedding she went downstairs. The cramped two-seater settee in the front room would be better than lying there in misery. She put on all the lights and lit the gas-fire to counteract the chill in the house.

Boris still cowered in the corner.

"The end is only a few hours away now. That's what Roger saw in your palm." Something was pressing down on her now, heavy, suffocating. She almost felt the house was falling in on top of her. *"We're going to kill you."*

"No!" she screamed and struggled up off the settee. With Boris at her heels she ran out into the road. The front door flapped open behind her, but she did not look back. 'The Pattersons. Yes, they would know what to do,' she thought wildly as she hammered on the door of Number Four.

David and Kim were sitting on the sofa watching the ten o'clock news.

"Claire! Whatever's the matter?" asked David when he opened the door.

"Is it Jasmine?" quavered Kim. "Is she worse again?"

"No, but I've got myself into such an awful mess. I'm terrified! Do you think your vicar would help a woman like me?"

"I reckon he'd be proud to," said David. "Why don't you come in and have a cup of tea."

"I don't want any tea!" snapped Claire. "They're going to kill me tonight. Take me to your vicar. Now!"

"But you can't go across Bakers Hill in your night

319

clothes," soothed Kim. "Why don't you go home and get dressed?"

"Don't you understand? I can't go back into that house. And what does it matter what I look like any more?"

"I'll go with her, Kim," said David.

When the door shut behind them, Kim went back into the sitting-room. 'I never imagined we were getting ourselves mixed up in anything like this,' she thought doubtfully. But she switched off the television and knelt down by the sofa.

10.15

Hazel and Graham were propped uncomfortably on the mattress which was usually a part of their four-poster bed. Around them lay the dismantled ruins of their elegant bedroom.

"I can't face it," said Graham suddenly.

"Face what?" snapped Hazel.

"Living with you."

"You've had too much gin," she said, throwing down the paper which she had been pretending to read. "You shouldn't touch gin, it always does this to you."

"Life isn't fun any more. Hasn't been for years."

"That's just the gin talking. Of course it's going to be fun when we get settled at Gresham Manor."

"That's what you always say. 'It's going to be great when . . .' But it never is because as soon as we get there, we have to start thrusting on towards the next thing. I'm sick of it all, Hazel, it's pointless." A shadow of anxiety crossed Hazel's face.

"That's what I thought the night of the storm." She sounded as if she was soothing a fretful child, but the anxiety still lurked in her eyes. "You remember when I got trapped in that damn beech-wood. I learnt a lot that night. You were stoned out of your senses then, too, if I remember rightly," she added. "You have to keep on driving at life, with your foot hard down on the accelerator – shunt obstacles out of the way otherwise life lands on you like a falling tree and crushes you flat.'' Graham did not appear to be listening and she was beginning to feel annoyed. ''You used to think that way, too – once, before you started drinking too much.'' Graham helped himself to another large dose of gin, but he still said nothing. She could feel anger mounting now.

''You've only got one life,'' she shouted as she firmly confiscated the bottle and marched with it towards the bedroom door. ''You damn fool! Can't you see, you've got to make the most of it?''

''You're a remarkable woman,'' said Graham unexpectedly.

''Do you love me?'' she asked, pausing uncertainly with her hand on the door knob.

''I'd have left you years ago if I didn't,'' sighed Graham and fell asleep.

11.45

Kim was sitting up in bed hugging her knees anxiously when David's key turned in the lock. She leapt out of bed and pattered downstairs.

''What happened? Where's Claire?'' she demanded.

''She's going to sleep in the vicarage spare room tonight. Richard's promised to go round every room of her house in the morning and spiritually fumigate the whole place.''

''But what happened? Don't you dare go silent and mysterious on me as usual. Could Richard help her?''

''It was all so easy it felt a bit like an anticlimax,'' admitted David as he climbed the stairs, unbuttoning his shirt as he went. ''We prayed first and then Richard explained that Jesus Christ is so powerful, nothing can stand against him. Claire was so upset by then she couldn't stop crying. She said she was uptight about all

321

the people she'd hurt, but Richard helped her to ask forgiveness and she calmed down a bit after that. Then he just told those evil things to get lost in the name of Jesus, and leave her alone for ever."

"Was that all?" said Kim, "No 'bell, book and candle'?" David chuckled.

"I reckon there's such power in the name of Jesus he doesn't really need any extra theatricals from us. Richard did warn her, though, that she's still in great danger. She can't keep fighting off the powers of darkness in her own strength." He was sitting on the bed now, pulling off his socks and frowning. "I'm trying to remember exactly what he said." David had never made such a long speech in his life. "Yes, that's it, he told her she must fill the void which the spirits had left with God Himself, and allow all His peace, love and joy to leave no room for the fear, hate and greed to come crawling back in to control her again."

"What did she say to that?"

"Well, she said she wanted to, but the poor old love was so bushed by that time, she could hardly keep her eyes open. They're going to talk it all through in the morning, but I'm sure she won't let Good Friday go by without giving herself over to God entirely."

"Won't that be wonderful for Jasmine!" exclaimed Kim.

"Shush, you'll wake the kids," warned David.

"It's good that there are so many of us at St Mark's nowadays, because she's going to need an awful lot of tender loving care after all this."

11.50

Hazel lay stiffly on the mattress; Graham's snoring made sleep quite impossible. He'd had so much to drink he'd be useless all day tomorrow.

Out in the road a bunch of patrons from the Prince Albert were kicking an empty tin-can about and shouting

322

raucously. Somewhere a baby cried and a dog kept on barking. The amber streetlight glared in at her through the uncurtained window, but what did it really matter? This time tomorrow they would be free of this squalid little Terrace and surrounded by five acres of privacy – their little kingdom. Things may have been difficult here, but they would be all right once she got Graham safely to Gresham Manor. 'I'll have everything I ever wanted then,' she thought.

Nigel was lying in the small, back bedroom of Number Three. Emmie's picture was propped up against his knees and he smiled at it lovingly. As usual he was completely happy.

In the next-door room his mother was also awake. Mrs Jardine never slept well. Everything was all right in the day, when she was busy, it was at night when the worry got hold of her. Those Pattersons over the road were so kind to her Nigel, letting him play with their children – making him feel wanted – but what if they moved away? Miss Dawson was good to him, too, but now the old lady was gone, she wouldn't stay round here much longer.

She pulled herself higher up on her pillows. Her heart was playing her up again, she couldn't breathe if she lay too flat. What if it got worse, suppose . . .? What would happen to Nigel then? He'd never cope in the world on his own.

Her mind always ran on like this in endless repeating circles. There was no escaping the fact the future was appalling.

"Grief, I'm tired," yawned David as he switched off the bedside light. "That 'all night vigil' with Richard in the church on Tuesday must be catching up on me."

"I love you," said Kim, reaching out for him in the dark.

"Do you really?" he said sleepily. "I always felt I was a bit of a let-down to you."

323

"It's been the other way round all the time, but I've been too blind to see it. I've got so fond of this funny little Terrace during the last year – I prefer it to Africa now, any day!" David was asleep already, so she kissed the back of his head and snuggled up against him. "Thank you for being so special," she whispered.

GOOD FRIDAY MARCH 27TH

4.55am

Gordon struggled and fought his way out of sleep, someone was calling his name. He slid out of bed and pattered across the cold lino in his striped flannel pyjamas. He must have been dreaming. It could not have been Alison's voice which had woken him, she had not spoken to him for days. He paused uncertainly on the landing.

"Gordon." The voice sounded oddly thin and wobbly, but it was Alison's all right and he cautiously pushed open the door of Amanda's old bedroom. His wife lay so still and flat in the bed, she resembled a corpse in the dim light of the bedside lamp.

"You not feeling too good, dear?" he said gently.

"There's no point in going on really, is there?" she said. "We've got nothing left now."

"Things always seem a bit worse early in the morning," he said as he pulled the covers up round her sagging chin. "Come on, old girl, buck up, and I'll make us a nice cuppa tea. How about that?" She made no response, but he padded off down the stairs anyway. 'Nasty things, nerves,' he told himself as he plugged in the kettle; they'd done this kind of thing to his mother, too. He'd give her a bit of a treat, find the best cups and put a nice cloth on the tray. Spoil her a bit. He almost felt happy as he pottered round the icy kitchen on his bare white feet.

5

Twenty-five miles away at Gatwick Airport, a Boeing 747 was being prepared for take-off.

The co-pilot glanced out of his window. To him this transatlantic shuttle was just another day's work. Down on the apron he could see the usual hectic activity which always surrounded the plane in the last half-hour before its departure. 'Security's tight this morning,' he yawned.

Of course there'd been the usual crop of terrorist threats, but it was always like that before a busy holiday weekend. He smiled grimly. If airline companies took note of them all they'd never get a single flight away.

A caterer's van was just backing up to the service hatch to deliver its stainless-steel food cabinets. Inside were the prepacked meal-trays which would provide breakfasts for the two hundred and twelve passengers on board.

5.10

Emmie opened her eyes in the darkness and peered at the luminous face of her clock. Why ever had she woken up this early when last night she had been so tired? She had forced herself to keep busy until late, sorting Rosie's possessions until everything was tidied neatly away – except the memories. Rosie's words would keep on going round and round in her head as she went upstairs. "Because you are afraid of being hurt you keep everyone at a distance." At last, in desperation she had knelt by the carved mahogany bed.

"Please God, show me what to do about Richard," she had prayed. "But you'll have to do it by tomorrow."

She had fallen asleep remarkably quickly after that, completely exhausted by the hard work of the day. Now here she was, wide awake with nothing to do but dread that afternoon appointment by the lake. Why hadn't God answered her prayer?

Quite suddenly she realised that he had. As she lay there, she knew *exactly* what she should do. She should marry Richard! God had not rejected her with all her faults, surely Richard who knew him so well, would behave just the same. She had also been given that special relationship with Rosie which had shown her she *could* go on loving someone, right to the very end. It was so simple she couldn't think why she hadn't realised it yesterday.

She padded into her kitchen and made a mug of coffee.

'I'm never going to be able to wait all those hours to tell him,' she decided as her mind began to frame a delicious plan. He got up early, too, so perhaps about seven she'd run up the Terrace, and tap on his front door. What would happen next was just too gorgeous even for her imagination. But how was she going to fill the two hours until then? She'd go for a walk with Gwyllum and watch the dawn.

She was pulling on her clothes as the last passenger boarded TC Flight 521 for Washington.

5.35

"Come on, old girl, drink up." Gordon was perched awkwardly on the edge of the bed; he was beginning to feel extremely cold now. He had fetched pillows from his own bed and Alison was sitting propped up gazing dully at the tray on her lap. She had not touched her tea.

"You used the best china," she said at last, "and Auntie Madge's crocheted tray cloth."

"Sorry," mumbled Gordon, "thought you needed a bit of a lift."

"It's nice," she replied, "thank you, dear." She lifted her cup at last and failed to see the expression of startled pleasure on her husband's face.

5.43

The bomb severed the wings and rear section of the plane
and scattered them over Ashdown Forest, leaving the
front fuselage to hurtle towards Laburnum Terrace. At
five forty-three and thirty seconds it hit the vicarage and
ploughed its ugly swathe towards the park railings.

For a long time Emmie stood staring stupidly at what had
once been her world. Her mind and body seemed unable
to react in any way. Noise. That was the first thing which
penetrated. The roar of the flames. Sirens converging
from all directions. Men shouting orders. Glass cracking
in the heat.

Out from Albert Gardens plunged a line of fire engines.
"Get out of here!" someone yelled. She moved back
and watched men like frenzied ants spraying feeble jets
of water at the flames of hell.

Fools! No point. Everyone's dead. No! She mustn't let
her mind start to think. Not now she'd seen the vicarage
blazing at the far end of the Terrace. Where's Gwyllum?

Her lethargy changed to frenzied activity as she began
running all over the park, screaming his name. It did not
strike her as odd to be upset over a lost dog when so
many men, women and children had just died close
beside her. Gwyllum was all she had left now.

She found him after half an hour, cowering under the
seat on the peninsula, whining pitifully. She snapped on
his lead quickly. Mustn't think of the kingcups. Mustn't
think of Richard. Mustn't think at all!

Slowly she stumbled up the hill again and along Acacia
Avenue, another little cul-de-sac higher up Bakers Hill.

It was so like Laburnum Terrace. Same houses. Same
gardens. But the people who stood around in little
frightened groups were not the right people. 'Her' people
were all gone. Gone, she thought, gone with all the things
which had mattered to them. Everything they had tried
to achieve. Gone!

"God," she cried out, "It isn't fair!"

"You all right, love?" said a woman with a baby on her hip. She wasn't Kim so Emmie pushed her away. "It isn't fair!" she repeated. Rosie had tried to explain it once. She must remember what she said — one day. Cling on to Rosie's faith — whatever happened to her own. When she reached the end of the road she was seized by a sudden surge of hope. Perhaps she had not really seen the vicarage on fire after all. Perhaps the plane had missed it altogether. She bounded out into the middle of Bakers Hill while the ambulances and police cars blasted their horns as they swerved to avoid her. But as she looked down the hill she could see that the flames had almost finished with the vicarage now. Richard! She had let him die without knowing that she loved him.

"Come on, luvvy," said a familiar voice. Warm woolly arms were pulling her on to the pavement. "I'm here. I'll look after you." Emmie didn't want anyone to look after her. Everything was pointless now.

"Come and keep warm in my milk truck. I was up here when it happened. Saw the whole thing."

Babs hoisted her up, and while the rescue vehicles surged by in the road, they sat side by side with Gwyllum squashed between them. 'Why can't you make clocks go backwards?' thought Emmie.

" 'Fraid there's not a lot of work for the ambulance men," remarked Babs ghoulishly. "No one's going to come out of that plane, or the Terrace for that matter." 'Doesn't she ever stop talking?' thought Emmie.

"The fire chief wants my help once he starts looking for bodies. I can tell from my order-book who was away from the Terrace on holiday. Tilsons moved out — for a start." 'No they didn't,' thought Emmie.

"And there was one miracle survivor."

"Who?" Hope felt sharp and painful.

"That Mr Coley of all people. They got him away within a few minutes of the crash. I talked to the ambulance driver who took him to hospital. Said they found him

329

right in the middle of Bakers Hill. He must have been out early – jogging. Plane went clean over his head.'' 'That's nice for Ann,' thought Emmie, and closed her eyes. She did not want to sit here looking at what was happening at the bottom of the hill.

''Terrible to think of those nice Pattersons, though, a real tragedy.''

Emmie knew she would mourn for Kim for the rest of her life, but just for that moment she envied her. What was it Rosie had said? ''Death's not the end, only the beginning.'' Well, the Pattersons were all together there now and out of this mess. They were more ready for this than most people in the road. 'Death's only a tragedy when it parts people.' She thought of Richard then, and had to hold her mouth closed with both hands to stop herself from screaming.

In the distance Babs was still talking.

''The plane took the roof clean off the vicarage, the vicar only just had time to get his family out before the fire started. I saw him getting them into one of the first ambulances. That hairdresser woman was with them. Can't think why the Almighty spared a woman like that!''

Emmie was out of the milk truck instantly.

''Hold Gwyllum!'' she shouted. ''Did you say the vicar went to hospital?''

''No, he stayed to help in the rescue. Here! Come back! You won't be allowed down there!''

But Emmie was already running down Bakers Hill, pushing her way through the chaos and confusion. Dodging knots of spectators and forcing herself through police barriers. She blundered unheeded past groups of rescue personnel and newsmen with cameras.

There, among the flashing blue lights, the debris and the horror he was quite unmistakable. Towering above the crowd in his ancient dressing-gown.

''Richard!'' she screamed. ''Richard!''